Y002561

BABY
SITTER

D1354026

THE
BABY
SITTER

SHERYL BROWNE

bookouture

Published by Bookouture in 2018

An imprint of StoryFire Ltd.

Carmelite House
50 Victoria Embankment
London EC4Y 0DZ

www.bookouture.com

ISBN: 978-1-78681-341-1
eBook ISBN: 978-1-78681-340-4

To my family, who offered their love
and support unquestioningly when I needed it most.

To my little brother. I miss you.

To Drew. You are my inspiration. Without you, this book
might have had one or two plot holes.

I love you all.

PROLOGUE

EIGHT YEARS AGO

Oblivious to the slimy, wet mud oozing between her toes, Grace took a faltering step backwards, away from the house. Her huge cognac-coloured eyes illuminated by the light of the fire, she watched, mesmerised and helpless, as the flames licked hungrily at her parents' bedroom curtains. She'd tried to tell them what happened to Ellie wasn't her fault.

Constantly around her ankles, while their mum and husband number three had partied, her younger sister Ellie had been watching as she and her friends lit up their sparklers and drew their names against the dark blue ink of the sky. Ellie had wanted to do it, too. Later, Grace had promised her; anything to placate her and stop her 'telling Mummy' she'd been smoking, which would only add to Grace's list of sins.

Ellie hadn't forgotten. Still awake when Grace had crept up to bed, her sister had whinged until, urging her to be quiet, Grace had given in and tiptoed back downstairs to fetch a packet of leftover sparklers from the box in the kitchen.

Her eyes like big brown orbs, Ellie had watched in awe as Grace struck the match and lit the sparkler, igniting a thousand crackling slivers of light in their bedroom. She'd squealed like the foxes that scream in the night when her flesh had singed, despite how hard Grace tried to shush her. Grace hadn't wanted to hurt her sister. But she knew nobody would believe her. They never did.

Grace took another step back, her heart skipping a beat as a figure appeared at the window, flames lashing at his flesh like hot vipers' tongues. It *wasn't* her fault. She'd *tried* to tell them. She'd *told* Ellie to hold the firework at arm's length. They hadn't been listening. Her mum's eyes had been as wild as the fire. She'd still been wearing her lipstick, blood red, like an angry red slash for a mouth, as she'd cursed and spat, 'You stupid creature. Look what you've done. *Look* what *you've* done!'

She'd been holding Ellie in her arms, clutching her plump little hand in her own and pointing it out towards Grace like an accusation. Ellie's fingers had been blistered, her thigh, too, where the sparkler had landed.

Her stepdad had started after her as her mum swept past Grace to take Ellie to accident and emergency. 'I'll drive you,' he'd offered, but he hadn't wanted to. Grace could tell by the way his gaze drifted lewdly towards her that he hadn't wanted to.

'Don't be ridiculous!' her mum had snapped angrily. 'You've drunk your own body weight in beer. Just… deal with her,' she'd added, causing ice-cold dread to pool in the pit of Grace's stomach. She hadn't wanted to be alone with him, to watch him draw the blinds and turn from the window, that liquid, faraway look in his eyes as he unfastened his waistband.

Hearing the wail of the sirens growing closer, Grace tore her gaze from the window. Panic twisting her stomach and thick, choking smoke gripping her throat, she backed towards the denser foliage at the bottom of the garden.

Pulling on the requisite hand and footwear protection, Mark sucked in a deep breath and braced himself to enter the premises. 'DI Cain,' he said, producing his ID and introducing himself to the uniformed officer in the hall, who was looking rather green around the gills. The guy was young – early twenties, Mark guessed, probably not long off probation. Mark had been about the same age, seven long years ago, when he'd encountered his first victim. He'd kept his breakfast down – just. This, though – a whole family incinerated, a young child included – was truly an initiation by fire. 'DS Moyes?' he asked.

'Child's bedroom. First left at the top,' the officer answered, and swallowed hard on his Adam's apple.

Mark nodded, glancing at him sympathetically. 'Take a break,' he suggested. 'Grab some air.' Not that the air out there was much less putrid than in here. As acrid as the smell of burned wood suffused with gunpowder was, it was doing little to hide the nauseatingly sweet stench of singed flesh. Like roast pork crackling on Sundays. Mark remembered well the times he'd looked forward to going to his gran's as a kid, escaping the endless violent arguments at home. He hadn't been able to go near a roast joint since he'd attended a road traffic accident where the unfortunate driver, entombed in his car, had gone up in flames.

'I'm good, sir,' the officer assured him stoically.

Mark was unconvinced. 'Humour me,' he said. 'I've done my own fair share of contaminating evidence. Trust me, I know the signs.'

'Sir,' the officer said, his look now a mixture of embarrassment and relief as he turned for the front door.

Mark watched him go, and then, steeling himself, he climbed the stairs and headed directly for the child's room. Lisa Moyes, his detective sergeant, was there, looking down at the small form in the bed. Detective Sergeant Cummings was also there, though Mark was buggered if he knew why. First responder, he wondered? Unlikely. The man was a lazy sod. More likely he'd been on his way back from some seedy liaison in the city and had stopped by out of idle curiosity.

'Cummings.' Mark nodded a curt greeting as he walked across to Lisa Moyes. He didn't like the man, a chauvinistic prick who obviously considered sexual harassment one of the perks of the job.

'What have we got?' he asked Lisa, who didn't meet his gaze. From the hand she ran under her nose, Mark guessed why. Petite in size, with blonde hair, which she purposely cropped short, and pretty, Lisa had had to work to prove herself in a largely male-dominated environment, determined to be as hard-nosed and detached as some of her male counterparts. As a mother herself, though, Mark suspected she didn't have a snowball's chance in hell of remaining detached now.

'A young girl,' Lisa answered, eventually, 'white Caucasian, aged approximately four. Cause of death—' Her voice catching, she stopped and fixed her gaze hard on the ceiling.

'Smoke inhalation,' Cummings supplied. 'The door was closed. She got lucky though, better than being burned alive. Can't imagine what must have been going through her mind hearing her mum and dad screaming. Poor cow must have been petrified.'

At that, Lisa turned around. 'You really are a prat, Cummings,' she muttered, pushing furiously past him and heading for the door.

Cummings watched her go, confounded. 'What was all that about?' he asked, looking clueless as he turned back to Mark.

Sighing, Mark shook his head. Married and divorced twice, Cummings had never had kids, but it didn't take a great leap of the imagination to guess what might have been going through that child's mind.

'Lisa has two children under five,' he pointed out exasperatedly, and turned his attention to the little girl, his heart constricting inside him as he did. Curled into a foetal ball in her child-sized bed, she had her thumb plugged into her mouth and a one-eyed Pooh Bear clutched close to her chest.

Mark took a second to compose himself. He didn't have kids either. They had had a child, he and his wife, Melissa, and though his son's life might have been too short, Mark had grieved more than he would ever let on. Melissa had needed him to be strong, Mark had realised that as he'd watched her nursing their premature child in her arms. Her heart had been breaking as Jacob's weak lungs had stopped fighting. In those bleak weeks afterwards, Mel had fought to stave off a deep, dark depression born of carrying a child, giving birth to a child and then having that child cruelly stolen away. Mark had been dying inside. Probably the only person who'd guessed how much he was hurting, and how frustrated and angry he'd felt after two subsequent miscarriages, was Lisa.

No, it didn't need a great leap of the imagination to envisage how terrified in such circumstances a small child might be. Swallowing back a tight knot in his throat, Mark closed his eyes, offering up a silent prayer for the girl, before turning back to Cummings. 'You might as well go home,' he said tiredly.

'Oh? Why's that then?' Cummings asked, eyeing him warily as Mark headed for the door. Ever since Mark had caught him in the act of groping a female member of staff and attempted to wipe the floor with him, Cummings had been jumpy around him. More so once he'd realised Mark was on to his little transgressions with confiscated items. Drugs mostly, nothing major, but there was no way it could be overlooked. Cummings had also been quietly watching him, Mark was aware, as if waiting for him to slip up; probably looking for ammunition to use against him should Mark bring his suspicions to the attention of their superior officers.

'You're surplus to requirements,' he clarified. 'I'm thinking this isn't a crime scene.'

Cummings looked doubtful. 'But aren't there traces of accelerant?'

'It's bonfire night,' Mark reminded him. 'Judging by the embers outside and the obvious signs of alcohol consumption, the family were partying. Chances are the accelerant was to make sure the party didn't get rained off.'

It had got the fire going all right, hadn't it, he thought jadedly. The idiots park the accelerant in the kitchen, a stray spark ignites the fumes, and bang, a fucking inferno. Mark quashed an overwhelming sense of anger. What were they thinking, taking that sort of risk with a four-year-old child in the house?

'I'll assess whether we need to drag the forensic specialists out of bed. DS Moyes and I can handle the rest. Once the coroner arrives, you might as well go and catch up on your beauty sleep. You look as if you could use it.' The last was added acerbically, bearing in mind Cummings' penchant for touring red-light districts.

Mark turned away from Cummings and headed for the main bedroom. There, the smell was more cloying; the coppery odour of iron-rich burned blood suffused with barbecued meat turned his stomach over. Supressing the urge to retch, Mark forced himself further into the room, almost stepping on what remained of one of the corpses as he did. The mother, he gathered. Burned where she lay, her body in much the same foetal position as the little girl, though through muscle flexion rather than fear, as she'd obviously been trying to get to the door.

Working to keep his nausea in check, he walked around the bed. The father had obviously headed for the window. Blackened and charred, clothes and curtain material melted into his flesh, his body was barely recognisable as human.

Mark couldn't begin to imagine the pain they must have gone through. Was smoke inhalation a less painful death, he wondered, his mind going back to the little girl. A forensic specialist had once assured him it was, marginally. Either way it was a fucking horrific way to go. *Dammit.* He needed to get out of here. He needed to breathe. Curtailing his anger, Mark headed back to the landing to concentrate on the practicalities of what needed to be done.

Gulping a lungful of slightly less stifling air as he exited the house, he glanced around, assessing the location. An isolated country property located on the Worcester and Herefordshire border. He'd already noted the absence of a fence or gate dividing the land from the road.

Pondering options for a perimeter, he was gazing into the woodland on the opposite side of the road when DS Moyes joined him. 'How's it going?' he asked her.

'Slowly.' Lisa sighed. 'I sent one of the first attending officers to the local pub. The landlord was pissed off at being knocked up, but he confirmed he was here last night and that there hadn't been any arguments or suspect incidents. Guests were mostly local apparently. He's going to let us have some names.'

'Right.' Mark nodded. 'I actually meant how's it going with you?'

'Good. I'm good,' Moyes assured him, her gaze fixed to the front.

Mark noted the determined set of her jaw. 'Bullshit.'

Lisa's shoulders deflated. 'Yeah,' she said, running her hand through her short crop of hair. 'Sorry about back there. It's just… Cummings can be a right tactless twat sometimes.'

Mark sighed empathetically. 'Tell me about it.'

'I could imagine it' – Lisa tugged in a tight breath – 'how terrified that little girl must have been. I don't know what I would do if I ever lost one of my children. I suppose the small plus is the parents won't have to go through the grieving— Oh God.' She squeezed her eyes closed. 'Sorry, Mark. I wasn't thinking. I—'

'It's fine,' Mark said quickly.

Lisa obviously got the gist. 'So, how's Mel?' she asked, her voice falsely bright.

'Good,' Mark assured her, happy to talk about his wife. 'Throwing herself into her work. She's managed to get a couple of commissions supplying local craft centres, so… Yup, she's doing okay.'

Outwardly, Melissa and Lisa were as different as chalk and cheese. Taller than Lisa, with long, softly curled hair the colour of soft copper, Mel was meditative, rarely outspoken unless with good cause, caring. As was Lisa, but there the similarity ended.

Lisa was definitely outspoken, and she could curse with the best of them. Inwardly, though, they were made of the same stuff, with a steely determination to keep going no matter what shit life dealt them. Having survived an abusive relationship, it was no wonder Lisa would have nil respect for a Neanderthal of Cummings ilk. Mark wouldn't say it to her face, but having grown up in the midst of an abusive relationship himself, he had a profound respect for her. Lisa had been a friend to Mel when she'd needed one, and Mark had been grateful.

Mark smiled as his mind drifted to Mel, who of late could usually be found at her potter's wheel. Somehow, she'd pulled herself out of the pit of despair she'd fallen into and built up a business, albeit a fledgling one, from scratch. Mark was in awe of her.

'Excellent,' Lisa said, looking pleased. 'And are you two still… um… you know.'

Noting the insinuating arch of her eyebrows, Mark got the drift. 'Yes, we're still trying,' he confided. And hoping, he added silently, that by some miracle that one day they would be blessed with the child they both desperately wanted.

'You're a handsome bastard.' Lisa smirked. 'Who could resist?'

Mark shook his head. 'I could think of a few.'

'And modest with it. Be still my beating heart.' Lisa fluttered her eyelashes theatrically. 'Well, you know what they say, practice makes perfect and all that. It'll happen,' she said, glancing over her shoulder as one of the first attending officers approached from the house. 'Probably when you least expect it. Keep it up, Detective.'

Mark's mouth twitched into a smile as she gave him a thumbs up and turned to liaise with the uniform. Praying it would happen, for both of their sakes, Mark pulled in a sigh and turned his attention back to the task of setting up the perimeter.

'I'm heading back in,' Lisa said. 'They're removing the bodies.'

Turning back, Mark arched an eyebrow, surprised she was so keen. He was all for facing fears head on – his biggest fear in his young life had been his own father, until he'd plucked up enough courage to confront him – but Lisa had been visibly upset in there. 'You sure?' he asked her. 'You can always take over out here while I go in.'

Lisa nodded resolutely. 'I'd like to be with her. Make sure she's all right, if that makes any sense.'

'Perfect sense.' Mark smiled, understanding. It was pointless, the little girl was dead, but making sure she was treated gently might possibly lay a ghost for Lisa.

Gesturing her on, Mark made his way around the side of the house to liaise with the officers out back, plucking his ringing mobile from his pocket as he went. It would be DCI Edwards calling, he assumed, wanting a progress report – i.e., checking up on him, after his psych report had labelled him borderline fit for work. Yes, he'd lost it with Cummings, and flooring a fellow officer hadn't been the proudest moment of his life, but the bastard had deserved it. And, yes, he might have been 'borderline' at the time – his emotional state hadn't been great after the funeral – but he was fit for work now.

But when he looked at the screen, it wasn't Edwards. 'Mel? What's wrong?' he asked, a knot of apprehension tightening inside him.

'Nothing's *wrong*,' Mel assured him. 'Does there have to be something wrong for a wife to call her husband?'

Mark glanced at his watch. 'It's six in the morning.'

'*Nooo*, really?' Mel said, in mock surprise. 'Funnily enough, that's exactly what I thought when I groped for your body and came up empty-handed.'

'Sorry,' Mark apologised distractedly, his attention drawn by activity further down the garden. 'I didn't want to wake you. I had a call-out. I left a note by the kettle.'

'I haven't been down yet. I was too busy lying in bed contemplating the thin blue line.'

'Sorry?' Mark said again, his attention now definitely elsewhere.

'Thin – blue – line,' Mel repeated slowly. 'Work it out, Detective.'

'What?'

'Well, actually, I have blue lines and pink lines and… I'd say you've done a very thorough job, DI Cain.'

Not sure he was hearing her right, Mark stopped walking. Was she saying… *Jesus.* Conflicting emotions assailed him, and he dragged a hand through his hair. He wanted to whoop and cry at the same time, to sound jubilant, for Mel's sake, but how could he? Here? Now? 'Mel, I'm going to have to call you back,' he said, his throat tight. 'I—'

'Mark?' Mel cut incredulously across him. 'Did you hear what I just said?'

'Yes. Yes, I did. It's… I can't talk now, Mel,' he said, kneading his forehead in frustration as two officers walked someone towards him. 'I…'

'Oh.' Now she sounded deflated. Bitterly disappointed.

'It's a house fire,' Mark explained quickly. 'A family. There've been fatalities. I have to—'

'Oh no.' Mel obviously realised his circumstances immediately. 'Go,' she urged him, as the officers, plus charge, stopped in front of him. 'Call me back when you can.'

'I will,' Mark promised gruffly, realising the absolute impossibility of remaining detached as he looked into the tearful, terrified eyes of another child. A child they'd been unaware of and had obviously missed in the pandemonium. Still dressed in her unicorn-print pyjamas, she was shaking from head to foot. Her cheeks, smeared in crap from the fire, were tear-stained, her cognac-coloured eyes wide and utterly petrified.

'*Shit*,' Mark uttered under his breath. 'Where was she?' he addressed one of the officers.

'Hiding out in the bushes,' he said, nodding at the trees behind him.

'Looks like she didn't want to be found,' the second officer observed.

'I'm not surprised.' His heart constricting for the girl, Mark looked back at her, unsure what to say, what to do that could possibly help. There was no way she would have even begun to process the enormity of what had happened. Nor would she for a long time to come – if ever.

'All right if we leave her with you, sir?' the first officer asked. 'There's some debris needs shifting on the landing.'

Mark nodded. 'Go,' he said. 'Get another ambulance here pronto and alert DS Moyes on your way, will you?' he added, as the officers skirted around him. Apart from the fact that he hadn't got a clue how to handle this, protocol dictated he should have a female police officer present.

'Hi,' he said, turning to the girl and trying to sound as reassuring as possible. 'I'm Detective Inspector Cain.' The girl peered at him through a straggle of mousey hair. 'Mark for short,' he added. 'Do you have a name?'

'G… Grace.'

'Grace. That's a nice name.' Mark smiled again, wishing he could do more than just stand there. 'Do you live here, Grace?' he enquired gently.

The girl glanced past him, nodded, and then hastily dropped her gaze.

Nice going. Despairing of his ineptitude in such a situation, Mark sighed inwardly, and then, removing his jacket, crouched down to her level.

She flinched as he moved towards her, her expression one of alarm, he noted.

'To keep you warm,' he said. 'You're shaking fit to break something loose.' Again, he smiled and prayed he wasn't doing anything to add to her terror and confusion.

The palpable fear in her eyes diminished a little as he wrapped the jacket around her, making sure to hold her gaze as he did. 'Can you tell me what happened, Grace?' he asked softly, pulling it close at the neck.

Warily, she searched his eyes. Her own were wide and dark, Mark noticed, as she glanced at the house and then back to him.

'I was asleep,' she said, her gaze flicking guiltily away for a second. No surprise there. Skinny under her pyjamas, her demeanour that of a frightened five-year-old, she looked around twelve, thirteen maybe. Too young to have to deal with this, but old enough, he guessed, to have realised her family had possibly perished. 'But something scared me,' she said. 'A crash.'

'Like breaking glass?' Carefully, Mark probed a little further.

She nodded, then, gulping in a breath, dragged a sleeve under her nose.

A break-in, Mark wondered, or a window popping? The latter, he suspected.

'I smelled smoke,' she said, swiping at her nose again. 'I didn't know what to do. I shouted and screamed but no one came. I tried to get to out, but I *couldn't*, and I got scared and—'

'Hey, hey, slow down,' Mark urged her, as the words tumbled from her mouth in a garbled, hiccupping rush.

'I didn't know what to do,' she repeated, choking back a sob. 'I was going to wake Mummy and Daddy, but… but…'

'Was there smoke on the landing, Grace?'

'Yes,' she sobbed. 'And fire. I couldn't get *past* it. I couldn't get through it. I didn't know what to do.'

So she ran. *What else was there to do but fucking burn*, Mark thought furiously.

'I left them,' she said, the sheer anguish in her voice cutting him to the core.

'You had no choice,' he told her firmly.

'My sister. She was screaming. I couldn't save her.' It came out little more than a whisper.

Useless. Feeling powerless as the girl's gaze hit the ground again, Mark ran a hand over his neck. *Stuff protocol*, he thought, getting to his feet, as she began to cry in earnest. It wasn't a criminal offence to hold a child while she broke her bloody heart, was it? Briefly, he hesitated, and then reached out to wrap an arm around her as another sob escaped her throat.

The girl, obviously in need of physical contact, moved towards him in an instant, her arms around him, her face pressed hard into his torso. Fresh, heart-wrenching sobs now wracking her frail shoulders, and Mark tried to soothe her, stroking her hair, offering her banal words of comfort.

'It wasn't your fault, Grace,' he said throatily, but she only cried harder.

She was glued to him like a limpet when Lisa appeared, running towards them, to Mark's huge relief.

'The ambulance has arrived,' she said, casting Mark a warning glance as she slowed her run to a walk.

Reading the look, Mark shrugged helplessly. Lisa was right, of course. This definitely wouldn't be listed as appropriate behaviour in the child protection and safeguard manual, but what else was he supposed to have done? 'Grace,' he said softly, 'you need to go with Lisa now. Just to the hospital,' he added quickly, as her startled gaze shot to his. 'I'll be in trouble with my superior officers if I don't ensure you get adequate medical attention.'

Again, the girl scanned his eyes, a new fear in her own.

'It will be all right, Grace.' Mark tried to reassure her, his heart sinking as he realised it was utter bullshit. Things wouldn't be all right for this child ever again. How could they be? 'I'll check up on you as soon as I can, okay?'

'Promise?' she asked uncertainly.

It meant he would get back home later than he wanted to, but… 'Promise.'

She seemed to accept that, giving him a small nod. 'I'm frightened,' she said tremulously, causing Mark's heart to constrict afresh.

'Don't be,' he said, making sure to hold her gaze now. 'You can always contact me if you need to, Grace. I'll always be there if you need someone to talk to or to protect you. That's an absolute promise.'

CHAPTER ONE

MELISSA
PRESENT

'Mark!' Hoisting their six-week-old baby girl higher in the crook of her arm whilst simultaneously hanging onto their wriggling seven-year-old, Melissa called frantically after her husband, who'd set off at a run towards the burned-out cottage diagonally opposite their own. The fire was doused now, fire officers wearily reeling in hoses, but it couldn't be safe to go near the property yet.

'Mark, come back!' she shouted, and he hesitated for a split second, obviously debating his options before deciding on access to the back of the cottage via the garden gate. And then he was off, the distressed mewl of a cat driving him to instinctively react, as he tended to.

Oh God, what was he *doing*? Melissa held her breath as he scaled the back gate and disappeared over it, then her heart lurched violently in her chest as their daughter tore her hand from her own and made a determined dash to go after him. 'Poppy!' she screamed.

'It's all right. I've got her.' Moving faster than Melissa, their neighbour, the owner of the property that had caught fire in the night, went after her, sweeping Poppy up into her arms.

The fire officers had cordoned off the lane, and Melissa would have caught her before she'd gone far, but even so… Her world had gone off kilter for a nauseating few seconds. 'Thank you.' Her heart rate returning to somewhere near normal, Melissa smiled gratefully at the woman as she walked back towards her. She'd moved in just before Evie had been born. Melissa had meant to pop over and see her, but then, with a new baby to care for and her business beginning to take off, providing she could fulfil her orders, she hadn't managed to make time. She should have. She was clearly the kind of person you would hope to have as a neighbour.

'I want to go with Daddy,' Poppy whimpered, kneading her eyes tiredly with her knuckles. 'I'm frightened.'

'He'll be back in a minute, sweetheart,' the woman assured her, gently coaxing her hand from her face. 'I think he knows how terribly frightened my cat is, too, so he's gone to try and rescue her. He's a very brave man, isn't he?'

Poppy surveyed the woman uncertainly for a second, then she sniffled and nodded over the thumb she'd plugged into her mouth. 'He's a policeman,' she said shyly.

'Is he?' The woman widened her eyes, looking impressed for Poppy's sake. 'Well, he's a very brave policeman indeed. I think he should have a medal, don't you?'

Poppy nodded happily at that. 'Yes,' she said, settling more easily into the woman's arms.

'I'll hold onto her, shall I?' The woman smiled and nodded towards Melissa's bundle. 'You seem to have your hands full.'

Melissa followed her gaze, down to the content little miracle in her arms, who, amazingly, had slept through the cacophony of noise around them. 'Thank you,' she said again, looking back to the woman, who was actually not much more than a girl in her early twenties at most. 'Are you all right?' she asked her worriedly. Just a few short hours ago, Mark, having noticed the ominous orange glow through their bedroom window, had raced outside to find Monk's Cottage thoroughly on fire and her sobbing in the lane.

'Well, you know.' Managing a tremulous smile, she shrugged. 'I suppose there's always a bright side. At least I'm alive.'

'Mummy, when's Daddy coming back?' Poppy asked, as Melissa pondered the stupidity of her question. Of course she wouldn't be all right, what with all her earthly possessions gone up in flames.

'Soon, sweetie,' Melissa promised, glancing from her daughter's huge chocolate-brown eyes, which were so like her father's, every emotion dancing therein, and then back towards the smoke-blackened cottage, praying that Mark hadn't gone into the building. No, surely not. Distressed cat or not, he would be well aware of the dangers. Nevertheless, Melissa's apprehension grew as she watched one of the fire officers heading that way after him.

'I don't know your name,' the woman said, chatting to Poppy, trying to distract her. Melissa was grateful.

'Poppy… What's your name?'

'I'm Jade. And I think your Daddy will be out very soon. Do you know how I know?'

Poppy furrowed her brow over the thumb she still had wedged in her mouth. 'How?'

'Listen.' Jade cocked an ear. 'What do you hear?'

Poppy tilted her head to one side, the little furrow in her brow deepening as she concentrated. Then, 'The cat's stopped meowing,' she said delightedly.

'That's right. Which probably means your daddy's found her, which means your daddy's a hero.'

'He is.' Poppy nodded importantly. 'He catches all the baddies and puts them in prison so we can all be safe.'

'I bet he does.' Jade exchanged a knowing glance with Melissa. 'I bet he rescues all sorts of animals and people from all sorts of dangers, too.'

'He does. *And* he shoos the scary bug monster from under my bed,' Poppy informed her, her little face earnest. '*I'm* going to be a policeman when I grow up, aren't I, Mummy?'

'That's right, sweetie.' Melissa smiled distractedly, her gaze still fixed on the gate.

'Daddy's going to teach me, isn't—'

'Oh, thank God.' Melissa blew out a sigh of relief as her husband finally reappeared, nursing the cat, which appeared to be subdued, miraculously. No doubt Mark had worked a little bit of his magic on it. The man was as soft as a brush when it came to animals and children. Melissa had no idea how he did the job he did, witnessing such despicable acts of cruelty sometimes, things that really could make a grown man cry. Mind you, she arranged her face into a suitably annoyed expression as he neared her.

Obviously sensing he might be in the doghouse, Mark did his usual trick, disarming her with that sheepish and far too winning smile of his, the look in his soulful brown eyes somewhere between contrite and teasing. DI Mark Cain obviously knew her too well, confident she would forgive him his sins – because she loved him, irrevocably. He was her rock, there for her when she'd been lost, gently helping her find the will to go on when depression had been a dark, cloying blanket threatening to suffocate her. She hadn't wanted to go on after losing Jacob. Wouldn't have, if not for Mark, whose heart had been quietly breaking too. Mark had loved their little baby boy, who'd been so outwardly perfect, but whose tiny lungs couldn't function independently. It had been there in his all-telling eyes. He'd so wanted the family she couldn't give him. The normal functional family that, with his awful, abusive childhood, he'd never had. He'd never made her feel inadequate, not with a look, not with a gesture, but she had felt inadequate. Especially after the miscarriages.

Mark had his flaws, a tendency to withdraw when he was immersed in some horrendous case, seemingly moody to those who didn't know the caring man underneath, but from the first time she'd met him, forcing herself to report her previous boyfriend, a manipulative excuse of a man who'd eventually shown his true colours and hit her, she'd known Mark was one of the good guys. He'd handled the case sensitively, checked up on her afterwards, become her white knight. He'd been a catch. This much Melissa knew, because, having told him that much once, Mark had never missed an opportunity to remind her he was. He didn't do a bad back massage either, she reminded herself, unable to stop her mouth curving into a reciprocal smile as he stopped in front of them.

'He's got her! He's got her!' Poppy exclaimed, bouncing excitedly in Jade's arms. '*Daddy!* You're a hero!' She extended her own small arms, obviously wanting to latch herself onto him, inconsiderate of the poor cat.

'Definitely a hero,' Jade agreed emotionally, her eyes filling up as she stepped towards him. Blue eyes, Melissa noticed – striking ice-blue. The sort of eyes you couldn't fail to be mesmerised by.

'Er…' His arms full of her cat, Jade's full of his child, Mark looked nonplussed at how to make the swap. 'Jump down a sec, Poppet,' he asked Poppy, giving her a reassuring smile. 'I'll pick you right back up as soon as Jade has her cat back.'

'Is she your baby?' Poppy asked, dutifully allowing herself to be lowered to the ground while Mark passed Jade his furry charge.

'Yes.' Jade nodded, reaching to take the cat gently from Mark's arms, and then leaning in to plant a soft kiss on his cheek. 'She's my whole world. Thank you, Mark.'

'My pleasure,' Mark said, looking ever-so-slightly embarrassed as he bent to swoop Poppy up into his arms. And then he almost choked when Poppy locked her arms around his neck and announced, 'Daddy's good at making babies, too. He made one with Mummy, didn't you, Daddy? He could make you a proper one if you asked him nicely, couldn't you, Daddy?'

'Um, I, er… *Ahem.*' Mark clearly didn't know where to look as Melissa and Jade swapped amused glances.

'I think Daddy's a bit too busy, Poppy,' said Melissa, deciding now might be a good time to rescue him.

'Busy causing chaos,' the chief fire officer added, a despairing look on his face as he approached. 'Don't do a solo again, hey, mate? You, above all people, should know it's not on. No one near the property until it's been cleared by the fire safety officer. I ought to report it. You'll land me in hot water up to my neck if you end up suffering from smoke inhalation.'

'Yes, sorry.' Mark looked contrite. 'I didn't—'

'She wasn't inside. She was in the tree. She got scared and ran before I could catch hold of her,' Jade interrupted, clearly seeing that Mark might need rescuing here too. 'When will it be? The fire safety officer's visit, I mean,' she added, neatly changing the subject.

The fire officer turned to her, and did a double take, literally. Melissa wasn't surprised. Wearing a nightie under the jacket one of the firemen had supplied her, albeit a modest winceyette affair, and with her long blonde hair tousled and just-got-out-of-bed gorgeous, Jade was undeniably attractive. 'I'm not quite sure,' he said, clearly taken with her. 'Do you want to come over to the engine while I make a call?'

Melissa watched them go, Jade cuddling her cat, looking fragile and vulnerable, despite her well-developed curves, the fire officer unable to resist looking sideways at her. 'Do you think he's trying to impress her?' she asked Mark.

'Undoubtedly,' Mark concurred. 'I doubt he'll get very far though.'

'Oh? Because she's beautiful, you mean?' She idly wondered if the girl had had Botox. Her lips and eyebrows were perfect. But then, she supposed, at her age they probably would be.

'Yes.' Mark nodded, keeping his gaze fixed forwards. 'And young,' he added, his mouth curving into a mischievous smile as Melissa glared at him.

'Uh-oh,' Mark said, winking at Poppy. 'I think I might be in the doghouse, after all.'

'Don't be silly.' Poppy sighed expansively, giving him a despairing roll of her eyes. 'Hercules doesn't have a house. He sleeps on my bed.'

'I think he might need to move over to make room for me.' Mark laughed, reading the now very peeved expression on Mel's face. 'I meant that he's twice her age,' he clarified, obviously realising he was on thin ice. 'And, yes, Jade is pretty, as you've just pointed out, but not half as gorgeous as you, Mrs Cain, is she, Poppet?'

'No's the right answer,' he whispered, as Poppy looked doubtful, making Melissa laugh. She couldn't help it. The two of them together were mischief in the making. 'Especially wearing my shirt,' Mark added, rescuing himself this time. 'Though I prefer it without the leggings under.'

'Hmm?' Melissa wasn't ready to let him off the hook yet.

'You don't wear leggings,' Poppy piped up, her huge eyes saucered in astonishment as she squirmed in Mark's arms to stare at him, which caused them both to burst out laughing.

'Only on Sundays.' Mark assured her, hoisting Poppy onto one arm to reach in his pocket for his beeping mobile.

'You've met her then?' Melissa asked, easing the shawl to one side to check on Evie, who was still sleeping soundly.

'What?' Mark looked up distractedly from his phone.

Work texting him, Melissa guessed. 'Jade.' She nodded towards where Jade was gathering quite a uniformed fan club. 'I noticed you knew her name, so I assumed you'd met.'

'Out jogging. She runs around the same time I do,' Mark confirmed, his mind clearly more on the text he'd received than their new neighbour.

'She is very young, isn't she? To own her own home, I mean?'

'That's what I thought,' Mark said, his brow furrowed in concentration as he thumbed in a reply. 'Her parents passed away recently, apparently. Left her a tidy sum.'

'Oh no.' Melissa immediately felt for her. Losing her own mum before she'd hit thirty was bad enough, but to lose both parents at Jade's young age would be terrible.

'You have to admire her pluckiness, buying a property, especially one in need of renovation.' Mark glanced at Melissa and then back to Poppy, who'd clearly figured out that Daddy's mobile beeping early in the morning meant he would soon be leaving, and who was now fastening herself more firmly around his neck.

'Especially now,' Melissa said, looking across to what had been reduced to an uninhabitable property and then towards Jade, who was walking back towards them, looking like a lost soul.

Noticing the fresh tears brimming in the girl's eyes as she reached them, Melissa's heart went out to her. 'I take it it's going to take a while?' she said sympathetically.

Nodding, Jade dropped her gaze and nuzzled her cat. 'It looks like it was probably an electrical fault, but they can't be sure until they've done all the checks.'

'So, what will you do?' Mel asked, trying to make eye contact with Mark, whose phone was now ringing.

'Start the renovation over, I suppose.' Jade sighed, and then, clearly seeing that Mark needed to take his call and Melissa was struggling to manoeuvre Evie into the crook of her arm, moved to coax Poppy down with promises of chocolate.

Again, Melissa was grateful, if not overjoyed at the chocolate temptation. 'She's allergic to dairy,' she said, smiling nevertheless. 'But she can have a vegan chocolate bar, since she's being such a good girl, hey, Poppy?'

Amazingly, Poppy allowed Jade to unlatch her from her father, who was incapable of being strict with her.

'Allergic?' Jade looked utterly stricken as she lowered Poppy gently to the ground and took hold of her hand, as Mark stepped away to take his call. 'God, how stupid of me,' she said, closing her eyes.

'Don't look so mortified.' Melissa laughed. 'You weren't to know.'

'No, but we covered food allergies on my course so it should have occurred to me to ask,' Jade said dejectedly. 'I did a childcare course in college,' she supplied, as Melissa eyed her curiously.

'Well, it will next time.' Melissa smiled encouragingly. 'I actually meant where will you stay?' The girl was standing in the road with barely a stitch to her name.

Jade shrugged disconsolately. 'I have a friend I could ring,' she said, looking uncertain.

Again, Melissa felt her heart twist for her. 'No family you can call?' she asked carefully.

At that, Jade quickly shook her head, and then looked down at Poppy with a reassuring smile. 'I'll sort something out, don't worry,' she said, giving her hand a squeeze.

Poppy, though, didn't look convinced. 'You can't go out in your nightie,' she said, her huge brown eyes aghast. 'It's not allowed.'

'Come home with us,' Melissa offered. It was the least she could do.

'Yay!' Jumping on the spot, Poppy immediately gave that idea her seal of approval.

'I'm sure I can find you something to wear. We're about the same size,' Melissa went on, as Jade hesitated, 'if you don't mind jeans or leggings, that is. I spend most of my life up to my eyes in clay when I'm not changing nappies or doing the school run, so it's jeans or evening wear, I'm afraid.'

'She can't wear a sparkly dress in the day, Mummy,' Poppy pointed out exasperatedly.

'Who can't?' Mark asked, a familiar faraway look in his eyes as he turned back from his call.

'Jade,' Poppy informed him. 'She's coming home with us. Mummy's going to share some of her clothes with her.'

'Good idea.' Mark smiled. 'Sorry, got to go,' he said, bending to plant a kiss on Poppy's nose and another gently to Evie's forehead.

'Um, haven't we forgotten something?' Melissa asked him, as he turned towards his car.

'Damn.' Squeezing his eyes closed, Mark turned back to kiss Melissa, now looking definitely distracted, she noted. The call must have been important. She'd seen that look many times before.

'I actually meant your car keys,' she said.

'Ah, right.' Realising he was minus said car keys, and work jacket, and his ID, having dashed out when he'd spotted the fire, Mark headed swiftly past her back to their own cottage.

Rolling her eyes good-naturedly as he disappeared through the front door, Melissa beckoned Jade and – with Poppy skipping happily alongside her – they strolled more leisurely in the same direction.

Thirty seconds later Mark bowled past them again. 'Bye,' he said, spinning on his heel to smile apologetically. 'Sorry, it's—'

'Urgent. I gathered. Go.' Melissa waved him onwards.

'Bye, Daddy!' Poppy called after him. 'Love you bigger than the sky.'

'Bye, Poppet,' Mark called. 'Love you bigger than the sky and all the stars.' Blowing her a kiss, he shrugged embarrassedly at Jade and then climbed quickly in the driver's side.

'He's nice, your daddy, isn't he?' said Jade, as Mark started the engine and pulled away.

'Yes.' Poppy nodded adamantly. 'Mummy says he's too nice for his own good sometimes, but I don't really understand what she means.'

'That people might easily take advantage of him,' Jade explained, with a knowing smile.

CHAPTER TWO

MARK

Scratching his unshaven chin, Mark swung into the main office to find DCI Edwards pointedly checking his watch. 'Problems on the home front, I take it?' he asked him acerbically, his expression one of despair as he looked him over.

Mark followed the man's gaze down to realise the front of his shirt hadn't fared too well after his encounter with the cat and his none-too-elegant scramble over the garden gate to rescue it. As if it mattered what he looked like, with a child on the missing list.

'House fire. Neighbour's,' he explained, heading straight to his own office and his filing cabinet for the clean shirt he kept there in case of emergencies – of which there were many lately, with a new baby in the house.

DS Lisa Moyes was two steps behind him.

'Can you bring me up to speed, Lisa?' he asked her, tossing his jacket on his chair and reaching for his shirt buttons.

'It seems the girl was taken from home – assuming she was taken.'

'Which is where?' Mark asked.

'Farley Village, close to the Herefordshire border.'

Just twenty miles or so away from his own house, Mark realised. God, it could have been one of his kids.

'Parents were celebrating last night, apparently,' Lisa went on. 'Wife's birthday party. It all went a bit pear-shaped when hubby decided to give her a big surprise and shag one of the young female guests.'

Mark arched an eyebrow. 'Thoughtful bloke.'

'Very. And doing it in their bed was a nice touch, I thought.' Lisa smiled flatly.

Mark nodded, tugged off his shirt and reached for the clean one. 'So, when did they notice she'd gone?'

'This morning.' Lisa sighed. 'Mum went up to check on her and found the bed empty. They checked the house and garden and then called us.'

Which basically gave them a timeframe that was wide open. Mark tugged in a terse breath. 'I take it they argued after the birthday surprise?'

'Volubly, according to the residents of the neighbouring property. At it half the night. Husband makes himself scarce at some point. Wife falls asleep on the sofa with a bottle for company. Fairly standard stuff.'

In which case, it was possible the girl had slipped out, seeking to extract herself from what might have been one of many arguments, assuming the husband made a habit of screwing around. Mark's inclination as a kid had been to do the same. Knowing the shouting was a prequel to his father's violence, he'd been petrified. But wherever he went, whatever space he squeezed into, the bastard would always find him. He'd been terrified of the dark, imagining zombies or vampires lurking in shadows, but he'd felt a hell of a lot safer walking the streets at night than he had at home.

'We've searched all the likely places – house and garden again, gardens of properties within walking distance of the house, fields beyond it,' Lisa continued. 'And we've also managed to contact the wife's sister, who says that she poked her head around the child's door before she left. She confirms Daisy was still in bed.'

Daisy. His thoughts immediately went to Poppy, imagining her missing and terrified in the company of some sick individual, and Mark felt something twist inside him.

'We've currently got uniforms going door to door throughout the village. And we're pulling up all local sex offenders,' Lisa said, holding the door open for Mark as he hurried with the last of his shirt buttons. 'There's something else,' she added, as they walked towards the incident room. 'Might be relevant, might not, but I'm thinking it makes the husband definitely worth checking out.'

Mark read her expression and guessed he wasn't going to like it. 'Shoot.'

'The young female he was caught *in flagrante* with, she was very young. Just three days past underage, to be precise.'

Mark felt his jaw clench. 'Tosser. Find out whether he's on the sex offenders' register and make sure we have his PC and phone. If he refuses to hand them over, pull him in.'

'On it,' Lisa assured him. 'Talking of tossers…'

Mark followed her unimpressed gaze to see DS Cummings strolling towards them, a sleazy smirk all over his face.

'Not interrupting anything, am I?' His gaze drifted from Lisa to Mark, who was hastily tucking in his shirt.

'Piss off, Cummings.' Mark eyed the man disdainfully and moved past him, only to meet the now decidedly despairing glance of his DCI.

'Problem?' Edwards asked him.

Mark got the message. Even now, years after he'd communicated his feelings to Cummings regarding his sexual harassment of female colleagues, Edwards never missed an opportunity to remind Mark of his 'tendency towards hot-headedness'.

'Not with me,' Mark assured him.

'Good,' Edwards said. 'DS Cummings will be working with you on this one. Given the gravity of the case, let's leave the personal feelings aside in favour of finding the girl, shall we?'

'Sir.' Mark nodded, determined to do just that. Every second spent here was time wasted, as far as he was concerned. This would automatically be escalated as a high-risk case. The fact was, though, if the child had slipped out for whatever reason, with March temperatures averaging seven degrees, death from exposure was probable if she wasn't found soon. Time, therefore, wasn't a luxury they had.

CHAPTER THREE

JADE

Her day at school having been cut short when a water pipe burst, Poppy was chatting excitedly to Jade about her teacher, who'd apparently fainted in morning assembly, as Melissa led the way into the kitchen to dump the shopping bags on the island worktop.

'We heard the headmistress say it was because she was having a baby,' Poppy said, attempting to scramble up onto a stool. 'But we didn't see one.'

Jade swapped amused glances with Melissa. 'That's probably because baby wasn't quite ready to make an appearance yet, Poppy,' she said, lifting her up.

Poppy nodded thoughtfully as Jade planted her safely on the stool. 'Like Hercules's puppies, you mean?'

'Hercules had puppies?'

'Yes,' Poppy informed her with a matter-of-fact shrug, as she peered into one of the carriers. 'He's a girl dog, but Daddy got mixed up.'

'Ah.' Jade widened her eyes, which had Melissa laughing.

'He brought the wrong puppy home,' she supplied, and then mouthed 'rescue dog' in Jade's direction.

Jade nodded, getting the drift. Presumably, they'd decided to get a rescue, but Mark had had to change their choice at the last minute. Perhaps the dog they'd originally chosen had died, or shown unexpected aggression. He really was a lovely man. Poppy didn't know how lucky she was, growing up with a father who loved her like a father should.

'Poppy had already chosen the name, hadn't you, sweetie?' Melissa said, rescuing the eggs from Poppy before they ended up scrambled.

'Yes.' Poppy extracted a pack of cookies from the bag – dairy free, as Melissa had pointed out in the supermarket. 'I chose the name Hercules, because he had huge paws and Daddy said he was going to grow up to be big and strong,' Poppy supplied. 'Hercules's puppies weren't very strong though, were they, Mummy?'

'No, sweetie.' Smiling sadly, Melissa reached to brush Poppy's too-long fringe from her face.

'They were teeny-weeny.' Poppy demonstrated thus with her thumb and forefinger.

'Oh dear. Poor little things. I don't think they could have been ready to make an appearance either.' Jade reached to give Poppy a cuddle, as Melissa pointed back to the front door, beyond which little Evie was still fast asleep in the car.

'They couldn't breathe properly,' Poppy said, with a shuddery sigh, causing Melissa to hesitate at the kitchen door.

Jade smiled and nodded her on. 'I bet that made you sad, Poppy,' she said, as Melissa, duly reassured, went to retrieve the child she'd momentarily forgotten about.

'It did,' Poppy said. 'But I didn't cry too much, because I didn't want to make Hercules sad.'

'Well, you're a very considerate, grown-up little girl. I'm impressed,' Jade said. 'Hercules is very lucky to have you as a friend. I wish I had a friend like you.'

'But I *am* your friend.' Poppy said, her face earnest as she turned towards her.

Looking into Poppy's huge brown eyes, framed by long, dark eyelashes – her daddy's eyelashes – Jade felt her heart constrict inside her.

She composed herself and arranged her face into a smile. 'Well then, I'm very lucky too. And we'll stay friends, I promise. I'm not sure where I'll be living, but as soon as I find somewhere, I'll be in touch. Deal?'

Poppy knitted her forehead into a frown. 'But why do you have to find somewhere? You can stay here,' she said, splaying her hands to indicate the vast expanse of Melissa's kitchen, which, tastefully decorated, with children's paintings adorning the fridge and colourful height charts pinned to the walls, was comfortable and homey. Jade hated it.

'What, forever?' She chuckled indulgently. 'I'm not sure your mummy would be very happy about that.'

'Yes, she would,' Poppy assured her, with an adamant nod. 'Mummy says we should share with our friends and look after those less fortunut than ourselves.'

'Fortunate,' Jade corrected her. 'I'd like to,' she said, uncertainly. 'We'll see how it pans out, shall we? If Mummy says she wants me to stay, then I'll think about it.'

'She will,' Poppy said confidently, stretching her arms out and leaning towards her to be helped down. 'I'll tell her I want you to stay because you're my bestest friend ever.'

'But only if Mummy suggests it first.' Jade lifted Poppy off the stool, swung her round and planted her on her feet. 'We don't want Mummy to think she's being ganged up on, do we?' she added, in answer to Poppy's obvious confusion.

Poppy shook her head sombrely. 'No. Miss Winters says it's cruel to gang up on other people at school.'

'Exactly.' Jade smiled. 'She's a wise woman, your teacher. And you're a sensible girl for listening to her. It's not nice being bullied, Poppy, trust me.'

Poppy scanned her face. 'Are you being bullied?' she asked her, her eyes clouding with concern.

'No,' Jade assured her. 'I was once, though, when I was little. It made me cry.'

Poppy looked alarmed at that. 'I won't let anyone bully you, Jade,' she said, sticking her chin up determinedly.

'Nor I you.' Jade reached out to brush her hair from her eyes. 'We'll look out for each other. Okay?'

'Deal,' Poppy said delightedly. 'Would you like to see my room?'

Jade extended her hand. 'I'd love to.'

Poppy slid her own small hand trustingly into Jade's. 'It's a bit messy. Nemo's water needs to be changed,' she said, as they headed to the hall. 'And Baby Annabell was supposed to tidy up her toys, but she forgot. You won't tell Mummy, will you?'

'My lips are sealed.' Jade mimed zipping her lips.

'And mine are sealed about your secret chocolate supply.' Poppy smiled up at her, doing likewise.

Jade smiled conspiratorially back. 'I think we have an understanding.' *Win the child over, win the parents over*, she thought, satisfied that she'd got the child on side. She'd felt a sliver of guilt for stuffing a whole chocolate bar down in front of Poppy while Melissa had been in the baby changing room.

CHAPTER FOUR

MELISSA

With Poppy and Evie fed and settled, Melissa gave Jade the guided tour of the house, before the poor woman was driven mad by Poppy's constant chatter and tea parties with an assortment of Peppa Pigs and scarily lifelike baby dolls. Poppy, it seemed, had taken to their guest, declaring Jade her 'bestest friend ever'. Jade had been wonderful with her, and Melissa could see why she'd chosen childcare as a vocation. She was obviously a natural.

'And this,' she said, leading the way into the detached brick garage at the bottom of the back garden, 'is what I grandly refer to as my studio. It still needs some work. The roof leaks when it rains and the window's rattling in the frame, but it's my sanctuary… when I can find time.'

'Gosh, you have your own kiln?' Jade said, obviously feeling the blast of warm air as they went in.

'It is a bit stifling, isn't it?' Melissa said, as Jade fanned her face with her hand. 'I normally have the air con on when I'm working.' Reaching to flick the freestanding unit on, she bent to lift Poppy into her arms, lest she wander in the direction of the kiln. 'I used to take my pieces to the art university to be fired, but they're extremely fragile once the clay's dried out. I did worry about the safety aspect of having my own kiln with little ones around, but at least it's away from the house. And, as Mark said, if I'm going to be a serious sculptor…'

'Impressive,' Jade said, gazing around. 'You even have a potter's wheel.'

'And a husband who understands my artistic temperament.' Melissa smiled, recalling how she'd caught Mark watching her from the doorway one night, before he'd wandered in and done a fair imitation of Patrick Swayze. It had been messy – gloriously messy – but hugely satisfying.

'Fortunately,' Jade said, her gaze flitting over her, making Melissa immediately aware of the staple workwear she usually wore – leggings or jeans and tops that wouldn't be ruined by clay or baby sick spatter. Was Jade being the tiniest bit facetious?

But then, seeing Jade's warm smile, Melissa despaired of herself. It was *her*, feeding her own paranoia. She had wondered sometimes how Mark had stuck with her through the dark times. He'd never stopped reassuring her he loved her – down days, artistic temperament and all – but she couldn't help thinking he might wish he was with someone more glamorous, someone who preferred to wear something slightly more alluring to bed than one of her husband's old shirts. She was just someone who 'scrubbed up well' – at least according to Detective Sergeant Cummings, who'd voiced such an observation at the last social function they'd been to together.

But then, Mark had been quite into her shirt last night. Melissa smiled quietly, recalling the wicked glint in his chocolate-brown eyes as he told her that imagining her naked beneath it was a serious turn-on, how he'd pinned her to the bed, with not much protestation from her, and worked excruciatingly slowly through each button, finally asking her to keep it on while he made deliciously slow love to her.

Phew. Stop. She'd be dragging him upstairs for a repeat performance as soon as he walked through the door at this rate. Dismissing her errant thoughts – which she absolutely shouldn't be having in company – she turned to her workbench to seat Poppy, who was growing heavy in her arms, at the end of it.

'And this is my latest masterpiece,' she said, indicating the sculpture on the bench. It was ceramic dipped in bronze, a kneeling, naked couple embracing, and Melissa was particularly proud of it. Still, she felt a flutter of trepidation in her tummy at showing it to Jade, which was mad considering her work was already stocking the shelves of the local craft centres and Garden & Homes store. Hopefully, the latter would stock her nationwide at some point, depending on whether she could fill the orders.

'Wow!' Jade looked the sculpture over and then back to Melissa in awe. 'That's really amazing, Melissa,' she said, hesitantly reaching out a hand. 'Can I touch it?'

'*Nooo*,' Poppy whispered, turning aghast eyes in Jade's direction. 'It's not allowed.'

'Not allowed with sticky fingers,' Melissa reminded her, reaching for the tissue she kept permanently up her sleeve, ready to mop the remnants of Poppy's coconut milk ice cream from her face, which would have the child wriggling like an eel in an instant.

'Go ahead,' she said, nodding Jade on. 'Sculpture is as much about tactile stimulation as visual, in my mind.'

Tentatively, Jade traced the soft curves of the figures with her fingertips. 'It's beautiful,' she said, sounding genuinely impressed. 'Nice pecs,' she added, turning to give Melissa a mischievous smile.

'Yes,' said Melissa, then, noting where her hand had come to rest, she laughed. 'And I enjoyed sculpting that bit too.'

'Mummy, what's pecs?' Poppy asked, temporarily distracted from Melissa's face-scrubbing endeavours.

'Muscles,' Melissa supplied. 'Large ones.'

Poppy looked at Melissa, astonished. 'But, *Mummeee*, that's a bottom,' she pointed out, correctly.

Melissa and Jade exchanged glances and then both laughed out loud. 'And a very tactile one, too,' Jade assured her.

'What's tactile?' was Poppy's inevitable next question.

'Pleasing to the touch. Now, come on, young lady, scoot,' Melissa said, lifting Poppy down from the workbench. 'Go and choose a DVD. Daddy will be back soon to get you into your jim-jams. You can have one hour of TV before bed. And don't wake Evie. She's not due a feed yet.'

'Yay! *Beauty and the Beast.*' Poppy whooped excitedly, charging through the workshop door and up the garden path.

CHAPTER FIVE

JADE

'Do you work in the evenings then?' Jade asked interestedly, as Melissa checked her kiln. The temperature in the garage was now stifling. With that and all these toxic materials about, Melissa's 'workshop' didn't appear to be a very child-friendly environment.

'To be honest, since having Evie, it's a case of grabbing time when I can. I have the baby monitor.' Melissa nodded towards the monitor parked on another bench, the surface of which was littered with various modelling tools – some of them quite sharp, Jade noted. There was also a dustbin, full of slip-sodden clay. Extremely dangerous, with an inquisitive seven-year-old about. 'I don't like to be too far away from her though,' Melissa went on. 'You never know, do you?'

'No, you certainly don't.' Jade sighed, looking appropriately concerned. 'You're not that far away here, though, are you? And little Evie's still at the sleep-and-eat stage. You might have to think about a babysitter later, of course.'

Melissa looked thoughtfully at her. 'Yes.'

Bait taken, Jade thought, pleased. 'So, you'll be working tonight then?' she asked, happy to leave the seed to germinate now it had been planted.

'I'm off to the university art class,' Melissa said, surveying her 'masterpiece' and then collecting up the workshop key from the bench. 'They have a new life model so I thought I'd grab the opportunity to make a few more sketches.'

Pausing before heading for the door, she looked around, as if checking all was in order, although there was precious little order in here. As far as Jade could see, the place was a mess. Not somewhere she'd want to spend time hiding away from her children. Jade would have cherished every second with her baby, if only…

Dismissing that thought, she smiled and widened her eyes in pretend surprise. 'What, as in *naked* life model?'

'As the day he was born.' Melissa smiled coyly. 'Quite a tasty model too,' she added, waggling her eyebrows suggestively, which was extremely irritating.

Jade smiled serenely. 'The one you've modelled your sculpture on?' she asked, nodding back to the clay monstrosity adorning the workbench.

'The very same.' Melissa looked pleased with herself.

'Hmm…' Jade cocked her head to one side, perusing the sculpture interestedly. 'Well, I must say I wouldn't mind measuring him up with my pencil.'

'You might need a big one,' Melissa quipped, and blushed. 'But whatever you do don't tell Mark I said that. 'I wouldn't want him measuring himself up and finding himself lacking.'

'My lips are sealed,' Jade laughed, zipping her lips. 'It's nice of him to help out with the kids. I mean, I know he's their dad and everything, but…'

'Some men wouldn't,' Melissa finished knowingly. 'True, sadly. Mark can't always, of course, but he tries, depending on his workload.'

Jade nodded. 'Worth holding onto then?'

'Definitely. And I intend to,' Melissa assured her, her expression smug. Like the cat that's got the cream – and knows it. Fittingly, she even had green eyes. They were quite nice, Jade supposed, in a beguiling, childlike way. It was no wonder Mark's natural instinct was to look after the woman. Jade had known him to be that kind of man the first time she met him. A good man. A caring man.

'Talk of the devil,' Melissa said, worry creasing her brow as she checked the number on her ringing mobile.

Mark calling, Jade gathered. And what was Melissa's reaction? Delight that he was calling? Excitement? No. She was worried, plainly only for herself. Mark didn't need a vulnerable woman in his life. He needed someone who understood him. Someone to protect him from women like this one, who was clearly taking advantage of him.

'Oh, Mark…' Melissa sighed disappointedly into her phone. 'I was just waiting for you to come…' Trailing off, she glanced at Jade, her expression changing to one of concern as she went on, 'No, no, it's fine. Of course I understand.'

Of course I understand, Jade mimicked silently. The woman wasn't capable of understanding anything but her own needs, as far as Jade could see. Presumably Mark's workload wasn't going to allow him to come home and babysit her children, after all. *Good.* That could work nicely to Jade's advantage.

'It's not the end of the world,' Melissa assured him. 'I can always reschedule. Just concentrate on what you have to do. Those poor parents. They must be going out of their minds…' Smiling in Jade's direction, she turned to walk down the path a little, in search of privacy.

As if Jade wanted to listen to her false sentiment anyway. Sighing contemptuously, she turned to close the workshop door. She was about to pull it to, when the cat that Mark had rescued slinked past her into the workshop. Jade glanced behind her to see Hercules, panting and prancing on the lawn. Obviously, the dumb animal had been chasing the cat, as if it could ever catch it.

'Scat,' she hissed in the dog's direction, glancing quickly over her shoulder, lest Melissa hear her. Hercules might just ruin things for her, Jade had realised. Were it not for the fact that Mark clearly doted on the dog, even talking to the flea-ridden thing when he was out walking it, Jade would have rid herself of that particular problem. She was beginning to wish she had. Rat poison would soon put a stop to it growling at her.

Stepping back into the workshop after the cat, Jade was about to call it – though she wasn't sure by what name, as it was actually a stray – when, in one swift feral leap, it sprang from the floor up to the workbench. *Whoops.* Jade winced as the sculpture teetered. And then surveyed the cat thoughtfully as it padded to the end of the bench and back again to weave itself around the sculpture, which really was rather close to the edge.

Damn. Jade's plan to close the door and let the cat do its worst was foiled as she realised that Melissa had finished her call. She couldn't afford for her to peer back and see that she'd shut the bloody cat in with her precious works of art. However...

'*Shit!*' she said out loud, hearing Melissa coming towards her, and then moved – with the agility of the cat – across to the bench. 'I've got it. Don't panic,' Jade said, her best relieved expression in place as Melissa followed her in. 'I saw it teetering.' She nodded towards the sculpture, which was now on its side, resting on her hand. 'Hercules chased Felix in.' She hurriedly christened the cat. 'I'm really sorry. I moved as quickly as I—'

'Oh God, don't be,' Melissa cut in, her concern only for her sculpture as she stepped across to unburden Jade of it. 'It was Hercules's fault. She's always up to mischief. It's like having another child sometimes, I swear.'

Righting the sculpture on the bench, she turned to look at Jade. 'Thank you,' she said. 'Thank God you were here.'

Jade saw the woman close her eyes, clearly immensely relieved, and considered that she'd earned herself another brownie point. 'But preferably catless?' she asked, turning to pluck the newly christened cat up.

'It wasn't Felix's fault, was it Felix?' Melissa drew a hand down the cat's back as Jade cuddled it. 'It was that naughty Hercules, wasn't it, sweetie?'

Oh no. Jade wasn't sure she could handle this woman baby-talking to animals, but she smiled brightly anyway.

'Bad Hercules,' Melissa said, leading the way out again and making sure to lock the door once Jade had exited behind her. 'Behave.' She scowled in the dog's direction. 'Or you'll be tied up.'

Jade mentally shook her head. She would swear to God the woman was waiting for the dog to acknowledge her as she wagged a finger at it.

'Problem?' she asked, as they headed back towards the house. 'Sorry, I didn't mean to eavesdrop, but I gathered it was Mark calling.'

'He's been detained.' Melissa sighed resignedly. 'It can't be helped,' she added quickly. 'It looks as if it might be a child abduction case.'

'Oh no. How heartbreaking.' Jade's step slowed. She glanced at Melissa, suitably stricken, though she imagined the only people the abusive, alcoholic parents would be heartbroken for were themselves.

'Dreadful.' Melissa shuddered. 'Having little ones, Mark always takes these cases to heart.'

'You're disappointed though, I bet,' Jade ventured sympathetically. 'I don't blame you. I would be. It can't be easy being cooped up with two little ones all day.'

'I am a bit,' Melissa admitted. 'But then, I should really be counting my blessings. I can't begin to imagine what the parents of that little girl must be going through. What the poor child might be going through.'

Stopping at the patio doors, Melissa wrapped her arms about herself, a troubled look clouding her eyes, as if she were imagining it. As if someone like her, living her perfect life, *could* ever imagine what it was like to be so traumatised as a small child that you prayed to God to make you dead and take you to heaven.

'Me neither.' Smiling empathetically, though she was sure the little girl was better off where she was, Jade gently placed a hand on Melissa's forearm. 'Poor Mark. I hope he finds her.'

'Oh God, I hope so, too.' Melissa pulled in a shuddery breath. 'He'll be absolutely devastated. He can't bear even the thought of children being hurt in any way.'

'I know.' Jade sighed, recalling again the first time she'd met him, the genuine grief in his eyes. 'You can see he's a caring man,' she added quickly. 'And he obviously adores his kids. I don't envy him. Look, it's only a suggestion, but why not let me babysit?'

Melissa looked uncertain.

'I have got my childcare qualifications, after all, so you might as well make use of me. And I can always call you if there's a problem.'

'Of course you do,' she said, still looking a little uncertain. 'But… are you sure? It's a bit of a cheek.'

'It's no problem at all,' Jade assured her. 'Like I said, I'm here anyway. It's the least I can do after all your kindness. And, to be honest, after this morning's events, chilling out with a DVD sounds like heaven.'

Melissa glanced through the patio doors to check on Poppy, who was already sitting cross-legged in front of the TV in anticipation of *Beauty and the Beast*. 'You've got the job,' she said, smiling gratefully.

'I wish,' Jade said, with a sigh. 'I'm job hunting at the moment. But I've no idea how I'm actually going to apply for any jobs now I'm homeless.'

CHAPTER SIX

MELISSA

'I usually let her catnap until eight, and then wake her for her feed,' Melissa said, dashing into the lounge to grab her sketch pad and pencil case from the coffee table. She looked around for her shoulder bag and then remembered she'd hung it on the stairs. Honestly, she'd swear to God that giving birth had addled her brain.

'There's milk in the fridge. I generally warm it in a bowl.' Realising she was running late, she checked her watch – and dropped her sketch pad. 'You'll find one in—'

'Melissa, I can manage,' Jade assured her, reaching to pick up the pencils that had spilled from the pencil case as Melissa bent to retrieve her pad. 'And anything I can't find, Poppy can point me to. Right, Poppy?'

'Yeth,' Poppy said, around the thumb plugged into her mouth. 'You can go now, Mummy.'

Dismissed, thought Melissa, eyeing the ceiling and then smiling gratefully at Jade as she handed her pencils back to her. 'Don't miss me too much, will you?' she said, going over to plant a kiss on Poppy's cheek.

'I won't,' Poppy said, attempting to peer around her at the TV.

'Well, that's reassuring.' Melissa sighed, theatrically rolling her eyes at Jade.

But rather than feeling put out by Poppy's apparent indifference to her presence, Melissa was pleased. Jade, it seemed, had definitely won her over, which was a huge relief. Their last babysitter, the daughter of a friend, hadn't been a hit, and Melissa had been reluctant to bring in another, which wasn't conducive to she and Mark spending any quality time together. Jade had also been fabulous with Evie, feeding her earlier without a hiccup. She really was a natural with children.

'Bed by seven thirty at the latest, young lady,' she said to Poppy. 'And don't forget to brush your teeth.'

'*Mummeee…*' Poppy sighed exasperatedly. 'We're missing the film.'

'Right, I can see where I'm not wanted.' Shaking her head in amusement, Melissa headed for the door. 'I'll be back in time for Evie's ten o'clock feed,' she told Jade, and then stopped. '*Damn!* I forgot to get milk out the freezer for the morning.'

'I'll do it.' Jade spun Melissa back towards the front door as she turned in the direction of the kitchen. 'Go. Not too much licking of pencils or drooling.'

Melissa laughed. 'I'll try not to,' she assured her, and then hesitated again at the front door. You know, you're quite welcome to stay a while if you need to, Jade. I mean, I wouldn't want you to feel obliged to babysit just because you're here, but… Well, we have space if you need it while you sort yourself out.'

Jade beamed. 'I'd love to, as long as you're sure. It would be a huge weight off my mind.'

'Positive.' Melissa smiled warmly. 'Just don't let madam here wrap you around her little finger.' She nodded towards Poppy, who was listening eagerly from the lounge doorway.

'Does this mean you're staying forever and ever, Jade?' Poppy asked, her eyes wide with excitement.

Jade exchanged a knowing glance with Melissa. 'Well, not forever and ever,' she said, turning back to her charge. 'But for the moment, yes.'

'Yippee!' Poppy jumped with glee. 'I told you. I told you.'

'So you did,' Jade said, steering her back into the lounge. She smiled at Melissa over her shoulder. 'See you when you get back.'

'Thanks, Jade. You're a godsend. I'm sure Mark will be pleased you're staying for a while,' she called, dashing out.

'Oh, I'm sure Mark will too.' Smiling, Jade settled down on the sofa, extending her arm for Poppy to snuggle comfortably under.

CHAPTER SEVEN

MARK

Driving home, Mark was thinking about Daisy Evans, the missing little girl. There had been no evidence of a forced entry, and he was considering the possible involvement of the parents in her disappearance, in particular the father's. Although Michael Evans had been caught having sex with a girl who was only just past the age of consent, Mark believed he hadn't known how old she was. The guy was an ex-footballer, and the girl was a member of his fan club. She was apparently besotted with him, and had told him she was eighteen. It didn't make what he'd done much more palatable, but her friends had corroborated his version of events. He'd had pornographic images on his PC, but nothing illegal. No suspect images or messages on his phone. He also had an alibi for the time in which his daughter disappeared. Mark wasn't enamoured of the man any more than he was of Cummings – who, laughably, had adopted a stance of moral outrage at Evans' 'obvious sexual exploitation of a sixteen-year-old' – but the guy's anguish had been palpable.

The meeting with the mother had been harrowing. Mark's initial assumption on learning the parents had been arguing, so drunk they hadn't noticed their child was missing, had been a kneejerk reaction, one born of his own childhood memories of cowering in corners as arguments escalated. It had prejudiced his thinking. Daisy's mother had been beyond devastated, blaming herself. She'd broken down as they left. Pausing on the drive of the house, a detached country property worth a fair sum, Mark had heard her heaving sobs as the front door closed. Whatever the future of their relationship, if Daisy wasn't found, God help them, the parents would both blame themselves for the rest of their lives.

Dammit. Frustrated, Mark banged the heel of his hand against his steering wheel. They *had* to find her. But *where?* Sighing, he ran a hand wearily over his neck. He needed some downtime. He needed to check his girls were warm and safe in their beds, and touch base with Mel. He wished he could do more than touch base… her warm body up close was an appealing thought right now. Whatever shit he was dealing with, he always felt safe in her arms. She reckoned he'd been her white knight; that somehow he'd saved her, but Mark knew it was the other way around. He'd had relationships before her – too many, because with no role models in his life, he didn't know how to do relationships – but Mel had shown him how, made him believe that love was possible, that he was a fully functioning, normal person, despite his dysfunctional background and his conviction that bad blood would out and he would inherit the traits of his abusive father. She'd made him believe in himself, because she'd believed in him. She'd loved him. His love for her… it scared him sometimes. The all-consuming love he felt for his children terrified him. His family were his lifeblood. He simply wouldn't know how to be without them.

Noting Mel's car wasn't there as he pulled into the drive, it took a second before Mark remembered her art class. It looked like she'd gone after all. Who was watching the kids? Their last babysitter, though she'd come recommended, hadn't been up to much. Or rather, she had, if coming home early to find her in a steamy clinch on the sofa with her boyfriend had been any indication. Neither he nor Mel were prudish, but the cider the guy had brought with him was definitely not on. Emily, a mutual friend, helped out when she could, but weren't the Chandlers away on holiday?

Mark checked his mobile as he walked to the front door, only to find the battery had died, which might explain why he hadn't received a text from Mel. She would undoubtedly have sent him one. The lights were on, he noted. The TV, too. Peering around the lounge door, he saw that it was empty, though the knot of worry in his stomach was quashed at the obvious signs of normalcy. He headed upstairs, figuring the kids would be in bed and the babysitter might be checking on them.

Poppy's door was ajar, and he could see her fast asleep in bed, Hercules curled up protectively at her feet. Mark breathed out a breath he hadn't realised he was holding in. Then, instructing Hercules to stay, he carried on towards the nursery, where he stopped and cocked his head to one side. Well that was a bloody relief. Tugging his collar loose, Mark listened for a second at the partially open door before going in. It seemed they did have a new babysitter, and she sang like an angel.

'*Hush, little baby, don't say a word*,' came a melodic voice from inside. '*Mama's going to buy you a mockingbird. If that mockingbird won't sing, Mama's going to buy you a diamond ring.*' Mark pushed the door open, and then, noting she had her back towards him, Evie nestled on her shoulder, he waited again rather than frighten her. He was mildly amused when she skipped straight to the last verse, obviously not knowing the words in between: '*Hush, little baby, don't you cry, Daddy loves you and so do I.*'

Smiling, Mark tapped on the door as she started the lullaby over. Jade spun around, the alarmed look on her face making it clear he had scared her, despite his efforts not to.

Shit. Mark stepped forward. 'Sorry,' he said. 'I should have called up from the hall, but I thought the kids might be asleep. Are you okay?'

'Yes, sorry. My fault. I should have been paying attention.'

'You were.' Mark smiled. 'To Evie.' He nodded towards his baby girl, who was awake but sleepy, and perfectly content on Jade's shoulder. 'I'll make sure to announce myself in future.'

Jade smiled back, though she still looked rather flustered at him looming in the doorway. With good reason. Averting his gaze, Mark stopped short of moving further into the room to say hello to Evie. That possibly wouldn't be a prudent move, what with Jade wearing a strappy top and pyjama shorts under her dressing gown. Obviously she was staying with them, which given her circumstances was fine, but… Christ, this was awkward. Mark really wished he'd remembered to plug his phone in earlier.

'She's been as good as gold,' Jade said, stepping towards him. 'Haven't you, angel?'

Pressing a kiss to Evie's soft downy head, she looked back to Mark. 'I was just about to pop her down for a nap before Melissa gets back, but I'm assuming you want to have a quick cuddle? Sorry about being in my PJs, by the way,' she said, handing Evie gently to him. 'I needed to wash the smoke out of my hair, so I grabbed a quick shower before I fed her.'

And Mark felt like a bit of an idiot. Clearly, he was the only one feeling uncomfortable. And clearly it showed. 'Thank you, I would very much like a quick cuddle,' he said softly, marvelling afresh at the perfect wonder of his tiny child as he gathered her close.

CHAPTER EIGHT

JADE

Making sure Evie was safe in his arms, Jade nodded towards the door. 'I'll just go and sort a few things out,' she said to Mark, offering him another bright smile as she took her leave.

Once on the landing, she looked back, her heart flipping and her pelvis dipping as she watched this tall, dark, broad-shouldered man nestling his baby close.

He didn't yet know who she was, of course. Jade had made sure he wouldn't. She'd thought it better that way initially. He was fundamentally a good man, after all. She wouldn't want him to do anything that went against his nature. He would have to be persuaded gently that the life he was living was all a façade. That, as much as he loved his children, he could never be fulfilled living with a woman who'd used those children to trap him. He'd sensed her, though. It had been obvious from the appreciative look in his eye as he'd glanced at her figure – which Melissa's pyjama set enhanced quite nicely. He, too, felt the undeniable chemistry between them.

In time, he would know. Smiling fondly, she turned to the bedroom the bitch wife had said she could use. Soon, Mark would realise they were two souls connected, destined to be together forever.

CHAPTER NINE

MELISSA

Mark almost bowled into Melissa as he came out of the front door – on his way back to work, she assumed. 'Hey.' He smiled. 'How's the new male exhibitionist?'

'Excellent,' Melissa said, with a mischievous wink.

'That good, hey?' Despite his best efforts to look annoyed, Mark's mouth twitched up at the corners. 'A lesser man might feel threatened, you know.'

Melissa leaned in to press a kiss to his cheek, allowing her hand to stray around back to clutch a handful of his very pleasingly toned rear as she did. 'Good job you're a bigger man then, isn't it, DI Cain?'

Mark furrowed his brow at that. 'Er, thanks. I think.'

'I take it this was a flying visit?' Melissa eased back to eye him seriously.

Mark nodded regretfully. 'Afraid so. Sorry.'

'No progress then?' Melissa asked, a shiver of apprehension running through her as she read Mark's gloomy expression.

'Not much, no,' he said, sighing wearily. 'I have to get back to the station. Organise available bodies for searches come first light.'

He really did look tired. Melissa noted the shadows under her eyes as he leaned to brush her lips with a kiss and move around her. She wished he could stay.

She wondered if they would despatch police divers to the river. Organise fingertip searches in fields and woods? She knew from experience how these things progressed.

'I'll see you soon. Take care,' she said, as he climbed into his car. It would be useless saying what she really meant: remember to eat, and try to get some sleep somewhere along the line. Learning the missing girl was around Poppy's age and knowing Mark as she did, she very much doubted he would be doing much of either.

'Oh, and Mark,' she called, as he reached for his door. 'I sent you a text earlier. Did you see it?'

'No, sorry. Mobile wasn't charged.'

'Jade's staying for a while. I thought I'd better let you know in case you run into her wandering around upstairs when you get back.'

'I've already had the pleasure.' Mark smiled wryly. 'She's qualified, presumably?'

'Abundantly,' Melissa assured him. 'She did a childcare course at college. I thought she might able to help out with the girls.'

'Have you checked out her references?'

'Of course.' Actually, she hadn't, but she could have hardly done that this evening. She'd do it first thing tomorrow. 'Mark Cain, you're not questioning my judgement, are you?' Melissa cocked her head to one side, eyeing him pseudo-disparagingly.

'Never. Wouldn't dare.'

Melissa laughed as Mark cringed in mock-terror and hurriedly closed his door. Watching him drive away, she turned to let herself in, trying not to mind that he was dashing off again. Policing was what he did, and she loved him for it, loved that he cared enough to want to try to make the world a safer place – but she missed him. And she worried incessantly for him, more so when he was dealing with cases involving children. With his own abysmal childhood, he seemed to feel their every hurt. But she wished he wouldn't blame himself when he couldn't fix that hurt. When he couldn't make their world a safer place.

He would slip out at night, sometimes, when sleep eluded him. Walking the streets, Melissa guessed, trying to get into the mind of a young child who might be a runaway, understanding why they might have run. He'd been reluctant to share his past secrets with her at first, imagining himself less of a man for admitting that his childhood ghosts haunted him still. He really was an enigma: strong and macho on the outside, yet deeply caring on the inside.

It had taken them a while to find each other again after Jacob. For her to come back to him. Mark had been patient – there to hold her when she'd needed holding, to catch her if she fell. And instinctively, no words necessary, he'd known when she'd needed him to move beyond holding. His lovemaking had been so gentle, so perceptive of her needs. And when she'd finally allowed herself to reach that sweet climax, he'd held her again while she sobbed in his arms. Held her like he might never let go.

She'd loved him more than she'd thought possible that night.

She hoped he was charging his phone. Dumping her sketch pad on the hall table and hanging her bag over the rail, she reached for her phone to text him again as she climbed the stairs to check on the children. She needed to remind him how much she still loved him.

Pausing at Poppy's door, she was about to go in when she noticed Jade emerging from the main bedroom. 'Jade?' she said, surprised to see she was dressed in no more than a short towel.

'Ooh, hell,' Jade whirled around. 'Sorry. I didn't hear you come in. I was just about to take a shower but I couldn't find any shampoo in the main bathroom. I *really* need to wash the smell of smoke from my hair.'

'Ah.' Melissa nodded, relieved. For a second, she'd thought… She'd no idea what she'd thought, actually. 'I'll fetch some from the en suite,' she said, making a mental note to stock up on bathroom essentials other than baby products. And to leave more than a hand towel out.

CHAPTER TEN

MELISSA

'Morning,' Jade said brightly, as Melissa came into the kitchen.

Melissa blinked, surprised to see everyone up and at it. 'Good morning,' she said, turning her gaze to Poppy, who, amazingly undistracted by early morning TV, was seated at the table, happily munching away on cereal – made with oat milk, of course.

'Morning, Mummy,' Poppy said, equally brightly.

Bleary-eyed, Melissa wandered across to plant a kiss on the top of her head, peering into her bowl as she did. 'I thought you didn't like cornflakes,' she said, noting the distinct absence of morning must-have Coco Pops.

'I do now.' Poppy shovelled in another spoonful. 'Jade said it will make my hair grow like hers.'

Melissa followed her daughter's wishful gaze to Jade's luxuriant blonde locks. It would certainly be some achievement, given that Poppy took after her father with her dark colouring and chocolate-brown eyes, but Melissa was happy to play along if it meant the battle of breakfast was no more.

Smiling, Melissa accepted the glass of fresh orange juice Jade handed to her, and headed towards the back door, where daughter number two also appeared to be content.

'She's had her early morning feed,' Jade said, as Melissa peered into the pushchair. 'You were fast asleep, so I thought I'd bring her down. I wasn't sure whether you liked her to have a bit of fresh air, but it's such a beautiful day. I hope it's okay?'

'Perfect. Wonderful, in fact.' Resisting the urge to plant a kiss on Evie's perfect cupid lips, Melissa tucked her shawl up and moved quietly away. She wasn't directly in the sun, but warm enough. Jade was right – it really was a gorgeous day.

Melissa looked her competent house guest over. Jade looked like a ray of sunshine, exuding vitality and health. She even made Melissa's clothes look good – a pre-baby striped yellow T-shirt, which Melissa didn't think suited her new, fuller breasted look, teamed with a pair of blue leggings.

'What do you fancy for breakfast?' Jade asked, heading to the toaster, where two hot slices popped on cue.

I'll have whatever you're having. Feeling the slightest bit wishwashy, and definitely mumsy, Melissa sighed inwardly. With her pale complexion and uninspiring ginger locks, which Mark kindly termed copper and which would be scarily frizzy at this time in the morning, she probably looked like one of the living dead by comparison. She couldn't believe she'd slept so long. The hot chocolate Jade had kindly made her last night appeared to have done its job. Obviously, she'd needed the sleep, but she didn't feel a lot better for it.

'I'll grab some cereal,' she said, yawning widely – and receiving a reprimand from Poppy as she did for not placing her hand over her mouth.

'Sorry.' Melissa stifled another yawn. 'I'm obviously more tired than I thought I was.'

'I'm not surprised, trying to run your own business with two little ones to look after – you must be absolutely frazzled,' Jade said, glancing at her sympathetically as she sailed by with a tray, on which was the toast, Melissa noticed, along with a tumbler of orange and a black coffee. 'Why don't you go and grab a shower? It might make you feel human.'

Now Melissa definitely felt like one of the living dead.

'I'll just pop this into Mark and then—'

'Mark?' Melissa gawked. 'He's here?'

Jade stopped, looking puzzled. 'In the lounge. He came home to get changed. He went to get a nightcap and the next thing I knew, he'd fallen fast asleep on the sofa.'

Melissa glanced at her, confused. She felt as if she'd slept the clock around and woken up to find herself in another time zone. It was stupid – paranoid probably – but… Mark never went into the lounge for a nightcap in the middle of the night. He'd previously had a spell of drinking more than was good for him once. They both had, when life had been cruel. Since then, though, he'd have wine with his meal, but rarely a nightcap. If he was keeping the hours he was now, it meant he was working a case that needed him to be clearheaded. He would grab a cold drink from the kitchen and then come straight upstairs. If he couldn't sleep, then he would walk – with the dog, if he could coax her out without waking Poppy.

'He looked so exhausted I didn't like to disturb him,' Jade went on. 'I didn't like to think of him charging off again without eating anything either, so… Are you all right, Melissa? You look a bit pale.'

Melissa was now feeling very baffled. She'd taken a paracetamol last night. At least she'd thought she had. She hoped to God she hadn't picked up the wrong packet. The sleeping tablets she'd been prescribed after losing Jacob were still in her bathroom cabinet. No, surely not. She'd checked the packet. Hadn't she? But still, she felt definitely woozy.

'What time did he come in?' she asked, aware it must have been after the last feed she'd given Evie. The baby had woken unusually early, at around two thirty rather than three thirty, which is when she'd taken the paracetamol.

'About five,' Jade said, looking puzzled.

And she was up? Melissa was growing more confused by the second.

'I heard someone downstairs.' Jade answered the question she hadn't asked. 'I was worried about the children so I crept down.'

'That was brave of you,' Melissa said, in all sincerity. Jade wouldn't have known it was Mark.

'It could have been a bug monster!' Poppy said, aghast.

'In which case, I would have poked his beady bug eyes out,' Jade assured her, looking fierce.

'With a big sharp knife,' Poppy said, narrowing her eyes in an attempt to look fierce too.

'Probably not a good idea, Poppy,' Melissa suggested, 'unless you want to end up in prison. It's not allowed.'

'But what about if it was a burglar?' Poppy asked, her eyes widened innocently.

'Still not allowed. In any case, it wouldn't be. Our house is very secure. Now, finish your breakfast, young lady. And then shoes on, please, or you'll be late for school.'

'Sorry,' Jade said, as Poppy huffed and went back to her cereal. 'I *really* should have thought that one through.'

Melissa looked up to the clock and wondered whether it would be acceptable to do the school run in her husband's crumpled shirt and leggings. Then she caught sight of Jade, still standing with the tray, looking uncertain and somewhat dejected.

And Melissa felt like a cow. The girl had let her lie in, obviously done her best to take over the helm while she'd been sleeping, and what had *she* done? Come over all proprietorial, as if her space were being threatened, and promptly burst her bubble. Her friend Emily had had a babysitter for a while, while she and Adam were busy setting up their holiday chalet business, and she'd once admitted she'd felt her nose had been put out of joint, even confiding she'd been the tiniest bit jealous at first, when the babysitter appeared to look after her child better than she did.

Chastising herself, Melissa smiled. 'It's okay,' she said, reaching to give Jade's shoulders a squeeze and then relieving her of the tray. It was nice of her to think of Mark, but if anyone was going to take him breakfast, it was Melissa. Not that he could expect such service on a regular basis. 'Poppy has a vivid imagination,' she said. 'She's very good at storytelling. She must take after her mad, arty mother.'

Jade looked relieved, though her smile was a little less zingy than it had been.

'I'll take this in and see if I can rouse my husband from his slumber,' Melissa said, supposing she'd have to get used to setting boundaries, but perhaps more subtly in future. 'You could do me a huge favour, though, if you wouldn't mind, and take Poppy to school. I'd hate to embarrass her in front of her friends.'

Jade's smile widened at that. 'You look fine,' she said. 'Great legs. But of course I wouldn't mind taking her. Come on, Poppy. Shoes on, sweetie. You can't possibly scrape that bowl any cleaner.'

Extending her hand, Jade waited for Poppy to scramble down and latch onto it.

'Jade…' Melissa stopped her, as they headed for the hall. 'Thank you. You've done an amazing job. I really would have been lost without you this morning.'

'No problem,' Jade assured her. 'Poppy and Evie have been as good as gold.'

Melissa hesitated. She hadn't been considering a babysitter just yet, though it was something she had on her future to-do list. She wasn't sure what kind of employment Jade might be looking for, but working here whilst overseeing the repairs to her own property might actually suit both of them, assuming she hadn't already scared her off. 'Jade, it's just a thought, but if it's a babysitting job you're looking for, I could certainly use some help here.'

'Really?' Jade looked hopeful.

'Really.' Melissa looked around, indicating the general bedlam. 'I was considering growing an extra pair of hands, but… I'd pay you the going rate, of course.'

'That would be brilliant. Perfect, in fact. Yes, I'd love to.' Jade beamed. And then she turned her smile on Mark, who had just appeared in the doorway, looking possibly more bleary-eyed than Melissa felt.

Smiling uncertainly back, Mark stepped aside to allow Jade to exit. 'Ahem,' he said, as Poppy skipped by without a word. 'I thought you loved me bigger than the sky?'

Melissa heard Poppy's audible intake of breath as she realised she'd ignored him, and watched with amusement as she abandoned Jade's hand and charged towards her father. 'I do!' she declared. 'Bigger than the whole moon!'

'Glad to hear it.' Only just managing to scoop her up as she threw herself at him, Mark laughed and smooched her neck, which had Poppy in wriggle mode in an instant.

'*Daddeee*,' she said, rubbing her cheek as she pulled back to inspect his face, 'you need to shave.'

'Yes, *ma'am*. Immediately, ma'am.' Lowering her to the floor, Mark planted her back on her feet, and then saluted. 'Bye, Poppet,' he said. 'Have a good day, and remember the Cain motto.'

'Be wise, stay vigilant.' Serious-faced, Poppy repeated the motto Mark drummed into her every morning. Translated: *don't go near strangers.* 'Wilco.' She nodded, blew him a kiss, then turned to catch up with Jade as she opened the front door.

'Whoops. Hang on a sec.' Mel put down the tray and turned to fetch a spare front-door key from the hooks on the utility door. 'In case I'm in the shower or out in the garage when you get back,' she said, handing the key to Jade.

'Brilliant.' Jade smiled. 'I might pop by the bank and order a new debit card, but I shouldn't be too long. Bye, Mark. You stay vigilant out there, too.'

'I will,' Mark assured her. Smiling as he watched them go, he turned to Melissa. 'I think our temporary house guest's a hit.'

'Um, actually, she might be more semi-permanent.' Melissa quickly picked up the tray, hoping to distract him from the fact that she hadn't discussed hiring Jade with him first.

'Oh?' Mark arched an eyebrow curiously. 'How so?'

'Well, I know we weren't thinking of taking anyone on just yet, but…' Melissa shrugged and smiled. 'She's our new babysitter. I hope you approve.'

Mark considered, and then nodded. 'Absolutely,' he said. 'If it means I get served breakfast on a regular basis.'

'Don't bank on it, Detective,' said Melissa, pinching a slice of his toast.

With Evie settled back into her cot, Melissa finally stepped into the shower, allowing the hot water to cascade over her and wash her awake. She was soaping herself luxuriantly when Mark passed by the en suite door. And then stepped back for a better view.

'You do know that could be deemed provocation, Mrs Cain?' he said, leaning against the doorframe, an arm across his chest, one hand grazing his unshaven chin as he watched her thoughtfully through the shower door.

Melissa smiled. God, he looked delicious, sexily dishevelled. 'And that, DI Cain, could be deemed voyeurism.'

'Guilty.' Mark smiled, stepping into the bathroom. 'I, er, don't suppose there's room for two in there, is there?'

'That depends on how good with the soap you are, DI Cain.'

'Very,' Mark assured her throatily, hastily stripping off his shirt and making short shrift of the rest of his clothes.

Melissa felt a thrill of anticipation as he stepped in behind her to demonstrate his skills. Burying his face in her neck, trailing his tongue over the already soapy wetness of her skin, Mark took his time, reaching around her to gently circle each sensitive nipple, touching her with slow, soft caresses and feather-light brushes with his thumbs, each touch so exquisitely pleasurable it was almost painful.

'Okay?' he checked with her, that alone almost bringing Melissa to sweet orgasm there and then, reminding her what a good lover he was, how caring of her needs. He hadn't been particularly sure of himself when she'd first met him – not surprising, given how his confidence had been knocked out of him. His uncertainty, though, had been nothing but endearing in a man so good-looking. And he'd learned fast. There was nothing they wouldn't do now, instinctively moving together as one. Nothing they hadn't done.

A low moan escaped her as he slid one hand over the soft round of her tummy.

'Have we got time for this?' she gasped, as he moved lower.

'Always,' he said huskily, hitching her towards him. She ached for him; she needed him. She wanted to slide her hands over him, soap his broad shoulders, to trail them down over his chest, his taut stomach.

Feel his body up close to hers.

She caught her breath as he slid a finger carefully inside her, his thumb now expertly circling, building her to heights of ecstasy she wasn't sure she could bear.

'Beautiful,' he breathed, with such intensity that, despite her baby blues self-doubt, she truly believed she was.

'Now?' he asked her.

Melissa could only moan her affirmation as he pulled her closer. With one hand propped against the wet tiles of the wall, his other supporting her, he eased himself inside her, pacing himself, checking with her, as if she were made of precious porcelain after all her body had been through. She loved him so much for that. And then he increased the rhythm, in tune with her, until he was plunging deep inside her.

CHAPTER ELEVEN

JADE

Bitch. Stunned, Jade backed silently out of their bedroom to press herself against the landing wall, her stomach clenching painfully inside her as she heard Mark's deep, throaty moan. Primal urges, that's all it was. He was a man. He had needs.

Jade tried to temper her fury, squeezing her eyes closed to block out the images of him making love to another woman. It was only because she was convenient. A convenient fuck! Why else would he?

Peeling herself from the wall, Jade tried to slow the rapid beat of her heart, and then, pausing at the nursery door, made her way quietly back to the stairs. She needed to be calm, she reminded herself. The epitome of niceness.

Notching up her chin, her back straight, Jade descended the stairs. Stopping in front of the hall mirror, she tried to compose herself, working to obliterate all emotion from her face.

Walking into the kitchen and calmly opening the dog food cupboard, she selected a chew from the plastic storage box therein and then headed for the back door, collecting the key for Melissa's workshop from the hook on the utility door as she went.

The cat was on the patio, basking in the sun. Whispering reassuringly to it, Jade picked it up. She actually couldn't wait to be rid of it. What was Melissa thinking, allowing a cat free run of the place? It could easily slink upstairs to lap at lips fresh with milk and end up suffocating her baby. Irresponsible cow.

The dog was on the lawn, its head plopped dejectedly between its paws. The stupid mutt had clearly realised the cat was too clever for it by far.

'Stay,' she instructed it, and then headed to the workshop with the cat. Once inside, she placed the cat on the bench, using a sliver of the chew to entice it to stay there, and then went over to the window. Melissa was right, it was definitely in need of repair. Jade eased the latch and opened the window, and then, scanning the tools on the workbench underneath it, she selected a knife-like sculpting tool, which pushed easily between hinges and frame. It took a couple of heaves, but both hinges came away from the rotting wood fairly easily.

'Stay, Felix,' she said sweetly, running a hand the length of the cat's back and up its tail as she passed it. Feeding it another nugget of chew, she moved to the sculpture, trailing a hand languidly over that, tilting it sideways, and then allowing it to fall and crash satisfyingly to the floor.

Alarmed, the cat jumped down, but Jade was already at the door, slipping sleekly out and closing it behind her. It didn't take much to push the window in. One hard shove was enough. Jade was impressed with the dog's agility skills, she had to admit, as she watched it sail through the windowless hole after the chew she threw into the workshop.

Jade furrowed her brow as she let herself out through the gate beyond the garage. Might it have cut its paws on the glass, she wondered. Briefly.

CHAPTER TWELVE

MARK

'I wasn't drinking on my own in the small hours,' Mark assured Melissa, as he towelled his hair with one hand and checked a text from Lisa Moyes with his other. 'We were out of coke in the fridge so I—'

Reading the text, Mark stopped: *Forensics back. Stain on stairs confirmed blood. DNA match to Daisy.*

Shit! Cursing silently, Mark tossed the towel aside. He was pulling on his clothes when he heard a distressed mewl and frenzied barking from the garden. Heading fast for the window, Mel close behind him, he looked out to see the cat scaling a tree as if its tail were on fire. Mark waited a second, expecting Hercules to come belting after it. More frantic barking but no sign of the dog. There followed a brief silence, followed by a sudden heart-flipping, high-pitched yelping that meant she was in trouble. Serious trouble, Mark realised, sensing the dog's escalating panic.

Turning, he raced to the landing, while Mel grabbed up her dressing gown, tugging it on and stuffing her feet into flip-flops to follow him.

'I'll go,' Mark said, nodding towards the nursery. He was probably being neurotic, but his inclination right now wasn't to leave the children on their own, and out of hearing distance.

Once in the kitchen, Mark stopped to search for the workshop key, but it wasn't hanging from its usual hook.

Dammit! 'Mel, the key!' he shouted, and headed out to the garden, where the dog's cries were growing more urgent by the second. What the hell had happened? All became clear as he neared the workshop and saw that the window – which he'd added to his mental to-do list but hadn't yet fixed – was missing. The cat must have gone in, chased by Hercules, who was now stuck inside the workshop.

'Stay, Hercules,' he said, calmly but firmly, as he approached the empty frame. 'It's okay, girl.' Mark peered in, and swallowed, hard. 'Okay, girl, stay. I'm coming.'

'Mark?' Evie in her arms, Mel was behind him as he hitched himself up to climb through after the dog. 'Where's the key?' she asked, as he was poised to drop the other side.

'Missing,' Mark replied tersely, noting Hercules had sunk to her haunches and was emitting no noise now but a low, pathetic whine.

'What's happened? Is she all right?' Mel called urgently, as he dropped carefully down to crouch beside the dog, talking softly to her and trying to coax her to turn so he could reach to apply pressure to the wound.

No, Mark thought. *She's very much not all right.* How in God's name was he going to get her out without injuring her further? 'She's bleeding,' he said, as calmly as he could. He didn't want to panic the dog, or Mel. 'Badly. Front leg. We need the key, Mel. Can you remember where you left it?'

'It's on the hook. I'm sure I hung it… Oh God.' Evie clutched close to her, Mel peered into the garage after him, clearly shocked when she saw the fountain of rich red blood Mark was trying to stem with his fingers.

'Ring the vet,' Mark instructed. 'See if they can send someone urgently. I'll have to try and lift her back through—'

'Melissa!' It was Jade, shouting from the other end of the garden. 'What is it? What's wrong?'

'Hercules!' Mel shouted. 'She's injured. I've lost the key. We can't—'

'It's on the hall table,' Jade cut in. 'I'm sure that's where you put it. Hold on. I'll go and look.'

Thank Christ for that. Mark thought, relief surging through him. The girl's timing was impeccable. From the amount of blood she'd lost, there was no doubt in Mark's mind the dog was going into shock. Lifting her back through the window would probably kill her. He should try to elevate the leg, he was aware, which would slow the bleeding. But how was he supposed to do that without an extra pair of hands?

Had Mel called the vet yet? Or the fire brigade, who could at least break the door down? A neighbour? Anybody would do. Where *was* the damn key? Frustrated, and trying hard to suppress his own panic, Mark leaned down to wipe the blood from his face against his shoulder. With combustible and toxic substances stored in here, the place was an accident zone. They'd discussed it. Agreed to keep the key on the hook, should it be required at short notice, and well out of Poppy's reach.

Yes, and he'd agreed to get the damn window fixed ASAP. If anyone was at fault here, he was. Mel had a million things on her mind with Poppy and Evie's needs to attend to alongside her work. Mark doubted he could perform the juggling act she did on a daily basis half as successfully.

'Hold on, girl,' he said softly. 'You're not called Hercules for nothing, you know.' Praying silently, he glanced upwards, and then snapped his gaze to the door as it opened.

'Mel's rung the vet,' Jade said, coming in and dropping down beside him. 'He said to keep pressure on the wound and take her straight there. Mel's just popping Evie back in her cot. What can I do?'

Mark nodded. 'I'll carry her. I'll need you to stay with me and take over the pressure bit. You'll need two hands, here and here.' He indicated where his own hands were placed. 'Are you okay with that?'

Jade immediately jumped to her feet. 'I'm right by your side,' she said determinedly.

Mark's mind was still on Hercules as he finally arrived at the station. And Mel, who was obviously blaming herself for what had happened. He shouldn't have been so short. He'd meant to apologise, but then he'd received another text from Lisa, informing him that DCI Edwards wasn't impressed by his absence, and Mel had slipped back to the workshop while he'd been replying.

At least it looked as if Hercules was going to be okay. Thank God for Jade, who'd certainly gone above and beyond her babysitting duties, even offering to pick the dog up from the vet's later while Mel tried to rescue what was left of her workshop and organise a glazier. Jade had only been with them ten minutes and already Mark was beginning to wonder how Mel had managed to keep all the balls in the air without her. She had though, allowing him to get on and do what he had to do. And by way of appreciation, he'd acted like a dickhead as soon as there was a blip on the domestic front, as if it was a major inconvenience to his work agenda. He'd left her in the workshop, plucking pieces of smashed sculpture from a pool of coagulating blood. She'd said it didn't matter when he'd asked her about it, but she hadn't looked him in the eye. She'd dragged her hair from her face, and kept her gaze fixed firmly on her task. Not sure what to do, what he could do, and running desperately late by then, he'd brushed her cheek perfunctorily with a kiss and said he had to go. No doubt Mel would quite like the freedom to sail out and leave someone else to pick up the pieces sometimes too. He really was going to have to apologise.

Pushing through the security door into the main office, Mark realised he needed to change the dressing on his hand. At first, he hadn't even realised he'd cut it while he'd been tending to the dog. But then, there'd been so much blood he'd have been hard pushed to identify any of it as his own.

'Crisis on the home front *again*?' DCI Edwards asked drolly as Mark headed past his open office door to the incident room.

That one was wearing a bit thin. Sighing inwardly, Mark offered an apology. He'd definitely been juggling crises on the home front at one point. With Mel ill, and everything falling apart around them, he'd taken to self-medicating, the odd nightcap growing into one too many. Mel had known it, which is why she was wary of him drinking late at night now. And Edwards had known it, reprimanding him on several occasions. He'd been right to – Mark's mind hadn't been on the job.

He'd lost sleep after messing up on a case, failing to notice one of his team hadn't followed the chain of custody, meaning evidence could have been contaminated. The vicious little shit who'd walked free had offended again, inevitably, kicking an old man almost to death because he'd refused to part with his phone. The old man had passed away a week later. Mark would never forgive himself for that. And Edwards, it seemed, would never let him forget it – which Mark couldn't blame him for, but he didn't need it, just as he didn't need Cummings constantly winding him up.

He hadn't lost too much sleep over his confrontation with Cummings. The man openly harassed women. He was a kerbcrawler. If anyone was a disgrace to the uniform, Cummings was. Mark couldn't prove it – yet – but he suspected Cummings had recently pocketed proceeds of a drugs bust he'd thought wouldn't be missed. The package he'd seen him passing to a sex worker had looked suspiciously like crack cocaine, which basically meant Cummings was fuelling the woman's addiction. Whether in exchange for sexual favours or information, Mark wasn't sure. Either way, the man was pond scum, end of.

Mark noted the cretin looking him interestedly over as he walked by his desk. He would swear the man was trying to goad him into losing it. Mark's guess was that Cummings knew he was on to him, and was trying to provoke Mark's 'emotional volatility', thereby making any accusations he made against him questionable. Mark's only real hope of nailing Cummings was to get enough evidence to make sure he was at least suspended pending investigation.

'Blimey, hope it wasn't a domestic,' Cummings commented behind him.

Shaking his head, Mark smiled sardonically. With supreme effort, he ignored Cummings and walked on. He had more important things to do right now than waste time on that prat.

'What have we got?' he asked, once in the incident room.

'The blood is definitely Daisy's,' said one of the team, confirming what Lisa had already texted him. 'She had an appendectomy about a year ago, so we were able to get a match from the hospital. I'm thinking we'll need to call the forensic experts back in.'

That wasn't going to be news the parents would welcome. Mark sighed disconsolately. 'Do the parents have an explanation for the stain?'

'She cut her foot in the kitchen a couple of weeks back, according to the mother,' said Lisa. 'The husband corroborates her story. We're still gathering information from possible witnesses, relatives and friends.'

'Thanks, Lisa.' Mark smiled wearily. 'Anything on the garage CCTV footage?' he asked, ignoring Cummings, who'd wandered in with nil sense of urgency and was now slouching on the edge of a desk.

Cummings, though, wasn't going to be ignored. 'Funny you should ask that,' he cut in.

Kneading a temple, Mark glanced towards him. 'Would you like to enlighten me?' he asked patiently.

'I've just been checking it,' Cummings said. 'I noted a car cruising past in the direction of the house.'

Lisa was obviously as impressed as Mark at that really useful piece of information. 'It's a road, Cummings,' she retorted acerbically. 'It's what cars travel on.'

Cummings glanced at her indifferently and then looked back to Mark. 'At four o'clock in the morning or thereabouts,' he went on leisurely. 'On three separate occasions over three consecutive weeks prior to the girl's disappearance.'

'And?' Growing more irritated by the second, Mark urged him on.

'And it looked familiar,' Cummings said, holding Mark's gaze.

'Oh, for fuck's sake, hurry it up, Cummings,' Lisa snapped. 'We haven't got all day.'

Cummings' mouth curved into a slow smile. 'It's a silver Audi Q5,' he said, and let it hang. 'Registered to one DI Mark Cain.'

CHAPTER THIRTEEN

MELISSA

'She's fast asleep,' Jade said, coming into the workshop. 'Do you need a hand with anything here?'

Mel glanced up from where she was mopping the last of the blood from the floor. It seemed to have been smeared everywhere. Mark had been saturated in it. Some of it, Mel had realised when he got back from the vets, was his own. She'd fetched him a bandage and tried to help him wrap his hand, but he was rushing. Late. Keen to be gone. Mel couldn't blame him.

He hadn't said much about her sculpture, which had been smashed to smithereens. But then, that was understandable. He'd hardly have been taking stock of the damage while desperately trying to stem the flow of blood from the dog. The sculpture didn't matter. It *was* important, to her, and it being irretrievably broken before she'd had time to make a cast was obviously upsetting. It was the statue the Garden & Homes store were considering stocking nationwide. But it was insignificant in the great scheme of things. Poor Hercules.

More upsetting, though, was that Mark had been so obviously annoyed about her forgetting to put the key back. She'd felt like crying when he dashed off, giving her no more than a peck on the cheek after all that they'd done together the first time he'd showered.

It was the shock, she supposed, catching up with her. Plus, she was still so damn tired. The fuzziness, like damp cotton wool in her head, just wouldn't clear. She needed to go for a brisk walk or something, get a grip. Mark was bound to have been frantic, and she was being oversensitive, her hormones playing havoc, more than likely. Thank God Jade had been there. Things could have been so much worse if not for her presence of mind.

'Mel,' Jade prompted. 'Do you need a hand?'

'No. Thanks, Jade.' Mustering up a smile, Mel attempted to pull herself together. 'You've been an absolute rock, I honestly don't know what I'd have done without you, but it's all pretty much cleaned up here now.'

'I'm so sorry about your lovely sculpture.' Sighing sadly, Jade walked across to where the remnants lay on the bench. 'It's such a terrible shame.'

Mel raked her hair from her face, which was a bedraggled mess. 'It's not the end of the world.' She shrugged. 'But it could have been, if not for you. I'll just have to start over.'

'Well, you just shout when you need some space to work,' Jade suggested. 'I feel so awful about it all. I'll obviously be more than happy to look after Poppy and Angel for as long as you need me to.'

'Angel?' Mel looked at her curiously.

'Sorry – Evie.' Jade shook her head apologetically. 'I minded a baby about the same age until her parents moved away.'

'Ah.' Mel nodded. 'Pretty name.'

'Yes.' Jade smiled. 'She was a beautiful little girl. A lot like Evie.'

Mel smiled at that. Evie was beautiful. The prettiest baby in the hospital ward, Mel had thought. But then, she had been the teeniest bit biased, she supposed. 'Look, Jade, there's no need for you to feel bad about any of this,' she assured her, leaning over to the bench and retrieving the key, which she would make sure to hang in its proper place. 'It's hardly your fault.'

'It is a bit. Felix was the cause of it,' Jade reminded her, following Mel to help her out with the dustbin full of debris. 'Hercules would hardly have hurled herself through the window if she hadn't been chasing the cat.'

'True, I suppose.' Mel took some small comfort from that. Glancing around, she satisfied herself that all that could be done was done for now, and pulled the door to.

'It's no wonder Mark was so snappy,' Jade said, with another heartfelt sigh.

Mel glanced at her, as she helped carry the bin towards the designated rubbish and recycling area. 'You noticed then?' she asked, her heart sinking.

'A bit,' Jade admitted reluctantly. 'But then, with everything that was going on and that woman constantly texting him…'

'Woman?' Mel arched an eyebrow as Jade trailed off.

'Lisa, I think I heard him call her from the bedroom when he went to get changed, before he left for work. I was passing, and I couldn't help overhearing,' she clarified quickly, as Mel shot her a questioning glance.

Realising who she meant, Mel smiled amusedly. 'She's a work colleague,' she explained. God forbid Jade should think Mark was in the habit of ringing women from the bedroom. She'd be wondering what kind of household she'd agreed to work for at this rate.

'Ah, I gathered it must be something like that.' Jade nodded. 'She's a bit keen though, isn't she?'

Is she? Mel hadn't noticed. Then again, she didn't really give his many texts and calls much thought, other than that they were work-related and therefore necessary.

'I'd better get back to Evie,' Jade said, stepping back to leave Mel to manoeuvre the bin into place. 'Unless you'd rather…?' She nodded towards the house.

Mel followed her gaze. She'd like nothing more than to retreat to the nursery, truth be told, to breathe in the reassuring smell of her little one and close her eyes for five minutes. Unfortunately, there was still the matter of the gaping hole where once was a rotting window.

'No.' Smiling wearily, Mel ran a hand over her aching neck. 'That would be great, Jade, if you wouldn't mind. I've still got to ring the glazier and I suppose I should tape something over the window until he can get here.'

'No problem.' Jade beamed her a smile back and turned to hurry back towards the house. 'Oh, I wouldn't worry too much about covering the window,' she called back. 'I've got rid of the cat.'

Got... What? Mel stared after her. 'Got rid of it how?' she shouted, but Jade was already disappearing through the back door.

CHAPTER FOURTEEN

MARK

He wasn't serious? Was he? Looking from Cummings, who was slouching against the window ledge, to DCI Edwards, who sat stony-faced at his desk, Mark laughed incredulously. 'You have to be joking,' he said, bewildered that his DCI would imagine he'd be doing anything in the area but driving by.

'Doesn't look very amused, does he?' Cummings observed wittily.

'Sit down, please, DI Cain,' Edwards instructed, casting a scathing glance in Cummings' direction, which was at least something.

Dragging a hand through his hair, Mark stayed where he was, his emotions swinging from disbelief to anger.

'We have to eliminate everyone from our enquiries, DI Cain. You above all should know that.' Edwards' gaze flicked towards him and then to the chair. 'Sit.'

This was fucking *nuts*. Mark counted silently to five, lest he was tempted to give in to his urge to wipe the supercilious smirk off Cummings' face, and then did as bid, where he waited, infuriatingly, while Edwards finished writing up whatever was so uber-fucking-important he felt obliged to ignore him.

Finally, Edwards downed his pen, leaned back in his chair and laced his fingers over his chest. 'Well?' he said, his expression impassive as he looked at Mark.

'Well, what?' Mark asked agitatedly. Did the man not realise what Cummings was up to? Looking for any and every opportunity to undermine him in front of Edwards. Obviously he didn't, because Mark hadn't yet filed his concerns about Cummings. Something he intended to rectify as soon as was humanly possible.

Edwards leaned forwards to eyeball Mark meaningfully. 'Don't be insubordinate, Detective,' he warned him quietly. 'I'd like details, please, of what you were doing driving through Farley Village in the early hours of the morning on three separate occasions.'

Tugging in a long breath, Mark curtailed his temper. 'I was trying to get Evie to sleep,' he said, locking eyes with Edwards and making damn sure to hold his gaze.

'Well, it's different,' Cummings sneered, 'I'll give you that. Definitely a new one on—' he stopped as Edwards glared in his direction.

'Would you like to elaborate?' Edwards asked, turning back to Mark.

Not really, no, Mark thought. But he had no choice, he supposed, galling though it was to talk about this in front of someone as contemptuous of marriage and children as Cummings was. 'Evie went through a phase of not sleeping between her three thirty and six thirty feed,' he explained, reluctantly. 'Mel needed to sleep. She was exhausted. Evie tends to nod off in the car, so I drove around with her.'

'Obviously going for father of the year award,' Cummings drawled sarcastically. 'In the habit of negotiating hairpin bends in the dark with your baby daughter in the car, are you?'

'I play music. Classical,' Mark answered tightly. 'It lulls her to sleep.'

'Right. No doubt while being filmed. Pay you well, do they, Audi, for starring in their smoother ride advert?'

Mark clamped his jaw tight, and didn't retaliate. Cummings would just love that.

Edwards picked his pen up, his forehead creased thoughtfully as he tapped it on his desk. 'And your wife will corroborate this, will she?'

'Bound to, isn't she?' Cummings muttered. 'May I suggest we get the video enhanced, sir,' he suggested, turning to Edwards. 'Just to confirm that the child was actually in—'

'No, you may not,' Edwards cut in bluntly.

Cummings stared at him, confounded. 'But surely you're—'

'That will be all, DS Cummings. Thank you.' Edwards turned back to Mark, something resembling a smile flitting across his face. 'Mark, get Melissa to give me a call, will you?'

Mark was taken aback for a second. 'Er, yes, no problem,' he said, watching bemused as Edwards went back to his paperwork. 'Is that it?'

'For now, yes,' Edwards confirmed.

Cummings glanced between them, shaking his head scornfully. 'I don't bloody believe this.'

'Dismissed, DS Cummings,' Edwards said, without looking up.

'What a fucking joke,' Cummings griped behind him, as Mark headed for the door to get on with what he was supposed to be doing – finding a missing child.

'Oh, that you definitely are, Cummings,' Mark grated, heading for his own office.

Lisa looked Cummings disparagingly over as she walked across to join Mark. 'Someone piss on your firework, did they, Cummings?'

'Just doing my job,' Cummings said, veering off towards his desk. 'I doubt DI Cain would have hesitated if the shoe were on the other foot.'

'Not for a second,' Mark assured him, wondering whether it might be worth an official warning in exchange for wiping the floor with the bastard.

*

Deciding positive action might be more productive than volatile reaction, Mark begged the use of a PC's personal vehicle that evening. He knew he should be using the time before the forensic specialist's report came back to be with his family, especially after the catastrophe that morning, but the cocky expression on Cummings' face as he'd sauntered out of the office had only made Mark more determined to catch the bastard in the act. Did the man really think that his car being picked up on CCTV amounted to anything? That he'd find *anything* in Mark's life or career – apart from the fact that Cummings' own repugnant activities had pushed him to the limit – that would make him a subject of investigation? Cummings had miscalculated, badly, if he'd imagined Mark would back off rather than risk being accused of pursuing a personal vendetta.

Following him at a discreet distance, Mark drove on by as Cummings parked up outside a 1960s high-rise, the seventh floor of which, Mark knew, was home to Tanya Stevens. Located just off the M5 into Birmingham on a notorious overspill estate, the decaying block of flats should have been demolished years ago, in Mark's opinion. Cummings wasn't paying Tanya a social visit, that was for sure. Normally to be found working the inner-city streets, Tanya only ever entertained her regular clients at home. Was Cummings one of them?

Driving around the block to allow Cummings time to go in, Mark planned to wait until someone turned up to allow him access into the foyer, but was surprised to find Cummings still parked up outside. So now what? Mark debated and then pulled into the car park of the adjoining block. There was a chance Cummings might have spotted him, but noting the open driver's side window and the billowing cloud of cigarette smoke, Mark thought not. The cocky bastard was clearly quite comfortable waiting there, for reasons which were pretty obvious in Mark's mind.

Sure enough, after a minute or so, Tanya appeared. She obviously didn't consider Cummings a regular, or else didn't trust him enough to allow him access to her flat. As a sex worker, Tanya was street savvy and choosy. Clearly, she had standards that excluded slimy, chauvinistic pricks like Cummings. Would she offer up any information about him, he wondered, given the right incentive? Mark doubted it. He'd first made her acquaintance after a girl who'd worked the patch next to her had gone missing, as, sadly, they sometimes did. Some of them had moved on, or more likely been moved on by their pimps. Some succumbed to drug abuse. Occasionally, missing girls would turn up having been hospitalised by their charming employers, or by the equally charming clients they hadn't been so streetwise about. Mark had a hard time convincing the girls he was more concerned for their welfare than how they earned a living. Realising he was on the level had earned him a grudging respect, and one or two informants. Not Tanya, unfortunately, who'd told him that, unless he could guarantee twenty-four-hour protection for her kid, she'd rather not piss off her pimp.

Watching as Tanya spoke briefly to Cummings through his window and then went around to the passenger side, Mark considered his next move. He had no wish to resort to taking snapshots of Cummings' nefarious sexual activities, but the fact was, if the man was passing drugs here, then he needed evidence of it.

Realising that Cummings had started his engine, probably to avoid whatever activities were about to go on in the vehicle being caught on CCTV, Mark did likewise. He doubted Cummings' 'liaison' with Tanya would be a long one. She'd want to be in and out of that car ASAP. Then Mark would need to talk to her – buy some of her time, if necessary.

Surprised when Cummings' car slowed again as it hit the street, Mark idled behind him. Either that was the shortest hand job in history or there was some negotiation going on. Serious negotiation, from the look of it. Mark narrowed his eyes, reaching to unfasten his seatbelt as he noted the animated body language inside the vehicle.

What the—? He watched as Cummings turned to Tanya, his hand shooting out to clutch her by the throat and force her head back against the passenger-side window. Mark was out of his door in a second flat.

He was almost upon the car when the door flew open and Tanya spilled from it to hit the kerb hard. *Bastard.* Hearing the rev of the engine, and guessing Cummings was about to step on the accelerator, Mark deliberated, and then, noticing Tanya wasn't moving, he went instinctively to her.

She was out cold. 'Tanya? Seeing a trickle of blood on the road, Mark crouched down and quickly attempted to assess the damage before moving the girl. He blew out a sigh of relief as her eyelids flickered open.

'Hi. How're you doing?'

Tanya blinked, disorientated for a second, and then clearly registered who he was. 'Fuckin' marvellous,' she grumbled, her face creasing into a scowl. 'How do you *think* I— *Ouch!*

'Don't move,' Mark said, as she tried to lift her head. 'You might need an ambulance.'

'Yeah, right. Blinding idea, Detective Cain. I'm lying in the gutter with me fanny on show and he says *don't move*.' Eyeing the sky, she heaved herself up regardless, amid much wincing and cursing.

Mark smiled, embarrassed, despite his years on the force. He debated whether to help her with the very short skirt she was tugging down, decided against, and offered her some assistance up instead. 'You've had a nasty blow to the back of your head, Tanya,' he pointed out, as she hung onto his arm, attempting to right herself on the pavement. 'You could be concussed.'

'Well, I never. I wondered why I was bleeding. It's no wonder you're a detective.' Sighing, Tanya rolled heavily made-up eyes, and then looked around for her missing stiletto, without which she was decidedly lopsided. 'Do us a favour, will ya?' she said, nodding towards it.

Dutifully, Mark obliged, offering his arm again as she wobbled while stuffing her foot into the shoe. 'I'll help you home,' he said. He guessed he'd probably get a load of verbal for his efforts, but he wasn't about to let her make her own way like this.

'Thank God for the freakin' cavalry,' Tanya muttered, as he steered her in the direction of his car. 'Wanker…' she added disdainfully.

Mildly surprised – he wasn't sure what he'd done to earn that – Mark glanced at her, and then followed her gaze to where Cummings was cruising slowly by.

'*Fuck!*' Mark swore, noting the quick flash of a camera and the smile on Cummings' face as he drove away.

CHAPTER FIFTEEN

MARK

Pulling up on his drive, Mark sighed wearily. Tanya had wavered, just for a second, obviously tempted to shaft Cummings and give evidence about how he was passing drugs… 'Yer living in la-la land,' she'd told him outright. 'What d'you think Eric'll have to say about me talking to the law, hey?'

Eric, the oily bastard that pimped her out, and had probably pumped her full of drugs in the first place, was highly unlikely to say anything, preferring to do his talking with his fists, or worse. It had been a non-starter. Cummings must have known he was behind him, and he'd played right into his hands. He'd obviously promised Tanya drugs as payment and then, knowing Mark wouldn't walk away, he'd decided to have fun of a different kind.

Idiot. Cursing his stupidity, Mark climbed out of the car and headed for his front door, trying to shake off the day as he did so. Mel really didn't need this – him miles away, contemplating where the missing girl might be, what Cummings might be up to. She needed him on board when he was home, focused on his family.

Wondering how the land lay, he let himself through his front door with a degree of trepidation. He'd checked in earlier, learning from Jade that Hercules was okay. He'd left a message for Mel, but she hadn't rung back, which was worrying.

'*Daddeee!*' Poppy, already in her pyjamas, immediately charged through to greet him from the lounge.

'Hi, Poppet,' he said, sweeping her up into his arms. 'How's my favourite seven-year old?'

'*Shhh.*' Poppy pressed a finger to her lips. 'Hercules is sleeping.'

'Is she?' Mark matched her serious look with one of his own. 'In which case, I'll be as quiet as a mouse, I promise,' he whispered, looking past her to Mel, who was smiling uncertainly in his direction.

Relieved, Mark walked towards her to offer a more affectionate kiss than he had this morning, although a rather awkward one, with Poppy sandwiched between them.

'How is she?' he asked softly, easing away.

'Good. She lost a lot a blood, but the vet thinks she'll be back to her old self in a day or two.'

'She has to have lots of rest for the first twenty-five hours, though,' Poppy informed him, with an important little nod.

'Twenty-five, hey?' Mark tried not to laugh, furrowing his brow thoughtfully instead. 'In which case, we'd better tiptoe upstairs and read our story very quietly. I think it's past a certain young lady's bedtime, don't you?'

Poppy immediately scowled at that, and then brightened as Jade came down the stairs. 'I'll take her,' she said. Poppy whooped, then clamped a hand to her mouth, lest she wake the dog. 'You look exhausted.' Jade smiled sympathetically at Mark.

'Are you sure, Jade?' Mel asked. 'You've already done more than your fair share today.'

'Always happy to help out in a crisis,' Jade assured her. 'Plus, it will give you two time to catch up.'

'Looks like we're outvoted,' Mark said, as Poppy reached out, clearly quite happy to latch herself onto Jade in lieu of Daddy. 'Night, Poppet,' he said, pressing a kiss to her cheek as he passed her over. 'Sleep tight.'

'Night, Daddy.' Poppy waved vaguely in his direction and then leaned back to study Jade's face as they mounted the stairs. 'Will you tuck me in, Jade?' she asked her.

'But of course.' Jade nodded reassuringly. 'I'm an expert tucker-in.'

'And Bedtime Peppa?'

'Well Bedtime Peppa might cry if I didn't,' Jade answered seriously.

'And will you check the bug monster's not there?'

'It wouldn't dare come near the place with me around. I've got my babysitter's bug-slayer badge. But, yes, I'll check anyway, just to make sure he hasn't snuck in.'

'I love you, Jade.' Poppy's voice drifted affectionately down from the landing.

Mark and Mel swapped amused glances. 'Looks like I might be surplus to requirements,' Mark said, loosening his collar as he headed for the lounge to check on Hercules, and actually feeling hugely grateful that Jade had volunteered after the day he'd had.

'Don't bank on it.' Mel pinched his backside as he walked past her, and then yawned widely.

'I don't think you're up to the job, Mrs Cain,' Mark observed, smiling over his shoulder.

'I won't be after a glass of wine, which I think we've both earned,' Mel assured him. 'In which case, you'll have to do all the work. But you'll have to do it quietly.' She lowered her voice as they walked into the lounge, where Hercules was snoring noisily on the sofa.

'Hmm?' Mark considered. 'Could be an interesting challenge.'

CHAPTER SIXTEEN

JADE

Poppy and Bedtime Peppa duly tucked in, Jade checked all was quiet in the nursery and then crept downstairs. She guessed they were in the kitchen, discussing their respective days over dinner together. How cosy.

Passing the lounge door, where the dog was still sleeping, which meant it at least wouldn't growl at her, Jade paused in the hall and listened.

'I really am sorry about losing the key,' she heard Melissa say. God, why didn't the silly cow just grow a pair and stop apologising, especially for something she didn't do? It was no wonder Mark despaired of her. Well, the woman could forget offering him her body by way of recompense for her sins. She was going to be asleep before her head touched the pillow.

'It's me who should be apologising,' Mark said, clearly about to take the blame. 'I could have behaved a little less like an arsehole and slightly more sympathetically. I'm so sorry about the sculpture, Mel. I don't suppose it was salvageable, was it? As a cast, I mean?'

He was obviously interested enough in her arty-farty endeavours to know something about the process then. Jade scowled, not sure she was very pleased about that. But then, he would be, she supposed. He had such a caring personality. He couldn't change that about himself and nor would Jade want him to.

'No.' Melissa sighed. 'But I've started another. Jade was great, looking after Poppy and Evie while I was in the workshop.'

Jade smiled to herself. She was all for Melissa singing her praises.

'I've been thinking though,' Melissa went on, 'maybe I should give up working. For a while, at least.'

Oh please. Jade rolled her eyes sky-high at that blatant play of the sympathy card.

'What?' She heard Mark choke on his wine. And no wonder.

'I mean, it's not important, is it?' Melissa continued, nauseatingly selflessly. 'Well, obviously it is to me, but it's not as if I couldn't put it on hold. Devote more time to the children.'

There was a pause. Clearly Melissa was waiting for Mark to give the right response, which, Mark being Mark, of course he did.

'It's important to me, too, Mel,' he said, with feeling. 'Your art is who you are. You shouldn't give up a fundamental part of yourself out of guilt. You're a fantastic mother. Poppy's a shining example of that. And apart from the blip when Evie wouldn't settle into her routine, she's about as content as a baby can be. This morning was nobody's fault. Shit happens sometimes.'

Melissa drew in a breath – and yawned. 'I know,' she said. 'I'm just tired, I suppose.'

'Looks like we've both had a shitty sort of day,' Mark empathised.

'Oh God, I'm sorry, Mark,' said Melissa – apologising, again. 'I'm so busy thinking about me, I forgot to ask about how things went with you.'

'Not great,' Mark said.

Hearing him scrape his chair back, Jade was primed to bolt for the stairs, but relaxed when she heard him walk in the other direction. He must be fetching more wine from the fridge.

'What on earth was all that about with DCI Edwards?' Melissa asked him, over the sound of wine being poured. If that was her glass, she would definitely be sleeping tonight. Like a dead thing.

Jade only wished it were that easy. 'I couldn't believe it when he asked me to confirm that you were driving Evie around rather than driving around on your own in the dead of night.'

Mark paused, then said, 'You did, though, right?'

'Of course,' Melissa assured him. 'I couldn't remember specific nights, obviously, but I told him you were driving her around to try and get her to go off to sleep.'

'Might have looked odd if you could remember specific nights,' Mark said, sounding distracted.

'So, why was he asking?' Melissa urged him.

Another pause, followed by a heavy sigh. 'Cummings,' Mark answered tightly.

'Your detective sergeant?'

'Unfortunately.' Mark sounded tense now. 'You remember we had an… er… altercation a while back?'

'Oh God, yes. The womaniser. I remember you told me. You hit him.'

'Not hard enough,' Mark replied angrily, and topped up the second glass. 'He has a penchant for younger women, outside and inside of work. Harasses female members of staff. It's way beyond acceptable.'

'But… has no one brought him to task? Reported him?' Melissa asked, disbelieving.

'Nope.' Mark laughed sardonically. 'Not even the girl who he was helping himself to a grope of when I clocked the bastard. Scared of losing her job. Long story short, I was reprimanded. Psychologically evaluated, not to put too fine a point on it.'

And she didn't *know* all this? Jade gawped at the kitchen door. What an uncaring, self-centred bitch.

Melissa gasped. 'What? Oh no…'

'It was just after Jacob. My emotions were all over the place.' Mark sighed audibly.

'Precisely because you had just lost your son! They must have known that. They must have known that you wouldn't *attack* someone, however emotional you were, without provocation.'

'He didn't exactly provoke me, Mel,' Mark said, less passionately. 'Pissed me off, severely, but in the eyes of my superiors, that wasn't provocation.'

'Idiots,' Melissa seethed. 'DCI Edwards is well aware of how losing Jacob affected you. He knows that you would do anything for your children, including driving endlessly around at night to try to get your baby to sleep. I honestly can't believe someone could be so vindictive as to try to make that into anything but what it is.'

'There's more to it than just the so-called attack,' Mark said, and then paused. 'This is just between you and me, though. I have no evidence.'

'Of?' Melissa waited.

'I saw him kerb-crawling. I've been keeping tabs on him. I think, but I can't yet be certain, that he's helped himself to drugs, possibly from various crime scenes, the evidence room maybe...' Again, Mark paused, as if debating how much information to divulge. 'It looks like he's supplying those drugs to sex workers, some of them clearly underage.'

'You're joking,' Melissa gasped, incredulous.

'I wish. Bottom line is, he knows I'm on to him. I suspect he's out to discredit me before I get enough to make sure he's kicked off the force and, hopefully, banged up.'

'So, he's a sexual predator and a drug pusher,' Melissa growled angrily. 'What a disgusting individual. I can't understand how he's been allowed to get away with it.'

Digesting this latest information, Jade gulped back a sudden overwhelming nausea. Hard though she tried not to, she felt it over again, the repulsion broiling in the pit of her stomach, the pain, the powerlessness of being at the mercy of such an individual, touching and pawing, salivating and thrusting and grunting. Closing her eyes, claustrophobic in the confines of the hall, she tried to block it out: the odious smell of him, body odour and beer; the look in his eyes as he studied her face, one of lust, his exhilaration fuelled by the fear of being found out, by her fear. The taste of him. She would never forget the sour, salty taste that would make her gag until she was sick.

Sweat prickling her forehead, her heart thrumming a drumbeat in her chest, she didn't hear the sound of Melissa's chair scraping back. She did register the sudden silence though. Sensing body contact in there, Jade snapped her eyes open. She couldn't allow that.

Time to announce her presence. Taking a few steps back up the hall, she started singing. It was the same song her mother had sung to her, a mother who actually couldn't have cared less if she'd cried. '*Hush, little baby, don't say a word, Mama's going to buy you a mockingbird. And if that*— Whoops! Sorry,' she said, pretending embarrassment at finding Melissa on Mark's lap. She was kissing him! Stuffing her tongue down his throat probably, the slut.

Melissa shot to her feet when she saw Jade. And Mark – poor Mark – looked as if he wanted to drop through the floor. Gathering herself, Jade beamed in his direction. It wasn't his fault, she reminded herself. He was trying to be a good husband. He would continue to try until he saw Melissa in her true light. That was simply who he was: a good man right to the core. She hadn't needed to hear his revelations about his detective sergeant to realise that. Jade couldn't force it. She had to handle it carefully, peel the scales from his eyes slowly. He would realise eventually that to deny his heart's desire for a weak woman who was using him as a cash cow was a ridiculous waste of a life.

As for this DS Cummings, who was trying to ruin Mark, Jade thought it was time the man got his comeuppance. She would make sure that Mark did get some evidence he could use against him. She couldn't entice the man to supply her drugs, as Mark would obviously become aware of her involvement, but Jade was quite sure she could entice him to other things. Yes, using his pathetic inclination to abuse women in order to ensure his downfall was entirely feasible. She needed to make the acquaintance of the delightful Cummings, Jade decided.

'No need to apologise, Jade,' Melissa said, as Jade went to fill up the kettle. 'We shouldn't have been canoodling in the kitchen.'

Canoodling? How twee. Jade tried to hide her immense irritation behind a sweet smile.

'We got carried away, I'm afraid.' Melissa smiled and yawned. And stretched, showing far too much boob over her low-cut top for Jade's liking. Mark could hardly avoid noticing them, could he?

'Why don't you go on up and run yourself a nice hot bath,' he suggested, averting his gaze as he got to his feet. 'I'll clear up down here.'

'Good idea,' Jade said, possibly a touch too enthusiastically. 'You look absolutely exhausted,' she added, fancying that, given the woman's age, saying she looked tired wouldn't go down very well. 'I'll give Mark a hand and then bring you up a hot chocolate.'

'Oh, don't bother, Jade,' Melissa said. 'It's really sweet of you, but you've done far too much for one day.'

'It's no problem,' Jade assured her, already on her way to the table to collect up the plates. 'I'm making one for myself anyway. A good night's sleep is what you need, isn't it, Mark?'

'Looks like it.' Mark smiled as Melissa tried and failed to supress another yawn, and then, conceding defeat, headed sleepily for the door.

CHAPTER SEVENTEEN

MARK

She really was exhausted. Mark looked down at his wife, sleeping on her tummy as she usually did, her face turned towards him. *Ripe for kissing.* His eyes strayed to her lips, her glorious copper hair, which was splayed sexily around her. He would very much like to make slow, sensual love to her but, despite her suggestion that he do all the work, he guessed that waking her up might not be deemed pleasurable foreplay.

Undressing quietly, Mark thanked God again for Jade, who he'd left downstairs in the lounge, making sure Hercules was well tucked up. True to her word, she'd made hot chocolate for Melissa and brought it up to her, checking on Evie and Poppy as she did. She'd practically shooed him up to bed when she'd found him dozing in the lounge. She really was a godsend, arriving just when they'd needed her.

Safe in the knowledge that Jade would turn off the lights – he'd already made sure that everything was locked up, twice – Mark slipped carefully in beside Mel.

She didn't stir. Mark searched her face again, before turning off the bedside lamp. Not a flicker of the eyelashes. Slow, sensual lovemaking definitely wasn't on the agenda tonight. She was dead to the world. Ah well, there was always tomorrow. Mark pulled the duvet up over her shoulders and dropped a soft kiss on her cheek, at which Mel finally did stir, wriggling onto her side and into their usual sleeping position, her back facing him, her bottom tucked well into him. Smiling, Mark wrapped an arm around her and pulled her close.

He was drifting in and out of sleep himself – fitful sleep, broken by stark images of the missing little girl, curled into a ball in some cold dark place. And other images: another time, another place, another child, curled up, eyes milk-white and empty, screaming in terror from the depths of the smoke-blackened room he couldn't reach. He desperately tried to wrench himself from the dream. Her heartbreaking sobs were growing louder… too loud. Too much to bear.

Rolling over, Mark pulled himself upright. Blinking hard against the dark, sweat pooling at the base of his neck, he realised the cries were real. Here. Not inside his head.

Evie?

Scrambling out of bed, Mark checked the bedside clock and realised it was nowhere near feed time. Feeling panicked, and not sure why, he headed for the landing. He was outside the nursery door when he heard the soft lullaby: '*Hush, little baby…*'

Jade. Mark felt his heart rate return to somewhere near normal. She'd obviously beaten him to it. A godsend. Definitely. Mark sighed, relieved, and then, remembering he was stark naked, he about-faced and headed back to the bedroom, where he found Mel still sleeping, amazingly. Normally she would wake if Evie or Poppy so much as sneezed.

CHAPTER EIGHTEEN

MARK

Two weeks she'd been missing. Fourteen days and cold nights and they were still no nearer to finding her. Mark studied the latest photo of Daisy: a pretty, rosy-cheeked child, similar in colouring to Poppy, she didn't look unhappy, scared or lonely. There were no shadows haunting her smile. She was just a normal, trusting little girl. A little girl whose innocence had probably been irretrievably broken. Swallowing back the bile in his throat, trying to dismiss the images that thought evoked, Mark dragged his hands through his hair. He didn't know why, but he was sure she was alive. The pictures that flashed through his dreams every night, elusive and wispy at first, were now so clear he could almost reach out and touch her; her fear so tangible, he could feel it. He could even smell her surroundings: mildew, damp moss, leather. Definitely a property in the countryside somewhere, but it could be anywhere. Was he being fanciful? Some might call this a hunch. Mark worried it was just wishful thinking.

Feeling utterly jaded, he sat heavily back in his chair. So where did he go from here? Forensics had found other spatters of blood, but they were so small as to be insignificant, and possibly from the foot injury the parents had offered as explanation for the stain on the stairs. Whilst not ruling them out yet, the parents looked to have played no part in her disappearance.

Searches were continuing locally and nationally, but Mark was running out of ideas. Unable to ignore the nagging instinct that she was still alive, he'd taken it on himself to revisit some of the neighbouring properties. Hawthorn Farm, a mile or so from his own house, was on his agenda later. The owner, a recently bereaved widow, wouldn't welcome another intrusion into her life, but he had to do something. She had enough on her plate with the farm up for sale and a son who was amiable enough but not the brightest tool in the box. He'd once been arrested, nine years ago, according to the details on file. The charge, indecent exposure, had been dropped when a local guy had marched his fifteen-year old daughter into the station. Turned out her and her mate had decided it would be a 'laugh' to remove 'drippy Dylan's' clothes while he'd been skinny-dipping in the river. Dylan, sixteen years old at the time, had never lived it down. Kids could most definitely be cruel sometimes. Now living in one of the small cottages on the farm, he seemed harmless, with no other misdemeanours or mishaps on his record. Impressionable, gullible, but harmless. Still, though, Mark wanted to revisit the farm in the vain hope that something had been missed.

Sighing, he looked back to his computer. Rereading statements wasn't likely to produce anything new, but he had to do something. Pulling up another file, Mark scrolled through it, reaching distractedly for his ringing mobile as he did.

'Mark, hi, it's me,' Mel said, over the noise of Evie crying, which immediately made Mark tense up. Evie was now waking several times most nights and Mel seemed permanently on edge. But then… Mark tried to suppress it, but the thought popped into his head anyway… Mel hadn't actually had to see to her at night over the two weeks since Jade had moved in. Jade's antennae always seemed to be on red alert. He'd met her on the landing a couple of times over the last week (he'd taken to wearing boxers at night now, just in case).

'Did you remember to book the table for tonight?' Mel asked him.

Crap. 'No, sorry.' Mark squeezed his eyes closed, realising he'd forgotten. They were supposed to be going out with the Chandlers to celebrate Emily's birthday, and it had completely slipped his mind. The broken nights, coupled with his increasing nightmares, were taking their toll on him too.

'Oh Mark, honestly… I thought you'd done it days ago.' Mel sounded utterly despairing.

'I'll do it now,' Mark promised.

'Forget it. *I'll* do it,' Mel said tetchily. 'I doubt they'll have a table now anyway.'

'Mel, I'll do it,' Mark assured her, concerned by her obvious agitation. He'd been trying not to worry about it, putting Mel's irritability down to stress, but, frankly, he was alarmed. Whether or not she was getting up in the night to see to Evie, she was exhausted. She *looked* exhausted. And where previously Mel would have been unfazed by something like a dripping tap – grabbing the tool box, in fact, and changing the washer herself – the one that was constantly dripping in the utility was driving her mad. Mark had put it on his weekend to-do list. It was no big deal – but to Mel it obviously was. She'd looked… edgy. It was the only way to describe it. It just wasn't like her.

He was about to reassure her again that he would ring the restaurant and then call her straight back when Mel practically growled down the phone, 'Oh for God's *sake*, now the bloody fuse box has blown. We really need to spend some serious money on this house, Mark, or move.' And with that, she ended the call.

Staring askance at his mute phone for a second, Mark shook his head. Mel had chosen the house. A detached farmhouse in the peaceful countryside, but with neighbours close enough for it not to feel isolated, she'd loved it on sight, particularly the outbuilding, which was perfect for her workshop. A fantastic family home, she'd said, her glorious green eyes dancing with excitement as she'd viewed it. She'd been willing him to love it too. Mark had, but with reservations. Despite the obvious attractions – oak flooring, oak joinery, stone fireplaces and the airy feel to it, thanks to the many windows looking onto the spectacular Herefordshire countryside – it was going to need a hell of a lot of money spent on it. Even with the small trust fund Mel had been left by her mother, the renovation was going to have to be done as and when finances allowed, they'd both been aware of that. That hadn't been a problem either. Until now, apparently.

Mark swallowed back an uneasy feeling, wondering whether her recent behaviour might be symptomatic of something more, something he hadn't realised she might be struggling with. She hadn't suffered postnatal depression after having Poppy, but might she be suffering with it now? Mark had no idea. He was debating whether to suggest Mel make a doctor's appointment, which he was loath to do, recalling how hard she'd worked to be free of doctors and psychotic drugs after losing Jacob, but...

'Hello, earth to Mark,' Lisa said, standing next to his desk.

'Sorry.' Mark shook himself. 'Miles away.'

'I gathered. Coffee,' she said, parking a mug next to his PC. 'You look like shit,' she added bluntly.

Running a hand over his unshaven cheek, Mark straightened himself up in his chair. He guessed he did, which wouldn't go down well with Edwards. 'Cheers, Lisa,' he said, then feeling in need of a caffeine kick, picked up his coffee. 'You do my ego the world of good.'

'I'm thinking a decent night's sleep might do you more good.' Lisa cocked her head to one side, studying him thoughtfully. 'I take it Evie's disturbing your beauty sleep? Not that you need much beauty sleep, obviously.'

'Obviously,' Mark concurred, his mouth twitching into a smile. 'Her routine's gone to pot,' he confided, glad, not for the first time, that he could talk to Lisa. It made life a whole lot easier at work, particularly now Cummings was back after his sudden mystery illness. It had been no surprise to Mark he'd gone off sick, probably hoping to avoid a confrontation with him. Mark's anger boiled afresh as he recalled his treatment of Tanya Stevens.

Rolling her eyes, Lisa empathised. 'Babies.' She sighed expansively. 'If anyone had told me what I was in for, I'd never have had sex.'

'Still, at least it was only the twice, hey, Moyes? Brave bloke,' Cummings commented crassly, winking over his shoulder as he swung by towards the coffee machine.

Lisa settled for giving him a finger rather than verbalising her thoughts. 'I take it you've tried all the usual tricks?' she asked Mark. 'White noise, temperature, lighting, varying the rocking, breathing deeply if none of the above work?'

'Yup, pretty much everything. Or rather, Jade has.'

'Jade?'

'The babysitter.'

'Ah.' Lisa nodded, but looked perplexed. 'I didn't know you had one.'

'We do now,' Mark said. 'Live in, thank God. She's amazing with the kids, but—'

'Night excursions in the car not working then, sir?' Cummings enquired sarcastically, as he sauntered back in the other direction.

'Fuck off, Cummings,' said Lisa, obviously noticing Mark's agitation and answering for him.

Mark glanced disdainfully after Cummings. He really was a piece of work. 'Do you mind if we, er…' Looking back to Lisa, he nodded towards the door, where he could hopefully grab some advice about Mel out of earshot of the creep. Lisa had been a friend to Mel when she'd needed one, and with two kids of her own, certainly had a good perspective on that side of things.

'With pleasure. There really is an obnoxious stench in here.' Curling a lip in Cummings direction, Lisa about-faced and headed for the door.

'So, what's up?' she asked Mark, once they were both in the corridor.

Mark started walking. The last thing he wanted was Cummings knowing any more of his business. 'Not sure,' he said, running a hand over his neck. 'Maybe nothing.'

'Which is why you're coming in late again, not shaving…'

'That obvious, is it?' Mark would have to do something about that. 'It's Mel,' he said. 'I mean, it might be nothing to do with her and all to do with me, but she's… I don't know… tired all the time, edgy.'

'Well, she's bound to be tired with Evie's feeding routine all over the place, Mark. It's bloody hard work getting up umpteen times a night.'

'I know, I know.' Mark sighed and massaged his temples. 'It's just, she's not getting up at night. That's the point. She's dead to the world. Doesn't even hear Evie. Jade sees to her. She usually gets to her before I do. There's plenty of milk in the freezer, so it's not a problem, but…' Not quite sure how to communicate what the problem really was, wondering again whether there even was one, he trailed uselessly off.

Lisa scanned his face. 'You're worried about her.'

'A bit.' Mark admitted, relieved. He felt like a traitor discussing Mel behind her back, but he really needed to know if he was being paranoid here – and Lisa would be the one to tell him if he was. 'I might be blowing things out of proportion, but given what happened before, well, I wondered if you'd drop by on some pretext or other. Tell me what you think.'

'Consider it done. I haven't seen her in ages. It'll be good to have a natter. I'm off early tonight – Anna's got a dance class. I'll pop by once I've dropped her off. And I'll check out that babysitter while I'm at it, see if she fancies a bit of moonlighting. She sounds too good to be true.'

CHAPTER NINETEEN

LISA

Babysitter?! Lisa gawked as a girl who looked more like she was auditioning for *Baywatch* than babysitting answered Mel's door.

'Hi.' Arranging her face into a smile, Lisa averted her gaze from the girl's breasts, not easily missed in the red tankini top she had on, which she'd paired with very short white shorts. Admittedly, there'd been a rare glimpse of early summer sun, but wasn't she a little underdressed for the job?

'Hi.' The girl didn't smile back.

'Is Mel home?' Lisa asked, feeling a bit spare on the doorstep. As if she were a ten-year-old kid calling for her mate and definitely under scrutiny from her mother.

'She's having a lie down.' Waving vaguely behind her, the girl continued to look Lisa curiously over. 'I'm not sure whether she's sleeping.'

'Oh. Well, I'm sure she won't mind me going on up,' Lisa said, nodding past her. 'We're old friends. I'm Lisa, Mark's—'

'Work colleague,' the girl finished, clearly not about to shift her pretty little arse and allow her access anytime soon.

Smiling patiently, Lisa waited a few moments before asking, 'And you are…?'

'Oh God, sorry.' The girl finally smiled back. 'Jade. Mark's babysitter. And Mel's, of course. And I've obviously forgotten my manners.' She moved aside at last, allowing Lisa access. 'Come on in. I'll go and give Mel a shout.'

'No worries, I'll just go on up,' Lisa assured her, feeling uneasy as she stepped in, and not sure why – apart from the fact that Mel had obviously taken leave of her senses, dangling that sort of temptation under Mark's nose. But Mark wasn't like that. Lisa reminded herself of her tendency to label all men the same, having been married to the kind of abusive Neanderthal who made Cummings seem positively charming, and having more recently hooked up with a wanker who turned out to be shagging anything in a skirt, the younger the better. Mark was devoted to Mel. He'd never even looked in another woman's direction, as far as Lisa knew. It didn't make him a saint, but his dedication to his wife had been obvious when his life had been a complete shit fest.

'I've got to go and get a jacket for Evie anyway.' She waved at Evie, who was in her stroller, all kitted up to go out. 'We're off to the park while Poppy's at her friend's. Just wait there, won't be a tick.'

Lisa watched her skip on up, trying hard not to judge her. She seemed friendly enough, after the initial hiccup on the doorstep. And she'd been right not to just allow anyone claiming to be a friend access to the house, Lisa supposed. She was obviously feeling the teeniest bit jealous.

Attempting to shrug off her concerns, Lisa crouched down to Evie's level. 'We can't all be beautiful as well as brainy, can we, sweetheart?' She smiled, relieved to note that Evie looked healthy enough. The blip in the sleeping routine was clearly just that, a blip.

'So, what have we been up to then, Little Miss Mischief?' she asked her, crooking a finger to stroke her peachy cheek. 'Are we keeping Mummy and Daddy awake, hmm? Would you like Auntie Lisa to come and sing you a lullaby?' Evie's mouth widened into a delighted, gummy smile as Lisa jiggled her caterpillar stroller toy.

'You really are a gorgeous little girl, aren't you?' said Lisa, reassured by Evie's gurgles and chuckles and flailing little hands. There was nothing wrong in the baby department. And with Mel's sparkling green eyes and delicate features, she was going to be a knockout.

'Lisa?'

She turned at the sound of Mel's voice, but her smile slipped a bit when she saw her. Far from sparkling, Mel's eyes were heavy with exhaustion. She looked more knocked out than knockout. Whatever was going on, she needed to get to the doc's, and fast.

CHAPTER TWENTY

MELISSA

'I haven't seen you in ages,' said Mel, smiling delightedly, despite that she felt a complete mess. She'd just climbed out of the shower when Jade came in to tell her Lisa was here, joking about her being Mark's frequent texter. Having been attempting to wash the cotton wool from her head, and failing, Mel had been ferreting through her wardrobe in hopes of finding something remotely sexy-looking to wear tonight. She'd given up when she'd seen Jade looking dazzling and thrown her leggings and old T-shirt back on. And now here was Lisa, looking trim and slim in her jeans, her short-cropped hair and huge blue eyes making her look like a little elf – a very attractive one.

Sighing inwardly, Mel brushed her damp hair from her face. She really was going to have to do something with herself. Take some vitamins, or energy pills or something. Go to the gym, or out jogging with Mark. Mel's heart dipped in her chest as she thought of him. She'd be surprised if he wanted to do anything with her. She'd been horrible to him on the phone. She really had no idea what was wrong with her. She felt like sleeping the clock around. They hadn't made love since the dreadful day of Hercules's accident, and Mark hadn't murmured a word. It was more than he dare do, she supposed, with her so snappy. When she wasn't sleeping or moaning or yawning, she was working. Or trying to. The blown fuse meant the kiln had stopped working, which had had her wanting to scream. She barely had time for the kids with her sculpture to remake, the casting of which still had to be done, and the orders to fill, which she hadn't even started on. It was a wonder any of her family wanted anything to do with her. Maybe she should go to the doctor's, Mel pondered. The thought didn't appeal. She'd steered clear of doctors and medication, even avoiding painkillers at the worst time of the month, since coming off her medication.

'My fault.' Lisa moved to give her a hug as she reached the hall. 'I've been so busy with work and the kids demanding my attention every two seconds. Anyway, I was passing after dropping Anna off at her dance class and I thought no time like the present. How are you?' Stepping back, Lisa looked her over, her brow furrowed. 'You look a bit…'

'A mess, I know.' Mel smiled and tried not to mind. Lisa tended to say it as it was.

'Frazzled,' Lisa finished diplomatically, whilst looking her worriedly over again. 'Are you okay, lovely?'

'Yes, fine,' Mel lied, waving a hand dismissively. 'It's a virus, I think. I can't seem to shake it off. I don't have an ounce of energy.'

'Unlike some,' Lisa observed, as Jade came bounding brightly back down the stairs.

'Got it.' She dangled the jacket and headed for the stroller. 'Come on, angel,' she said, peering down at Evie and steering her towards the door. 'Let's go and get some fresh air and leave Mel to catch up with her friend, shall we?'

'She's referring to you as Mel, not Mummy?' Lisa eyed Mel sideways as Jade tipped the stroller back and headed on out.

'Slip of the tongue probably.' Mel smiled in Lisa's direction, and then scooted to catch up with Jade. 'Hold on,' she said, crouching to kiss Evie's perfect little cupid lips. The baby promptly wriggled and looked fretfully upwards in search of Jade. Trying not to mind that either – she was getting things so out of proportion lately, she'd drive herself as well as everyone else mad – Mel got to her feet, allowing Jade to go on her way.

'Have you got her water?' she called after her.

'Yes.' Jade waved behind her. 'And a spare nappy and the sunscreen. We'll be fine. You worry too much, Mel.'

And lately she was worrying more than ever, when she wasn't too tired to think at all. Mel really did despair of herself. She had the perfect babysitter. A beautiful house, albeit in a constant state of repair. A good husband, whom she loved, very much. Two perfect kids. Everything in her garden should be rosy. So why did she feel so… down?

'Pretty, isn't she?' Lisa commented, as they watched Jade head jauntily off down the lane. 'Slim, too. Makes me feel like a flipping heifer.'

Mel laughed at that. 'In which case I must look like the back end of a bus.'

Lisa looked her over as they walked back in. 'Hardly,' she said. 'You've lost weight.'

'Have I?' Mel looked down at herself. That was a silver lining in the gloom, she thought, and then she felt her heart sink all over again. Why was she thinking this way? Feeling this way?

'I take it she's the new babysitter?' Lisa enquired, as they walked to the kitchen for coffee and a catch-up. 'Live in, I gather?'

Information conveyed by Mark, Mel guessed. 'That's right. She'd bought Monk's Cottage just up the lane – moved in with us after it caught fire. It was totally burned out. You must have noticed as you passed.'

She checked the wall clock – aware it might take some time to make herself gorgeous – and then headed for the kettle, as Lisa parked herself on a stool at the kitchen island.

'I did,' Lisa said. 'She was literally on your doorstep then?'

'Yes.' Mel spooned coffee into the mugs – or, rather, missed, cursing silently. 'We hadn't had much to do with each other really, but with her house going up in flames…'

'You got talking?'

'Obviously.' Coffee successfully made, Mel picked up the mugs and carried them over, without spilling any, thankfully. 'It was awful. All her worldly goods gone up in smoke. I offered her a roof for the night and, as we'd been considering a babysitter… Well, you could say she fell into our laps. I hate to say it, but the timing couldn't have been better, to be honest. She's an absolute godsend.'

'So Mark says.' Lisa sounded sceptical. 'And she's qualified, presumably?'

'Of course. She has her childcare qualifications. I wouldn't have entertained the idea of employing her otherwise.' Reminded that she hadn't got around to asking Jade about her references, she dismissed a flicker of guilt. The girl had more than proved herself in Mel's eyes.

'Right.' Lisa nodded. 'But don't you mind having another woman around?'

Mel eyed her with amusement. 'You mean having a pretty young woman around?'

'Just saying.' Lisa shrugged.

'Not all men do what Paul did, Lisa,' Mel said, kindly, aware that Lisa's last boyfriend had dumped her for a younger model.

Lisa gave her a look as she dipped into the biscuit barrel. Her 'Yes, and pigs fly' look.

Mel wasn't sure she liked the inference. Cautioning herself not to overreact, she pulled in a breath and reminded herself she'd been doing that a lot recently, reading things into things that weren't there. She'd even imagined that Jade had had the cat she'd supposedly loved put down. It had taken her ages to ask her. Jade had been horrified. She'd asked a friend to take it in, it turned out. Mel had felt awful.

'So,' she said, mustering up a smile, 'what else have you and Mark been discussing, apart from the attributes of the babysitter?'

Lisa's eyes flicked to hers. 'Nothing much. This and that,' she said vaguely.

'Such as?' Mel asked, watching her carefully over the rim of her mug.

Lisa put down her coffee and looked up to eye Mel levelly. 'He's worried about you, Mel,' she said, searching her eyes, a curious look in her own.

'Oh.' Definite unease was now gnawing at Mel's stomach. 'I see,' she said, taking stock. 'So, you've been discussing me then, clearly.'

Lisa looked away awkwardly. 'Well, yes, naturally you come up sometimes. But Mark was only confiding in me out of concern, Mel. He—'

'Our intimate relationship?' Mel felt her mouth go dry, her cheeks heat up. 'Does that come under discussion during these cosy conversations you have?'

'No!' Lisa refuted. 'Mark wouldn't do that. You know he wouldn't. He's just been concerned about you—'

'You text each other a lot, don't you?' Mel cut in angrily. It seemed to her that Lisa knew an awful lot about what Mark would or wouldn't do. And, clearly, *she* didn't. She'd never imagined her husband would discuss their personal details with all and sundry.

Lisa splayed her hands, looking incredulous. 'Only on work matters. For God's sake, Mel, you don't honestly think that I—'

'Or, rather, *you* text him.'

'Oh, come on, Mel.' Lisa eyed the ceiling. 'You know very well I only ever text him about work.'

But she didn't know, did she? She trusted Mark, implicitly. Or she had. There had been something between Lisa and him once, at least Mel had suspected there had. He'd gone out with her, Mel had been sure of it. Her mind raced back to the first time she'd met Mark, when she'd been giving her statement about her ex. 'Thanks for last night,' Lisa had said. She'd threaded an arm around his waist as she passed him in the corridor and given him a squeeze. Thanks for last night! Mel had heard her, loud and clear. She'd assumed they'd had a thing. She'd been wrong, or so she'd been led to believe. She'd asked Mark about it, trying to sound casual. Lisa had needed a shoulder, he'd said. Still married to her abusive husband, she'd been having some problems. Yes, and what else had he offered her, Mel thought, fuming now at the obvious lie. Regular little white knight, wasn't he?

She narrowed her eyes. 'Did he ask you to come here?'

Lisa didn't answer. Plainly not knowing how to. Plainly meaning he had.

'Well, did he?' Mel demanded, a distinct wobble to her voice.

'No.' Lisa sighed, at length. 'As I said, I was passing. I'm concerned about you, too, you know. I am your friend. I just wanted to check—' Lisa stopped as her phone beeped inconveniently in her pocket.

Or rather, bang on cue, Mel thought, humiliation bubbling furiously away inside her. That Mark had discussed the intimate details of their relationship at work, even with a supposed friend, was incomprehensible. Who else had he discussed it with? The entire police force? 'Aren't you going to check it?' she asked Lisa, now studying her intently. 'It might be one of the kids.'

Knowing she had no choice, Lisa reluctantly retrieved her phone.

'Is it Mark?' Mel asked, cold certainty gripping her insides.

Lisa checked the text. Again, she didn't answer. Nor would she meet her gaze.

Mel tried very hard to hold onto her temper. '*Well?*'

Sighing heavily, Lisa closed her eyes and nodded.

Caught in the act. Seething inside, Mel didn't say anything, but coldly extended her hand.

Lisa waited a beat. 'We haven't been discussing anything *intimately*, Mel,' she said, reluctantly handing the phone over. 'Mark was just worried, that was all.'

Ignoring her, Mel took a breath and read the damn text that she didn't want to see, absolutely didn't want to read anything into. And her world shifted completely off kilter.

Off to Hawthorn Farm shortly. Hope all went well with Mel. Thanks for the ear. Talk to you tomorrow, preferably in private. Promise to be clean-shaven and looking my beautiful best.

CHAPTER TWENTY-ONE

MARK

Leaning towards him, Mark planted his fists either side of Cummings' desk while he waited for whatever pathetic explanations the man thought reasonable for assaulting a woman.

'She's an informant.' Cummings laughed incredulously, but Mark didn't miss the nervousness flitting across his eyes. They were alone, with no witnesses if he lost it big time this time and did what he really wanted to.

'And that justifies you forcibly ejecting her from your car how, exactly?' he said, through gritted teeth, making sure to hold eye contact with the detective sergeant.

'For *fuck's* sake, what is this? A bloody interrogation?' Cummings pushed his chair back and rolled his eyes at the ceiling. 'She had a hold of my balls, all right!' He looked back to Mark, his expression one of humiliation. 'What would you have done?'

If I were Tanya? You really don't want to know, Cummings. 'Why?' he asked shortly. 'Why did she have a hold of you?'

Cummings splayed his hands. 'How the fuck do I know? Off her head on coke probably.'

Yeah, right. Mark didn't believe a fucking word of it. Straightening up, he pushed his hands into his pockets. Still, he kept his gaze fixed hard on Cummings. 'Supplied by you.' It was a statement, not a question.

'Uh-uh. *No* way.' Cummings got furiously to his feet. 'I pay my girls cash.'

Mark couldn't keep the contempt from his eyes. 'Including the girls you have sex with?'

'Sometimes.' He shrugged, looking back to Mark. 'Some of us don't have the convenience of a wife to go home to, do we? *Sir*.'

Mark sucked in a breath. *Don't*, he cautioned himself, swallowing back the hard knot of anger climbing his chest.

'I'm presuming you have some evidence to back up your accusation?' Cummings asked, his eyes defiant, his tone holding a challenge.

Mark glanced away, disgust broiling inside him.

'Thought not,' Cummings sneered, turning to reseat himself at his computer.

Mark counted, silently, steadily. He was an inch away from dragging the man back to his feet, stuff the consequences. 'And the photos?' he asked, sorely tempted to forcibly retrieve the phone from the man's pocket.

Cummings looked disinterestedly up from his screen. 'What photos?'

Mark clamped hard down on his jaw. 'The photos I saw you taking, Cummings. You might do better to turn your flash off if you want to take covert photos in future.'

Cummings knitted his brow, confused, supposedly, and then nodded as if realisation had just dawned. 'It was my lighter. I was lighting a cigarette.' He smiled flatly. 'You could probably do me for that, since it was a pool car – depending how desperate you are.'

Looking him scornfully over, Cummings dragged his gaze away, safe in the knowledge that Mark couldn't touch him.

Not yet. But soon, Cummings. Some time very soon.

His gut twisting inside him, Mark turned to slam out of the office. His still had to check out Hawthorn Farm before hurrying home to shower before going out with Mel. Lisa was right, there really was an obnoxious odour around here.

CHAPTER TWENTY-TWO

JADE

'I still can't believe what he did,' Dylan said, gazing down at Evie, who was contentedly sleeping after her feed. Jade sighed inside, wondering whether the idiot boy was worth the effort. He really was as thick as pig shit. He hadn't even recognised her from their school days. Mind you, with her changed facial appearance, blue contacts and once unremarkable mousey brown hair now a head-turning shade of blonde, he wasn't likely to. He even looked like a plank, with that perpetual gormless expression. But a pliable plank, she reminded herself, which was why she needed to stroke drippy Dylan's ego, along with certain other parts of his anatomy. When it was time to lose little Evie for a while – or, rather, for poor muddled Melissa to lose her for a while – Dylan could be trusted to keep his mouth shut. He'd already proved that much.

'I was young.' Collecting up her baby bag, Jade walked across the barn, sighing wistfully as she joined him. 'He was helping me out, really.'

'What?' Dylan turned to her, his heavy forehead furrowed disapprovingly. 'By making you have his babies?'

'Paying me, Dylan. I wouldn't have had a roof over my head otherwise,' Jade reminded him. Dylan had offered her his roof, of course, when she'd tearfully confided in him. Thankfully, he'd realised it wouldn't be at all suitable for all of them, the cottage being so tiny and with basic amenities, and that, in any case, she couldn't possibly leave without her baby. More importantly, when she did leave, she had to be secure in the knowledge the child's father wouldn't try to grab her back.

'Yeah, well, it's still taking ad…' Dylan stopped, his frown deepening as he struggled for the word.

'Advantage,' Jade kindly supplied.

'Yeah, that.' Dylan nodded piously, puffing up his big barrel chest as he did. 'It's just wrong, innit, him being a policeman and all. He should be setting an example. My mum always said that people in positions of authority should be beyond…'

Dylan trailed off, apparently at a loss for what policemen should be beyond.

'Reproach.' Mentally rolling her eyes, Jade helped him along. 'And your mum's right, Dylan. But I didn't have anyone else, did I. No mum. No dad. I only had him. You haven't said anything about the babies, have you?' she added quickly. 'To your mum?'

Dylan shook his head adamantly. 'No, Scout's honour.'

Jade winced as he actually held up two fingers in a scout salute. 'Or anyone else?' she asked, scrutinising him carefully. Dylan's cheeks flushed like a set of brake lights if he was ever embarrassed or uncomfortable. She'd soon know if he was lying.

'Haven't breathed a word,' he assured her, with another exaggerated shake of his head.

'Good.' Jade gave his cheek a pat, her other hand straying to his groin, causing Dylan to suck in a sharp breath. 'We wouldn't want anyone to come between us, would we? And they would, you know, if they found out I'd had his babies before I was old enough.'

'I didn't say anything, honest.' Dylan's voice went up an octave as she gave his testicles a gentle squeeze, giving him an instant hard-on.

'You're a rock, Dylan.' Jade leaned in, panting breathily in his ear. 'I'm so lucky to have you as a boyfriend.'

Dylan nodded. 'I like being your boyfriend,' he said, the flush to his cheeks indicating his awkwardness as his eyes flicked to hers and back. 'You shouldn't be living with him, though, Jade. Not if you're my girlfriend.'

Jade stopped her ministrations in favour of lifting his chin to gaze lovingly at him. Dylan might be pliable, but now he'd discovered what his penis was for apart from pissing, he was showing signs of becoming proprietorial. God forbid his male ego might drive him to do anything unpredictable. 'It's only for a while,' she assured him, blinking kindly. 'Just until my house is rebuilt. And at least this way I get to see my children.'

Dylan ran a hand under his nose. Still, he looked disgruntled.

Damn. Jade hoped she wasn't going to have to go the whole hog and give him a blowjob by way of distracting him. It wouldn't take long but she really needed to be getting back. 'And then you can move in with me, remember?' She dangled the prize carrot instead. The prospect of having her next to him in bed every night was enough to make sure he stayed on track.

'And the kids?' Dylan said, eyeing her uncertainly.

'And the kids,' Jade assured him, smiling her sweetest smile. 'And your mum can visit as often as she wants. She could even move in with us if she liked.'

Dylan brightened at that. 'She could cook our dinner.'

'We'd be one big happy family,' said Jade, though she was having to force the smile a bit now.

Dylan nodded happily, and then frowned, again. 'But what about the other one?' he asked. 'I'm not sure it's good for her, being away from you and all.'

'Oh, she's fine.' Jade waved a hand, irked now. Given how unemotional he was when it came to shooting vermin or snapping chickens' necks, she hadn't banked on him becoming attached to the girl. 'She's much better off staying with you than with me.'

Dylan didn't look convinced.

'You know *he* doesn't want her, Dylan.' Jade blinked at him beseechingly. 'It's best she stays where she is for a while. Just make sure your mother doesn't go poking her nose— *Shhhh.*' Hearing a car drawing up in the farmyard, Jade cocked an ear.

Perplexed, since drippy Dylan and his depressing-looking mum hardly ever had visitors, she pressed a finger to her lips and tiptoed across the floor to peer through a popped knot in the barn door, and then... *Shit!*

CHAPTER TWENTY-THREE

MARK

Mark climbed out of his car, deciding to take a look around before knocking on the farmhouse door. If there was anything they'd missed, he was hardly going to fall over it, but he just couldn't shake the feeling that Daisy was still alive and being held close to home. She haunted his dreams. But then, the small girl who'd died in the cruellest way possible came to him at night too, her tiny form curled into a ball, clutching her one-eyed Pooh Bear close to her chest, calling out to him. And the smell, before the unbearable screams snatched him back to consciousness: thick, cloying smoke, scorching his lungs, suffocating him.

In dreams of Daisy, it was always the same rural smell. Mark had no idea why the nightmares kept coming, robbing him of what sleep he might get in between Evie waking. It was because he had children, he supposed. Because he lived in fear of something too unbearable to comprehend happening to his baby girls, and that, despite having police resources at his fingertips, he would be powerless to save them.

Shaking himself, Mark looked around. Once a well-kept, thriving dairy farm, the place was now abandoned, the cow house and stables sadly bereft of inhabitants. He decided to start with the smaller of the two barns, frightening scrawny chickens who'd obviously escaped the poultry yard into a flutter of wings and piercing skirls as he walked. Once inside, he wondered why he'd come. Like the rest of the farmyard, it was empty, dusty and derelict. Original beams supported the roof; ropes and chains hung from a crossbeam. Nothing much else inside; nowhere to hide.

The smell though – damp, earthy and pungent, of mildew and soft hay – was so familiar. Mark sighed, despairing of himself. He was supposed to be dealing in facts, not wild flights of the imagination. He was triggering childhood memories, that was all. One in particular, where he'd been selected as one of the school's deprived kids to go on some pony-trekking holiday. Turns out he hadn't been much safer away from home. He'd heard him before he saw him, his old man, pissed, ranting incoherently in the small office situated next to the stables – Christ only knew how he'd driven there. He'd come to fetch him back. Mark hadn't been about to go back though. Even as a kid, he'd known he wouldn't make it. Not that time. He'd hid instead – spent half his life hiding. Deciding the hayloft was too obvious a place, he'd bolted for the stable block, curling himself into the corner of one of the stalls. The stench of leather and hay and horse manure had been overpowering. He'd been more terrified of his father finding him than the horse's hooves, which had seemed pretty menacing to a ten-year-old-kid. He'd been lonely, too. The other kids' cruel taunts had intensified after that. *Forget it*, he told himself. It was the past, dead and buried.

Consigning it to history, telling himself he needed to stop chasing shadows, Mark turned to walk back across the yard, pained by the sense of isolation the disused property evoked.

CHAPTER TWENTY-FOUR

JADE

'Don't move.' Jade whispered, her heart thrumming manically against her ribcage. Fear, and an undeniable frisson of sexual pleasure, surged through her as she watched Mark walk towards the barn. 'He can't find me.' Turning imploring eyes towards Dylan, whose face was now set in a hard scowl, she pressed a finger to her lips and stole a glance at Evie.

Hell! Why had she come looking for Dylan when she hadn't found him at the cottage? She'd already been pushed for time. She should have just left.

Please don't wake up, Angel. Seeing Evie twitch in her sleep, her eyelids fluttering, as if she might wake at any second, Jade prayed hard. He *couldn't* find her here. He absolutely couldn't. Panic mounted in her chest. She could lie through her teeth, but nothing would excuse exposing his baby to danger. He'd never forgive her. She couldn't risk that. There was also the risk that he wouldn't leave it there. That drippy Dylan might drop her in it, even though she'd coached him and coached him. And then what? Mark was a detective. He might take Dylan to the station, question him. How long would it be before Dylan spilled his guts and told him where the little girl—

Jade closed her eyes with relief, gulping hard, as she noticed the farmhouse door opening. Glancing over his shoulder, Mark turned towards it, and then stopped to fish his phone from his pocket.

Evie stirred as he spoke, as she naturally would on hearing the rich, deep timbre of her daddy's voice. Quickly, Jade turned to gather her from the stroller. '*Hush, little baby, don't say a word,*' she recited silently, rocking her gently. Then, grabbing her pacifier from the stroller tray and feeding it to her, she turned back to the barn door, hardly daring to breathe as she listened.

'Oh Christ… You're joking.' She heard Mark's shocked tone. 'But why the *hell* would she think that?'

Jade waited as Mark listened to whoever was on the other end of the line.

'But you told her the texts were only ever work-related?' Mark went on, running a hand agitatedly through his hair.

Jade felt a thrill of excitement spiking inside her. Melissa had obviously got the hints she'd been dropping about Lisa's persistent texting. And it was about time. Jade had been wondering whether she was going to have to paint the woman a bloody picture.

'Apart from the one I sent while you were there. Right.' Mark sighed despondently and stared up into the sky. 'Okay, thanks, Lisa. No, not your fault. I'd better get back.'

Jade watched as Mark ended the call, studied the phone for a second, as if debating making another, and then walked towards Dylan's mother, standing in the farmhouse door. Poor Mark. She could almost feel his hurt. She so wished he didn't have to suffer all this. It was just so cruel. But then, she had to be cruel to be kind. There was no other way. They were two souls destined to be together. She would soothe away his troubles with sweet, tender kisses, take his seed inside her, gladly give birth to his babies. He would thank her, eventually, for opening his eyes.

CHAPTER TWENTY-FIVE

MELISSA

'So, what do you think?' Mel asked Poppy, turning from the front door after waving off Poppy's little friend and her dad, who'd kindly delivered Poppy safely home. He'd clearly appreciated her new look. Mel might have been out of circulation for a while, but she could still read the signs. Poppy, however…

Peering over Baby Annabell, clutched to her chest, she looked up at Mel uncertainly. 'You look like Jade,' she whispered, her huge chocolate-brown eyes filled with awe.

'Do I?' Mel fluffed up her new blonde locks, courtesy of a mad dash to the supermarket. 'Well, there's a compliment.'

Smiling, she held out her hand and waited for Poppy to take hold of it. Poppy hesitated for a second, which was only natural, Mel supposed, on finding a different-looking mummy greeting her at the front door. She actually wasn't trying to look like Jade. She'd been going more for the Lisa look, on the basis that Mark obviously preferred blondes. She'd stopped short of cropping her hair short, although she'd felt like it, closely followed by slicing into his shirts.

She toyed with the latter idea. But no. She was going to rise above it, she'd decided. She wasn't even going to question him about it. She was going to be the epitome of calm. Sitting in the corner sobbing like a baby wasn't an option. She had cried, bitter tears of hurt and soul-crushing humiliation. She felt too tired for this, too tired to fight it. And then she'd caught sight of herself in the mirror, looking pathetic, looking exhausted, and thought *fuck him*. And Lisa, her so-called friend. She wasn't going to scream and shout, she didn't want to hurl raging accusations in front of their children, she just wanted to get back to where she was a few short weeks ago. She wanted to feel well, to feel in control again. And to that end, she did need to fight. She'd stocked up on vitamins, throwing them in her shopping basket arbitrarily. Starting tomorrow, she would set her alarm and make sure to get up early. Eat sensibly, exercise, and then get back to work in earnest. She wasn't going to go down the medication route. There was absolutely no way was she going there again, so far down the bottomless pit she'd had to claw her way out of it by her fingernails. Wouldn't Mark love that, his wife comatose to the point of oblivion, enabling him to do what he liked, *who* he liked? But… She swallowed back a tight lump in her throat. He wouldn't. Not the Mark she knew. He'd always been dependable, there for her, the one solid thing in her life when everything else seemed to be sliding away from her. Her rock.

But he was human, wasn't he? Perhaps he was tired, too. Emotionally depleted. Perhaps he needed support, and she just hadn't seen it. She wouldn't fall apart, Mel promised herself. She wouldn't accuse him or attack him. She would wait. She would watch. And she would see. Because, if her worst fears were true, if he no longer loved her, which was possible – love wasn't forever, was it? – it would be there in his eyes.

Deep in her thoughts, Melissa hadn't realised Poppy was tugging on her hand. '*Mummeee*,' she said, scowling up at her, 'why are you standing in the middle of the hall crying?'

'I'm not,' Mel said, blinking quickly.

'Yes, you are. You've got wet cheeks,' Poppy pointed out, her innocent eyes wide and now dark with worry.

'I'm not crying, sweetheart,' Mel assured her, quickly bending to pick her up. 'I got shampoo in my eyes when I washed my hair, that's all.'

Pressing her close, she gave her world-wise seven-year-old a firm hug, and tried to quiet her own rising panic. Poppy had looked at her as if she were mad. Was she? Or on her way to being? There had been a time when her grip on reality felt as elusive as sea slipping through sand. Simple, everyday tasks had been beyond her.

She couldn't allow that to happen again, to be so emotionally dysfunctional she couldn't care for herself, let alone her family. Her chest tight, she studied Poppy's confused little face and steeled her determination. She would not to drift off to that faraway place and abandon her children.

Poppy leaned back, searching her face curiously in turn, as if she didn't quite know what to make of her. 'Where's Jade?' she asked.

Mel mustered up a smile. She couldn't blame the child for that, she supposed, given her own odd behaviour lately. 'On her way,' she said. 'She popped out to see a friend, but she'll be back before Daddy and I go out. Let's go and get your jim-jams on, shall we? And then you can help Mummy put some make-up on and make herself beautiful. What do you think?'

Poppy studied her for a second longer. 'But you *are* beautiful, Mummy,' she said, her expression concerned and earnest all at once.

Mel swallowed hard.

CHAPTER TWENTY-SIX

MARK

Mark drove home fast, cursing his thoughtlessness all the way there. He'd gone behind Mel's back. There was no point in denying it. The whys and wherefores wouldn't matter to Mel. He had. And he was sorry. But if Mel imagined, for one minute, that he would *ever* use anything that had happened between them as an excuse to… No way. Mel *must* know him well enough to know he would never risk losing his family, losing her.

Pulling haphazardly up on the drive, he took a breath and then pushed through the front door, cautioning himself to calm down. He was the one at fault here. He had no idea what was going on with Mel – he was worried about her, now more than ever – but, whatever his motives, he'd obviously made the situation a whole lot worse.

'*Daddeee!*' Poppy greeted him as usual, gleefully barrelling into him as he stepped into the hall, closely followed by Hercules, who seemed to be back on form.

Mark patted the dog and then scooped Poppy up into his arms. She was in her pyjamas, also as usual. The make-up though? Mark studied his daughter's glossy red lips and smoky grey eye shadow with bemusement.

'I'm beautiful!' Poppy announced, pressing her small hands to her blushed cheeks and beaming at him.

Mark widened his eyes. 'Undoubtedly.' He smiled, pressing a kiss carefully to her nose so as not to smudge her. 'Where's Mummy?'

'Trying her wardrobe on,' Poppy supplied.

'Ah,' Mark nodded. 'Not sure it will suit her, but…'

'Not *really* the wardrobe, silly.' Poppy rolled her eyes. 'She's trying some *clothes* on so she can look gorgeous.'

Mark quietly thanked God for the apparent normalcy – apart from Poppy's makeover – that seemed to prevail. 'In which case, I'd better go up and make myself gorgeous in case I'm too scruffy to be seen out with her.' He smiled, turning for the stairs.

'Wait.' Poppy jiggled and pointed to the lounge, where *Scooby-Doo* was in full swing, judging by the sounds from the TV. 'Mummy said I could watch the end of my programme.'

'Bed as soon as it's finished,' Mark said, lowering her to the floor. Straightening up, he watched her scoot back to the lounge, and then turned back to the stairs with a shake of his head – and stopped dead.

'Well?' Mel asked, searching his face as she paused partway down.

'Um…' Loosening his collar, Mark looked her slowly over, taking in the five-inch heels, the long shapely legs, the tight, short red dress that fitted her every curve, and which Mel had previously declared made her look tarty. Mark had disagreed, he recalled, assuring her it made her look red-hot. His gaze travelled higher, pausing at her breasts over the low-cut neckline, and then upwards to her face. She was wearing makeup – plenty of it, unusually. It was the hair that really grabbed his attention, though.

'Wow,' he said.

'Wow in a good way, or a bad way?' Mel asked, studying him carefully. From her expression, however, Mark felt she wasn't seeking his approval.

'Good,' he assured her. 'You look… stunning.' He didn't lie. She looked breathtaking. Slightly perturbing, though, was that she didn't look like Mel. Mark didn't dare say he'd loved her hair the way it was, a fiery hot copper.

'I thought I'd try a new look,' Mel said. 'Variety's the spice of life, after all,' she added, holding his gaze as she joined him in the hall. '*Isn't it?*'

Noting the innuendo in her tone, Mark wasn't sure what to say. He'd hoped to apologise, but here in the hall, with Mel scrutinising him, a defiant expression on her face, and Jade looking on from the galleried landing, didn't seem quite the right time.

'I'd, er, better get changed,' he said, nodding upwards. 'I'll be two minutes.' Smiling uncertainly, Mark headed on up, puzzling over this change in Mel. She'd smiled back, but… there had been something there, hiding beneath her cheerful expression. But she did look good, fantastic, and she seemed in control. Mark couldn't help thinking it was forced though, that she seemed to be working hard at it.

Meeting Jade at the top, on her way into the nursery, Mark followed her in to have a quick check on Evie. Finding her sleeping, he breathed a sigh of relief, and turned back to the door, almost falling into Jade in the process. He hadn't realised she was standing behind him.

'Sorry,' he said, catching hold of her forearms as she stumbled backwards. 'Did I hurt you?'

'No,' she assured him. '*Shhhh.*' She smiled, pressing a finger to her lips and gesturing him out of the room.

'You'd better get a move on,' she whispered, once they were on the landing, pointing down to where Mel was now heading for the lounge, calling Hercules to go out for a wee as she went, 'or you'll be in even more trouble.'

Clearly he was in trouble then. 'Yeah, I think I might have some apologising to do.' He smiled half-heartedly, guessing that Mel had 'shared' with her what an idiot he'd been.

'Chocolates,' Jade suggested. 'They work for me.'

Mark nodded and dipped his head in appreciation. Chocolates were a no. With Poppy's dairy allergy, they made it a rule not to have any in the house. Maybe flowers, he thought, and then wondered how they might be interpreted.

'If it's any consolation, I gathered you were just trying to get a female perspective,' Jade offered astutely.

'I was. Backfired a bit, though, didn't it?' Mark rolled his eyes at his own ineptitude. 'I'll try a grovelling apology, I think. And the most expensive thing on the menu. We shouldn't be too late back,' he said turning to the main bedroom. 'You have all the numbers in case of emergencies, yes?'

'All to hand,' Jade assured him. 'I'll ring you if I need to, but don't worry. I'm sure there won't be any problems.'

CHAPTER TWENTY-SEVEN

JADE

Well, there wouldn't be any problems here. As for what might happen in the restaurant…

Jade watched Mark walk towards his bedroom, looking troubled, as he would be by his wife's peculiar behaviour and trollopy appearance. Then, humming softly to herself, she headed along the landing to her own room, where she retrieved a shoebox from the top of her wardrobe. Pondering the side effects of the various drugs, she was replacing the packet of slow-release capsules under the few bits of memorabilia she kept there when someone tapped lightly on her door.

Quickly snapping the lid back on the shoebox, Jade stuffed it well back on the shelf. It was Mark at the door – Melissa always called out 'just me' in an irritating singsong voice. Jade's mouth curved into a smile. Turning for the door, she hitched her T-shirt over her head, tugged it off and unsnapped her bra. Then, reaching for the dressing gown Melissa had so kindly provided her, she pushed her arms into it, holding it loosely enough at the front to expose a good expanse of milky white breast as she yanked the door open.

'Oh, my!' Jade blinked, suitably mortified, as Mark got the desired eyeful before turning away. 'I'm really sorry,' she mumbled, the door now partly closed as she peeped shyly around it. 'I thought it was Melissa.'

'My fault,' Mark said, as a gentleman would. 'Please accept my apologies. I'll announce myself next time.' He was kneading his forehead in that way he did – flustered, obviously. Bound to be.

'Apology accepted,' Jade assured him, tying her dressing gown tight to expose a lot less of herself. 'I'm decent now. You can turn around.'

Nodding, Mark turned back, looking decidedly uncomfortable. That was to be expected, she supposed. Jade continued smiling, her gaze grazing over him as he stood there, looking achingly sexy in a navy linen jacket with a light blue shirt underneath, dark jeans and leather belt. Her eyes rested briefly at belt level before travelling back to his face. Tall, dark and heart-stoppingly handsome; he was hers. Or he very soon would be.

'I just wanted to let you know we were leaving.' He smiled nervously. 'Poppy's still in the lounge. We'll be back around eleven.'

'I'll come right down and fetch her. Enjoy,' Jade said brightly, as he headed for the stairs. 'Don't drink too much.'

'I won't. I'm driving.' Mark waved a hand as he went on down.

'All the more for Melissa then,' Jade called after him. *The whole bottle would be good.*

Poppy fell asleep in record time, Bedtime Peppa tucked cosily up with her and Hercules lying protectively at her feet. Jade scowled at the dog and then tiptoed out. Then back in again to feed the goldfish. Sprinkling the requisite pinch of food into the bowl, she bent down to peer at the fish, eyes wide and making a guppy mouth as she did. The water was getting dirty again, she noticed. Sighing, she tipped another more generous dollop of food in. *Knock yourself out, Nemo.* What kind of a life was it, swimming around in circles in shitty water anyway? Cruel, Jade thought. She gave him another sprinkle for good measure, and then, turning to poke out her tongue at Hercules, eased the door quietly shut behind her and crept out.

Peeping into the nursery, she noticed a little hand flailing in the cot and realised it was time for Evie's feed. 'Coming, sweetheart,' she assured her, and then, humming, she went back to her room to collect her Boots bag before carrying on down to the kitchen, where she picked up the sealed container of milk Melissa had left in the fridge and tipped it down the sink. It was a good job she'd started weaning Evie as soon as she'd moved in – she congratulated herself on her foresight as she prepared the formula. With her careless mother stuffed full of drugs, breast milk would obviously harm the poor little mite.

Milk in the microwave, she slipped back upstairs and lifted Evie out of her cot. She was now wide-eyed and alert, looking forward to her bath, followed by a warm, cosy feed and a soft lullaby.

'She'd probably let you slip through her hands and drown you in the bath, wouldn't she, Angel, hmm? Or stuff you in the kiln and fire you. Silly Melissa.' In sweet singsong tones, she addressed Evie by her proper name, which suited her far better. She laid her carefully on the changing mat to undress her.

'You're a gorgeous little girl, aren't you?' Pulling her little sausage arms and legs gently from her pink stripy sleepsuit, she saucered her eyes and smiled down at her, laughing as Evie smiled back. Then she blew on her tummy, causing Evie to chuckle delightedly.

'Mummy's perfect little Angel, aren't you?' she said, standing up and hoisting the naked little baby high in the air. 'Don't you worry, sweet girl, Mummy won't let naughty Melissa hurt you. Daddy would be heartbroken, wouldn't he, hmm?'

Holding her as high as she could, which Evie just loved, Jade twirled her around and around. 'Piss off,' she hissed over her shoulder, as Hercules growled at her from the landing.

CHAPTER TWENTY-EIGHT

MELISSA

'She's absolutely amazing. I have no idea how I managed without her,' Melissa said, regaling Emily and Adam with tales of their perfect babysitter. 'She's fantastic with the kids, isn't she, Mark?'

'Er, yes. You already said so, though, Mel.' Mark looked worriedly from her to her wine glass.

Mel ignored him. She'd only had a couple of glasses. And someone had to fill the awkward gaps in the conversation, since Mark didn't seem to have much to say for himself, unsurprisingly. 'She literally fell into our laps,' she gushed on, talking to their friends, rather than to him. 'I mean, it was just dreadful, her house catching fire like that, but the timing couldn't have been better from our point of view. Mark likes her too, don't you, Mark? Then again, he's quite partial to blondes. Thus...' Plucking up a strand of hair, Mel indicated her own transformed locks.

'It's different,' Emily said, glancing between Mel and Mark. 'I still think I prefer your own colour, though. In fact, I was saying to Adam I wished—'

'Can't afford to let things shlide, see, we women.' Mel waggled her wine glass in Emily's direction. 'I mean, having a baby's the most natural thing in the world, isn't it? We should just pop 'em out...' Poking a finger in her mouth, she attempted to pop her cheek. It didn't quite pop, but they'd get the drift. 'And then bounce back to our beautiful, slim selves. Course, we'd have to be beautiful to start with. And slim.' Mel furrowed her brow, pondering her pre-baby body forlornly.

'Good job you're both of the above then.' Adam paid her a compliment, bless him, in the absence of one from her husband, whom she was obviously embarrassing, judging by the uncomfortable look on his face. Mel didn't much care. She was *so* bloody angry. How dare he sit there in judgement of *her*.

'But it has to be effortless,' she went on determinedly, knocking back the contents of her glass and planting it on the table. 'Lisa's effortless, isn't she, Mark? Like an adorable, natural little pixie.'

Mark glanced down at that, drawing in a long breath – quite clearly embarrassed.

'I can't believe she can hold her own as a police officer. Ooh, pardon me, I mean a *detective sergeant*.' Mel flapped her hand, pseudo-apologetically. 'Probably holds everyone else's, as well,' she added bitchily. Then, chuckling at her wit, whilst biting back a sudden urge to burst into tears, she reached for the wine bottle.

'It's all gone, Mel,' Mark pointed out gently, glancing warily at Emily as he did so.

'Oh well, we'll just order another then.' Mel waved the bottle by way of attracting the waiter's attention.

'The time's getting on, Mel,' Mark started. 'Maybe we should—'

'We'll have another Pinot Grigio, please,' said Mel, smiling sweetly and fluttering her eyelashes at the waiter as he came across to their table.

The waiter nodded politely and, apparently oblivious to her subtle flirtations, reached to relieve her of the empty bottle. *Ah well, his loss.* He was probably gay. Far too good-looking not to be. Mel looked him over, giving Emily a conspiratorial wink. 'Adam' – she turned to him – 'another red?'

Adam glanced at Mark and then back to her. 'No. Thanks, Mel, I've had more than enough,' he said, with a gracious smile.

'But you're not driving,' Mel reminded him. 'You came in a taxi. What was the point of that, for goodness' sake, if you didn't intend to have a drink? Go on, go wild. You only live once.'

Adam reached up a hand and scratched behind his ear. A habit he was prone to when he was agitated, Emily had once confided. He looked a bit agitated. Mel squinted at him. Probably because of Mark sitting there looking so bloody po-faced.

What had he got to be miserable about? It was *she* who was supposed to be miserable, wasn't it? Was *she* spoiling everyone's evening? No. Shooting Mark a scornful look, Mel reached to grab his still three-quarters-full glass. 'Here then. You might as well finish Mark's,' she said, pouring the remainder of the red wine into Adam's glass. 'He's obviously not going to.'

'Doesn't look like I am either,' Adam pointed out, pulling back out of splashing distance as most of the contents of the glass spilled onto the pristine white tablecloth.

'Whoops, sorry!' Mel closed one eye and smiled wanly. 'Never mind. I'll order you a single glass instead.'

'Mel…' Mark caught hold of her arm as she waved the glass in the air. 'He doesn't want one.'

'Oh?' Mel turned to glare at him. 'And *you've* decided that for him, have you? Clearly you're a mind reader now, as well as perfect in every other possible way and a genius when it comes to women's feelings. I mean you're just so flipping clever, I'm in awe. Particularly at how you *cleverly* managed to text Lisa about the little secret between you while she was sitting in *my* kitchen!'

The silence that followed was profound, made more obvious by all the diners in the restaurant seeming to stop clattering cutlery as one and turn heads in their direction. Mel didn't care about that either. Was *she* at fault here? For what, exactly? Making a monumental effort to have a good time when the man she'd thought she could trust implicitly had betrayed her? Did he really expect her to believe Lisa's feeble attempts to convince her they'd done no more than swap intimate texts? *Hah!*

Swiping a tear from her face, she snatched the new bottle of wine from the ice bucket as the waiter brought it across. 'Come on – cheer up, everyone, for goodness' sake,' she said, topping up her glass. We're supposed be celebrating Emily's birthday.'

Glancing at Mark, who wouldn't meet her gaze, and then at Adam, who averted his in favour of studying his phone, she leaned across to refill Emily's glass. 'We should leave these killjoys here and go clubbing,' she suggested, casting another meaningful look in Mark's direction. Obviously, they've forgotten how to have a good time.'

Emily, though, placed her hand over her glass. 'Actually, I think we need to go, Mel.' She smiled apologetically. 'Kayla's not so happy with her babysitter. You know what eleven-year-olds can be like.'

'Oh.' Reminded of the fact that she had children of her own, Mel dropped her gaze. 'Yes. Of course. Sorry, I… wasn't thinking.'

'The taxi's outside.' Emily reached to squeeze her arm. 'I'll give you a ring tomorrow, Mel. Take care, hon.'

Giving Mark a pointed look, Emily got to her feet and walked around to give Mel a firm hug. The two men stood simultaneously, leaving Mel feeling bewildered, still seated at the table. She had spoiled her friend's birthday. Spoiled everything. *No!* It was Mark's fault, not hers. She was only trying to be cheerful. What was the *matter* with everyone?

'I'll give you a ring. About that holiday chalet,' Mark said, shaking Adam's hand.

'Do that.' Adam smiled. 'We have some new log cabins being built by the river. It would be great to have you and Mel over to dinner one evening. I'll give you the guided tour.'

Emily went around to Mark then, giving him a hug. A very firm hug. Mel watched, jealousy and incomprehension warring inside her. Incomprehension at her own volatile emotions. Mark wouldn't. She *knew* in her heart that he wouldn't. His family were the world to him. So, why was she hurting so much? Why did she want to hurt him? Because it had been too good to be true? *He'd* been too good to be true? Her white knight had probably got tired of the battle. Tired of her. And who could blame him?

Adam and Emily left, and Mark rushed to settle the bill before she disgraced herself completely.

'Okay?' he asked her, slipping his wallet back into his pocket as he walked back to her, then leaning down to wrap an arm around her shoulders. He tried to make eye contact, but she looked away. She didn't want to see the pain in his eyes, the humiliation that would undoubtedly be there. She'd only been trying to have a bit of fun. It wasn't her fault. He'd caused all this, *not* her.

Her heart, which had been sinking steadily all evening, settled like a cold stone in her chest. She reached for the bottle of wine, drawing it proprietorially closer. People were looking. She could feel the prickle of their disapproving, hostile stares. But she didn't care.

'Go then. I'm staying,' she announced, getting precariously to her feet as the too-handsome-not-to-be-gay waiter came over. 'I'm going to dance on the tables with Miguel.'

Stumbling forward, one leg decidedly shorter – it turned out she was missing a shoe – she snaked the hand still clutching the wine around the startled waiter's neck. 'Dance with me, Miguel,' she said breathily, attempting to lock come-hither eyes on his, but found she couldn't quite focus.

'Mel?' She felt a hand slide around her waist. Another trying to ease her arm from around the man's neck. 'We need to go home, Mel,' Mark said, close to her ear, as the room tilted and shifted. His voice wasn't angry. It was soft. Concerned. Frightened.

Oh, dear God. She was frightened.

Mel felt the floor shift violently beneath her, saw a thousand slivers of green glass shoot across the floor in slow motion as her legs melted, like soft butter, beneath her.

CHAPTER TWENTY-NINE

MARK

Mel didn't speak as Mark helped her into the car. She'd been subdued since the doctor at A&E had suggested that he might like to make sure his wife didn't drink so much in future. She'd looked out of it as they'd dressed the cut to her arm, which fortunately hadn't needed stitching. She still looked out of it, as if her mind was wandering to some dark, lonely place he couldn't follow. Mark had seen that look before. Guessing it would be fruitless to try to talk to her now, he made sure she was comfortable and went around to the driver's side. Climbing in, he reached gently around her to fasten her seatbelt, then took a breath, mentally steeling himself for what might be to come. 'All right?' he asked her, not sure what else to say, what else he could trust himself to say.

Mel nodded, a small uncertain nod, but kept her gaze fixed on her hands, which were resting lightly in her lap. Sighing inwardly, Mark started the engine, wondering where the bloody hell they went from here.

As he flicked the wipers, which swiped hopelessly against the sudden deluge of late spring rain, Mel spoke. 'Are the children all right?' she asked him, her voice barely a whisper.

You've finally remembered you have kids then? Mark thought, his emotions swinging from despair through anger to immense guilt. In truth, he felt like resting his head on the steering wheel and weeping. He had no idea what to do next. How to fix this. Bitter experience told him he couldn't, but he needed to. God help him, he couldn't let Mel sink so far down he was unable to reach her again. How had this happened? How hadn't he noticed the signs until now?

His jaw set tight, Mark gripped the steering wheel hard, reversed sharply and swung out of the car park. 'They're fine,' he said, after a pause, during which he'd had to work at composing himself. It would do no good to heap guilt on her shoulders, which would only add to the wretchedness she would undoubtedly be feeling. 'Jade has everything under control. Don't worry.'

She didn't look at him. Couldn't or wouldn't. Swallowing back a tight knot in his throat, Mark hesitated, and then tentatively reached across to squeeze her hand. 'We'll talk tomorrow,' he said gruffly. 'Let's just get you home for now. You need to rest.' He resisted saying that things would look better in the morning. He had a feeling that they wouldn't. That things wouldn't look better for a long time to come.

Mel didn't answer. Turning her gaze to the passenger window, she fell silent instead, watching the bleak night pass by as they drove.

Fat splodges of rain now plopping moodily against the windscreen, Mark concentrated on the road. Silently, he thanked God, yet again, that they did have Jade. As horrendous as the circumstances were that had forced her to move out of her house, Mark was bloody glad she'd arrived in their lives when she had. He'd managed last time Mel had been ill, but with two children to care for now, Mark doubted he'd cope without help. But wasn't he jumping the gun? Imagining the worst-case scenario? Her odd behaviour was reminiscent of her previous severe bout of depression, but his thoughtlessness at involving someone else in their problems had added to her upset tonight. She'd obviously convinced herself that he might actually be involved with Lisa.

He had to take things one step at a time. The first thing he needed to do was persuade Mel to get a diagnosis. Alongside that, he had to make sure she knew he was here for her. Shocked though he was by the sudden onset of symptoms, she had to know that she was much more to him than the mother of his children. She was the woman he loved. The woman who'd loved him back, despite his insecurities and flaws. If the sunny, independent person he knew her to be was momentarily eclipsed by the darkness, then so be it. He'd fight alongside her until the fucking sun came back out. He was here for the long haul. Somehow, he had to convince her of that.

Pulling up on the drive, Mark killed the engine and waited. Mel seemed reluctant to move. Guessing she would be struggling with her own conflicting emotions, Mark gave her a moment before softly prompting her. 'Ready?'

Jade was waiting in the hall when they went in, her dressing gown belted tight, her expression apprehensive as she looked down at the shoes Mark was carrying. Mel had refused to put them back on, but even without them she was still unsteady on her feet.

Supporting Mel around the waist with his free arm, Mark shrugged, guessing he didn't need to communicate more than he had from the hospital.

Jade smiled sympathetically. 'I'll make us some tea,' she said, clearly attempting to give them some space.

'Thanks,' Mark said, parking the shoes in the hall and steering Mel gently towards the stairs. He wasn't sure she would be able to drink any, but it might help. She'd vomited up what little food she'd eaten in the ambulance.

Mel stopped. 'Are Poppy and Evie all right?' she asked, looking at Jade.

Jade stepped back, her concern obvious, as she looked Mel over. 'Fine. Both fast asleep and dreaming happy dreams,' she reassured her with a smile. Mark was grateful.

Mel nodded, smiling tremulously, and then wrapped her arms about herself and allowed Mark to guide her up the stairs.

She paused on the landing, looking first towards Poppy's door and then Evie's. Mark prayed she didn't insist on going in, and then breathed a considerable sigh of relief when she walked on. Aside from the fact that they would be bound to wake them, he doubted Mel would want Poppy to see her like this.

She still had her arms about herself as she walked into the bedroom.

'I'll get you something to sleep in,' Mark offered, as she stopped in the middle of the room, seeming uncertain.

Walking to the en suite, he unhooked the shirt she wore from the door, considering whether to offer to help her to shower and quickly discarding the idea. His heart twisted afresh as he recalled the last time they'd been in there together, when everything had seemed so right between them. The morning Hercules had been injured, he reminded himself, realising now that things hadn't been as right as they'd seemed. He'd just been too damn wrapped up in his work to see it.

'I'll give you a hand,' he said, walking back towards where Mel still stood, unmoving. 'Fancy sitting on the bed?' he asked, standing behind her, ready to catch her if she stumbled. 'It would make life a lot easier.'

Still, Mel didn't move. 'I'm sorry,' she said instead, her voice so small and full of remorse, Mark felt like crying for her.

Briefly, he hesitated, and then wrapped his arms around her. 'It's okay,' he assured her, easing her towards him. 'The world's still turning.'

'So, *so* sorry,' Mel said, her voice catching, causing Mark's chest to constrict.

'It's okay, Mel,' he repeated throatily, turning her gently to face him as a sob shook through her. 'We'll get through this, I promise.'

Another sob escaping her, Mel leaned into him, dropping her forehead to his shoulder.

Mark pressed a hand to her hair – her gorgeous, copper hair, now blonde. Not Mel's. This illness was part of her, and Mark realised he'd have to accept it might always be. But it wasn't the biggest part of her, the person she was. Somehow, he'd deal with this. Help Mel deal with this.

'Can you promise me something, Mel?' he asked cautiously.

Mel nodded into him.

'Will you make a doctor's appointment?'

Mark prayed hard as he waited again. She hated the damn place. She would go for the kids, no qualms. But when it came to herself, she wouldn't go to the surgery unless she absolutely had to. He couldn't make her go, but hoped she would see that this was one of those times.

'Yes,' Mel said at last, with some effort. 'I will, I promise.'

Breathing deeply, Mark pulled her closer. 'Good,' he said, overwhelming relief washing through him. 'So, how about we get good and cosy together? I don't know about you, but I'm dead on my feet.' Dropping a soft kiss to her head, Mark eased back, gently lifting her chin to look into her beautiful green eyes. The colour of ferns after the rain, they were peppered with such anxiety and uncertainty it tore him apart. 'I do excellent cuddles.' He mustered up a smile.

Mel laughed, a rather strangulated laugh. 'My white knight,' she said, her expression now one of immense sadness.

'At your service,' Mark assured her, hoping he could be all she needed him to be. That he was strong enough. He would be. He needed to be. There was simply no other option.

Mark helped her wash her face, brush her teeth and get changed, the body-hugging dress being impossible to get off single-handedly even when stone-cold sober, he imagined.

Now, trying to find the balance somewhere between husband and carer, he eased the duvet up over her. She was facing away from him, curled into a tight ball. Mark's heart wrenched inside him. Checking the baby monitor, which, mercifully, had remained quiet, he deliberated for a second and then switched it to mute, before quickly undressing and slipping in beside her. She might not need a lover right now, but she needed not to feel alone. He hoped she needed him.

Brushing her cheek with a soft kiss, he slid an arm around her. He closed his eyes as he felt the tension run through her body, heard her trying to stifle her tears. Mark wasn't sure what to do, what to say. He couldn't make it go away. 'I love you, Mrs Cain,' he eventually murmured, close to her ear, wishing he could show her, but that would be insensitive beyond belief. He settled for holding her instead, waiting until her tears subsided and she relaxed into him. Waiting again, until he heard her breathing slow and felt the steady rise and fall of her chest, he eased quietly back out of bed.

He was desperately tired, but he needed to check on the kids. He also needed to let Jade know the monitor in here was switched off, at least for tonight. He'd heard her going back downstairs and guessed she'd been too disturbed by the evening's events to easily drift off. He just hoped she wasn't put off. He hadn't realised how much they would need her, but they did, now more than ever.

Mark found Jade in the kitchen, preparing a feed. And clearly, he'd caught her by surprise. She jumped as he came through the door, dropping the lid of the pedal bin faster than she'd intended and wincing as it clanged.

'Sorry,' she said, blushing. 'I didn't hear you.'

'My fault. Sorry I startled you,' Mark said, apologising for the second time in twenty-four hours.

Jade smiled brightly. 'No problem. I was just making sure Evie's feed was ready. I didn't want her crying for too long and waking Melissa. How is she?'

'Okay… ish.' Mark shrugged uncertainly. He wasn't sure how much he should divulge, given his mistake of confiding in Lisa, but, assuming Jade wasn't already thinking of moving out, she would have to be aware of at least some of what was going on.

'I made Mel some tea.' Jade indicated the mug as he walked across to her. 'It might need a quick blast in the microwave though.'

'She's spark out,' Mark said wearily. 'I could use one though.'

'Not this.' Jade swept up the mug, tipping the contents down the sink before he had chance to reach for it. 'Sorry. It's got loads of sugar in and I know you don't take it.'

Mark furrowed his brow. Since when did Mel start taking sugar?

'She thought it might help with her energy levels,' Jade said, though he hadn't asked. 'I'll make you another.'

Ah. Made sense, Mark supposed. As much as anything made sense tonight. 'No need. Thanks, Jade, but I think I might have a nightcap instead.' He shouldn't, but, frankly, he needed something stronger than tea. 'Don't suppose you fancy joining me while you have your tea, do you?' he asked, noting her mug, which was still half full.

Jade hesitated for a second. 'I'd love to,' she said. 'Evie's due to wake soon anyway. There's not much point going to bed.'

'No.' Mark guessed she wouldn't be getting a great deal of sleep tonight either. 'Sorry about all of this, Jade. Mel doesn't make a habit of drinking. She has the odd glass of wine, but… Well, there's a bit more to it, to be honest.'

Mark sighed despondently. He really didn't have a clue where to start.

Jade reached to squeeze his arm. 'Come on,' she said. 'You can tell me all about it while you have your nightcap.'

Picking up her mug, she headed for the lounge. Mark followed, grateful for her understanding, and for the fact that she didn't seem to be about to give her notice and bolt for the door.

Curled up on the sofa, Jade waited while Mark poured himself a large whisky. Taking a breath, he swilled the amber liquid contemplatively around the glass and then swigged back a large gulp.

'You looked as if you needed that,' Jade commented, as Mark waited for the whisky to hit the spot.

'Yeah.' Mark ran his hand through his hair and took a seat in the armchair. 'Strange night.'

'Do you want to talk about it? I mean, I know you probably feel like a bit of a traitor with Melissa lying asleep upstairs,' she added intuitively, 'but I'm a good listener, if you need one.'

Mark nodded. Traitor pretty well summed it up, but what choice did he have? Jade clearly knew there was a problem anyway. He just hoped she wouldn't think it was too big a problem to deal with.

'I suspect Mel might be suffering symptoms of depression. I'm not sure yet, but the signs are there. She's suffered with it before. Severe depression.'

He paused, looking at Jade for her reaction. The sad fact was, some people simply couldn't cope with mental illness, which was the basis of Mel's fury with him for discussing it behind her back. The rest, her imagining that he might be having an affair, was fuelled by the negative view of herself she would have right now. Mark was aware of it, but it didn't make it any easier to deal with.

Seeming to digest the information, Jade nodded.

Her expression was concerned, but not shocked, Mark noted. He took a breath and went on. 'We lost a child. A while back. A son, six months old.' Having studied the subject endlessly in his attempts to help Mel get through it, he was also aware that there might not be an apparent cause for the onset of symptoms, that the sufferer might not even be aware of it, but he felt Jade should know the circumstances around it, for Mel's sake.

Jade paled, now definitely looking shocked. 'Oh God, Mark, that's awful. Poor Melissa.'

'It was.' Mark took a swig of his whisky. 'Bloody awful, to be honest. There was a point where I thought I might lose Mel as well. I felt I'd already lost her emotionally. She came back to me, eventually, but…'

Mark trailed off. He hadn't realised he'd finished his drink until Jade walked across to relieve him of the glass. 'Another?' she asked him kindly.

Mark glanced from her to the glass. Alcohol was small comfort, in reality. He'd depended on it too heavily in the past, but now he felt the need to anaesthetise himself, at least for tonight. 'Better make it a small one.' He smiled. 'Thanks, Jade.'

'You were saying?' Jade urged him on, as she poured a small measure.

'It's not something you just get over,' Mark confided. 'Mel really had to work hard at it. She took antidepressants, prescribed on a trial and error basis, had psychoanalysis. She hated it. Hated herself for it. She's lived in fear of slipping back there since. I suppose we both just hoped it had gone away.' He'd certainly hoped, desperately. Obviously, he'd buried his head in the sand, rather than realise she might never be truly 'cured'.

Leaning forward, Mark dragged his hands exhaustedly over his face, and then looked up, surprised, as Jade placed a hand on his shoulder. 'I'm sorry, Mark,' she said sympathetically. 'I know how difficult that must have been for you. It's hard on the sufferer, but it's hard on loved ones too.'

Accepting the drink she offered him, Mark eyed her curiously.

'My mum,' Jade elucidated, smiling sadly. 'She struggled with depression for years. I do understand, honestly.'

Mark felt a huge surge of relief, and then concern, as he recalled her personal circumstances. 'That's not how she...?' He stopped, not sure how to ask whether she'd had to deal with the worst kind of loss possible.

Jade shook her head. 'No, I lost my parents in a car accident,' she said, heading back to the sofa. 'The car caught fire, actually,' she said, seating herself in the corner and drawing her legs up underneath her. 'A gruesome coincidence.'

Christ. A graphic flashback slamming violently into him: images of the dead child who haunted his dreams, calling ceaselessly out to him. Mark almost choked on his whisky.

'Are you all right, Mark?' Jade asked, unfurling herself and getting to her feet. 'You look as if you've seen a ghost.'

Mark drained his glass. 'Yes,' he managed, nodding. 'Just exhausted.' Definitely exhausted, he realised. He needed to sleep. And he really needed not to be drinking this stuff on top of endless nights broken with nightmares bordering on hallucination. 'You must be, too.'

'A bit,' Jade admitted.

'I'm sorry, Jade. About your parents,' Mark offered. 'That must have been so hard to deal with.'

'It was. But we cope when we have to, don't we?' Smiling stoically, she shrugged, and then turned quickly to the door as the unmistakable sounds of Evie waking reached their ears.

'I'll go,' Mark said, dumping his glass on the coffee table. 'You try and get some sleep.'

Jade caught his arm as he joined her in the hall. 'I have her feed ready,' she reminded him. 'Go to Melissa.' She smiled reassuringly. 'She might need you. And don't worry, Mark, I'm not going to run at the first family hiccup. The children will need support too.'

Hearing her humming sweetly as he bypassed the nursery five minutes later, Mark couldn't help but be in awe of her. How she had coped, losing her parents like that and yet remaining positive and cheerful, he really didn't know.

He peered quickly into Poppy's room. Hercules was alert, looking up at him when he popped his head in, as usual. Everything seemingly normal. Yet normality was slipping away. Again.

Climbing in beside Mel for a second time, Mark reached gently for her. He needed to feel the wholeness of her, to reassure her he was here, though he doubted she would wake, given her sleep patterns over the last few weeks and the alcohol in her system. Mark was pretty sure she must have been hitting the booze earlier that day. The few wines she'd had while they were at the restaurant wouldn't have rendered her inebriated to the point of unconsciousness.

How long might she have been secretly drinking, he wondered. What might have precipitated it, caused her to reach for alcohol as a crutch, as she had done once before? He had no way of knowing. If only he'd been aware, been paying attention, then maybe, just maybe, he could have done something to help her.

Mel stirred a little in his arms. No more than that. Mark moved closer, pressing a soft kiss to her cheek, and then dragging a hand across his face to wipe a salty tear from his own.

CHAPTER THIRTY

JADE

For God's sake! What now? Jade was halfway through a phone conversation with drippy Dylan, who was fretting about the girl, who apparently looked 'sickly', when she heard the commotion from the other end of the landing. Storming from her room, she only just managed to wipe the scowl from her face as Mark emerged from his bedroom. Looking worse for wear after his horrendous night out with his mental wife, followed by two sizeable whiskies, precious little sleep, and obviously panic-stricken, he hadn't bothered pulling on anything but his tracksuit bottoms.

Appreciating the view, Jade turned the flash off on her phone and took a photo to inspect more thoroughly at leisure, and then bolted after him as Mark headed for Poppy's room, where the child was howling like a banshee.

'Poppy? What on earth?' Mark faltered inside the bedroom door, clearly bewildered. Jade, one step behind – and contemplating poisoning the dog, who was emitting a low growl at the sight of her – could see why.

'What's happened, Poppy?' Concerned, as obviously he would be, Mark walked over to where Poppy was sitting cross-legged in the middle of the bed, cradling the goldfish bowl.

'Nemo's died,' Poppy wailed, dragging an arm under her snotty nose as she looked up at him. 'He's floating on the water. He's dead, Daddy. He's dead!'

Little brat. She'd make her eat the fucking fish for breakfast. Seething quietly in the doorway, Jade noted the foul-smelling water had soaked through Poppy's nightie and into the duvet beneath her, which would now have to be washed by yours truly, with Melissa about as much use as a fart in a spacesuit.

'Hey, hey. Come on, Poppet.' Mark joined her on the bed, wrapping an arm around her and kissing the top of her head. It was such a tender gesture, Jade couldn't resist taking another photo. 'Let me take a look,' Mark gently cajoled her. 'He might just be sleeping.'

'He's not sleeping!' Fresh tears sprang from Poppy's eyes. 'He's dead!'

Nodding understandingly, Mark squeezed her closer and then reached into the water.

Ugh. Jade recoiled as the slimy fish floated onto the palm of his hand. She watched in wonder as Mark blew softly on it. He really was the nicest, kindest person she'd ever known. He looked a bit crestfallen when it didn't twitch so much as a fin, despite several attempts at resuscitation.

'I think he might be, sweetheart,' he eventually conceded, with a sympathetic sigh. 'I'm guessing that means God must have wanted him for Baby Jesus' aquarium.'

Mark looked down at Poppy, shrugging sadly.

Judging by the stubborn little crease in her forehead, though, Poppy wasn't buying it. 'But why does God want him for baby Jesus' aquirum?' She looked querulously up at him.

To feed the five thousand, thought Jade, mentally rolling her eyes – though she had to admire Mark's ingenuity.

'Because…' Stopping, Mark furrowed his brow, clearly struggling for what to say next.

'Because Baby Jesus' aquarium is the ocean,' Jade supplied, as he glanced helplessly in her direction.

Poppy looked towards her, blinking huge, hopeful eyes.

'One of the walls of his nursery is made of glass,' Jade went on, walking across to kneel in front of her, rather than perch on the side of the wet bed. 'He watches over the fish to make sure all the lost little ones find their mummies and daddies and swim in fish heaven together forever.'

Poppy looked, awestruck, from Jade to Mark and back again. 'Like Dory? She found her mummy and daddy,' she whispered, and warming to the idea, judging by her expression.

'Just like Dory.' Mark smiled at Jade, looking hugely relieved.

'They based the film on it, didn't they, Mark?' Her heart skipping a beat at the warmth in his decadent chocolate-brown eyes, Jade got to her feet before she melted in front of him.

'Yup.' Mark played along perfectly. 'It's a true story.'

Poppy looked up at him and then to Jade – her wide eyes so trusting, it could almost be touching. 'Will you help me bury him, Jade?'

'Of course I will,' Jade promised with a reassuring smile. 'I'll just go and see to Evie first.' She indicated the nursery, beyond the door of which Evie was crying, having woken up far too early.

'And I'd better see to you, young lady.' Mark placed the fish carefully back into the bowl and got to his feet. 'We'll leave him there for now, where he's safe,' he said, reaching to relieve Poppy of the bowl.

Parking it on the dressing table on the opposite wall, he gave Jade a conspiratorial wink as she headed for the door. Something deep within her swooped in response. Mark turned back to his daughter, who, in Jade's opinion, was demanding far more of his time than was healthy. 'Come on, Poppet, up we come,' he said, plucking her up from the bed. 'We can't send Nemo to fish heaven wearing a wet nightie, can we? Arms up,' he instructed, giving Jade another photo opportunity as he tugged the soggy nightie up over Poppy's head.

Jade didn't particularly want a wriggling, shivering, naked child in the photo, but with Mark's state of undress... How was a girl to resist? And Mark might like the photos, she supposed, later, should Poppy no longer be around.

Humming happily, she turned to the nursery, nipping deftly inside when she glimpsed Melissa stumbling from the main bedroom. Jade shuddered as she closed the door. Bleary-eyed and white-faced, and with her bleached blonde hair scarily all over the place, the woman looked like something the cat had dragged in. She thought fleetingly of the feline fleabag they'd assumed was hers. She really hoped Dylan didn't get it into his head to go poking around in the depths of his freezer. Preferring his mummy's home-cooking to his own culinary disasters, he wasn't likely to, and she had wrapped her parcel securely, first in polythene, then a carrier bag, before finally sealing it in a Perspex box and marking it Baby Milk. She'd told him it was imperative the box wasn't opened until the milk was ready to use, but still, she really ought to move it soon.

Jade hurried across to lift Evie from her cot. 'Hello, my gorgeous baby girl.' She flashed her a smile. 'Let's get you changed and fed, shall we? We don't want silly Melissa interfering, do we, Angel? No, we do *not*.' Jade's smile widened as, clearly delighted to see her, Evie chuckled gleefully and gave her a gummy grin.

Catching one excitedly flailing hand, Jade cradled her in the crook of her arm and pressed a kiss to her tiny fingers. 'We want her gone, don't we, my precious?' she whispered. 'Out of our lives forever and ever.'

CHAPTER THIRTY-ONE

MARK

The local search for Daisy had now been widened, concentrating on woodland, orchards, beer factories and cider mills. Mark, meanwhile, was painstakingly going through historical maps and small-scale ordnance surveys, looking for abandoned buildings with basement access and properties that might no longer exist above ground level, in particular those with concealed septic tanks, or any conceivable place that might be used to secrete a small body.

'How's it going elsewhere?' Lisa asked him, coming back from a call-out to the town centre, where a group of local youths had decided to break the tedium of hanging around looking bored and had phoned in a sighting of the girl. Another false alarm.

Mark guessed she was asking after Melissa. Edwards had pulled him up twice this week for tardiness, now the norm for him with pandemonium on the home front. Mel had gone from sleeping heavily to waking several times in the night, thus insisting on taking over the night feeds. Mark would have been glad of it, grateful, were it not for the fact that he felt he had to watch her like a hawk, which really didn't make him feel great. Plus, it had thrown Evie's routine into chaos. Jade must have the patience of a saint, Mark had decided. She hadn't said so, but he'd guessed, from the look in her eyes, that she wasn't happy trusting Mel with the baby. Mel was also trying to catch up and fill the orders that had come in from Garden & Homes head office. Mark had been relieved, until he'd helped her load some ceramic stuff into her car, only to discover a carrier bag full of empty wine bottles.

'One day at a time.' Mark smiled wearily in Lisa's direction, glad she was concerned enough to ask. He'd discovered from Lisa the full extent of Mel's reaction to his ill-timed text last week. Apparently, Mel had been reasonably calm, asking Lisa to leave and then telling her she didn't think for one minute he'd fucked her, because he preferred younger women with tits. Mark still winced when he thought about that scenario. Lisa obviously didn't text him early in the morning any more, which meant he was rarely up to speed when he did finally arrive at the station.

'He's still imagining the girl's alive,' Cummings said as he walked past Mark's desk, heading for the door. Obviously, he had assumed they were discussing Daisy.

'There's always the possibility,' Lisa pointed out.

'No chance,' Cummings called back from the corridor. 'She's pushing up daisies, mate.'

'Crass bastard,' Lisa tossed after him. 'Can't we do something about him?' She turned back to Mark, visibly agitated. 'I mean, do we have to share an office with the twat?'

'It's not easy when his old man's Edwards' golfing buddy, but, trust me, I'm trying,' Mark assured her. Frankly, he'd rather work from the toilet than share an office with the man, but he was stuck with him, for now.

Sighing, he got to his feet. He'd pulled up a possible location – a pre-existing cottage on the perimeter of the Hawthorn Farm land. He needed to get uniforms together to check it out.

'Maybe I'll just hire a hitman,' Lisa muttered moodily.

Mark's mouth twitched into a smile. 'Nice idea. Not allowed, unfortunately.'

'Plan B then,' Lisa said.

Mark arched an eyebrow.

'Laxatives in his coffee, since he's so fond of spouting crap.'

Mark shook his head as he collected up his jacket. 'Messy,' he said.

'Mark… if you need anything, an ear anytime, you know where I am. Right?'

'Cheers, Lisa.' Mark nodded appreciatively. 'I might take you up on that. But I think we have things pretty much under control for the moment.'

Assuming Mel accepted help getting things under control that was, and kept her doctor's… *Shit!* Mark checked his watch and hurriedly pulled out his phone. He'd meant to call and remind her what time her appointment was.

CHAPTER THIRTY-TWO

MELISSA

After several unsuccessful attempts to feed Evie, to the exasperated stares of some of the patients in the waiting room, Mel gave up, close to tears. Hurriedly, she got to her feet, pressing Evie to her shoulder. She'd already tried rocking her, changing her, pushing her around in her stroller, waving the few toys they had in the surgery at her, walking around with her, but still Evie wailed as if she were being murdered.

Growing more and more fraught, Melissa almost had a heart attack when her phone rang, hurriedly grabbing it from her coat pocket. Seeing it was Mark, she hit answer and snapped into it, '*What?* I'm here!'

'I thought I'd just check,' Mark said. 'Make sure you made it okay.'

'It's a trip to the doctor's, Mark, not an Antarctic expedition. I do *not* need checking up on.'

'Right.' Mark paused. 'Is that Evie crying?'

Mel was tempted to end the call. Who the hell did he think it was? 'Yes,' she said shortly. 'I'm trying to feed her.'

Mark paused, infuriatingly. If he could hear Evie crying, why didn't he just go? 'I take it Jade isn't with you then?' he asked cautiously.

'No. I don't need a babysitter either, Mark.' Mel felt her hackles rising. 'I'm an adult. I'm quite capable of driving myself to the doctors.' She felt tears welling afresh, even as she said it. She *did* need a babysitter, for Evie. Clearly. But *she* was her mother. Why couldn't she seem to do anything right for her?

'You *drove* there?' Now Mark sounded disbelieving.

Pulling the phone away from her ear, Mel stared at it and then ended the call. Why didn't he trust her? Why did he keep watching her, as if waiting for her to fall? Was she falling? Had she only imagined she'd been happy and content such a short while ago? That Evie had? Her family?

Was it possible she was going mad? That she'd been the only one not to notice it, until now? Cold fear constricted her stomach, icy fingers tugging at her heart, at her mind. In this room full of people, she suddenly felt utterly alone.

'What is it, sweetheart?' she whispered, pressing her face to the top of Evie's soft, downy head, breathing in the smell that was supposed to bind mother and baby together forever. Yet Evie didn't want her. It was as if she could see, through her innocent child's eyes, that her mummy wasn't who she was supposed to be.

Mel wasn't aware of the fat tears sliding down her cheeks, the anguished sob escaping her throat. She didn't hear her name being called, until Dr Meadows spoke right next to her, slid an arm around her shoulders and steered her gently towards one of the nurses' rooms.

Watching a nurse cooing to Evie, who was now gurgling happily, having drained a bottle of formula feed, Mel waited for Dr Meadows to finish going through her notes. She almost hadn't come – but for Mark's insistence, she wouldn't have. She was glad she had now. Dr Meadows had been kindness itself, somewhat restoring Mel's faith. Despite a growing queue of ever more disgruntled patients to see, he'd taken time out to make sure she was looked after, and, more importantly, that Evie was. He'd waited until she was composed and then fetched her personally back to his office, thus allowing her to avoid the hushed whispers and sympathetic glances in the waiting room. Mel really didn't need those.

He'd listened while she'd garbled an apology, and waited while she explained that she had no idea why she was feeling this way, that things had been good in her life and that this feeling hadn't crept up on her so much as hit her like a bombshell.

He'd asked her to explain how she was feeling. After a brief hesitation, Mel had, summarising symptoms she knew only too well: lack of energy, exhaustion, sleeping too much, too little, loss of appetite. She was irritable, easily agitated, apathetic in turns. Each admission tightened the knot of fear inside her. She had problems concentrating and making decisions. Mel ticked all the boxes for the bleak depression she'd thought she'd escaped. The scariest box of all was the feeling that she was unable to look after her own baby. That she might even harm her own baby.

'And you're struggling with feelings of guilt?' Dr Meadows asked astutely, turning towards her. His eyes were full of compassion, with no sign of the judgement Mel had been so worried about. She felt guilty all over again for not seeking help sooner.

Drawing in a long breath, she nodded.

'Feelings of hopelessness and self-blame? Thoughts of suicide or self-harm?' he probed gently. 'It's nothing to be ashamed of, Mrs Cain,' he added quickly, when Mel dropped her gaze.

Again, Mel nodded. She'd tried not to allow her mind to drift down that path in the dark hours, tried so hard, but seeing the hurt in Mark's eyes, the confusion, yet perversely feeling compelled to hurt him more because of it, she had started to believe he would be better off without her. Knowing that he'd felt the need to talk to someone else, a female someone else, only compounded those feelings. Mel guessed Mark would never really understand how devastated she'd been, realising he hadn't been able to talk to her.

Dr Meadows leaned back in his chair, his hands steepled thoughtfully under his chin. 'I know you've struggled with these symptoms on a previous occasion, Melissa. The road to recovery isn't an easy one, is it?'

'No.' Mel agreed wholeheartedly with that. The road she'd travelled had been a long and tortuous one, full of mountains to climb and potholes to trip her up.

'Half the battle is admitting it, of course,' he went on. 'People can be judgemental. It's human nature, I'm afraid.' He paused and sighed. 'Don't judge yourself through their eyes. That's the important thing to remember. Postnatal depression is common. If only mental health issues weren't still thought of as a stigma, I'm sure many women would admit to feeling like you do.'

Would they, Mel wondered. Weren't new mothers their own harshest judges?

'We have the technology, we can fix it,' he joked, winking.

Mel relaxed a little, which was obviously what he'd intended. If only it were that easy, though. 'A brain transplant, you mean? Perfect.' She smiled back. It felt good to do that. When did she lose her smile?

'A short course of antidepressants initially, I think,' he said. 'Counselling possibly, if you feel the need to talk. It might help. Is your husband supportive, Mrs Cain?'

'Yes,' Mel answered hesitantly. 'But… he's been down this road before too.' She let it hang.

He nodded. 'If you don't mind my suggesting, I think you'll find he'd like to be. He arrived enquiring after you while you were with the nurse. He's waiting for you.

Watching Mark's expression change as he walked across to his child, Melissa felt joy tinged with unbearable, palpable pain. It felt as if her heart might tear apart inside her. This wasn't fair.

This wasn't Mark's fault. It was her. *Her* problem. *Her* stupid, dysfunctional brain.

And now, where once he had been free to walk away, he would feel obliged to stay, because his love for Evie and Poppy was unequivocal. But could he really cope with this? Again?

'Hey, little miracle,' he said, taking Evie carefully into his arms and gazing wondrously down at her, as if he couldn't quite believe her. Mel swallowed a tight lump in her throat.

'She's beautiful,' the nurse said, sighing audibly as Mark bent to place a soft kiss on Evie's forehead.

Mark smiled, the kind of warm, adoring smile fathers reserve for their children. 'Like her mother,' he said throatily, turning to face Mel.

Seeing the love in his eyes, peppered with crushing anxiety, Mel caught a sob in her throat. She *had* to get better. For Mark's sake, for her children's sake, she had to get well.

CHAPTER THIRTY-THREE

MARK

Unfastening Evie's car seat, Mark lifted her out, and then breathed a sigh of relief as Mel's car turned into the drive.

'Here she is, baby,' he said softly, waiting for Mel to pull up before he went inside. He couldn't stay. Lisa had covered for him, but he needed to get back soon. He wished Jade was home. He wished to God Mel wouldn't insist on driving. The last thing Mark wanted was for Mel to think he was trying to take away her independence, but, in his estimation, she shouldn't be, particularly with a child in the car. She was exhausted and distracted, and he also feared that she'd started drinking during the day.

As if to demonstrate his point, Mel climbed out of her car, walked past him to the front door, and then went back for her keys. And then back for a second time for Evie's baby bag.

'Thanks for coming, Mark. We'll be fine now,' she said, walking past him again to unlock the front door. She reached for Evie's carrier, as if expecting him to hand it over and go back to work.

'I'll bring her in.' Mark smiled and stepped towards the house.

Mel nodded tightly, but moved aside, allowing him to carry Evie through. 'Shall I take her up?' he asked, as Mel followed him into the hall.

'No.' Mel returned his smile, but still she seemed miles away. 'I thought I'd have her with me in the kitchen for a while. I've missed her company.'

Mark hesitated, thinking that Evie might be tired after all the excitement, which would probably make her fractious later.

'I'll take her up in a little bit,' Mel said, pulling off her coat.

Mark nodded and carried Evie through to the kitchen, heading for the island in the middle of the room, where he hesitated again. Would she be all right parked up there? Of course she would, he chastised himself. Mel wasn't likely to accidentally knock baby plus sizeable car carrier onto the floor. Still, though, he pushed the seat well into the centre of the work surface.

'Have the assessors been yet?' Mel asked, coming in after him as Mark eased Evie out of her coat.

'Sorry?'

'The fire assessors. I wondered if Jade had managed to get the go-ahead on the work to her house?'

Mark tried to think. He'd noticed that Jade didn't seem to show much interest in the house. She'd barely been near the place. But then, it couldn't be easy sifting through the burned-out remnants of your life, future plans turned to ashes. 'A couple of weeks ago, I think. She said she was getting some estimates together. Why?'

'No reason. I just wondered.' Mel shrugged, looking preoccupied as she walked across to the kettle. 'Do you like it?' she asked out of the blue, leaving Mark struggling to keep up.

'Like what?' Checking Evie didn't need changing, he headed for the fridge for her water.

'My hair.' Mel turned to him, her pretty green eyes awash with worries Mark had no clue about and felt powerless to help her with.

He looked her over, noting her pale complexion, which the hair colour did nothing to improve. 'Truthfully,' he said, hoping he wasn't about to put his foot in it, 'I prefer your natural colour.'

Seeming unperturbed, Mel nodded. 'Coffee?' she asked, turning away.

'No. Thanks.' Concerned at the seemingly random conversational leaps, Mark watched her carefully. 'I have to get to work.'

'Sorry. Yes, of course you do.' Mel paused. 'I'm thinking of changing it back.'

The hair, Mark assumed. 'Good idea,' he said, going back to Evie, who Mel hadn't so much as glanced at since she'd come in.

'Would you lie to me, Mark?' Mel asked, completely out of left field.

'Never,' Mark answered straight off. In actual fact, he felt he was lying, right there, going along with her insistence in ignoring the elephant in the room. He wanted to talk to her about what was happening, not skirt around the issue, having this stilted, staccato conversation. How could he hope to help her if she wouldn't confide in him? 'Where did that come from?'

Mel ignored that, too. Or maybe she hadn't heard him. From the impassive expression on her face, Mark wasn't sure. Making her coffee in silence, she wandered to the back door, opened it and went out to sit at the patio table.

Minus coffee. Mark noticed it still sitting on the work surface. 'Back in a minute, sweetpops.' Evie seeming to have satisfied her thirst, he grabbed a paper towel to mop up the drips, and then followed Mel out with her drink.

'I have to go soon, Mel,' he reminded her, placing the coffee on the table and checking his watch, debating whether he should ring in and claim some emergency. But how many times could he do that? Perhaps he should keep it up his sleeve, in case there was another day when Mel needed him more. He shook off the thought. 'Will you be all right?'

She didn't respond.

'Mel?'

'Yes, fine,' Mel said, looking up at him but not seeming to see him.

'Evie's had some water,' he tried, wishing she would talk to him; wishing that by some miracle this would all go away.

Mel smiled. 'Good,' she said.

Exasperated, Mark glanced back to the kitchen, where Evie was on her own, content for the moment, though he doubted she would be for long. He wasn't happy about leaving her there and Mel out here. 'Will Jade be back soon?'

'Should be,' Mel said. 'She went to the dentist with a tooth. She's picking Poppy up on the way.'

A toothache, Mark presumed. And she must be picking Poppy up from school on the way home, not the way there. Growing more concerned at Mel's emotionless responses, Mark pulled out a chair to sit opposite her. 'Are you okay with the medication, Mel? The antidepressants?'

Mel answered with an indifferent shrug.

'Have you taken any? Your first dose, I mean.'

Mel's answer this time was a shake of her head.

And yet, she seemed more out of it than ever. Frustrated, Mark pressed on. 'Do you think it's a good idea to drive on them, Mel?' He had to broach the subject of her driving, whether she might think he was being controlling or not. His only other option was to take the car keys, and he really did *not* want to do that.

Mel looked at him at last, guardedly. 'If I felt I couldn't drive, I wouldn't.'

Mark nodded. 'You'll have to report it to the DVLA if it does affect your driving.'

Mel frowned, and then shrugged again, as if only half-interested, which increased Mark's apprehension. So, what now? This was getting him nowhere.

Deciding he had no other option, Mark breathed in deeply and took the bull by the horns. 'And you'll avoid alcohol, yes?'

'Avoid…?' Snapping her gaze to his, Mel searched his face. 'Are you serious?' She laughed incredulously.

Mark held her gaze. 'Deadly,' he assured her. He would do anything and everything for her. He believed, hoped, that she knew that to be true. Risking his children, though, was something he couldn't do.

'Since when did getting drunk, *once*, for the first time in I don't know how long, become a criminal offence?' She stared at him, her expression somewhere between bemused and angry.

'Spectacularly drunk,' Mark reminded her, for want of a better word.

'Yes, spectacularly!' Mel's voice rose. 'And I'm sorry I embarrassed you. Sorry that, for whatever reason, I couldn't handle it, but… Oh, for God's sake, Mark. How many times am I supposed to apologise? I haven't had so much as a sip of wine since.'

'Right.' Mark sighed, heavily. He hadn't expected her to admit it, but he'd hoped she wouldn't deny it outright.

'What does *that* mean?' Mel asked, her anger obviously escalating.

Mark ran a hand over his neck. 'Nothing. I'm just concerned, Mel, that's all.'

'About me driving while taking medication?'

'Obviously.' Mark locked eyes with her. Mel's gaze was fiery, her eyes slightly bloodshot. He studied her, noting her pupil reaction time seemed to be slowed, and steeled his resolve. 'I don't want you taking risks while—'

'Driving under the influence of alcohol?' Mel finished furiously.

'Both of the above,' Mark supplied disconsolately.

'I *don't* drink and drive!' Mel snapped, her tone now aggressive. 'I never have!'

Tugging in a terse breath, Mark squeezed the bridge of his nose hard with his thumb and forefinger.

'*Mark?*' Mel waited for him to answer, but he couldn't say what he truly felt: that he couldn't trust her, and it was killing him.

'I don't bloody believe this!' Mel shoved her chair back and stormed into the kitchen. 'Why don't you bloody well breathalyse me and be done with?'

Berating himself on his abysmal handling of the situation, Mark hurried after her.

His heart dropped as he watched her banging around, opening cupboards. All of the fucking cupboards.

'Take a look,' she said. 'Go on!'

'Mel, don't.' He glanced towards Evie, who had been startled by the loud crashing of doors opening and shutting.

'Don't forget the fridge.' Mel marched over to it, yanking that open too. 'I mean, I'm bound to have a bottle chilling in there for…' She stopped, staring hard at the contents, and then slammed the door shut. '*Fuck!*'

Mark bit back his own anger. He wasn't sure where this was going, but wherever it was, it wasn't happening in front of Evie.

'Who turned the fridge off?' Mel yelled, as he walked across to her.

Mark stopped, confused. 'What?'

'The fridge. It's off at the wall!' Mel waved a hand in the direction of the socket and then reached for the freezer door. '*Shit,*' she muttered. 'Shit, shit… *shit!*'

Oh Christ. 'Mel…' Hearing the sob in her throat, and realising immediately what was wrong, Mark started towards her. But he stopped as Jade came in, with Poppy, wide-eyed and wary, holding tight to her hand. She was holding a goldfish in her other hand, Mark noticed, his heart sinking further as he realised his little girl's bubble was about to be rudely burst.

'What's happened? Mark? Mel?' Obviously puzzled, Jade trailed off.

Mark held up a quieting hand. Then, seeing Jade had understood, he nodded towards Evie and then went over to Mel.

'It's ruined,' she said, crying now in earnest. 'All of it.'

Mark reached out, gently stroking her back, attempting to ease her towards him. He had no idea what else to do. He couldn't fix this.

'Why is Mummy crying?' Poppy asked Jade in a worried whisper.

'I think she has a headache,' Jade answered quietly, moving towards Evie, who was now demonstrating her distress vocally.

Mark nodded his appreciation and tried to comfort Mel, but she was fighting him, pulling away from him. 'Did you do it?' she asked, swinging around to level an accusing gaze at Jade.

'Do what?' Jade looked confusedly from Mel to Mark. 'I'm not sure, I…'

'The freezer,' Mark explained, feeling worn out already, to his very bones. 'Someone's switched it off.'

'Not me.' Jade looked alarmed. 'At least I don't think I—'

'Well, someone did!' Mel snapped, causing both Jade and Poppy to step back.

Glancing at Jade apologetically, Mark wrapped an arm around Mel's shoulders. 'It was an accident, Mel,' he said softly, aware of how distraught she would be. Determined to breastfeed Evie, she'd expressed milk religiously every day, making sure the freezer was always stocked up.

'It's all ruined,' Mel said again, her sobs stilling to a shudder as she heaved air into her lungs.

'I'm so sorry, Mel.' Mark tried to pull her closer, but Mel didn't want to be held. Didn't appear to want him near her. Her body language was stiff, her emotions all stuffed precariously inside. Like a watch spring, Mark felt, wound way too tight and ready to uncoil in an instant.

'It's okay.' She drew in a shaky breath. 'I was going to wean her anyway. I can't feed her myself now, can I? That would really be putting my child at risk, wouldn't it? You'll be pleased to know I'm in possession enough of my faculties to have thought that one through, Mark.'

The medication. Mark squeezed his eyes closed. *Dammit.* It hadn't even occurred to him, but it had to Mel. And she was devastated. She shrugged him off and walked away.

Mark hesitated for a second and then, hearing her climbing the stairs, he moved to go after her. He couldn't leave her, not like this.

'I'm sorry,' Jade said tearfully, as he walked past. 'I honestly don't think I did switch it off, but if I did…'

Noting how crestfallen she looked, as if holding herself responsible, Mark stopped and placed a hand on her shoulder. 'It was an accident,' he repeated firmly. 'Anyone could have inadvertently knocked the switch.' Even Mel. In her present state, Mark had to concede that she might have done it herself.

Jade nodded, still looking unhappy. Very. Mark hoped this didn't cause her to leave.

'I'll go to the chemist,' Jade offered, dredging up a smile from somewhere. 'Get some formula. I'm sure Evie will be fine, Mark. Don't worry.'

Mark closed his eyes, relief surging through him. If anyone knew what to do here, it was Jade. 'That would be great. Thanks.'

'No problem,' she assured him. 'Do you want to come with me, Poppy?'

'Uh-huh.' Poppy nodded quickly, looking as if she'd rather be anywhere than home right now.

'I could take Evie, too,' Jade suggested. 'We shouldn't be too long. It might give you a chance to…' She nodded diplomatically towards the stairs. 'If Mel wouldn't mind me taking her car, that is?'

'I'm sure she won't.' Mark nodded to the keys on the work surface, and then crouched to give Poppy a firm hug. 'Be good, Poppet,' he said, his heart twisting as he noted the bewilderment in her eyes. 'And remember, Jade's in charge while Mummy's not feeling well. Make sure to do everything she tells you to. Okay?'

'I will,' Poppy promised, with a brave little nod.

'Good girl.' Mark kissed her forehead and straightened up.

Hearing Jade shushing Evie and chatting to Poppy as he went up the stairs, assuring her that Dory would be fine, left in her special fish water in the sink, Mark counted his blessings. He'd worried about her qualifications when Mel had employed her so quickly. That had been one long month ago, and clearly his worries had been unfounded. Not only was she competent enough to care for the children in a crisis, she was caring enough to want to. She was indispensable. Mark knew that now with certainty. He'd need to do all he could to make sure she had access to everything she needed, including Mel's car. If Jade stayed – and he prayed that she did – she would need to drive it on a regular basis.

Mark's first reaction when he woke in the small hours was surprise at the complete silence. His second was panic as he reached for Mel to find her side of the bed empty.

He threw back the duvet, almost falling over it in his scramble to pull on his tracksuit bottoms before heading for the landing. Seeing no glimmer of light from downstairs, he went straight to the nursery, glancing into Poppy's room as he did. She was fast asleep, Hercules lying loyally at the foot of her bed. She'd obviously been fighting with the duvet too. Bidding Hercules to stay, Mark crept quietly in to ease the covers back over his daughter's small form.

The nursery door was closed, unusually. Both he and Mel preferred it left open a fraction. Warily, Mark listened outside and then, hearing no sound, he pressed down the handle and went inside, looking apprehensively over to the cot as he did.

Evie, lying on her tummy, one tiny hand to the side of her face, appeared to be sleeping. Needing to reassure himself, Mark took a breath and stepped further in. Seeing his baby girl's eyelids flutter as her mind chased her dreams, he closed his own eyes and allowed himself to breathe out.

Mel was standing in the middle of the room, though she gave no indication she knew he was there. She was quite still, her arms wrapped tightly about herself. Not sure what to do next, wondering whether she might even be sleepwalking, Mark hesitated for a second, watching her watching Evie, and then, noticing her shoulders tense as she breathed deeply in, he walked quietly across to her.

'I wouldn't hurt her,' Mel murmured, as he stopped behind her.

'I know.' Hearing the wretchedness in her voice and wondering how long she'd been standing here, quietly crying, Mark felt his heart hitch. 'I know you wouldn't, Mel,' he said, placing his arms around her and desperately trying to quash the feeling that, if he let go, he might lose her.

CHAPTER THIRTY-FOUR

MELISSA

Melissa willed her body to respond, her mind screaming. Her heart constricted inside her; she tried to run, to breathe, but her feet were weighed down by the swirling nothing beneath her. The air was too thick, too putrid; choking smoke seared her lungs. Petrified, she tried to reach Evie. Tried to push and prise them away, the hands that clutched and clawed at her legs, disembodied arms rising and writhing like pale grey vines from the mire. She was crying. Pitiful whimpers turned to terrified tears – her baby was crying. Someone was shaking her, hurting her, and she… couldn't…

Hush, little baby, don't say a word…

Jade?

'Morning,' Jade greeted her cheerily.

Prising heavy-lidded eyes open, Mel blinked hard against the bright light the girl seemed to be bathed in.

'Morning,' Jade said again, standing over her. 'I brought you some tea.'

Attempting to focus, Mel gulped hard against the parched dryness of her throat, and struggled to lever herself up.

'Hold on,' Jade said, taking a step to the side.

Squinting, Mel registered the sunlight filtering through the slatted blinds. Her blinds at her bedroom window, she realised, immense relief washing through her.

'You were sleeping like a baby.' Jade bobbed back into view. 'We didn't like to wake you, so—'

'We?'

'Mark,' Jade clarified, leaning down to help her with her pillows. 'He said you hadn't fallen asleep until after three, so we thought it was best not to disturb you.'

There was that 'we' again. Mel wasn't sure she liked it. Or being left to sleep until some ridiculous time. Her sleep patterns had been erratic, to say the least, when she'd been unwell before. She'd had no reason, not even the will, to get out of bed then. But things were different now. She had a family, and suddenly, paranoid though it might be, she felt excluded from it. Routine was what she needed, to get up and get on with it. She didn't want to give in, to lie in bed, battling nightmares that seemed too real to be dreams and slipping further into her black hole. 'Where is he?' she asked, pushing the duvet back and attempting to pull herself into a sitting position, no easy task with her brain and body seemingly immersed in soft treacle.

Jade reached a hand out to steady her. 'He's taken Poppy to school. And Evie's due her check-up, so he—'

'Mark's taken her?' Mel asked, surprised. 'But doesn't he need to be at work?'

'He said he wanted to spend some time with her. I was ready to take her, but—'

'Wanted to keep her out of harm's way, more likely,' Mel growled. Seeing the alarmed expression on Jade's face, she felt immediately guilty. Again.

'He means well, Melissa,' Jade said, tentatively, obviously wary of being interrupted or snapped at. 'I know how you feel, honestly I do. Sometimes you just want people to go away and not treat you as if you're incapable, but he is trying to be helpful.'

He was. She knew he was. Mel sighed inwardly, and then looked at Jade curiously as her thoughts caught up with her. 'Do you? Know how I feel?'

Jade hesitated, and then reluctantly nodded. 'I was on medication, too,' she admitted, now looking awkward. 'Only for a short while, after my parents…' Mel searched her face, attempting to digest this new information about her babysitter. 'I'm fine now. I probably should have mentioned it before, but…' Dropping her gaze, Jade trailed embarrassedly off.

'You thought I wouldn't employ you?' Mel finished, empathising completely. There was more understanding of mental illness nowadays but still there was prejudice and fear of the unknown. Mel had experienced it herself. She'd never imagined Mark might think her incapable of looking after her own children though.

Jade nodded slowly. 'Sorry,' she said, in a small voice.

And Mel despaired utterly of herself. The girl had been efficient, genuinely caring towards Poppy and Evie, falling over herself to help out. More than that, she was prepared to stick around when many people wouldn't. Most people, in fact. And how had she shown her appreciation? By accusing her of sabotaging her milk supply, when it had obviously been just an unfortunate accident. Jade must feel awful.

'Don't be sorry.' Mel reached out to take her hand, and the poor girl looked as if she might burst into tears. 'For the record, I would have employed you, and, also for the record, you're doing a fantastic job, Jade. I'm immensely grateful.'

'Really?' Jade beamed at that. She had a gorgeous smile.

'Really.' Mel gave her hand a squeeze. 'It's me who owes you an apology. I shouldn't have jumped to conclusions about the freezer. The switch is in the perfect place for getting accidentally knocked. I've done it myself with the kettle. Anyway, I'm sorry.'

'Apology not necessary,' Jade said, reaching for the tea and passing it to her. And then the tablets. Mark must have given them to her. Plainly, he was worried she'd forget to take them, or leave them lying around. Mel dearly wished she could forget to take the bloody things. She already felt woozy to the point of drunkenness.

It was no wonder he'd thought she was secretly partaking of the odd tipple. She wished he hadn't accused her of that though. It felt as though he didn't trust her.

Mel stared at the tiny, innocuous-looking tablets Jade offered her.

'They'll help,' she urged, as Mel hesitated.

'Not for the next few weeks.' Aware of what the side effects were, which would only get worse before she got better, Mel sighed, but took them anyway and washed them down with the tea. 'As long as you don't mind coping with the mood swings,' she said, feeling a little easier confiding in Jade now that Jade had confided in her.

'I'll look the other way if you throw a wobbly,' Jade promised.

Mel smiled. 'I'd walk the other way, if I were you. I might be about to throw one.'

Jade widened her eyes worriedly. She had nice eyes, Mel thought. True baby blue, and as innocent as a baby's too.

'The hair.' She rolled her eyes upwards. 'What on earth am I going to do with it?'

Jade cocked her head to one side. 'Dye it back,' she said. 'In fact, I might join you. I quite fancy going copper. Meanwhile, wear it up. Come on, I'll show you.'

Taking hold of Mel's hands, she pulled her to her feet and steered her towards the wardrobe mirror, where she proceeded to gather her hair and pull it into a topknot.

Ouch! Rather too roughly, Mel thought, but felt it impolite to point out.

'Like this, see?' Jade smiled, and waited for her reaction.

Mel studied her reflection. It was an improvement, she supposed, but she doubted she'd look as bright and bouncy as Jade any time soon. *Jaded* is how she looked – pale and drawn. How had this happened, she wondered again, her resolve waning a little, which wasn't helped by the room spinning in slow revolutions around her. Mel wondered about that, too. How it was she'd felt so spaced out before she'd even started the medication.

'You should wear some blusher,' Jade said, surveying her thoughtfully. 'Until you get the colour back in your cheeks.'

So she'd noticed her sallow complexion too. 'I can imagine what Mark will think about that,' Mel said, with another roll of her eyes. Other than a little concealer beneath her eyes, she hardly ever wore make up around the house, clay spatters on top of blusher not being a good look. He'd probably think she was off to proposition another waiter. Recalling her drunken endeavours at seduction, the waiter's horrified expression and Mark's clear mortification, Mel winced inwardly.

'Think about what?' Mark asked, eyeing her curiously as he came through the open bedroom door.

'Mel wearing her hair up,' Jade supplied, diplomatically leaving out the pale and uninteresting bit. 'What do you think?'

Mark looked at Mel through the mirror as Jade demonstrated her proposed up-do. 'Sexy,' he said, smiling.

It didn't reach his eyes, though, Mel noticed. There was no mischievous glint there, no subtle innuendo. He looked wretched, as pale as she was, and utterly exhausted.

'I, er, should go. Running late,' he said, reaching for his mobile. Out of habit, Mel wondered, as he pocketed it again without checking it, or did he not want to check his messages in front of her? 'Will you be okay, Mel?'

'Yes. Why wouldn't I be?' Irked by what felt like his patronising concern, Mel replied sharply – and then immediately regretted it.

'I'll go and see to Evie,' Jade said, tactfully excusing herself from the situation. 'Is she still in her carrier, Mark?'

'In the lounge, fast asleep,' Mark confirmed, turning his confused gaze away from Mel towards Jade. 'She's due a feed soon, so I thought I'd leave her for the moment.'

'Brilliant.' Jade headed towards the door. 'That'll give me a chance to get it ready.'

'Thanks, Jade.' And this time his smile was one of relief, tinged with palpable sadness.

Mel felt her heart sink. He didn't want to be here. How could he? And then her stomach lurched as she noticed Jade reach out to brush his arm with her hand. Bewildered, Mel turned away from the mirror. Why would she do that? Commiseration? Reassurance? It was too intimate a gesture. She must know that. *He* must. Right here in front of her. In her *bedroom*.

'Mel? Are you all right?' Mark asked, as she turned swiftly to the en suite.

'I'm fine! For God's sake…' *Please, just stop asking.* Mel closed the door and turned to lean against it, desperately trying to hold back the useless, *pathetic* tears. To convince herself it was just her paranoia at play, misinterpreting things, yet again.

CHAPTER THIRTY-FIVE

JADE

Jade had no idea why she hadn't got rid of the girl sooner. She'd felt sorry for her, initially. How could she not, with her mother seething and raging, embarrassing her in the middle of the supermarket? The woman had been a complete witch, dressed like a trollop: short skirt, tits on show, blood-red lipstick, like an angry red slash for a mouth. Watching from across the aisle, seeing the woman's rubbery lips exaggeratedly moving as she'd cursed and berated the child for accidentally knocking over a display stand – 'You stupid girl! Look what you've done!' – Jade had felt goosebumps prickle her skin. She recognised the child's fear. The same fear she'd felt when her own bitch mother had snarled and scorned and walked away, leaving her with *him*. She felt again the ice-cold dread pooling in the pit of her stomach, the repulsion, the pain; the powerlessness as he'd pushed into her, groaning and thrusting and grunting. The hopelessness, trying to make her mother understand. *It wasn't her fault!*

Daisy had said the same thing. 'It wasn't my fault, Mummy,' she'd cried, huge, salty tears sliding down her cheeks as she'd looked beseechingly up at the spiteful, self-centred cow. Looking for comfort, where there was none.

It could have been her.

Irresistibly drawn, Jade had followed them, cruising past the house in the car she'd since disposed of – a car of her own being superfluous to requirements once she'd secured employment with the Cain family. Approaching on foot on her subsequent vigils, she'd watched and she'd waited. She'd seen the hysterical mother hurling accusations at the father, so drunk after a boozy party she couldn't stand up straight. 'You're disgusting,' she'd screamed, lashing out at him, her face twisted, her eyes full of hatred. 'A fucking disgusting paedophile!'

Jade had made her decision then. They didn't deserve to be parents. They didn't deserve Daisy. They deserved to burn in hell. First, though, they needed to learn, to realise what they'd done. They needed to lose the child, whose innocence they were stealing, whose childhood they were breaking, whose love and trust they were abusing.

Obviously frightened of them, Daisy had come willingly when Jade had told her she was going to keep her safe – which she'd every intention of doing then. The girl had reminded her of her little sister. Annoyingly, just like her little sister, she was becoming a nuisance. Poppy had, too. But Poppy, of course, had also turned out to be spoiled beyond belief and far too demanding of Mark. Jade still hadn't come to a decision about her. She'd so hoped Poppy would have some redeeming features. She didn't want Mark to go through the unbearable grieving process of losing another child unless he absolutely had to.

This one, though… It was hard work, keeping the girl occupied and fed with Dylan constantly fretting and ringing her. And now things were moving on with Mark, she'd become a liability Jade didn't need.

Jade sighed as Dylan fussed and twitched behind her, scared to death his mummy would discover his secret and realise what kind of a pathetic idiot he really was. She peered down at the girl, who was sleeping contentedly enough, thanks to a large dose of Calpol. 'She's fine,' she told him, turning from the bed. 'It's just a cold. She'll feel better after a nap.'

Dylan stared at her stupidly for a second and then, wiping his shirtsleeve under his nose, he followed her to the bedroom door. 'You sure?' he asked, once on the landing. 'It's just, she didn't seem to be breathing right when I looked in on her last night. Chesty-like, you know?'

Jade looked him over, taking in the worry lines furrowing his brow like a five-bar gate, his jeans which were an inch too short – obviously turned up by his mother – and the wet patches under his armpits, and suppressed her immense agitation. 'I'm her mum, Dylan. I'm also a qualified nursery nurse. I think I should know, don't you?'

Smiling sweetly, she stroked his cheek – God forbid she should have to stroke any other part of him today – and then, feeling nauseated at the stench of body odour mingled with pig shit that seemed to permanently emanate from him, she turned quickly for the stairs.

Grabbing up her bag, she headed across the tiny living room and straight for the front door.

'You going already?' Dylan asked, following her like an annoying little lapdog as she stepped out and breathed in some blessed fresh air.

'I have to pick Poppy up from school.'

Jade sighed as she watched him lumbering after her, wondering again how a man who was built like a brick shithouse came to be scared of his own shadow. It was useful, of course, along with the fact that he'd obviously been born stupid, but she did worry it might be her downfall. Dylan would undoubtedly spill the beans if he were cornered – he couldn't lie convincingly to save his life. Jade would probably have to do something about him too, which was a shame, but needs must.

'So, will you be taking her soon?' Dylan asked, shrugging his huge round shoulders awkwardly. 'It's just that me mum comes out to talk to the pigs sometimes.' He nodded to where the disgusting creatures were snuffling and grunting in the field adjoining the cottage,

Jade had to stifle a laugh at that, the image of his sour-faced, frumpy mother talking to the pigs. Mind you, she wasn't surprised, with only Dylan for company.

'I will, I promise. It's just…' Jade faltered. 'You know he doesn't want her,' she went on, looking tearfully back at him. 'He's bound to do something awful to her. She really is much better off here for now.'

'He' being Mark, who Dylan believed to be the father of the girl, and who was as capable of doing something awful to a child as he was his needy wife. His inexhaustible patience was becoming a bit of a concern. Jade needed Mark to realise that Melissa was nothing but a ball and chain around his ankles, pulling him down. He needed to leave her. Jade had no intention of sharing him for much longer.

Puffing up his chest manfully, Dylan looked her over and nodded. 'I know,' he said sympathetically, placing a huge paw around her shoulders. Jade's skin crawled. 'It's okay,' he said gruffly. 'She can stay a bit longer. I'll try and keep me mum away.'

'Thanks, Dylan.' Jade smiled at him, and silently thanked God she'd convinced him to change the locks. With his miserable mother wandering around, she was going to have to do something about the girl sooner rather than later, she realised. 'I knew I could depend on you. I'll see to her soon.' Checking her watch, she sighed regretfully. 'I'd better go.'

Giving him a peck on the cheek, Jade turned, resisting the urge to wipe her mouth. She wasn't sure how, exactly, she would see to her. Feed her to the pigs? Pondering her options, Jade hummed softly to herself as she went. *Hush, little baby…*

CHAPTER THIRTY-SIX

MARK

'Hey, Poppet.' Mark swept Poppy up as he came through the front door. He was late. Way later than he'd expected to be, having been on site at a demolished property within the search radius for Daisy Evans. Discovering the building had a basement, it had been worth checking out, but to no avail. Now, Mark felt exhausted and frustrated. 'Shouldn't we be in bed?' He nodded to the hall clock, where Poppy could see that the big hand was way past the half past seven mark.

'I *was* going.' Poppy made huge eyes at him as he put her down. 'But Mummy said she would come up and tuck Dory in.'

'Ah, I see.' Mark nodded, then furrowed his brow, pondering how, exactly, one tucked a goldfish into bed. 'So where is Mummy?'

'Working,' Poppy said, following him towards the kitchen. 'She'll be utterly sausted,' she added, with an elongated sigh.

'Exhausted,' Mark corrected her, looking curiously towards Jade, who was busy loading bottles into the steriliser.

'She's been in the workshop since this morning,' Jade explained, turning to flick on the kettle, which was now plugged into a socket well away from the freezer, he noted.

'She's been working all day?' Mark was surprised. He'd worried the side effects of the drugs, which he knew to be difficult to handle for the first few weeks, might make it impossible for her to work. But then, Mel was a fighter, he reminded himself. He'd never known her to give up on anything easily, an attitude of which their two beautiful kids were evidence. Plus, she found her work therapeutic, which might actually help. Staying out there the whole day and half the evening, though? He hoped she wasn't overdoing it.

'She's been in to check on Evie once or twice but that's about it,' Jade said. 'Do you want me to take Poppy up and read her a bedtime story while you go out and have a chat with her?'

'That'd be great. Thanks, Jade.' Mark guessed Poppy wouldn't be too devastated at having Jade read her a story in lieu of him. Mark was grateful for Jade's help, and amazed at how adaptable she was prepared to be. Grateful also for the effort she made to be a friend to Mel. She would certainly need one, particularly now her friendship with Lisa had cooled. Mark still couldn't get his head around what the hell had been going through Mel's mind. But that, he suspected, was probably a subject best left alone for now.

'Yay! *Lily the Little Mermaid*!' Poppy clapped her hands glee-fully.

Definitely not devastated. 'I take it she does Lily better than me?' Mark asked.

'She's a *girl*, silly. Lily's a girl mermaid,' Poppy informed him.

Mark sighed theatrically. 'A lesser man would be crushed, you know.'

Poppy pressed her hand to his cheek as he leaned down to kiss her goodnight, searching his eyes worriedly, and then giggling when Mark went cross-eyed. 'You're teasing,' she said, trying very hard to do likewise and make her pupils meet in the middle.

'A bit,' Mark said, planting a kiss on her cute button nose. 'Good job I know you love me bigger than the sky, isn't it?'

'And the moon.'

'And all the stars. Night, Poppet. I'm assuming you've had no further trouble from the bug monster?'

'No. Jade slayed him,' Poppy said airily, as Jade led her to the door.

'With a single blow of my bug-slayer sword,' said Jade, rolling her eyes good-naturedly over her shoulder.

'A single blow? Wow. You're a braver man than I am,' Mark said, looking suitably impressed as he headed for the back door.

'*Daddeee*, she's a *girl!*' Poppy called from the hall.

'I know, I noticed.' Mark called back.

Rather than barge in and possibly frighten her, Mark tapped on the workshop door and waited.

'It's open,' Mel shouted, after a moment.

'How's it going?' Mark asked, going in.

Mel stepped away from the sculpture she was working on. 'Truthfully,' she said, brushing her fringe from her face with the back of her hand, 'crappily.'

Mark looked her over, hopefully not too obviously. She had clay on her face. He might have wiped that off with his thumb, a few weeks back, brushed her soft lips with his own. Now? He felt he was walking on eggshells, never quite sure how she'd react. He might do better to check how the land lay first.

'You're probably pushing yourself too hard,' he ventured. 'You should take a break.'

Mel glanced at him despairingly. 'Thanks for the advice, Detective,' she said, with a definite hint of sarcasm. 'In case you hadn't noticed, I'm miles behind with my orders. But then, you've obviously been too busy elsewhere to notice.'

It looked like the ground underfoot was going to be tough going. Mark sighed. 'Which means?'

'Nothing.' Mel shrugged, picked up a modelling tool and went back to her work. 'It's just you've been a bit distracted lately.'

Mark looked at her askance. 'That's hardly fair, Mel,' he said, wondering how to point out that the only thing he'd been distracted from was his job.

'No, nor is being treated like an invalid.' Mel shot him a look, a flash of fury in her eyes. '*Or* an idiot.'

Mark staggered inwardly at that. He hadn't been. Had he? He sifted through his memory – though he was so bloody tired, he could hardly think – and realised he probably had. Her *I don't need a babysitter* comment came to mind, her obvious annoyance at him asking her if she was all right every two seconds. He needed to pull back. Give her some space. Stop acting as if *he* was her babysitter.

'Right.' He nodded, running a hand through his hair. 'Well, if I have, I'm sorry. I'm concerned, that's all. You can't blame me for that, Mel.'

Mel looked him over – guardedly, Mark noticed. 'So why so late?' she asked him. 'If you're so concerned, I mean, why work so late?'

Because I have to catch up, too. I'm not exactly having a picnic here myself, Mark thought. 'Work,' he said. 'The missing girl. We located a property that might have been a possible location. I needed to check it out.'

Mel looked momentarily saddened by that. Then she frowned. 'With Lisa?'

And there it was, whatever was eating away at her. 'Yes, with Lisa,' he said exasperatedly. 'I work with her, Mel. What do you want me to do?'

'Tell the truth,' Mel suggested, with another casual shrug.

'The truth?' Mark stared at her, completely confounded. She really did think he been screwing around, didn't she? '*Jesus Christ, Mel!* I have no idea what's going on in your head, but—' He stopped, realising that what he was about to say would seem way below the belt.

Mel didn't speak. Just carried on sculpting.

This was useless. 'I should go and check on the kids.' Kneading his temples, Mark sighed heavily and turned away before he said something he would certainly regret.

He got as far as the door before Mel stopped him. 'I'm sorry!'

Mark took a slow breath and turned back. He needed to stay calm, he reminded himself, however bloody angry he felt. The fact was, Mel wasn't likely to be rational right now. He knew that. It didn't make it any easier though.

'The kiln's still not working properly, and everything seems to be going wrong – even the sink's blocked up.' Mel waved a hand in that direction. 'And... *me*! Me, Mark! I'm going wrong,' she shouted, clamping a clay-caked hand to her breast. 'I can't do a thing right for Evie. She seems to think Jade's her mummy, and Poppy seems to prefer Jade's company too. I... I can't *think* straight any more!'

Mel looked at him, her eyes beseeching, her chest heaving, clearly desperate for understanding.

Mark wished he did understand. That he could. Right now, he felt confounded, shut out, utterly impotent. 'I love *you*, Mel. You! I don't *look* at anyone else, I don't *want* anyone else. Can you *please* try and hold on to that?'

Mel pressed the heel of her hand to her forehead. 'I know,' she said eventually. 'I know you do. It's just...'

She looked back at him, scanning his face hard.

Just what? Apprehension twisted inside him. She hadn't said she loved him. Did she? Love didn't come with a lifelong guarantee, did it? Might she want out? Could that be part of what was going on here? Mark took a step towards her – and there was a loud thump on the door behind him.

Fuck! He cursed silently, glanced back to Mel and then, arranging his face into something less than a scowl, turned to open it.

'Sorry. I had to kick the door, rather than knock it,' Jade said, holding a tray aloft. 'Hope I'm not interrupting, but I brought Mel some tea out. She said her kettle wasn't working earlier.' She smiled past Mark to Mel. 'I brought your tablets out, too, Mel. Just in case you forget to take them.'

CHAPTER THIRTY-SEVEN

JADE

Jade wasn't surprised to find Mark still in the lounge, drinking what appeared to be his second glass of whisky. He'd drained his first when he'd come downstairs, looking dishevelled yet sexy in his tracksuit bottoms and a T-shirt. Mel had drifted off to sleep before he'd come out of the bathroom and he hadn't wanted to disturb her, he'd said. He really was a kind, caring man. Selfless. His own nights had been disturbed constantly, first by Evie waking, then by needy Melissa insisting on seeing to her and only succeeding in making her more fractious, and now by the silly bitch's screaming nightmares. Still, though – Jade tried to be charitable – she couldn't help those. Considering the amount of medication she was on, she'd been surprised Melissa had stayed the pace today, working on her stupid pottery in the garden. Jade did hope she was swallowing all the tablets. She'd have to keep her eye on that.

'Do you mind if I join you?' she asked, going on in. She couldn't leave the poor man sitting there on his own, looking so utterly dejected, so desperately lonely. He was studying the bottom of his glass as if looking for answers. He needed company, the comfort of a good woman's arms around him. *Soon, my love. Soon.*

Mark looked up at her, smiling wearily. What Jade would give to press her lips softly against his and soothe his worries away. 'That bad, hey?' he asked her.

'No.' Jade smiled reassuringly back. 'I thought one red wine wouldn't hurt, though, if that's okay? It might help me to relax. Busy day.' She yawned and stretched, making sure to expand her chest, showing off her breasts, covered only by a flimsy strappy top, to maximum advantage.

Mark looked at her, his eyes travelling fleetingly lower before moving back to her face. He smiled again, obviously having appreciated the view. 'Help yourself,' he said.

Jade was *so* tempted to invite him to do the same, but… it was too soon. He was clearly worrying himself silly about Melissa, imagining himself responsible for her, indebted to her in some way for giving birth to his children, as if she'd done something miraculous. Well, Jade supposed it was a bit of a miracle that she'd managed to produce two, given that the woman was useless at the fundamentals. He must have been so relieved when she did finally manage to get pregnant and hang on to it – he wouldn't have to keep going through the mechanics of having sex with her. Jade doubted he would have got much satisfaction there. And he certainly wasn't getting any now.

Jade might have to do something about that, she decided. Fuck him long and slow. Jade's insides clenched at the thought of him coming hard inside her. She could almost feel it.

'Another?' She turned, waving the whisky bottle, sure he would see the burning desire pooling in her eyes, possibly throw his principles to the wind and stride across to take her there and then. Mark's gaze, though, was unfortunately elsewhere, studying the happy-fucking-family snaps lined up on the mantelpiece. Bloody Melissa. Jade reined in her irritation. It wasn't his fault. It was *hers*, digging her claws in and holding on to him, manipulating him. The sooner the man stopped torturing himself and made up his mind to leave her, the better.

'Mark?'

'What?' Mark snapped his gaze back to her. 'Oh. Sorry. I, er…' He looked from her face to the bottle, taking in her breasts, which she was holding the bottle strategically in front of, and then back to her face. 'Why not?' he finally said, handing the glass to her.

The poor man was beyond exhausted. He needed a massage, firm hands to ease away the knots in his muscles. Pouring his usual small measure, then adding another good splash, Jade carried the drink over. His fingers brushed hers as she handed it to him, sending an electrifying jolt of sexual tension right through her.

'Thanks,' he said, such longing in his eyes as he smiled up at her that Jade was tempted to throw her own carefully laid plans to the wind and peel off her top there and then. But no. The decision had to be his. She couldn't rush it. She couldn't give him cause to lay the blame at her feet should he lose his children. Though that was highly unlikely – there was no way Melissa would be deemed capable of looking after them, assuming she didn't do them all a favour and end her sad little life before custody was an issue – but it was still better to err on the side of caution.

Offering him an encouraging smile, Jade walked across to the seat opposite him, making sure to swing her hips seductively, but not too overtly, as she did. Curling herself up on the chair, she watched him pondering for a while – probably questioning how he'd come to be trapped in such a destructive relationship. 'I'm a good listener,' she said.

Mark turned his attention back to her, his expression pensive. 'I hadn't realised how bad things were,' he said quietly.

Jade waited, hoping he'd say more, but Mark fell silent, kneading his temple instead.

'I'm glad I can be here,' she said. 'To help.'

Mark nodded, once.

'And how's the investigation going?' she asked, keen to show some support with the obvious lack of any from his wife.

'Not great.' He sighed and took a large gulp of his drink. 'I thought I was on to something, a possible location on Hawthorn Farm, but…'

Oh shit! Alarm bells rang loud in Jade's head. 'No luck, I take it?' she asked, trying not to sound too interested, as her brain scrambled for a plan. She'd have to speak to Dylan, enlist his help, bribe him or goad him. It wouldn't be a problem, she assured herself. The man was as malleable as Melissa's clay, but she'd have to do it soon.

'No.' Mark shook his head disconsolately. 'Turned out to be a wild goose chase. I was so bloody sure.'

Sighing again, he got to his feet and walked to the cupboard to top up his glass.

'Is that why you were late?' Jade asked.

'Yeah, sorry about that. I was later than I thought I'd be. If I'd known Mel was working I would have tried to get back sooner.'

'It's not a problem,' Jade assured him. 'I get that you'll be detained sometimes. I mean, with a missing child investigation underway it's bound to happen.' She hesitated, then decided to go for it. 'I'm sorry Mel didn't seem to understand.'

Mark looked at her quizzically as he sat back down.

'I overheard, when I brought the tea out.'

Mark nodded, his jaw set tight. 'She used to,' he said, taking a small sip of his whisky. 'For some reason, she doesn't seem to trust me right now. I'm still not sure I understand why.'

'Does that worry you?' Jade probed carefully.

Mark hesitated, as if not sure how much to confide. 'Frankly,' he said, after a second, 'it bloody terrifies me.'

'Why?' Jade asked, gently urging him on.

Mark ran his hands up over his face. 'I don't... I know she's ill, but I'm beginning to wonder whether she still...' He paused, picked up his whisky, put it back down, then got to his feet.

'She seems to be pulling away from me,' he said eventually. 'I'm not sure how I'd handle it if we split.'

What? Her heart flipping violently inside her, Jade stared hard at him.

'I've seen the damage a broken home can wreak,' he went on, plunging his hands in his pockets and walking to the window, staring out at nothing. 'I don't want that for my kids,' he admitted, his voice tight.

And Jade's heart settled clunkily back into its moorings.

And he wouldn't have to, she decided, steeling her resolve. There would be no broken-home scenario. Angel was hers. She loved her. She was *her* child. She would *never* see her without her father. He must know that. Poppy, who was now grating seriously on her nerves, she hadn't made up her mind about yet, but she could tolerate her, at least for a short while, if Mark was really going to be so heartbroken without her.

'Crap!' Mark said suddenly, moving away from the window and heading for the door.

Jade started after him, and then, realising Evie was crying, rushed into the hall. 'I'll go,' she said, catching his arm as he mounted the stairs. 'You've had one or two whiskies,' she pointed out kindly, searching his eyes. Such troubled eyes, it tore at her heart.

Mark nodded and stepped back down, a little unsteadily on his feet, Jade noted. 'One or two too many,' he admitted, looking ashamed.

'I think you probably needed them,' Jade sympathised. 'I'll look in on Melissa as soon as I've settled Evie. Why don't you have a lie down on the sofa? You're obviously a bit tiddly. It might be an idea not to disturb her tonight.'

Knowing Melissa would be cooped up in the workshop for some time, Jade finished her tasks in the kitchen the next morning. She'd struggled a bit with the U-bend under the sink, but the lump of clay was now successfully wedged in place.

Having realised she needed to bring things to a head, Jade had lain awake in the night pondering how, and finally come to a conclusion. She had to shatter Mark's white knight image once and for all, make Melissa believe that he wasn't the perfect husband she had always thought. But the woman wouldn't go of her own volition, not without the children, and Jade would never allow her to take Angel. Nor would Mark. He was obviously scared for his fragile demented wife, but his children came first. If Melissa wasn't going to leave willingly without them, then Jade had to make sure she left unwillingly.

To which end, she had to make sure that Mark started being less concerned for his wife and more concerned for himself. He had to get good and angry, and Melissa needed to see it, to realise how utterly disillusioned with her he was. She had to learn that he was concerned for his children, as any caring father would be, and that having her sectioned might be his only option. Melissa would react, of course – irrationally and violently, hopefully. Yes, the more she pondered, the more she liked the idea. Melissa would go, and soon, one way or another.

And Jade would step seamlessly into her shoes.

We'll all be together soon, sweetheart. She mentally addressed her precious Angel. *Just you, me and Daddy. Won't that be lovely?*

But what about Poppy? She was already a needy child, and she would only get worse with her mother gone. Jade knitted her brow. She hadn't considered that until now. She would have to get rid of her. There was no other option. But… Mark doted on her. He would be inconsolable.

Yes, but then he would need an awful lot of comforting, wouldn't he? Jade's mouth curved into a smile at the prospect of that. And if she got pregnant soon, which she would, after sex, sex and more sex, Mark would soon have something else to occupy his mind.

Checking the wall clock – she needed to be off soon if she was going to enlist Dylan's help in getting rid of Daisy – Jade made the tea, and then reached up to the cupboard to extract Melissa's tablets, popping one in the cup and one on the tray, which Melissa would dutifully swallow.

She'd take her a biscuit, too. There wasn't a lot of point in the woman watching her figure, after all, when Mark was clearly appreciating the view elsewhere.

Now, what had she forgotten? Ah, yes. The vodka, Melissa's tipple of choice – the perfect drink for an alcoholic trying to hide the smell of booze on their breath. Humming happily, Jade went to the hall to extract the half-litre bottle from her handbag, one of several she'd purchased, and then, removing the top, she headed to the downstairs toilet to tip a good measure down the sink. Going back to the kitchen, she placed what now appeared a half-drunk bottle in the under-sink cupboard, far enough back to be hidden. Until one emptied the cupboard, that was, which Mark would have to do in order to unblock the pipe and avert a disaster.

CHAPTER THIRTY-EIGHT

MELISSA

'It's open,' Mel called, hearing a tap on the workshop door, and then, realising it could only be Jade, who'd no doubt come bearing tea and biscuits, she wiped the clay from her hands and walked over to open it.

'How's it going?' Jade asked, with her usual radiant smile.

Mel smiled back, rather less joyously. 'Painfully.'

Holding the door for Jade to come in, she beckoned to Hercules, who'd decided she preferred curling up in the workshop during the day, rather than in the kitchen with Jade. Mel couldn't fathom why the dog had taken a dislike to the poor girl, growling if ever she was around her. As Jade had said, it was probably because she was nervous around dogs, having been bitten by one as a child. The dog obviously sensed it, she'd suggested. Still though, it was a bit of a mystery, Hercules being such a placid animal.

'Come on, girl, outside.' She beckoned again to the dog, who was watching Jade warily as she deposited the tray. 'Hercules, come *on*,' Mel tried, patting her thigh when the dog didn't budge. She was growing irritated, she realised. She was doing that a lot lately – not surprising, when she was so perpetually exhausted. She felt like a zombie. Maybe she should ask Dr Meadows about changing her medication, or reducing the dose? Her nightmares were terrifying, and so real, as if she were living the dreams and the daytime was an illusion. Mel knew she'd terrified Mark, too, on several occasions, screaming out in her sleep. The last thing she wanted, though, was to resort to taking sleeping tablets on top of antidepressants, which was her only option if either of them were going to get a decent night's sleep.

'All right. You can go out later. But don't blame me if you end up crossing your paws.' Mel sighed, closing the door, and walked across to where Jade was looking her sculpture over, probably coming to the same conclusion Mel had.

She was sculpting like a zombie too.

'You've finished it,' Jade said with enthusiasm. 'Well done, Mel.'

'Finished, yes, but unfortunately not so well done.' Emitting another sigh, Mel surveyed her endeavours with a critical eye. Her couple seemed to be holding on to each other in petrified desperation, rather than loving embrace. Where was the passion? The sensuality? The desire?

'But it's beautiful.' Jade sounded surprised. 'Really evocative.'

'Evocative of what though?' Mel said glumly. 'They're supposed to be in post-coital ecstasy, limbs, hearts and bodies entwined, two lovers as one, not two people grieving.'

Jade considered her passionless lovers quietly for a moment. 'Maybe he wasn't up to the job.'

It took Mel a second to catch up. 'Oh God.' She laughed. 'More work needed then?'

Jade shrugged noncommittally. 'Well, I think it's fab, but I know it won't be right until you're happy with it. I'll leave you to massage his ego,' she said, turning for the door. 'I thought I'd go out for a while before collecting Poppy.'

'Oh?' Mel tried to quell an immediate sense of panic. Panic that she'd be left alone to care for her baby, she realised, with an overwhelming sense of dismay.

'I'm off to the DIY store,' Jade went on, oblivious. 'I thought I'd try and get a few ideas for the cottage, if ever the work gets underway. Don't worry, I'll take Evie with me so you can get on.'

Mel's panic gave way to relief, followed swiftly by trepidation. What would she do when Jade wasn't here on a permanent basis? How on earth would she cope?

Jade paused at the door. 'What do you fancy for dinner? I could pop by the supermarket and get something nice, if you—'

'No!' Mel said quickly. And then she stopped herself, taking a deep breath. What the bloody hell was wrong with her? She had to get a grip! Of course she'd *cope*. Evie was *her* child. She loved her with her very bones. She'd lost her way, that was all. Postnatal depression wasn't something she should feel ashamed of, or guilty about. She simply needed to find her way back, to regain control of her emotions, her life, her child. One step at a time.

Calming herself, she glanced towards Jade, who was blinking bemusedly in her direction. 'I thought I'd cook tonight,' Mel explained. 'I'm really grateful for all your help, Jade. I'm sure we'd have starved without you, but it's not fair to expect you to do it every night. You're already doing far too much.'

'I don't mind.'

'I insist,' Mel said, with a decisive nod. 'It will give you a break, and, to be honest, I could do with a break from my moody lovers.'

'No problem,' Jade said, smiling understandingly. 'So, what will you cook?'

Mel thought about it. 'Spaghetti bolognese,' she decided. She could defrost the mince in the microwave and she probably had the other ingredients in. Enough to make a reasonably tasty dish anyway, served up with garlic bread, which Poppy and Mark both adored.

'Perfect.' Jade said, looking impressed. 'And I'll be around, so you can give me a shout if you need a hand.'

Mel steeled her determination to do nothing of the sort as Jade bounced brightly out of the door. She could manage to produce a meal in her own kitchen, for God's sake.

Meanwhile... Her clay man needed more than his ego massaging, she fancied. He needed major surgery.

With the kiln still not working properly – meaning she'd have to transport everything to the university and beg the use of their kiln – she'd be more behind than ever if she started over, but… It was no good. The piece was substandard. Sliding her sad lovers reluctantly into the bin, she went to fetch a fresh lump of clay, which she could at least knead in readiness to start afresh tomorrow. Leaving the biscuit unguarded, however, with a Labrador in sniffing distance, turned out to be a fatal mistake.

'Hercules! Bad girl!' Mel scolded the dog, dumping her clay and tugging at her collar. But the dog resisted her attempts to heave her away, knocking the cup over and lapping greedily at the dregs. 'Out. Go on, out!' She marched the dog to the door, ready to throw her out. She was furious, and no one could accuse her of getting this out of proportion. What if Hercules jumped up to snatch at Poppy's food? Or, God forbid, she tried to take food from Evie?

That dog really was getting away with too much. Sleeping on Poppy's bed with Evie only yards away across the landing might even be too risky. But Mark seemed to have this hare-brained idea that Hercules would protect her if they were broken into. The only chance of that would be if the dog licked a burglar to death.

Honestly, if Mark was going to allow her the run of the house the least he could do was train her. If he couldn't do that, then he should think about rehoming her. Jade had rehomed her cat quickly enough, after all, she thought crossly, retrieving the cup from the floor and finding it was cracked. Muttering, Mel crashed the cup back on to the tray – and then stopped, and breathed, realising her anger was escalating. It was a cup. Not even an expensive cup. God, was she really getting things so out of proportion, again, that she was contemplating letting Hercules go to complete strangers?

She thought of the ease with which Jade had got rid of her cat. Mel still couldn't help wondering how the animal had disappeared so quickly. Surely she wouldn't have had the poor thing put down? No, she said friends had taken it.

Feeling more guilty than ever that she'd considered Jade capable of having the cat disposed of in such a way despite her determination to give that particular emotion short shrift, Mel turned to mop up the tray, only to realise the capsule she should have taken was soggy with tea, its powdered contents spewing out.

On the bright side, at least Hercules hadn't swallowed it. Despairing of herself, Mel shifted the tray out of the way and set about taking her frustration out on her lump of clay. She'd take another tablet when she went in to make dinner, which hopefully wouldn't turn out to be as disastrous as everything else she attempted to do.

CHAPTER THIRTY-NINE

JADE

Oh, you have to be joking! Jade stopped short of the cottage, realising that Dylan's mother really *was* talking to the pigs. And not just in a 'Who's a pretty porkie?' sort of way either. She was having a whole fucking conversation with them. Obviously, she was as soft in the head as her drippy son was.

'Careless farming they said it was, Inky,' the woman was saying mournfully. 'Said we'd managed our farm in a way that encouraged floods. I've never heard the likes. Killed my Charlie, they did, worked him to death, with their rules and regulations. Left me with nothing. Except our Dylan, of course.'

Sighing forlornly, the woman stopped and gazed off over the fields. Probably contemplating suicide, Jade thought despairingly, if Dylan was all she'd got.

'I'll be glad to see the back of the place,' the woman went on, bending to pick up a metal bucket full of foul-smelling swill to chuck to the beasts.

Ugh, disgusting. Jade screwed up her nose. It was probably the leftovers of the piglets they'd given birth to. Where the hell was Dylan? Realising there was no sign of the man – who was obviously more moronic than she'd suspected, allowing his mother to wander around with the girl not thirty feet away – she stepped quickly forwards. The woman hadn't got a key, but God forbid she got it into her head to go peering through the windows.

'Morning, Mrs Jackson,' Jade said brightly, at which the woman jumped, literally, and whirled around, dropping her bucket in the process.

'Is Dylan here?' Jade asked, wearing her sweetest smile.

A hand clutched to her ample chest, Mrs Jackson took several slow breaths and then narrowed her eyes. 'Why?' she asked suspiciously.

'I thought I'd ask him if he fancied going into the village,' Jade improvised. She wouldn't be seen dead with him in the village, or anywhere else for that matter.

'Why?' the woman repeated.

'Because we're friends, Mrs Jackson,' Jade said patiently.

Mrs Jackson folded her arms and cocked her head to one side. 'Right. And my Inky's priming his wings as we speak,' she said, attempting to be clever, which really didn't suit someone dressed in crap-covered dungarees and whose personal hygiene was obviously on a par with her son's. Mind you, Jade could understand her cynicism. Dylan, who only ever attracted the wrong sort of attention, had about as many friends as he had brain cells.

'He looks out for me, Mrs Jackson,' Jade explained, less patiently. Evie was asleep in the car. The window was open, so she'd hear her if she cried, but even so, she hadn't got all bloody day. 'I feel safe with him when other idiots come sniffing around.'

Mrs Jackson arched an eyebrow at that, obviously trying to work out whether Jade was being sincere.

'Is he home?' Jade asked again, growing perturbed now. Surely Dylan hadn't actually gone off the premises and left the girl on her own?

'He's fixing the barn roof,' the woman said, turning disinterestedly away.

Jade stared at the rude bitch's back. And then – *oh fuck* – past her to a movement at the cottage's upstairs window. The girl was walking around. If she looked out of the window, the woman was bound to spot her.

Irritated, having been delayed while she took necessary action to ensure Mrs Jackson didn't discover the girl, Jade parked outside the pub and texted Dylan back. He was worried, because his mother had apparently gone out without telling him. Definitely tied to her apron strings. Jade shook her head despairingly.

She obviously couldn't find you. She's probably visiting friends, or gone shopping or something. Bit tied up with children today. See you tomorrow first thing.

She would have to be there early, she decided. She couldn't have him throwing a wobbly now. She needed him. As well as helping her move the girl, she had other plans that required Dylan's participation. He was tall and dark, and therefore easily mistaken for Mark at the wheel of Mel's car. He was going to need careful handling, though, with lots of physical and emotional reassurance.

One eye on the entrance to the pub, she waited patiently for her phone to ping back a reply and then breathed out a sigh of relief when it did.

Okay. C U then. Xxx

Rolling her eyes at his use of abbreviated text words, and fully expecting him to text again before the day was out, Jade sent him a smiley face back, with three reciprocal kisses, and then emitted a sigh of relief as DS Cummings exited the pub, bang on cue. Having googled his details and then followed him, she'd learned he liked a pint with his lunch, and one or two once he was off duty. He was also obviously everything she'd overheard Mark confiding to Melissa he was – a womanising, sexist wanker, led by his penis, which, Jade suspected, would make him just as malleable as Dylan.

Waiting for the right moment, Jade watched him pause in the car park, picking his teeth and leering after two scantily clad girls half his age as they teetered on vertiginous shoes towards their car. 'Hope you've been watching your alcohol intake, Taylor,' he called after them. 'Wouldn't want me having to arrest you now, would you?'

'Depends…' said one of the girls, smiling coquettishly back over her shoulder.

Yeah, depends on how much he's paying. Jade curled a lip and sighed inwardly, supposing it was time to flash her own assets in his direction. Clearly the man couldn't resist a pair of tits. Glancing over her shoulder to check on Evie, who was soundly sleeping, bless her, Jade adjusted her plunge bra and tugged down her strappy top to show off maximum cleavage, and then climbed out of her car. Her phone clutched to her ear, she swept her hair from her face and stared down at her flat tyre, looking suitably flustered. And then, bending from the waist, she leaned to examine it. As she was wearing her tightest skinny jeans, she guessed he'd be enjoying the view.

'An hour?' she said despairingly, talking to no one into her mobile. 'No, it's just that I have a baby in the car and I have to get her back to her parents. Yes. Okay, I'll wait. No choice really, have I?'

Sensing a certain someone approaching, Jade sighed and ended her 'call'.

'Problem?' Detective Sergeant Cummings said behind her, not that Jade had imagined he would be the slightest bit concerned unless he fancied getting into her knickers.

Jade turned, making sure to look girly and wary for a second, and then hugely relieved when he flashed his ID. Plainly, he was thinking she'd be impressed, the full-of-himself prat. 'Slow puncture,' she said, with a helpless shrug. 'I don't have a car pump with me, unfortunately, and I have to get my charge back to her parents.'

DS Cummings followed her gaze to Evie in her baby carrier. 'Can't you ring them?' he asked.

Clearly *not* Sir Galahad then. 'Well, I will, obviously, but her mum's due to go out soon.' Jade checked her watch. '*Hell!* I'll probably get the sack.'

His gaze roving over her, Cummings ran a hand contemplatively over his chin. 'I don't have a pump in the car, but…' He glanced at her tits, then down to her tyre, and then nodded behind him. 'Tell you what, I'll go and ask in the pub. The owner's bound to have one.'

'Would you?' Jade all but wilted with relief. 'That would be so kind. I'd be really grateful.'

'No problem,' Cummings assured her, glancing down to the hand she'd placed on his arm and then back to her face, lingering appreciatively at her breasts again on the way up. 'Why don't you wait in your car? You never know what sort of cretins might be hanging around a dive like this.'

Oh, I have a pretty good idea. 'Thank you, I will.' Jade fluttered her eyelashes and turned back to the car.

Cummings held the door open, all the better to ogle her as she climbed demurely inside, bum first, threading her legs slowly in and smiling suggestively up at him.

'Don't go anywhere.' He winked, looking pleased with himself, as he turned to jog keenly back to the pub.

Five minutes later, Jade looked on in suitable awe as DS Cummings inflated her tyre. 'So strong,' she said, smiling coquettishly, God help her. 'You have a wonderful pumping action,' she breathed, her voice loaded with sexual innuendo.

He paused in his wonderful pumping action to scan her eyes questioningly. 'So I'm told,' he said hopefully, and most definitely weighing his chances.

Jade lowered her eyes, perusing the length and breadth of him slowly before coming back to his face. 'I can see why,' she said, running the tip of her tongue provocatively over her lips.

At which the guy looked positively orgasmic and pumped harder.

'You're an absolute hero,' Jade said, once she was good to go, her eyelashes now unashamedly in overdrive. 'I honestly don't know how I can thank you.'

At that, his mouth curved into a lurid smirk. 'Oh, I can think of a way,' he said, taking the bait. 'How about you let me buy you a drink?'

'It should be me buying you one,' Jade pointed out.

'Tomorrow night?' he said, pushing it. 'I could pick you up, if you'd like?'

'Better not. I'm a babysitter – live in. Might not go down well with my employers. I'll meet you here. Seven thirty.'

'Excellent,' he said, having a last inspection of the goods he no doubt fancied sampling. 'I'll look forward to seeing you then.'

Job done. Jade was going to enjoy seeing this disgusting, drug-pushing creep get his just deserts. 'See you tomorrow,' she said, planting a soft kiss on his cheek and noting his sharp intake of breath with satisfaction.

CHAPTER FORTY

LISA

'In your own time, Cain,' DCI Edwards said, drumming his fingers impatiently on Mark's desk and looking hugely unimpressed.

'Yes, sir. It's here somewhere.' Mark scrolled through his inbox again, obviously not finding what he wanted, and looking like shit. Dark circles under his eyes, four o'clock shadow, he looked as if he hadn't slept for a month. The distinct whiff of whisky Lisa had already caught wasn't going to go down well either. Edwards, who had a nose like a sniffer dog, was bound to notice that.

Lisa glanced across to Mark, rolling her eyes as Edwards exaggeratedly checked his watch, as if he'd been waiting half an hour rather than a couple of minutes. 'Got it,' she called across. 'Sending it over now, sir,' she said, emailing the forensics report Edwards had asked for across to him.

'Thank you,' Edwards said curtly. 'My office, DI Cain. Now, please,' he added, twirling around to march in that direction.

Leaning back in his chair, Mark thumped the heel of his hand against his forehead, and then looked royally pissed as Cummings, who'd just strolled in late from lunch – a liquid lunch, by the looks of him – walked past with a smug smirk on his face.

'Sleeping on the job, sir, *tsk, tsk*. More water with it, mate,' he suggested. 'And maybe a few less night-time excursions?'

'You should do stand-up, Cummings, you really should. Preferably in the middle of the motorway,' Lisa snapped, reaching into her desk drawer for her emergency supply of extra-strong mints. She'd had occasion to sit up pondering her problems through the bottom of a glass herself. Mark, however, looked as if he'd been brooding over his at the bottom of the bottle.

'Make sure you swallow it before you go in,' she advised, tossing the mints across to him.

'Cheers, Lisa,' said Mark, getting wearily to his feet.

'Fancy a drink after?' Lisa asked as he bypassed her desk, thinking he might need to offload a few things.

Marks smiled wryly. 'Probably not a good idea, but thanks. And Mel's cooking anyway.'

'Ah.' Lisa nodded. 'Another time then. Good luck,' she added, as, running a hand through his hair in a vain attempt to smarten himself up, Mark headed for the high jump.

Cooking? Lisa knitted her brow. Well, that was progress, she supposed. From what she'd gathered from Mark, life on the home front had lurched from bad to worse, though she only had to look at his dishevelled appearance to realise that. His decision-making was a bit awry, as well. Yesterday he'd deployed uniforms to premises that had already been thoroughly checked. Walking away from his computer and leaving confidential information on the screen, Lisa had noticed that too. All of which had given her cause to worry, particularly about Miss Baywatch Babe, who'd appeared on the scene around the same time things started going pear-shaped. It had been convenient for Mel and Mark that she'd just happened to be there – a homeless, fully qualified babysitter, looking for a job – but Lisa couldn't help thinking that the situation had been extremely convenient for Jade as well.

Could the au pair, whose house renovations seemed not to be imminent anytime soon, be causing problems between them?

Mark loved his wife and kids more than life itself, Lisa had no doubt about that, but it was a bit of a coincidence that Mel was suddenly imagining that Mark was having an affair – albeit with *her*. Mark Cain was a good-looking bloke, and under other circumstances, Lisa might have been tempted, but they were nothing more than good friends. She wondered at Mel's madness, allowing a pretty young woman to live with them. And, although she really shouldn't be judging her, from what she'd seen when she'd met her, the babysitter had been a little underdressed for the job.

She glanced towards Edwards' office, where Mark was shuffling awkwardly on the spot as Edwards bollocked him, loudly, to Cummings' amusement. She might be barking up the wrong tree, probably fuelled by the fact that she was upset about her own cooled relationship with Mel, but…

Lisa was only marginally surprised when Google coughed up sweet FA about Jade Hart. Had Mel done all the checks? Had Mark? Had they actually seen the woman's paperwork? Though, she wouldn't have any paperwork, would she? Not hard copies anyway. All burned to a cinder, presumably – and also too conveniently for Lisa's liking. Mel might not have pursued it once they'd decided Jade was an angel sent directly from heaven.

Guessing at Jade's age, Lisa was checking yearly college student intakes when she heard Edwards raise his voice. He wasn't happy. By the sound of it, neither was Mark. 'I was out last night,' he yelled heatedly back. 'Yes, I had a few drinks. Since when did that become a criminal offence?'

'Since you're obviously so hungover you can't see straight! You're exhausted. Go home!'

Wincing, Lisa glanced in Cummings' direction. He was just loving this, the smug bastard.

'Immediately, DI Cain,' Edwards called after him, as Mark emerged furiously from his office.

Lisa closed down her search window and hurried over as Mark yanked his jacket from the back of his chair. 'That went well then?'

'It just gets better. I'll text you... ring you tomorrow.' He stormed to the door, and Lisa saw his jaw clench as Cummings stood to open it for him.

CHAPTER FORTY-ONE

MARK

Attempting to calm down, Mark selected some soothing music as he drove around for a little while before going home. Chopin's 'Piano Sonata No. 2', though, served only to heighten his anger and frustration. Was he being monitored on overhead cams by Cummings, he wondered, for whatever perverse reason that would no doubt become clear? Probably. Bastard. Blowing out a frustrated sigh, Mark selected Vaughan Williams' 'The Lark Ascending' instead – one of Evie's favourites – and tried to get some perspective on his life. Edwards was right, of course. He wasn't capable of doing his job. Mark dearly wished he hadn't dragged him over the coals in earshot of that wanker Cummings though, who would probably get off on it.

He *was* exhausted, weary to his bones. He needed to do as Edwards had advised and take some time. He was no use to anyone like this. At least he wasn't being put on 'voluntary' gardening leave for the foreseeable future, as he'd half expected to be. That was something.

Feeling more in control, Mark turned for home. He couldn't help wishing it felt more like a home, that he could turn the clock back, or forward. That he could make this whole mess go away. He couldn't. No one could. All he could do was be there. And he would be. If Mel was fighting, he'd fight alongside her.

Mel's car wasn't there, he noticed as he pulled up, which meant that Jade and the kids weren't back yet. That was good. As much as he loved his children, it would be nice for Mel and him to have some space.

Mark parked up and let himself in, and his heart nose-dived. Cosy conversation wasn't going to happen, he realised, any more than dinner was. Clangs and curses were coming from the kitchen, followed by 'For God's sake, Hercules, get out of the way!' Mark headed in that direction, stopping confounded in the doorway as a scene of utter chaos greeted him.

'Mel?' he said. The first thing he noticed was the open red wine bottle on the island, half empty, he noted, his heart plummeting further. Warily, he turned his gaze towards Mel, who appeared to be fishing wormlike spaghetti from the overflowing sink. 'What's happened?' he asked, trying hard to reserve judgement.

'This bloody house happened!' Mel swiped her hair from her face, clanged the colander on the drainer, and turned to glare at him. 'The bloody sink's blocked up. I *told* you the plumbing was packing up. Everything's packing up. Hercules! Get out!' She scowled down at the dog, who was helping herself to the spaghetti on the floor.

Mark's heart skipped a beat as Mel grabbed her roughly by the collar and attempted to drag her out.

'*Jesus*, Mel, don't.' Mark stepped in, herding Hercules towards the back door. 'She's just doing what dogs do.'

'Yes, scavenging!' Mel snapped, dropping down to scrape up the spilled spaghetti. 'Because *you* didn't take her to training lessons, because you were too busy working! As usual. She's been asleep in the middle of the kitchen floor for the last hour. I've had to keep walking around her while I'm trying to cook. She's completely out of control.'

What? Mark definitely couldn't get his head around that one. The demands of work meant he'd missed one or two sessions, but the dog had been to training lessons. Not eating spaghetti off the floor hadn't been covered, but he decided for the sake of argument not to point that out. *Christ!* About to help her clean up, he headed fast for the gas hob instead, where he realised there was a pan close to catching fire.

'Shit!' he cursed, grabbing the handle without thinking and then dropping it as fast as he'd picked it up. It landed with a crash, spewing the contents across the ceramic tiles to add to the mess already there.

Mel looked up sharply. 'Why in *God's* name did you do that?'

'It was hot!' *Dammit.* Shaking his scalded hand, Mark headed for the sink to run it under the cold tap. He cursed silently when he realised he couldn't.

'Are you hurt?' Mel asked, concerned now she'd realised he'd hurt himself.

Mark reached for the tea towel, wetting it and wrapping it around his hand. 'No,' he said tightly, turning to face her. 'Have you been drinking?'

Mel shook her head, confounded. 'What?'

Mark looked at the ceiling, willing himself not to lose it. 'The wine?' He nodded towards the bottle.

Cocking her head to one side, Mel studied him curiously. 'It's one you opened. I put a spoonful in the bolognaise sauce. Would you like to breathalyse me? Scrape some up from the floor and get your forensics team to test it?'

Great. Mark blew out a long breath. 'Mel…' He stepped towards her. 'I'm sorry. I just…'

'Assumed?' Mel finished.

Sighing, Mark nodded wearily. 'Wrongly,' he admitted. 'I'm sorry. I…' He trailed off, not sure what else to say.

Mel studied him a second longer. 'So am I,' she said disappointedly, pulling her unimpressed gaze away from his and walking into the hall.

*

Mark had cleaned up, fetched his toolbox, and was about to investigate the situation under the sink when Jade and the kids arrived, Poppy chattering excitedly as they bustled through the front door. About her teacher's big belly, Mark gathered, as they came towards the kitchen.

'But how did the baby get *in* there?'

Mark winced as he heard her ask.

'Little baby Jesus put it there to keep safe and cosy until it's fully grown,' Jade answered smartly.

'Like we put Dory in the fish bowl to keep safe and cosy till she's grown?' Poppy asked.

'Just like that.'

Well done, Jade, Mark thought, smiling as the babysitter and her charges arrived in the kitchen. He wasn't sure how he would have fielded that one.

'Daddeee!' Poppy did her usual and flew over to him, regardless of the under-sink paraphernalia Mark had in each hand.

'Hi, gorgeous girl. How was your day at school?'

'Good.' Poppy nodded, unhooking herself from his neck and allowing him to straighten up. 'We felt Miss Winters' tummy. It's huge!'

So were Poppy's eyes. Mark couldn't help but laugh.

'They're learning about the birds and bees early,' Jade said, as she lowered Evie carefully down in her carrier.

'God, I hope not.'

'The child-friendly version, I think.' Jade smiled as she walked over to him, and then frowned as she peered in the sink. 'Oh.' She eyed him sympathetically.

Mark shrugged, feeling for Mel. He owed her one hell of an apology. He just hoped she'd accept it, once he'd unblocked the sink and sorted out an alternative to spaghetti bolognaise.

'What's for dinner?' Poppy stood on tiptoe and peered into the sink.

'Takeaway McDonald's,' Jade said, steering her away. 'You can come with me to fetch it.'

'Yay!' Poppy whooped, obviously all in favour of that.

Mark breathed a sigh of relief. 'Thanks, Jade,' he said, feeling indebted, yet again.

'No problem,' Jade assured him. 'I'll take Evie too. She's not due a feed for another hour or so. We should be back by then.'

Grateful, Mark went back to the under-sink cupboard. 'Fuck,' he uttered, extracting something that didn't belong there.

'Daddy!' Poppy whirled around. 'That's a really naughty word.'

'I, er… It is. An extremely bad word. Sorry, Poppet. I banged my head.' He smiled tightly, his eyes travelling to Jade, who'd clearly gathered the reason for him cursing out loud.

'Oh no!' Looking alarmed, Poppy hurried across to him. 'Does it hurt?' she asked, her little brow now creased with sympathy.

'Yes. It does. It hurts quite a lot,' Mark said throatily, turning to park the bottle of vodka he'd fished from the cupboard on the work surface.

CHAPTER FORTY-TWO

JADE

Noting the number of the incoming call, Jade left Poppy to her cereal and dashed out the back door to answer it.

'It's my fault!' Dylan blurted in her ear, before she had a chance to speak. 'It's my fault. She's just lying there, and I—'

'*Whoa*, Dylan, slow down. What's happened? What's your fault?'

'Me mum! She's… *dead*! She's…' Emitting a guttural sob, Dylan broke off.

'Stay where you are,' Jade said firmly. 'Don't touch anything or say anything. Not to anyone, Dylan.'

Dylan choked back another distraught sob. And another.

Hell, he was losing it. 'Dylan!' Jade felt panic twisting inside her. 'Do you hear me?'

'It's my fault!' Dylan repeated, sounding like a distraught parrot.

'Dylan, it is *not* your fault! You weren't even *there*,' Jade barked. 'Were you?' she tacked on quickly.

Dylan sniffled snottily. 'No,' he said timidly, after a second. 'I was fixing the barn roof, and when I finished I couldn't find her. I thought she'd gone out, like you said, but…' He broke off with another sob.

'No one will blame you, Dylan, I promise.' Jade softened her tone. She needed him to get a grip. God forbid he should get it into his thick head to dial 999. 'But you have to listen to me. You need to stay calm, stay there and not talk to anyone – don't even use the phone. Can you do that for me?'

There was a hiccuppy pause. 'Uh-huh,' Dylan replied uncertainly. 'Will you come?'

'Of course I will. I'll be there as soon as I've dropped Poppy off at school,' Jade assured him. 'It will be fine, my love. I'll help you sort it all out. Just make yourself a cup of sweet tea and sit tight. Okay?'

'Okay,' Dylan said, sounding somewhat relieved.

Thank God for that. Dylan subdued, for the moment, Jade hurried back inside to finish making Mark's coffee. She needed to be gone, but first she needed to check how the land lay here. They hadn't kissed and made up, she was aware of that. Other than to say goodnight to Poppy and Evie, Melissa had stayed in her bedroom. And no wonder. Clearly, she'd decided to keep a low profile. Mark had been white with anger when Jade had left to fetch the McDonald's, and then subdued when she had arrived back. She'd learned from Melissa when she'd taken her some warm soup, with the necessary extra ingredient, that they'd argued about the catastrophe that was dinner. He'd been avoiding her since, Melissa had said shakily, meaning Mark had valiantly restrained himself rather than tackle the ridiculous woman about her drinking habit. Probably because it would lead to the inevitable argument, which Jade knew Mark desperately didn't want his children to witness. He really was a lovely man. After helping Poppy with her Peppa Pig construction kit before her bedtime, he'd spent the rest of the evening listening to his music – trying to distract himself, Jade guessed. Then he'd spent the night on the sofa, fetching a pillow and sheets from the airing cupboard this time, which meant it might be becoming a more permanent arrangement.

Perfect. Jade hummed happily to herself. Who would have thought a little lump of clay could wreak such havoc?

'All finished?' She smiled brightly at Poppy as she passed by with the coffee.

'Yup,' Poppy said, picking her bowl up and tipping the last dregs of milk towards her mouth.

'Good girl,' Jade said, though she felt sorely tempted to slap her. Ill-mannered glutton. She really did have to go. 'Go and get your shoes on then, sweetheart,' she urged her. 'I have an appointment this morning. If you're really quick getting ready, I'll bring you some sweets later. How does that sound?'

'Yay!' Poppy clapped delightedly, slid off her chair and skipped happily to the stairs.

Spoiled little brat. Quashing her irritation, Jade went quietly into the lounge. There was a chance Mark might still be sleeping. After all that had gone on, Jade doubted he'd had a very restful night.

But she found him sitting on the sofa, contemplating the bottle of vodka on the coffee table, obviously debating how to tackle his self-centred, needy wife about it. *Poor Mark.* Jade's heart went out to him. 'Morning,' she said, toning down the cheeriness. She didn't want to appear insensitive.

Mark dragged his hands tiredly over his face and got to his feet. 'Morning.' He forced a smile, for her sake, bless him.

'I made you a coffee,' Jade said, walking across to put the mug on the table. 'With extra caffeine. I thought you could use it.' Glancing at the vodka, she smiled sympathetically.

'I could.' Mark sighed, a world-weary sigh. 'Cheers, Jade,' he said, moving to bundle up his sheets, which were in a bit of a tangle. Definitely not a restful night then, Jade deduced.

'How are you feeling?' she asked, reaching to help him.

'Okay,' Mark lied. 'A bit tired.' He paused, a wretched look in his eyes. 'I'm sorry about all this, Jade,' he said, glancing embarrassedly away and back again. 'If you wanted to hand in your notice, I'd quite understand.'

'And leave you in the lurch? I wouldn't dream of it. The children need stability above all else right now. I don't want to add to their troubles.' She flapped a sheet and folded it briskly. 'I could cancel my arrangements, though, if it would help. Under the circumstances, I mean.'

'Arrangements?' Mark's expression was one of confusion. And mild panic, Jade noticed, gratified. He was going to miss her. But not half as much as she would miss him.

'I mentioned it to Mel. My friend, Samantha… she gets the result of her biopsy today. I said I'd go with her.'

'God, no, don't cancel,' Mark said emphatically. 'Go. I'm sure we can manage for…?' he trailed off on a question, his look now hopeful.

God love him. He really was in an intolerable situation. The sooner Jade could get him out of it, the better. 'Just the one day,' she assured him. 'She lives in London though, so I wouldn't be back until quite late.'

'No problem.' Mark smiled, relieved. 'I'm off for a couple of days, so I can look after Evie and collect Poppy. I'm guessing you could use a break anyway, although that's probably not much of a break. Give your friend my best. I hope it all turns out okay for her.'

Even now, he was thinking of others. Jade's heart fluttered inside her. A gem, he really was. 'I'll take Poppy to school on my way,' she said. 'Evie's fast asleep. She's due a feed at nine. You have my mobile if you need it. Good luck with…' Pausing, Jade glanced again at the vodka. 'Everything.'

'Yeah, thanks. I might need it.' His look now, Jade noticed with quiet satisfaction, was one of utter despair.

Seeing Dylan standing at the far side of the pig field, Jade called to him as she climbed out of the car. When he didn't respond, she called out again, and then cursed and heaved the gate open to head towards him.

'Dylan!' Jade was seriously irritated now. Squelching through mud and pig shit in her trainers was most definitely *not* on her list of favourite things to do.

Finally, he turned towards her as she skirted around the pig house, careful to give Inky and bloody Oinky a wide berth. 'It's my fault,' he said pitifully, his face the colour of damp putty and slick with sweat.

'Dylan…' Jade tempered her tone and tried to hide her annoyance. Could he not hear himself? He sounded like a two-year-old, for God's sake. 'Whatever's happened, it is *not*—'

Jade stopped, gulping back a violent bout of nausea as she followed his gaze down to the ground. *Bloody hell.* They'd eaten half her face.

'Oh my God!' Dylan!' Jade looked away from the woman, genuinely horrified. She was going to step carefully amongst those carnivorous little fuckers in future. 'What the hell have you done?'

'Nothing!' Dylan widened his eyes in obvious terror. 'She was upset,' he blurted defensively. 'We had a row, yesterday morning. She wanted me to phone Uncle Bob and ask him for a job, but I didn't want to work on a building site. I told her I wanted to stay here, on the farm. Uncle Bob doesn't like me and Eric is always taking the mickey. I don't *want* to work in Birmingham. I told her and she got all upset. She wasn't talking to me and I—'

'Dylan, stop.' Jade moved closer, clutching his shoulders with both hands. He was blinking rapidly, close to hyperventilating or wetting himself. 'Slow down. Who's Eric?'

'Me cousin. He's always winding me up.' Dylan dragged an arm under his nose and glanced embarrassedly down.

Gosh, I wonder why. Supressing a sigh, Jade arranged her face into suitably annoyed. 'He's obviously an idiot,' she supplied what he needed to hear, whilst bracing herself to bend down and examine the woman at closer quarters.

'She's gone, Dylan.' Hoisting herself quickly to her feet, she looked at him, oozing sympathy.

'Dead?' Dylan squeaked.

Yes, idiot, dead. Jade nodded solemnly. She looked dead enough, but, having found the faintest of pulses at the base of her neck, Jade suspected she wasn't yet, quite. So, what did she do with her now? Finishing the job would be the kind thing to do, but she could hardly do that with Dylan looking on. The pigs would probably chomp their way through the rest of her eventually. But that would take time and they could hardly leave her here meanwhile.

'It's my fault.' Dylan gulped hard.

Jade gritted her teeth. If he said that one more time, in that wimpish tone, he'd be joining his mum as the bloody pigs' lunch. 'Dylan, it's not,' she stated firmly. 'But… it is possible they might blame you.'

Holding his gaze, Jade tried not to notice his Adam's apple bobbing grotesquely in his throat. 'She probably passed out or had a heart attack or something. Did she mention she'd been having pains in her chest?'

Dylan's face drained of what little colour he had. 'After Dad died,' he said, his voice now a croaked whisper. 'She said her heart was hurting.'

'Well, there you go then. It wasn't your fault. It might even have been brought on by Mark Cain sniffing around again.'

'Cain?' asked Dylan, his thickset brow furrowing. And then a spark of fury glinted in his eyes. *Good*, Jade thought. That's what she needed – Dylan angry, not cowering and bawling like a baby. Ready to do whatever it took. She had a plan, and it involved Mark being 'seen' to be driving around certain areas. If Dylan pulled it off, she'd succeed in tarnishing Mark's 'white knight' image in Melissa's eyes. She had to get that bloody woman off the scene before it was poor Mark who ended up on medication.

'With all the stress she's been through, worrying about why he's snooping around could easily have caused her to have a heart attack. Bastard. He might even come back,' she said, forcing the point home.

'Oh shit.' Dylan looked fearfully past her, as if expecting Mark to arrive any moment, blue lights flashing.

'We have to move her.' Jade nodded determinedly.

'But…' Dylan looked uncertain. 'Shouldn't we call an ambulance or something?'

'She's dead, Dylan,' Jade reiterated. Or she soon would be, judging by how much blood she'd lost. 'And we don't have much time. He might come back,' she reminded him. 'We can't just leave her here for him to find, can we? Even if he doesn't blame you, he's bound to set you up, especially if he has an inkling about us, and he must have. Why else does he keep coming here?'

Glancing back at his mum, Dylan thought about it. He was going to go for it. Jade could almost hear the cogs creaking. 'And we have to move Daisy, too. Today. We'll take her in the car and put your poor mum in the barn where she'll be nice and safe until we can bury her properly. How does that sound?'

Dylan still didn't look a hundred per cent certain, but he seemed placated by the bury her properly bit.

'Don't worry.' Jade pressed a kiss to his cheek, though with Dylan's sweat glands in overdrive and that faceless old hag staring up at her, she actually felt like vomiting. 'I'll help you, I promise.'

By which she meant she would offer moral support. Jade had no intention of getting her hands dirty. She was meeting the delightful DS Cummings tonight. And, as much as the thought of being anywhere near him made her skin crawl, she intended to look her provocatively enticing best.

'We have to go, Dylan,' Jade said gently an hour or so later, watching him sobbing in earnest, chest heaving and huge round shoulders shaking as he looked down at his poor soon-to-be-deceased mother.

Realising he'd be there for the foreseeable future if she didn't hurry him up, Jade stifled a despairing sigh and attempted to comfort him. Placing a hand on his arm, she rubbed it gently, sending goose pimples up her own – and not in a good way. 'Come on, my love,' she coaxed, encouraging him away. 'We need to move Daisy. Your mum's at rest now.'

'Do you think she's happy?' Dylan looked at her beseechingly.

Delirious, I should think. Jade really had to work at keeping her face straight. 'Of course she is. She's with your dad now, isn't she? Her heart won't be hurting any more, Dylan. She won't be in pain.'

Appeased, Dylan nodded slowly. 'Bye, Mum,' he said gruffly, running a hand under his nose and finally turning away. *Thank God*, Jade thought, taking his hand as they walked back towards the cottage. They needed to get a move on if they were going to get this done while Mark was collecting Poppy from school. Melissa shouldn't be a problem. She'd dosed her up with enough drugs to knock out a horse.

CHAPTER FORTY-THREE

MELISSA

Mel was lying down when Mark finally came into the bedroom. She didn't want to be. She'd tried so hard to get up, to get dressed. But with the room spinning around her, she'd made it halfway to the bathroom before giving up and crawling back to bed.

'Mark?' Mel struggled to sit up. She was desperately trying to piece the events of the last few weeks together, trying to work out how in God's name she ended up here, but everything was fragmented, disjointed. She couldn't seem to separate dream from reality any more, memories slipping away from her like wisps of smoke on the air.

Easing her legs over the edge of the bed, Mel summoned up what little energy she had and heaved herself to her feet. Taking a step, she stumbled, and her heart, already heavy with guilt and confusion, plummeted like a lead weight in her chest. Mark didn't move to help her, as he would have done a short time ago. His face white, his expression inscrutable, he stayed where he was by the door, watching. Waiting? For her to fall? Mel swallowed hard.

'Here,' he said, walking across the room after a second, during which time Mel had sunk heavily back down on the bed. 'If you need it so badly, take it.'

Stopping in front of her, he lifted his hand and tossed a bottle onto the duvet.

Vodka? Mel glanced at it, bewildered. 'I don't…' She drew her gaze back to his. 'We don't drink vodka.'

'Apparently one of us does,' Mark said, scanning her eyes, his own dark, thunderously dark, and… *accusing?*

She blinked at him, stupefied for a second, before the disturbing realisation dawned. 'You think it's mine?' she asked, incredulous.

'It was in the cupboard under the sink. I sure as hell didn't put it there,' Mark said coolly. 'So, tell me, Mel, who else might have?'

Mel stared at him, stunned. He didn't really think…? No, surely not. She never drank vodka. She didn't even like the stuff. 'It's not mine. Whoever put it there, it wasn't me.'

Mark held her gaze. Apart from a telltale tic in his cheek, his expression didn't flinch. 'Right,' he said, shortly, and turned away.

'Mark! I didn't. It's not mine!' Mel sounded desperate, even to herself.

Mark stopped.

'It's not, Mark. I swear it's not.'

Mark pushed his hands into his pockets, his shoulders tensing.

'Why would I put it there?' Mel implored him. 'Why would I do that, and then tell you the sink's blocked? Why would I *do* that, Mark?'

Mark shrugged. 'Because you forgot you'd put it there?'

'It's not mine!' Mel screamed it.

Mark whirled around. 'So, who *did* put it there then, Mel?' he demanded angrily. 'Hey? Jade? Poppy? Evie?'

Mel shook her head, confused and scared – by the tone of his voice as much as the nightmare her life had become. She was losing him. He was pulling away from her. Second by second, right there in front of her, he was pulling away. And there was nothing she could do about it.

'*Hercules?*' Mark shouted when she didn't answer, causing her to jump. 'The *fucking* fairies?'

Mel bit back her tears. She wouldn't. She wouldn't cry in front of him. Her heart twisted painfully, because, truthfully, she knew he wouldn't come to her now if she did. 'I… I don't know,' she stuttered, desperately scrambling through her dysfunctional brain, acknowledging, not wanting to acknowledge, that there was only one person it could be. 'Jade,' she whispered finally. 'It must have been Jade.'

'Right.' Mark laughed bitterly. 'Without Jade,' he said, his eyes now burning with fury, 'this house would be falling apart.'

The comment hit her like a low blow to the stomach. Mel didn't speak. She couldn't.

Mark sucked in a breath and looked away, absolutely disgusted. 'I'm going,' he said hoarsely. 'I can't do this.'

'Who *else*?' Mel shouted, behind him. 'Who else could it have… Oh God.' She stopped, cold foreboding sweeping through her. 'It was you.'

Mark didn't answer. His step faltered, but he didn't turn around.

'You want me gone, don't you?' Mel swallowed back a sick taste in her throat. 'Is that it, Mark?' she asked him, her emotions swinging violently. 'Is that why you're trying to convince me I'm going out of my mind? Why you're driving me away? So you can be with Lisa?' Someone else, if not her? Who, Mark? How many other women do you have *intimate* conversations with?'

Still Mark didn't say anything. Her heart now beating a rapid drumbeat in her chest, Mel watched as he walked calmly out of the room without uttering even a word.

CHAPTER FORTY-FOUR

MARK

Mark sat at the kitchen island, his head in his hands, wondering whether it was him who was going out of his mind. She believed it. She really did believe he was having affairs. Worse, she believed him capable of such horrendous manipulation. And to what end? To move someone else in in her place? *Jesus.*

Swallowing hard, he pulled himself to his feet. Going to the kitchen cupboard, he extracted the prescription drugs, pulled out the leaflet and studied it, yet again, desperately trying to find some explanation as to what was happening.

His wife was delusional, paranoid to the point of insanity. Hallucinating. Having screaming nightmares most nights, for most of the night, and then suffering insomnia when she wasn't. The drowsiness, dizziness, obvious depression and irritability, those symptoms could be put down to the medication, but not this. This was extreme. He needed to speak to her GP; he hoped data protection wouldn't prevent Meadows from speaking to him. Somehow, though, Mark doubted changing the medication would make any difference. She needed help, more help than he or her GP could offer. She needed professional help. God help him, she might even need sectioning. Mark could hardly stand the thought, but if he had to, for the sake of their children… How much was this damaging them?

Thanks to Jade, Poppy seemed almost oblivious, although she had asked him why Mummy was strange when he'd read her a bedtime story the other night. Last night, she'd prayed to God to 'make Mummy smile again'. Mark swiped angrily at an errant tear on his cheek. Evie was fine, sleeping better than she had been. She'd sat in her bouncer for a good hour after her eleven o'clock feed, smiling and gurgling and reaching a hand towards her mobiles. Her hand–eye coordination was good. She was content. She was unaffected. For now.

Deliberating whether to take Mel a drink up, he decided against it. She'd been out of it, dead to the world, when he'd retrieved the lunch she hadn't eaten. He'd taken the opportunity to check the bathroom cabinets. He'd never imagined, even when she'd been at her lowest ebb, after Jacob, that she would ever contemplate taking an overdose, but he was imagining it now.

Time to bite the bullet, he supposed. Searching the house for hidden bottles – Mark had never imagined himself doing that either. He didn't want to prove anything, confront her again – he just needed to know.

Three bottles, all partially drunk. Feeling sick to his soul, Mark lined them up in the kitchen. One stuffed down an armchair – Mel's chair. One in the airing cupboard, nestled between the sheets. Another secreted in a Perspex storage box in a rarely used cupboard. Mark might have missed it, if he hadn't been looking. How many more were there? One under the mattress maybe? A couple in the workshop? No doubt she would have booze hidden away there. *Fuck!*

Grabbing the first bottle, Mark squeezed his hand hard around it, sorely tempted to smash it against the nearest wall. Only Evie's presence in the house stopped him. Breathing hard, he unscrewed the top. Mel wouldn't hurt her. He recalled her saying it. But *why* had she said it? Because the thought had occurred to her? Because the urge had possessed her? Not bloody surprising, putting this lot away on top of the pills. Mark furiously ditched the second bottle, and then the third, down the sink that had been blocked.

Blocked with clay. Mark stopped, the final bottle still poised. How had it been blocked with clay? From Mel washing her hands there, he'd thought. Hadn't she said the sink in the workshop had been blocked too? From washing her tools there, he'd thought. He'd assumed the clay had accumulated in the U-bend. Except it hadn't been particles of clay, collecting at the bottom of the bend like sand. It had been a solid lump.

Mark thought about it as he headed for the back door to dump the bottles and search the workshop. He was halfway out when he paused, thinking of Evie. She *wouldn't* hurt her, he assured himself, carrying on out.

Still, though, Mark searched with haste. He checked the kiln, the shelves and cupboards, workbenches and the spaces beneath them. He was heading back to the door when he remembered the clay bin. She wouldn't, would she? But then, it was precisely what addicts did. Mark had been a copper long enough to know that. Crouching, he made sure his sleeve was out of the way and delved down into the slip-sodden clay. *Bingo*, he thought bitterly, as his hand made contact with what felt like a polythene-wrapped package.

Tightening his grip, Mark attempted to pull it out, but the clay seemed reluctant to part with it. Bloody hell, what was it? A two-litre bottle? He pulled harder. The package finally unsuckered itself with a squelch, causing Mark to fall back on his haunches. Retrieving the parcel from where it had landed on the floor, he eyed it curiously, wiped some of the muck from it, and then dropped it, scrambling backwards.

Jesus Christ. Mark's heart slammed into his ribcage, his stomach turning over as his mind registered what his eyes refused to believe.

The cat's eyes were wild, wide and terrified, its fanged mouth wide open, the polythene clinging to its face.

Mark's hand shook as he poured a whisky. Knocking it straight back, he poured another and was about to swallow that when he remembered what time it was. *Shit! Poppy.* Mark pressed the heel of his hand against his forehead, breathing in hard and trying for some kind of composure, some equilibrium in a life that was fast careering out of control.

Attempting to pull himself together, he dumped the glass back on the table and headed for the kitchen, where he heaped coffee granules into a mug. He made it strong and black, topping it up with cold water so he could swill it down as fast as he had the whisky. How much had he had? Two fingers? Three? Mark couldn't recall. His hands were still shaking. Badly.

He raced for the stairs, cursing the creaking floorboards on the landing as he approached the main bedroom door. He wanted to check Mel was all right, but he desperately didn't want to wake her. He couldn't have a conversation of any kind with her until he'd got his head around what was going on. As if he could. As if anyone other than a trained psychiatrist could make sense of any of this.

His breath hitched in his chest as he went quietly into the bedroom. Mel was on her stomach, her normal sleeping position, and not one that would normally worry him, except he couldn't tell whether she was breathing. Going closer, Mark hesitated, and then crouched down and studied her face. Seeing the rapid eye movement behind her eyelids, he dropped his head to his hands, relief sweeping through him. He wanted to cry. He wanted to scream. To berate the god he wasn't sure he believed in. A god who could do *this*! *Why?*

He needed to be at the school. He needed to take Evie with him. There was no way he could leave her here, not now. Quickly rechecking the bathroom, praying he hadn't missed anything, Mark went into the baby's room, talking softly to her as he gathered her warm, fragile body from the cot. Evie whimpered sleepily, but she didn't cry. Mark was grateful for this smallest of mercies.

The tablets. He couldn't risk leaving them. But he couldn't empty the whole house of possible suicide tools either. What the hell was he going to do? Thinking of the long row of carving knives in the kitchen, Mark knew he couldn't do it. Not on his own. Glancing down at Hercules, who was nervously wagging her tail, Mark closed his eyes against the stark image of the startled, petrified cat. Was it even safe to leave the dog?

CHAPTER FORTY-FIVE

JADE

Jade very nearly had a heart attack as she saw Mark pulling out of his drive. Parked in the lane, her skin prickling with apprehension, she held her breath and waited. Then she closed her eyes with relief as Mark turned in the other direction. He must be running late to pick Poppy up from school, Melissa no doubt demanding his attention. As if the poor man hadn't got enough on his plate without having to deal with his drug-addled wife's drink problem. Jade understood why he felt he should stay – of course she did, she knew him – but surely he must realise by now that exposing his children to that kind of environment might be worse than the damage a broken home could wreak? But Mark would carry some guilt if he simply walked away from the needy cow. He couldn't help his caring nature, which was obviously why he hadn't sought further professional help yet. She would talk to him about it, subtly, when the time was right. Meanwhile, she had to up her game. If Mark was reluctant to do what it was blatantly obvious he should do and get her sectioned, then Jade had to make damn sure Melissa had every reason to leave him.

'Are you sure it wouldn't have been better to just take her in? You know, just tell him,' Dylan asked, irritating Jade immensely. Hadn't she already explained in great detail that Mark didn't want the child?

Curtailing her impatience, Jade turned to him. 'It would be too risky, Dylan,' she said, arranging her face into a suitably sad smile. 'He's… unpredictable. And don't forget, he'll have his colleagues behind him whatever I say. Trust me, it's better this way. She'll be safer at my house, for now.'

'But… Isn't your house burned out?' He was looking in the direction of her cottage, which was little more than a blackened shell. God, he really had been the last in the queue when they handed out brains.

'I've made a nice space in the basement,' Jade assured him. 'I've got her favourite duvet and all her favourite toys. She'll be fine.'

'She looks a bit pale,' Dylan said, glancing worriedly back to the girl.

Jade had to concede she definitely looked peaky, her complexion the shade of a delicate white lily. But the Calpol would help. And she'd probably feel better after a nice sleep. At least she wasn't suffering at the hands of the bitch mother and paedophile father who'd made her short life such a misery. With any luck, she might slip off quietly, which had to be better than being stuffed in a kiln while still alive.

'She needs some sun on her face, that's all. And she'll soon have it. As long as you do your bit tonight. I can count on you, can't I, Dylan?' Sighing soulfully, Jade made sure to look uncertain and vulnerable.

Dylan melted. 'You can rely on me, Jade,' he said manfully, reaching out a big paw for her hand. 'I won't let you down, I promise.'

'Nor I you.' Jade smiled tremulously. 'I just can't wait for all this to be over. For us to be together, as we should be.' Aware he might need a little reminder of what their being together meant, she moved closer, one hand pressed to his cheek, her other seeking his groin, which had Dylan squeezing his eyes closed and emitting a low throaty groan in an instant.

Shit! Jade's eyes sprang open as Dylan pressed his lips hard against hers and, clearly excited, proceeded to stuff his tongue deep into her mouth. Shuddering inwardly as he probed deeper, his tongue sliding around like a repellent slug, Jade moved her hand lower, applying just enough pressure to his balls to leave him wanting more, rather than with irreparable damage. 'Tomorrow,' she said breathily, easing away before he got it into his head that she was going to go the whole hog and give him a blow job.

Dylan emitted something between a wince and a moan. 'Promise?' he asked hoarsely.

'Most definitely,' Jade said, lowering her eyelashes and leaning in to press a placatory kiss to his overripe cheek. 'Now, you know where you're going, yes?' she asked him, unclipping her seatbelt and climbing out.

'Uh-huh.' Dylan nodded, climbing across to the driver's side of Melissa's car, grimacing a bit as he went. 'I'm following the satnav, and then when I reach my destination, I'm going to drive around a bit.'

'And?' Jade prompted him.

Dylan knitted his brow. 'I'm going to drive slowly,' he managed, with a decisive nod.

'That's right. And what else?' Smiling, Jade encouraged him on.

'I'm going to stay close to the kerb,' Dylan said, looking pleased with himself.

'Perfect.' Jade beamed him another smile. 'And remember, you're doing this for your poor mother too, Dylan. We owe it to her to make sure that DI Cain gets hurt where it hurts most. We need to make sure his reputation is under suspicion. That he's labelled unfit to be a policeman and a father. They'll take him in for questioning. And as soon as they do that, I'll be free. I can take my children and leave. No one will believe his word against mine once they realise what kind of person he is. Especially when

I have a stable home with you if social services come snooping, which they're bound to.'

She hoped the halfwit didn't mess this up. Evidence Mark had been touring red-light districts was all Jade needed. She knew Melissa couldn't possibly tolerate it.

'Don't forget to drive past the speed cameras fast,' she reminded Dylan. 'But not too fast.' She wanted him to clock up a speeding ticket or two in the suspect part of the city, not get stopped. If that happened, Jade would have to claim he stole the vehicle, or kill him.

'I won't.' Dylan fastened his seatbelt and clutched the steering wheel, his expression now one of steely determination.

Man on a mission, Jade thought wearily, rolling her eyes as she walked around to the tailgate to collect the bag Mark would have assumed was for her London trip, but which, in fact, had contained her necessary change of clothes for her meeting tonight. The question was, what to do with him when he'd accomplished his mission and she had no further need of him? A fall from the barn roof, possibly? No. She'd have to climb up there with him, or drug him and haul him up, which would be nigh on impossible without winching equipment. Hauling him over a beam in the barn, however? Yes, that might be an option. He'd murdered his mother, after all. That he'd chosen to hang himself rather than live with his conscience would be the natural tragic conclusion.

CHAPTER FORTY-SIX

MARK

Dr Meadows wasn't being majorly helpful. And with Evie in his arms, Mark was attracting attention he could do without. He moved away from a group of mothers, all of whom were smiling indulgently in his direction, no doubt thinking he looked lost, like a fish out of water. If only they knew how lost he was.

'I'm not asking you to break patient confidentiality, Dr Meadows,' he said into his hands-free as he walked. 'I'm asking you to listen. She needs psychiatric evaluation. She needs it now. I'm concerned. Very.'

'Is she a danger to herself, Mr Cain?'

'Yes. No.' Mark sighed heavily. 'I… don't know.'

'Has she tried anything?'

'No, but I think she might,' Mark answered honestly.

'Has she had any psychotic episodes?'

What the fuck defined psychotic episodes? With one eye on the school gates whilst trying to placate Evie, who was growing fractious, Mark tried to think. How to explain. Where to start. How the hell to get some urgency injected into this.

'Hallucinations?' Dr Meadows went on. 'Delusions?'

'Both of the above,' Mark confirmed.

'Do you think she might be a danger to her children, Mr Cain?' Meadows asked pertinently, causing Mark to draw in a sharp breath. 'I'm sorry to ask these questions,' he went on when Mark hesitated, 'it's just that in order to make a proper evaluation…'

Mark glanced down at Evie, catching hold of one of her tiny hands as she flailed it, pressing a soft kiss to her hair. Mel's hair. She was going to be just like Mel. Beautiful.

'There was a cat,' he said throatily, after a second. The words, the thought of what he was doing, almost choked him, but Mark knew he had to. He might be wrong, hoped to God he was, but the risk was one he just couldn't afford to take. 'In her workshop. Wrapped in polythene. Suffocated, I think.' Mark didn't dare imagine when she'd done it, or where she'd stored it, the episode with the freezer still stark in his mind. I was searching for hidden bottles. She's… drinking – a lot – and I…'

Mark stopped. This sounded insane. It was insane.

Dammit. Seeing kids spilling out into the playground, Mark headed quickly back the way he'd come. 'I have to go. I'm picking my daughter up from school,' he said, determined not to leave Poppy waiting, or for her to overhear. She didn't need to know any more than she already did, not yet.

'Get your wife to make an urgent appointment, Mark,' Dr Meadows said, sounding more understanding. 'Or better still, make one for her and try to make sure she keeps it. I'll text you some numbers. Psychiatric crisis intervention team, helplines, etc.'

Mark's heart plummeted to the pit of his stomach. What choices did he have, though? None, it seemed. If only Mel would talk to him. Let him in. If only she would be honest with him.

CHAPTER FORTY-SEVEN

MELISSA

Realising the shrill cry piercing the silence wasn't part of her nightmare, Mel snapped her eyes open. Her phone was on the bedside table, its persistent ring dragging her from sleep, sleep that was no escape from the insanity her life was becoming.

It stopped as she reached for it. Lethargic, her limbs too heavy, she couldn't even manage to take a phone call. Close to tears, Mel summoned up what little energy she could and disentangled herself from the duvet, woozily sitting up and reaching for the phone as it started ringing again. She'd almost hit answer when she realised who was calling. *Lisa.*

Anger and humiliation welling up inside her, Mel let it ring. Staring at the phone as it went again to voicemail, she wiped a salty tear from the screen, swiped another determinedly from her face, and then steeled herself to listen. Both voicemails were from Lisa, along with several texts. The gist of it all was that whatever Mel was thinking, she was wrong. Mel swallowed back her heart, which seemed to be wedged painfully in her windpipe, seeing again the fury in Mark's eyes, the coldness, the accusation. She hadn't got that *wrong*. She hadn't imagined the vodka bottle he'd tossed at her, the disgust on his face. She hadn't imagined that, any more than she'd imagined she *wasn't* drinking.

Sinks blocking up, kilns breaking down, the freezer… A hand going involuntarily to her breast, Mel drew in a long breath. The key. Poor Hercules.

She breathed out. Mark confiding in another woman, the excessive texting between them, the lies. She had not *imagined* any of it.

The only thing that was *wrong* was this house, which she'd once loved the very bricks and mortar of, and everything in it. Mark was wrong. What he was doing was *wrong*. He had two children, for God's sake. Evie was so tiny, so vulnerable. Poppy worshipped the ground he walked on. Why would he do it? Why would he send the woman she'd once considered a friend to check up on her, and then blatantly text her while she was in the house? Why would Lisa go along with it? Were they colluding to drive her out of her mind, or to leave? *Why?* She had no money. Her inheritance was tied up in the house. Unless it was the house he wanted? She had nothing else, nothing worth…

The children?

Was that it? He knew she would never part with them. *Ever.* And he wanted – needed – to be part of a family. But if he didn't want her, as a wife, as a mother to his children, what better way to eliminate her from that role than to label her an unfit mother? To label her insane? Have her sectioned? Take power of attorney over her affairs. Take everything. Mel's stomach tightened, certainty running coldly through her like ice in her veins.

She had to get out.

Mel pulled herself to her feet, nausea immediately washing over her. She had to go. Reeling, she forced herself unsteadily on, another bout of dizziness assaulting her as she made it to the bathroom. She needed to shower, but there was no time. Jade would be back soon with Poppy. She needed to be ready.

She needed not to take the *fucking* tablets.

Leaning over the toilet, Mel tried to make herself regurgitate those she had taken, but only managed to retch painfully. Her stomach was empty and raw. As raw as her heart.

Evie. Turning to the sink, Mel ran the taps full force and splashed cold water over her face. Stumbling back to the bedroom, she tore off her shirt, Mark's shirt, feeling as though her chest might tear in two as she did. She pulled on jeans and a clean T-shirt, and stuffed her feet into her flip-flops. She would come back for the rest. All that mattered now, though, all she wanted now, were her children.

Going to the nursery, mentally listing the few essential baby items she would need to take, she went straight to the cot – and stopped dead. *Empty.* The cot was empty. But where…? Jade hadn't taken her. She'd heard her crying earlier, and *not* in her dreams. She'd heard her.

Mark. He'd been here when he should have been at work. She'd lost track of time, but she was sure of that. He'd taken her. But where? Would he come back? Again, she saw the impenetrable coldness in his eyes, dark and unforgiving. He would keep Evie close, hold on to her. She couldn't fight him physically. She couldn't call the police. Couldn't call anyone. Couldn't…

She couldn't fight him.

Oh God… A sob escaping her, Mel clamped her hand to her mouth and stepped away from the cot. *Please don't let him do this.* Sick, giddy with nausea, she staggered back another step, felt for the wall behind her and sank to her haunches. *Make it stop. Please, make it stop.*

CHAPTER FORTY-EIGHT

MARK

Hearing Hercules whining sorrowfully upstairs, Mark parked Evie in the hall. 'Go and get yourself some ice cream, Poppet,' he said, nodding Poppy towards the kitchen.

'Yes! Vlanilla and Gorilla.' Poppy dumped her bag and shot off.

'Yup, that'll do,' Mark called after her, knowing that was a safe food option for her. 'Just the one though.'

Going on up, he paused apprehensively on the landing. Realising where the sound was coming from, he closed his eyes and offered up a silent prayer. But when he stopped at the nursery door, a mixture of disbelief and relief washed through him.

She was crying. The dog's head resting gently in her lap, she was sitting on the nursery room floor, quietly sobbing.

'Mel?' His heart breaking for her, Mark crouched down in front of her, as Hercules looked dolefully up at him.

Mel met his gaze. Her eyes, frantically searching his, were swollen and red, awash with hurt and confusion. 'Where is she?' she asked him, running a hand shakily under her nose.

'Who?' Mark asked gently. Noting the way she was looking at him, guardedly, mistrustfully, he felt the foundations beneath him shift another inch. 'Where's who? Mel, what's—'

'Where's my *baby*?' Mel shouted desperately over him. 'Where *is* she?'

'Downstairs!' Panic gripping him, Mark answered quickly. 'She's downstairs,' he repeated, as Hercules sat up and barked, clearly as concerned as he was. 'I'll fetch—'

'Mummy,' Poppy interrupted worriedly from the doorway, 'what's wrong?'

Mark snapped his gaze to her. Her ice cream was dripping, little white rivulets running down her chin, down her hand. She was close to tears. 'Nothing's wrong, Poppet.' Mark got to his feet and went to her. 'Mummy's…' *What?* What could he say to explain this away?

'I'm fine, sweetheart.' Wiping a hand over her eyes, Mel smiled shakily towards her daughter. 'I tripped over one of my flip-flops, that's all. I landed on my bottom. *Ouch!*'

Frowning, Poppy surveyed her uncertainly for a second. 'Are you hurt?'

'A little bit.' Mel's voice caught in her throat.

'Don't cry, Mummy.' Propelled by her obvious anguish, Poppy flew towards her, throwing her arms, plus dripping ice cream, around Mel's neck. 'Daddy will rub it better. He has magic hands. He can make the hurt go away.'

They would have laughed at that once, until they'd both cried. Together. But now, Mel didn't even glance at him.

'I think I prefer cuddles from you,' she said instead, burying her face in Poppy's hair and hugging her tight.

He'd lost her. Mark's heart cracked in his chest. There was no way to reach her. 'I'll fetch Evie,' he said, turning for the stairs. He didn't feel comfortable leaving Poppy alone with her, but she was safe, he felt, for now. Still, he unbuckled Evie quickly.

CHAPTER FORTY-NINE

JADE

'So, you're thinking of running your own nursery then?' the delightful DS Cummings asked. Taking a huge gulp of his pint, he wiped his hand across his mouth and addressed Jade's breasts, prominently displayed in her minuscule top.

'Eventually,' Jade said, leaning forward to offer him plenty of cleavage as she picked up her wine, which she'd made sure he paid for. She'd already had to fork out for a taxi to get to here. Still, it would be worth it. She was sure their meeting would be productive. 'It really depends on whether I can get the planning requirements through.'

'Ah, well' – Cummings finally focused on her face – 'that's where you'll find me a handy copper to have around. Friends in the right places,' he said, tapping the side of his nose and then giving her a slow wink.

'Really?' Jade said, looking hugely impressed.

'I know a few people. Reckon I could pull a few strings.' Cummings picked up his glass, swishing the contents around and holding her gaze meaningfully.

His meaning was clear: he would coerce a few people and expect to be amply rewarded for his efforts. Jade got the not-so-subliminal message. 'That would be amazing,' she gushed. 'I'd be *so* grateful for any help you could offer.'

Lowering her eyelashes coyly, Jade looked up at him with eyes full of innuendo.

Cummings' mouth curved into a slow smirk. Clearly, he'd got the message: you scratch my back, and you get certain parts of your anatomy serviced in return. 'Let me have the details. I'll make sure any requirements go through,' he said, his gaze drifting lustfully down again, before coming back to her face, or rather her lips.

'You're an absolute hero,' said Jade, and then, smiling apprecia- tively, she flicked her hair back and adjusted her top, thrusting her breasts forward and further whetting his disgusting appetite. God, the man was transparent, and utterly loathsome. The thought of him slobbering and sucking away at her caused her stomach to recoil, but needs must.

'At your service.' Cummings winked again and picked up his glass. 'So, where are you working now?' he asked, tipping his beer to his mouth.

Jade hesitated for a second, and then decided that, contrary to being put off by her disclosing who she worked for, the cocksure bastard would probably be turned on.

'For a colleague of yours, I think,' she said, taking a casual sip of her wine. 'Detective Inspector Mark Cain and his wife. Do you know them?'

At that, Cummings promptly choked on his beer. '*Shit!*' he spluttered, lowering his glass and wiping a dribble from his chin. 'Sorry,' he mumbled. 'Er, yes, I do. He's my boss.'

Jade noted the look: irritation bordering on contempt, though he tried to hide it. 'Your boss?' She widened her eyes, feigning surprise. 'Oh.' She paused, chewing worriedly on her bottom lip. 'I hope that's not going to be a problem. It's just, well, I like you, and…'

'No, no problem. My personal life is my own,' he assured her, folding his arms as he leaned back in his chair to appraise her once more; the look in his eyes, Jade detected, now one of quiet triumph. He was definitely getting off on the thought of fucking his detective inspector's babysitter.

And fuck him she would. Entice him to games that even in his most perverted fantasies he wouldn't have dreamed of. And then she would gain her own satisfaction from presenting herself at the station with substantial bruising as evidence of his sadistic attack. Given his reputation, Jade suspected his colleagues, particularly his female colleagues, would believe him capable of anything. *No one messes with my man and gets away with it, soon-to-be-ex detective.*

'Good.' Holding his gaze, Jade ran a finger around the rim of her glass, dipped it into her wine and then pushed it slowly into her mouth.

No one.

CHAPTER FIFTY

MARK

Mark had worried about leaving Poppy and Evie with Mel, even for the time it took to fetch Mel's tablets. Now he was regretting it bitterly.

'Mel, for Christ's sake, open up!' He banged on the bedroom door again, aware he'd be frightening Poppy, but not sure what else to do. *He* was frightened. He thought about ringing one of the numbers Dr Meadows had texted him, and felt himself free-falling into a dark place from which there would be no return.

'Mel, please,' he begged. 'Just for one second. I need to talk to you. I don't want to shout it through the door. The kids…'

No answer.

He could hear Poppy whispering inside. Mel was telling her it was a game. *A game!* Trying to stay rational, Mark pressed his hands either side of the door and leaned his head tiredly against it. What could he do? Force it? He felt like dropping to his knees and weeping. Who else could he call? Talk to? He'd lied to Edwards – said he was fine, just overwrought, would be back at work within the week. He'd avoided telling Lisa too much in case she tried to talk to Mel, which would only make matters worse.

For the sake of Poppy and Evie, he couldn't let this go on.

Resigned to make the only call he could, Mark tugged in a deep breath and took a step away. Then the door squeaked open.

'I want the children with me. They're staying with me tonight,' Mel said coolly.

Seeing the gritty determination in her eyes, knowing there was no way to get the kids out of there without arguing in front of them, Mark nodded slowly and looked away.

'Okay,' he said, his throat tight. 'Okay. Just…' He looked back at her, imploring her, through whatever madness was in her mind, to understand. 'Please don't lock the door, Mel.'

Mel didn't say anything, just looked him over as she might a stranger.

'I'm terrified there'll be a fire, Mel,' he admitted hoarsely. 'Please, don't lock the door.'

CHAPTER FIFTY-ONE

JADE

Finding the house in semi-darkness, Jade was intrigued. But finding Evie and Poppy's rooms empty and Mark sitting on the landing floor, his head resting on his arms and apparently fast asleep, she was furious. What had that pathetic excuse for a wife been up to now?

Jade crouched to gently shake his shoulder, and Mark almost shot out of his skin.

'*Christ.*' He ran his hands over his face and glanced towards the bedroom door beside him.

'Mark?' Jade looked him over, concerned. 'What's—?'

Mark pressed a finger to his mouth, and quietly eased himself to his feet, gesturing her to follow him to the stairs.

She'd follow him anywhere. To the ends of the earth. The poor man looked like death, he really did. That *bloody* woman. Jade might bring all this to an abrupt halt and strangle her and be done with it.

His gaze constantly flicking towards the bedroom, Mark outlined what needy Melissa had been up to, telling her about the extra bottles he'd found. It confirmed Jade's suspicions, she admitted reluctantly, that she had been a bit tipsy on occasion.

'There's more,' Mark said, looking suddenly nervous, as if scared what her reaction might be. 'The cat…'

'Felix?' Jade prompted him, a surge of excitement running through her as she guessed what he might be about to confide.

'Mel said you, er… She said you got rid of him?' Mark looked at her questioningly.

Jade furrowed her brow. 'I said he'd run away,' she said, pondering appropriately. 'It was a bit strange, because he was a homey sort of cat. I wondered if he'd been run… Oh no.' She clamped a hand to her mouth. 'Has something happened to him?'

Nodding sadly, Mark closed his eyes. 'He… It looks like he was suffocated. I'm sorry, Jade.'

'Suffocated?' Jade repeated, aghast. 'But… how? Where?'

'Polythene,' Mark said, his voice almost failing him. 'I found him in the workshop. In the clay bin. Jade, I am so, so sorry. I couldn't not tell you. I…' Blowing out a breath, Mark trailed wretchedly off.

'Oh God.' Looking horrified, Jade searched his face and then allowed her grief-stricken gaze to fall slowly to the floor. 'Poor Felix,' she said tearfully. 'Poor *Mel*.' She glanced back at him, and then came over quite faint.

Mark reached for her immediately, helping her as she lowered herself shakily to sit on the stairs. 'I'll fetch you some water,' he said, as she clamped her hands to her tummy and dropped her head to her knees.

Smiling gratefully, Jade took the glass when he returned, sipping the water and taking several slow breaths.

'Okay?' Mark asked, his expression so anxious, it was all Jade could do to stop herself reaching for his hand.

She nodded sadly, as if accepting the tragic news about her beloved cat bravely. 'I'm all right, Mark. Honestly, I'm fine. It's Mel we need to worry about. Has she had her medication?'

Mark trailed a hand through his hair and shook his head. 'She's refused it,' he said, looking sick to his soul. 'She's refusing to eat. I think she thinks I'm trying to poison her. She won't let me near the kids.'

He stopped, squeezing the bridge of his nose hard between his thumb and forefinger. 'I have no idea what I'm going to do, Jade,' he admitted, his tone wretched. 'None.'

Jade got to her feet and stepped towards him, her heart aching. She couldn't keep his children from him! That was just too cruel, the callous bitch. 'Let me try,' she said, keen to ease his obvious anguish. She was also keen to find out just how far needy Melissa was from the edge. A few more little pushes in the right direction and she would do something drastic – jump or leave him. It was a matter of days. Jade felt a bubble of sweet anticipation growing inside her.

'I'll make her some soup. She might take it from me, and she'll at least keep that down,' she said, taking the opportunity to press a reassuring hand to his worried face. She looked into his eyes, the pain she saw there cutting her to the core. He didn't look convinced, but he nodded wearily.

Yearning to wrap her arms around his broad shoulders, which were far too burdened with the weight of all this, Jade restrained herself. 'I was thinking…' she said, her brow knitted thoughtfully. 'You might not agree, but… You don't have any sleeping tablets, do you?'

Mark looked curiously at her. 'They're in the top kitchen cupboard. Why?'

From his wary expression, though, Jade guessed he was one step ahead of her. 'I think it might be an idea to crush one up and pop it in her soup,' she suggested, making sure to look reluctant. 'I know that looks like you're doing exactly what she thinks you are, but… At least she'll sleep, until morning hopefully.' Or longer. Jade had no intention of putting just one tablet in there. 'Which means Poppy and Evie will get a decent night's sleep, too. God knows they must need it.'

Mark drew in a tight breath and eyed the ceiling. Obviously, he would be unwilling, being such a naturally kind man, but eventually he acquiesced with a tired nod.

Jade tapped lightly on the bedroom door. 'Mel,' she called, 'it's me. Can I come in?'

There was a brief silence before Melissa padded to the door to pull it open an inch, peering warily past her as if expecting to see Mark about to charge in. This was good. The woman was definitely close to cracking or leaving. But she couldn't take Evie with her. Jade couldn't allow that.

'I brought you some soup,' she said, going in as Melissa eased the door further open.

Melissa wrapped her arms about herself, eyeing the mug suspiciously as Jade turned to face her.

'I know a bit of what's happened.' Jade smiled at her under-standingly. 'Mark's version, at least,' she said, hinting that she didn't necessarily believe him, which would hopefully encourage Melissa to open up and spill her guts.

'It's kind of you, Jade, but…' Still eyeing the mug, Mel hesitated, and then shook her head. 'I don't think I should.'

'You can't stay up here without any sustenance, Mel,' Jade pointed out, oozing compassion. 'You need to stay strong, for the children.'

She nodded over her shoulder to where Poppy and Evie were tucked up on the bed, fast asleep. It really was a heart-warming scene, Poppy with her thumb plugged in her mouth, one little arm protectively around her tiny sister. Such a pity they'd have to be separated.

Melissa turned to the bed, and stopped. 'He's trying to drive me away,' she blurted out tearfully. 'Or drive me insane. I'm not sure which. Both probably.'

Well, she was well on the way to the latter, Jade thought, following her to put the soup down on the bedside table – and make damn sure she drank it. She looked demented. A bedraggled mess. Not quite the bright-eyed, bushy-tailed, smug cow Jade had first met.

'*Mark?*' Jade feigned disbelief. 'But… he seems so nice. So normal.' She blinked confusedly. 'I can't believe he's—'

'Been overmedicating me?' Mel turned to her, her eyes full of hurt.

Jade looked at her boggle-eyed. 'Really?'

'You don't believe me.' Melissa searched her face, her hope fading.

Jade stepped towards her. 'I didn't say that,' she said, placing a hand on her arm. 'I've been in an abusive relationship myself, Melissa. The man was a complete control freak, a sociopath. Presented a perfectly respectable front to the outside world, but behind closed doors… Believe me, I know how deceitful and hurtful men can be.'

Melissa studied her, her pale face flooding with obvious relief. Then, nodding, she closed her eyes and sat shakily down on the bed. 'He's accused me of drinking,' she confided. 'Excessively. But I haven't been. He's even planted bottles.'

'Bloody hell.' Jade widened her eyes in mock horror.

'He was vile – so angry, so cold.' Melissa tightened her hold around herself. 'I think… he's trying to get me certified. Trying to take the children away from me.' Her expression was now one of fear. A bit like the fleabag cat, Jade recollected, as she'd pressed the polythene bag over its pretty, green-eyed little face.

Melissa notched up her chin. 'I won't let him.'

You won't have much choice. Jade sat down as a cold shiver ran through Melissa's body, which was looking a bit scrawny, Jade noticed. She really ought to drink the soup.

'Thank God you alerted me to his affair with Lisa.' Melissa looked miserable. 'He might have got away with it if you hadn't. Oh, God' – she gulped back a sob – 'what am I going to do, Jade?'

Jade squeezed her shoulders and held her tight for a second, which was frankly a second too long for her own liking. 'Drink your soup,' she said. 'Get a good night's sleep, and then make a doctor's appointment.'

Melissa turned tear-filled eyes towards her.

'You need to change your medication,' Jade went on firmly. 'Whether or not Mark is feeding you drugs, God forbid, the medication you're on obviously isn't helping your symptoms. You need to change it, and stay on top of it yourself. You also need to let your doctor know what's happening, for your own sake, so he'll have it all on record.'

Jade prayed it sounded plausible. The ridiculous woman couldn't just stop taking her medication. That would be a complete disaster.

'You have to get yourself right, Mel. For the children.' Jade passed her the mug, and then gave her shoulders another squeeze. 'If you need some support, I could always come with you.'

'Would you?' Melissa's hopeful look was back.

'If you want me to, yes. Don't worry, I'm on your side, Mel.'

'Thank you.' Melissa breathed out a heavy sigh – and took a sip of the soup. 'I was going to go. Take the children and leave,' she said, glancing uncertainly towards Jade. 'But you had my car.'

'Oh, Mel, I'm so sorry,' Jade said, looking suitably distraught. 'If I'd known about any of this, obviously I wouldn't have taken it. I wouldn't have gone.'

'It's all right. I shouldn't be driving anyway, not like this, not with the children. In any case, I don't think I should.'

'Oh?' Jade felt suddenly apprehensive as Melissa took another sip from the mug.

'I've been googling it, on my phone.'

Googling what, for fuck's sake? Jade was growing agitated. Immensely.

'I shouldn't leave the marital home. I would if I thought the children were in danger, but I honestly don't think Mark would hurt them. So' – she took a heartier drink of her soup – 'I've decided. I'm going to fight back. I'm staying.'

Shit.

CHAPTER FIFTY-TWO

JADE

Thank God for that. Jade offered Melissa her new tablets with a smile. She'd eased off the drugs she was feeding her, but she couldn't hope to up them again without drawing suspicion if Melissa wasn't taking any medication at all. She'd been able to continue with the sleeping tablets, however. She couldn't watch her 24/7, and Mark desperately needed some sleep. He could do with a good meal inside him, too. He'd said he would get himself something for dinner, but Jade doubted he had actually eaten anything over the last two days while she'd been babysitting his needy wife. He looked dreadful. He would make himself ill at this rate.

'Why don't you have a nice bath,' she suggested, 'light some candles and put loads of bubbles in. You could dye your hair back, too.' She nodded towards the copper dye Melissa had purchased from the chemist, determined as she was to try and 'get back to normal', as if she ever had been normal. Listening to the nonsense the woman had spouted in the surgery this evening had been painful. The doctor had nodded in sympathy, given her various abuse helpline numbers, but he'd clearly thought she was off her trolley. Jade had made sure to back up his inclinations, looking appropriately concerned and doubtful in turns.

Melissa, who was now sitting on the bed, feeding Evie, to Jade's annoyance, looked up at her, smiling wanly. 'Nice idea,' she said, 'but Poppy needs bathing. Then there's her bedtime story.'

'I'll see to Poppy.' Jade smiled warmly, though she could cheerfully strangle the woman for alienating Mark from his children in his own home. He'd have to learn to live without Poppy eventually, but she didn't want him further upset now, on top of all of this. Jade had tried to convince her that Mark wouldn't just snatch them, that he'd know how upsetting that would be for Poppy, but still Melissa was wary, insisting on moving the cot into the main bedroom and telling Poppy she could sleep with her because she was feeling lonely with Daddy sleeping downstairs because he wasn't feeling well.

'Or… you could let Mark help out,' she suggested, deciding to try again. If Melissa had decided to 'fight', then Jade had to up her game. She had to ensure there was no doubt in Mark's mind that this woman was a danger to Poppy and Evie. To which end, Jade needed him to be hands-on with the children.

'No.' Mel shook her head adamantly as she lifted Evie to her shoulder. 'If he insists on staying here, he stays on my terms. He's given up any rights to his happy family life. I still can't believe he's done the things he's done. He ought to be locked up. If only I could prove it.' Stroking Evie's back, she pulled her possessively closer, and Jade's heart constricted inside her.

'I know,' Jade said, turning to get her little angel's cot ready, her face flushing with jealousy and anger as she did. 'The thing is, though, Mel, it's Poppy who's suffering. She doesn't understand. She misses him.'

Melissa stood, turning to lower Evie into the cot. Jade couldn't quite read her expression, but suspected she was wavering. 'Where is he?' she asked.

'Out running.' Trying to run his frustrations off, she knew. He couldn't hope to, though, when the source of it was under his roof. 'You're not on your own with this, Mel,' she reminded her. 'You can rely on me to keep an eye on things.'

'I know.' Melissa smiled sadly. 'Okay. I'll have a bath,' she relented.

Good, Jade thought. Pity she hadn't taken her sleeping tablet. With a bit of luck, she might have drowned in it.

'And make myself beautiful while I'm in there.' Mel rolled her eyes. 'Well, presentable, anyway,' she said self-effacingly, causing Jade to wince. 'Even though there doesn't seem to be much point any more.'

Jade moved to give her a hug as the inevitable tears welled up. God, she really was a weak specimen. 'You're doing it for *you*, Mel,' she said forcefully. 'For the children.'

Mel nodded. 'Thanks, Jade,' she said, smiling gratefully this time. 'I don't know what I'd do without you.'

'No problem. That's what friends are for,' Jade assured her, squeezing her hand and turning for the door. 'Indulge and enjoy. I'll go and extract Poppy from in front of the TV before she gets square eyes.'

CHAPTER FIFTY-THREE

MARK

'How are things?' Lisa asked, when Mark picked up her call.

'On a scale of one to ten, eleven.' Coming through the front door, Mark sighed and wiped an arm across his forehead. He'd run until he thought his lungs would give out. He'd thought it would help channel some of his anger and sheer bloody frustration. It hadn't.

'That bad, hey?'

'And some,' Mark answered honestly. 'How're things with you?'

'Wonderful. I love being in an office with Cummings strutting about like a dog with two dicks. Seems there's a new lust in his life, poor cow. She's obviously short-sighted or in serious need of counselling.'

Mark laughed, and then wondered when he'd last done that. 'Any developments on the Daisy case?' he asked her seriously. Even with the madness his life had become, he hadn't been able to stop thinking about the little girl, to shake the nagging feeling that somehow, somewhere, she was alive.

'Nothing. It's gone cold. Looks like the powers that be will be scaling the investigation down. Sorry, Mark,' Lisa said, dashing his hopes that someone might come forward with fresh information, that one of the team might come up with something in his absence.

Mark's stomach knotted inside him. He'd let the girl down. He should have been on top of it, he thought, his frustration growing.

He should have been on top of what was happening here, too, right under his nose, before it spiralled out of control. Before he lost the woman he'd loved with all of himself. Still loved.

'Look, Mark, I've been meaning to ring you about something else. It might be nothing, but…'

'Clearly you think it's something,' Mark prompted her, tugging his damp T-shirt over his head as he headed for the kitchen for a cold drink.

'I've been doing some digging and—'

But Mark cut her off mid-sentence. 'I have to go. I'll call you back,' he said quickly, abruptly ending the call.

'Lisa?' Mel asked him, from where she was standing by the fridge.

Mark cursed inwardly. 'A work call,' he said, feeling guilty, with no clue why.

'Of course it was.' Mel's tone was flat. She didn't look at him so much as through him. 'Just orange,' she said, indicating her glass pointedly, and then walked past him to the hall.

'Shit…' Mark muttered, fetching himself a coke from the fridge, and finding himself wishing he could have a whisky – or several. Consume so much alcohol he'd be comatose and oblivious to any of this. 'Sod it,' he said, parking himself heavily at the kitchen island. What happened? What in God's name went so wrong? *How?* He stared upwards, as if there were a God up there who might answer him.

He wasn't aware of Jade coming into the kitchen behind him.

'Oh dear, I take it things are getting to you?' she asked him sympathetically.

'Just a bit.' Mark smiled disconsolately.

Jade pressed an arm around his shoulders. Being half-naked, Mark felt somewhat awkward, but wasn't sure how to extricate himself without offending her.

Jade saved him from any potential awkwardness. 'Poppy's ready for her bath,' she said, giving his shoulders a reassuring squeeze and then moving towards the cooker. 'She wants *The Wheels on the Bus* for her bedtime story.'

Mark looked at her with surprise.

'She said to tell you to hurry up.' Jade smiled and nodded him towards the stairs.

He was being allowed contact with his own kids? That was something, Mark supposed.

CHAPTER FIFTY-FOUR

JADE

'And then we had gymnastics…' Jade could hear Poppy chatting to Mark about her school day as she crept along the landing. 'But I don't like it.' Jade peeked around the bathroom door to see Poppy wearing her petulant, annoying little frown.

'Oh, why's that then?' Mark asked.

'Because I like swimming better,' Poppy said, her little face pointing upwards as Mark carefully rinsed the soap from her hair. 'Miss Winters calls me her little mermaid,' she informed him importantly. 'Cos I can hold my breath for seven whole… *Ouch! Daddeee…*'

'Oops, sorry, Poppet. Hold on a sec.' Mark got hastily to his feet as Poppy clamped her hands to her soap-stung eyes. '*Damn,*' he muttered, turning for the towel to find it wasn't there.

The missing towel in hand, Jade took a step back down the stairs as he emerged from the bathroom to head for the airing cupboard, Poppy whingeing behind him. 'Daddy, it's *stinging*.'

Jade sighed and, covered by the outwardly opening airing cupboard door, stepped quickly back up towards the bathroom. She didn't have to dunk her, thankfully. Poppy had already taken it upon herself to look like a drowning mermaid.

Disappearing in the nick of time, as Mark reappeared, Jade waited at the top of the stairs. And sure enough… 'Poppy!' Mark shouted urgently. '*Poppy!*'

'What the *hell* were you *doing*?' he snapped angrily, plucking her from the water and swinging Poppy towards him, who clearly *wasn't* drowned. More was the pity. Peering back around the door, Jade watched jealously on.

Startled by his tone, and the shocked look on his face, Poppy squirmed in his arms, attempting to wriggle away from him.

'Poppy, stop.' In danger of dropping her, Mark tried to hang onto her. 'Poppy!'

'I was holding my breath!' Poppy cried, and promptly burst into tears.

'Christ…' Mark hugged her close. 'I'm sorry, Poppy,' he murmured throatily into her wet hair. 'I thought…'

She was rewarded, of course. Melissa fussed and fawned all over the little brat, while Mark, who'd almost suffered a heart attack, lingered awkwardly in the background, looking shocked – and guilty. As if it was his fault. Honestly, did the woman who'd promised to love and cherish him really have to work so hard at compounding his guilt? Obviously, if the child had drowned, it would have been an accident. Yet, Melissa, who'd previously thought Mark was her knight in shining armour, was looking at him as if he were a complete monster, nothing but contempt in her eyes, which was all to the good, Jade supposed.

Poppy, oblivious to the trouble she'd caused, was now busy licking her bowl free of vanilla ice cream. Little pig. They ought to have christened her Pinky.

'Come on, sweetie, let's get you tucked up in bed.' Melissa, who still had a towel wrapped around her hair, shot Mark another venomous look as she plucked Poppy from the stool at the island, as if the child had lost the use of her legs.

Mark said nothing, just kneaded his forehead in that frustrated way he did. Jade knew why. He was trying to avoid arguing in front of his children. Did the woman not have eyes? A brain in her rusty-haired head? Could she not see how much he cared for his children?

Jade pulled in a breath, blowing it angrily out through her nostrils, as she headed for the kettle. 'I'll make some hot chocolate,' she said, working to keep her tone in check. 'Would you like one, Mark?'

But he just stood there, looking for all the world like a lost soul. A lost, lonely soul.

'It wasn't your fault,' Jade said, walking across to him and pressing a hand softly to his chest. 'She didn't come to any harm.'

Mark glanced down. He didn't seem to mind her hand there. 'She could have done,' he said, his tone hoarse, as if he were holding back tears. 'I shouldn't have left her.'

The kettle boiled behind them. Jade smiled again affectionately and turned to it. She had no idea what to say to him. Words couldn't make his pain go away. He needed comfort, holding. He needed to be loved. To be needed. She was treacherously close to telling him the truth; that bitch had never wanted him for more than his seed, his money, his status. That she'd used him, mercilessly. Never loved him. Not like Jade loved him.

'Chocolate?' she said instead, the kettle poised over a mug.

'What?' Mark looked up distractedly. 'Oh. No, thanks.' Smiling sadly, he turned to the lounge.

For something stronger, Jade suspected, and she didn't blame him. How she wished she could sit next to him, lie next to him, press her ear to his chest and listen to his poor heart beating. Sighing, she popped two pills into Melissa's hot chocolate, stirred longingly, and then froze. *The hot chocolate wasn't dairy-free, was it?*

CHAPTER FIFTY-FIVE

MELISSA

'Poppy, shuffle over, sweetie.' Mel came out of the bathroom, where she'd finally managed to rinse the colour from her hair, to find Poppy lying sideways across the bed.

'Poppy?' Glancing at her through the mirror as she gave her new copper locks a last rub with the towel, Mel guessed she must have fallen asleep – not surprisingly, after the evening's events. She knew, in her heart, that Mark would never hurt their daughter. And she'd done it herself, dashed out of the bathroom for a towel or a toy, she thought guiltily. She hadn't admitted that to Mark, of course. She didn't want to give him any more ammunition to use against her.

Why was he doing this? Mel paused, gulping back the heartache, the horror and disbelief that she could have been so terrifyingly wrong about him. Why didn't he just *go*? Be with Lisa, if that's what he wanted? Accept that, in destroying his marriage, he'd be giving up his children? He was crushing her, little by little. Killing her. She hated him for it. Hated herself for allowing him to.

'Poppy, come on, my lovely,' she whispered to her daughter, who was well and truly asleep. Mel walked across to her, bending to ease her around. And she stopped dead, her heart lurching violently in her chest.

'Poppy!'

Her lips were swollen. She wasn't breathing properly.

'*Poppy!*' Mel screamed, hoisting her into her arms. '*Mark!*'

Hearing a distinct wheeze in her chest – *Please, God, no, not my baby!* – Mel turned, nausea sweeping through her, her heart beating as though trying to burst from her body.

Mark banged through the door before she'd reached it.

'*Jesus Christ!* What's happened?' He reached immediately for Poppy.

Mel didn't protest, but fed her into his arms. 'I don't know. I thought she was asleep. I… She…' She gulped back a sob. 'She must have eaten something. I don't *know.*'

'She has a rash.' Mark's eyes flicked quickly over Poppy. 'Fetch her auto-injector.'

Shocked, Mel was frozen to the spot.

'Mel. Go!' Mark shouted urgently, bending to lower Poppy quickly to the floor.

Mel turned, and flew. They had several. Emergency supplies. *Where?* She tried to fit her disjointed thoughts together in her head. Bathroom. Poppy's schoolbag. *Handbag!* Her gaze falling on her bag hanging from the en suite door, she seized on it, fumbling with it until finally turning it over and spewing the contents on to the floor.

Clutching two EpiPens, she raced back to where Mark was putting Poppy in the recovery position. Her throat hard and tight, Mel watched him. His face was pale, but his movements were precise and calm. Her own hands shaking, her legs feeling as if they might fail to support her, Mel passed him the pen. Mark injected it, straight through Poppy's pyjamas and into her thigh.

'Mark?' Jade appeared, hovering uncertainly behind him on the landing. 'Oh my *God*, what's happened?'

'Dial 999,' Mark instructed, his gaze still on Poppy as he held the EpiPen in place for the required ten seconds. Would Mel have remembered to do that?

'Just say anaphylaxis. A child,' Mark added, as Jade punched the number into her mobile. His tone was quiet but authoritative, his expression taut with worry as he pulled the injector pen out, concentrating his efforts now on massaging Poppy's small thigh.

'Baby?' Mel dropped to her knees, stroking Poppy's sweat-dampened hair back from her face.

'Come on, baby. You can do this,' Mark said, his voice cracking as he gently took their daughter's tiny hand in his own.

He closed his eyes briefly, massaged her back, checked his watch, trying to stay composed, Mel knew. 'We need to know what's caused it,' he said, checking his watch again. 'The ice cream?'

Mel shook her head. 'No. It's safe.' She could barely get the words out. But what? Searching frantically through her sluggish mind, Mel tried to think. She hadn't had anything that might cause… 'Oh no.' Poppy had chocolate stains around her mouth.

Mel scrambled to her feet and stumbled to the bedside table, and her insides turned over. But… Poppy wouldn't. 'The drinking chocolate,' she said shakily, cold fear running the length of her spine as she turned back to her unconscious child. 'She's—'

'Oh, sweet fucking Jesus.' Mark heaved in a breath and snapped his gaze to Jade, who'd come quietly in to take Melissa's place, softly caressing Poppy's cheek with the back of her hand. 'Did you…?'

'No.' Jade shook her head adamantly.

'Mark?' Melissa moved falteringly towards them. This was her fault. *Hers*. She needed to know what to do. She needed to do *something*.

'We need to get her to the hospital. Now!' Mark said tersely, gathering Poppy into his arms. 'Jade, go and start my car. Mel, make sure you have another EpiPen. You might need to use it on the way.'

Mel focused through her guilt and confusion. The paramedics would have oxygen, but Mark, who'd grown a shade paler, must be thinking they might be too late.

CHAPTER FIFTY-SIX

JADE

'*Hush, little baby, don't say a word…*' Pressing a kiss to Evie's forehead, Jade lowered her gently into her cot. 'Mummy will be back soon, my sweet Angel,' she said, caressing her peachy cheek as she smiled down at her.

She really was a content little baby, Jade thought, which was thanks to *her* calming influence in a sea of madness, obviously. She really did despair. If she phoned social services herself, she'd bet they'd whisk the children away from their demented mother in a flash. But she couldn't do that, of course. The vicious cow would no doubt hurl accusations at Mark, making him out to be anything but the good, loving, patient father that he was, and he would be denied access to them too. But not to worry: Melissa was almost at breaking point. Jade almost felt sorry for her.

Humming, she made her way downstairs, reaching into her pocket for the credit card she'd slipped from Mark's jacket during the pandemonium. Now then… which sites to browse, she wondered. Nothing extreme, she'd decided. She didn't want Mark to get into serious trouble. They would have to be sites with sexually graphic images though, where she would purchase certain goods used in the pursuit of certain pleasures – or rather Mark would, before saving the sites to his bookmarks. Melissa would be bound to go apoplectic, undoubtedly leave or demand that Mark did. Undoubtedly also, Mark would refuse to leave without his children. At which point, Jade would step valiantly but reluctantly in to help him remove them to a safe place. Or one of them, at least, depending on the evening's outcome.

Mark could save himself all the hassle if only he'd intervene and have his mental wife sectioned. In time he would see it was the only kind thing to do, for her own and everyone else's safety. Meanwhile, though, Jade had no choice but to ramp up her efforts, even if she did have to manufacture the proof that Mark found his needy wife about as exciting as cold tapioca.

Collecting Mark's laptop from the hall, Jade extracted the luxury bar of chocolate from her handbag, peeling back the enticingly shiny wrapper and settling down at the kitchen island to browse at leisure. Mark and Melissa would be ages at the hospital, which gave her plenty of time.

Popping a chunk of chocolate in her mouth, Jade sucked slowly. *Mmm.* It really was as delicious as she'd mentioned to Poppy. Hopefully, after the trauma of her collapse and hospitalisation, the brat wouldn't remember eating it, but if it came out, then Jade would just play her part – innocent and apologetic. And of course, it had never occurred to her to imagine the thieving little brat would sneak into her bag and help herself to it.

Up bright and early the next morning, Jade hovered at the kitchen window, intending to catch the postman before Mark or Melissa came down. They weren't likely to surface early after the dreadful night they'd had at the hospital, opting to stay by Poppy's side.

She'd survived, probably due to Mark's quick thinking in getting her there. Mark had rung her, as he would, to let her know they were keeping her in for observation for at least eight hours. He really was so thoughtful, assuming she'd be worried. Her blood tests had been clear, he'd also told her, which had perturbed Jade a bit. Having given his consent to Jade spiking needy Melissa's bedtime drink once, he'd perhaps suspected Jade might have thought he was condoning it on an ongoing basis, therefore inadvertently feeding Poppy a sleeping tablet. As if she would. It was tempting. Very. But it would have been monumentally stupid, when he plainly loved Poppy, as a father should love a daughter.

Quashing a pang of jealousy twisting inside her, Jade spooned coffee into the mugs and popped a pill into Melissa's.

She'd been hoping the chocolate might do the job. But... *c'est la vie*. Jade had been disappointed, naturally, but pleased for Mark, who, despite being exhausted to the point of dropping when they'd arrived home, had look so heartbreakingly relieved, Jade could have cried.

Aha, at last. Noting the postman heading for the front door, Jade took the eggs she was scrambling off the heat. She was going to feed them a hearty breakfast – and Melissa another pill – after their traumatic experience.

'Good morning,' she said brightly, beaming the postman a smile. He smiled delightedly back, his eyes trailing lustfully over her – as men's eyes did – and handed her the post.

Moron, Jade thought, her smile widening nevertheless as she closed the door and looked at the envelopes, one of which contained a green document, which, if she wasn't mistaken, was a certain speeding ticket.

Glancing quickly up the stairs, as she heard someone rising, Jade tore the envelope open, quickly scanning the contents. *Oh, well done, Dylan.* The man had excelled himself. Clearly, he did have a brain cell rattling around inside that dense skull of his. Jade noted the perfect location and timing of the speeding offence, which was well after she'd arrived home – courtesy of a lift to the end of the lane from 'Call-me-Pete' Cummings – and everyone had been tucked up in bed, apart from Mark.

CHAPTER FIFTY-SEVEN

MARK

'Morning,' Mark said, tugging his shirt on as he came into the kitchen.

Jade, fixing them up a late breakfast, turned to smile tremulously at him. 'Morning,' she said quietly, and then turned sadly back to her task.

Narrowing his eyes, Mark looked her over as he walked across to the fridge for orange. 'Something smells good.' He nodded towards the bacon cooking under the grill.

Jade didn't look back at him. 'I thought something a bit more substantial might help, after spending the night at…' She broke off, looking close to tears. I'm so sorry, Mark. I had no idea there was dairy in the hot chocolate powder. I—'

'No… It wasn't your fault.'

Mark ran a hand wearily through his hair as he noted a tear slide down her cheek. He'd thought… As he'd watched Mel with Poppy, not letting go of her tiny hand, not moving from her side for a second, he'd wondered just how accidental the shit that kept piling on top of them really was. His imagination had run riot. He'd got it wrong, looking for someone to blame, he guessed. There wasn't anyone. Not even God.

Sighing, he pulled his beeping phone from his pocket to mute it, wondering only briefly why Lisa would be texting him to 'chat' when they'd agreed to send no texts unless it was urgent.

Jade was chopping at the mushrooms. Chopping blindly, if the now steady flow of tears was anything to judge by. 'I prefer less salt with mine,' he joked, attempting to lighten things.

Clearly not appreciating his efforts, Jade just cried harder, dabbing at her cheeks, before going back to the mushrooms with a vengeance.

'I'm not into fried fingers much either,' Mark tried.

Jade stopped chopping. 'I'm so sorry, Mark,' she said again, looking utterly miserable. 'I'll go if you want me to. I'd understand. I...'

Mark hesitated as she heaved in a breath and pressed the back of her hand to her nose, and then he reached out to tentatively wrap an arm around her shoulders. 'I'd be in one hell of a mess if you did,' he said truthfully.

Jade turned and buried her face in his shoulder. 'I'm sorry,' she repeated, with heart-wrenching anguish.

'I think I got that.' Awkward though he felt, Mark gave her a squeeze, and then carefully moved to put a little distance between them. 'Poppy's home safe now. Let's just put it behind us, shall we?'

Jade nodded and smiled up at him. It wasn't her usual radiant smile, but at least she didn't look consumed with guilt any more. 'How's Mel?' she asked.

'I think she's feeling as guilty as you seem to be, to be honest.'

Mel hadn't actually said much while they'd waited at the hospital, but Mark had read the body language, the arms wrapped tightly around herself, seen the torment in her eyes. She didn't need him to drive it home. 'Stuff happens.' He shrugged. 'At least she's relented a bit on the accident in the bath. I think we've both realised we could lose her.'

Jade looked up at him. 'You're a nice person, Mark Cain. Do you know that?'

'Yeah.' Mark smiled ruefully. 'I only wish my wife thought I was.' Mel hadn't looked at him much either, apart from with sheer relief when they'd realised Poppy was going to pull through. She hadn't come to him, ruling out any body contact between them, if only to offer each other comfort. But at least she had finally looked at him. Maybe there was hope, he thought wearily.

Reminded of his close proximity to Jade, which might be misconstrued, given Mel's current suspicions, he moved quickly away from her.

Jade looked at him confusedly.

'It's probably not a great idea for Mel to see us… Well, you know,' Mark explained, finishing clumsily. Offering Jade a reassuring smile, he prayed that they could all put this behind them, that the small improvement he'd noticed in Mel's physical symptoms might mean they could move forwards and somehow find their way out of this nightmare.

'I'll take Mel's breakfast up,' Jade said, her smile definitely brighter as she turned back to the chopping board.

CHAPTER FIFTY-EIGHT

JADE

So, they'd had a little bonding session at the hospital, had they? Well, she'd soon nip *that* in the bud. Jade restrained herself from banging things into the dishwasher, placing them just so, lingering over the extremely sharp knife she felt like chopping certain little fingers off with.

Spoiled, that's what she was. *A wilful, overindulged little…*

'Do we need anything?' Mark said behind her, pulling his jacket on as he came back into the kitchen.

'Meds,' Jade said, quickly stuffing the knife in the cutlery basket and turning to retrieve Mel's prescription from the notice board. 'I thought as you were going to the chemist…'

'Cheers,' Mark said, smiling a little more easily than he had earlier that morning. Jade doubted he'd be doing that for long. 'I'll only be half an hour or so. The kids are in with Mel.'

Where else, thought Jade, suppressing her growing urge to tiptoe in and suffocate that woman with the pillow, take her baby and be done with. But that wasn't a good idea. Being a detective, Mark was bound to cotton on to something.

'See you soon,' he said, heading towards the front door, obviously feeling safe to go out for five minutes now he didn't think he was in danger of being thrown out.

Closing the dishwasher with a bang, Jade went to the window, making sure Mark had pulled out of the drive before retrieving the speeding ticket from behind the toaster.

Now to do the deed, while Melissa was disorientated, which she would be by now, and still shell-shocked after almost losing her precious Poppy.

Collecting up the rest of the post – plenty for Melissa about her arty-farty crap – Jade went upstairs, tapped on the bedroom door and went on in to find Melissa sitting on the edge of the bed, her hands pressed to her forehead and plainly feeling woozy. Evie was fretting, Jade noticed despairingly. The woman really was a useless cow.

'Hi, Mel,' she said, making sure not to sound too cheerful in light of last night's events. Placing the post on the bed, she went across to lift Evie from her cot. 'How are you feeling?'

'A bit queasy, to be honest.' Mel smiled feebly in her direction. So she wasn't about to start pointing fingers for a tragedy which was clearly her own fault, which was a relief. Jade needed Melissa on side if she was going to pull this off.

'Would you like some tea?' she asked her. 'You haven't eaten much.' She'd picked at her toast earlier, but had eaten a good portion of the egg, thank goodness.

'I'm not very hungry, Jade.' Mel offered her another weak smile.

'I'm not surprised after last night.' Jade pressed Evie close to her shoulder; she'd stopped fretting the second she had picked her up. Clearly, she knew whose shoulder she preferred. 'I'm really sorry about what happened, Mel.'

'Not your fault. Poppy's curiosity obviously got the better of her. I still can't believe it…' She brushed Poppy's hair lovingly back from her face, causing the little brat to stir in her sleep. 'She's all right, that's the main thing.'

'I'll go and change Evie,' Jade offered, heading towards the door. 'Give you time to get yourself together.' She'd only had half the day already. God help the woman's family if they had to rely on her for sustenance. 'Oh… I brought your post up.'

Melissa glanced at the envelopes on the bed half-interestedly, noting the one on top was from her Garden & Homes store and emitting a soulful sigh, which possibly had something to do with the orders she hadn't managed to fill. Aspirations beyond her dubious talents, that was Melissa's trouble, Jade thought with a satisfied smirk. Perhaps she should have channelled more of her energies into looking after her husband, rather than ensuring he looked elsewhere.

'I, um, opened one of the envelopes in error,' she said, looking apologetic as she nodded towards them. 'I thought I'd better let you know in case you wondered.'

'Oh?' Melissa leafed through the envelopes.

Jade stepped back towards her. 'It's just… Well, it's a speeding fine, and I was worried you might think it was me. It was your car, you see.'

Melissa looked at her in surprise. '*My* car?'

'It's dated two o'clock in the morning,' Jade went on, as Mel found it and read it. 'And as I was back here by ten thirty, obviously I was concerned.'

Melissa scanned it, her expression growing more puzzled by the second.

'Particularly when I noted the location.'

Melissa still looked puzzled. Gormless cow, she probably wasn't familiar with the area, even though she was a policeman's wife. Honestly. 'It's in the red-light district.' Mentally rolling her eyes, Jade waited for the significance to sink in.

'I thought maybe someone had stolen the car. You know, for joyriding or something.'

Got her, Jade thought, supremely pleased as Melissa's expression turned to disbelief, swiftly followed by palpable fury.

'What, and then returned it?' she seethed. 'No doubt they washed and valeted it too! That absolute bastard!'

Poppy, who'd been blissfully sleeping, oblivious to the trouble she'd caused, shot up. 'Mummy, what's wrong?' she asked, kneading her eyes worriedly.

'Nothing,' Melissa said shortly, finally managing to stand upright. Pretty quickly, all credit to her. Jade watched interestedly.

'But *Mummeee*, why are you angry?' Poppy whined, shuffling towards the edge of the bed to go after her.

'I'm not!' Melissa snapped. Then she closed her eyes and drew in a tight breath. 'I'm not, sweetheart,' she said, attempting a smile. 'Mummy has a headache, that's all. Go with Jade, darling. I have some things I need to do.'

'Come on, Poppet.' Jade extended her hand. 'You can help me feed Evie.'

Poppy's gaze flicked worriedly to Jade. 'But I don't want to,' she whimpered, bringing her knees up and shuffling towards the headboard, as though trying to make herself smaller. Yes, and Jade knew why.

'Go!' Melissa barked. 'Now, Poppy, before I lose my temper.'

'Come on, Poppet, come with me.' Smiling reassuringly as Melissa turned back to whatever mad mission she was on, Jade walked towards the bed. She plucked up the speeding ticket, stuffing it in her pocket, before grabbing hold of the disobedient little brat's arm. Poppy was shuffling further away, her face set in that infuriating petulant scowl she had.

'We'll watch a nice DVD later. How does that sound?' Jade asked her sweetly, all but dragging a tearful Poppy to the door. Melissa, fortunately, was too busy pulling Mark's clothes out of the wardrobe and going through pockets to notice.

Once on the landing, Jade whirled Poppy around to face her and leaned in to eyeball her meaningfully. 'Who did your father say was in charge?' she hissed, squeezing the child's arm hard.

Poppy gulped back a sob. 'You,' she answered tremulously.

'That's right,' Jade growled. 'Now, do *not* cause me any trouble, *sweetheart*. Not unless you want me to tell your daddy you've been stealing. And, trust me, you don't want me to do that. He's already *very* annoyed with you.'

CHAPTER FIFTY-NINE

MARK

As he came through the front door, Mark knew there was something wrong. Poppy didn't come bounding excitedly to him. Instead, thumb in mouth, she sloped dejectedly towards him, glancing warily over her shoulder as she did.

'What's up, Poppet?' Dumping his carrier bag, Mark crouched down to her level.

Poppy scanned his eyes, her own uncertain and... *guarded*?

'Poppy?' Mark eyed her questioningly.

'Mummy's angry,' Poppy whispered, her wide eyes now brimming with tears.

Mark looked to Jade, who had appeared in the kitchen doorway. Evie in her arms, she shrugged helplessly and then looked nervously upwards as something crashed onto the floorboards above them.

'Stay here, sweetheart,' Mark said, giving Poppy a reassuring smile. 'Do as Jade says. I'll be back in a minute.'

Heading swiftly up, Mark went straight to the main bedroom, not bothering to knock.

'Mel? What in God's name are you doing?' he asked, bewildered, as he saw Mel picking up clothes from the pile strewn on the bed. *His* clothes. 'Melissa...' Anger unfurled inside him as he watched her go through his pockets, tossing aside a pair of trousers and picking up another pair. 'Would you like to tell me what's going on here?' he asked, now trying very hard not to lose it.

Mel didn't answer him, just kept right on searching. But for what?

'Melissa! What the hell are you looking for?'

'I don't know!' Mel's expression as she glared at him was one of sheer contempt. 'Why don't *you* tell *me*?' She threw one of his jackets down and picked up another item. Realising it was a shirt and would yield nothing, she dropped that to the growing pile on the floor

Mark felt his jaw tense, felt his life slipping away from him, like sand through a timer. 'You need to stop this, Mel – *now*,' he said, making no attempt to hide his growing fury.

Mel ignored him. 'What will I find, Mark, hey?' She walked stiffly over to his dressing table drawers, dragging them out to spew the contents onto the shirts. 'Condoms?' she spat. 'Lube? Tell me' – she whirled around – 'what other dirty little secrets am I likely to find?'

What the…? Mark was stunned, in utter disbelief at this new twist in the madness. 'Mel, stop,' he said shakily. 'You need to talk to me.'

'You do *use* condoms, I take it?' Mel spat venomously. She was killing him. She was fucking well crucifying him.

'Mel! Stop!' Mark caught hold of her arm, but Mel yanked it away.

'Or is it more of a turn-on fucking prostitutes naked?'

'For God's sake! Where the *hell* is this coming from? You're completely insane.'

'Ha! Oh, yes, of *course* I am,' Mel yelled, gesticulating wildly. 'It's all in my mind, isn't it? I'm imagining it all, aren't I?'

Mark didn't speak. He couldn't. His temper was way too close to spilling over.

'Just like I imagined your sordid little affair with *Lisa*!'

Mark ran his hand hopelessly through his hair. He had no idea what to do. None.

'Did I imagine you've been overmedicating me? Putting extra drugs in my drinks? Did I imagine *that*?'

'*What?*' Mark looked sharply back at her. 'Look, Mel,' he moved towards her, felt the foundations rock this time, crumbling beneath him. 'I don't know what you think I've done, but can we please—'

'Do *not* try to deny it!' Mel stepped back. 'I have evidence!'

'Evidence of *what*?' Mark yelled, torn between guilt and gut-wrenching despair as he watched his wife dementedly dragging clothes from the bed, fumbling around, picking up envelopes, tearing them up.

'*God!*' She stopped, clutching handfuls of her hair. 'Evidence of your nocturnal activities,' she seethed, turning towards him. 'Your therapeutic trips out at night, kerb-crawling.'

Kerb-crawling? Mark felt his stomach turn over. 'Fuck,' he uttered, his anger shifting as he realised there was only one place any sort of so-called evidence could have come from. Cummings, the bastard. The photos he'd taken. It had to be. 'It's bullshit, Mel,' he said. 'Whatever you've seen or heard, it's—'

'You make me sick.' Mel looked him over, disgusted. 'Get out.'

'Mel, you need to listen,' Mark tried, taking another step towards her. 'There is *no* way—'

'Get out!' Mel screamed, reaching for whatever came to hand from the bedside table. The alarm clock. Her aim was good. Mark winced, his hand going to his face as she hit her target. 'Just take your bloody things and go! Or I swear to God I'll call the police.'

'And tell them what, Mel?' Mark asked calmly. 'That I assaulted you?'

Mel held his gaze. 'Yes,' she said, her expression resolute, her eyes burning with hatred.

'Right.' Mark pulled his bloodied fingers away from his cheek. 'It wouldn't be true though, Mel, would it?'

His heart free-falling into the vast space between them, Mark shook his head and turned away.

'I want you out, Mark,' Mel said coldly behind him.

Clearly, she was prepared to believe a slimy piece of shit like Cummings over him. Had her illness caused *this*? Caused her to be so suspicious of him, so paranoid, she'd believe such complete crap, even *knowing* him? Or were they headed this way anyway? Mark had no clue. Maybe he didn't know her. Maybe he never really had. Either way, he was going nowhere. She really must be insane if she thought he'd leave his kids to this.

'No way, Mel,' he said, squaring his shoulders as he walked away. 'Call who you like. I'm staying.'

CHAPTER SIXTY

JADE

What did she have to do to get him to leave? Get her to plunge a knife through his heart? And did Melissa have a victim mentality or what? Jade was feeling a need to lie down, she really was. Skidding away from the door as it opened instead, she made as if she'd just been settling Evie as Mark emerged from the room, the look in his eyes one of pure murder.

Oh no! He had blood on his cheek. Jade noted the sharp cut on his cheekbone and her anger boiled inside her. What had the bitch done to him now?

'Did she receive any calls?' Mark demanded. 'Did Melissa receive any telephone calls or texts?'

Jade, uncertain where this was going, didn't immediately answer. 'I… I'm not sure,' she stammered. 'Possibly. I don't pay much attention to Mel's calls.'

'Right. Of course, you wouldn't. Sorry, I er… Sorry.'

'It's fine,' Jade assured him. 'I realise you're a bit fraught. You're, um, bleeding.' She indicated his cheek, which really did look sore. Jade could see it swelling already.

'Yeah.' Mark pressed his fingers to his wound. 'Steadily.' He eyed her thoughtfully for a second, before hurrying down the stairs.

His heart. Jade placed a hand over her own. He meant his poor broken heart. She really didn't think she could bear it.

CHAPTER SIXTY-ONE

MARK

Poppy had been missing when he'd come down after the fiasco upstairs. His mind conjuring up all sorts of worst-case scenarios, Mark had felt sick to his gut when he'd finally found her, curled as tight as she possibly could be, hiding behind the armchair. Hiding from him.

Gulping back a large swig of whisky, Mark looked across to the chair now, his breath hitching in his chest as he saw again his baby's face. Obviously, having heard the argument and sensed the unbearable tension between him and Mel, she'd been petrified. So she'd tried to find a safe place to hide in, just as he'd once done. She wouldn't budge when he'd asked her to come out. 'No. I want to stay with Mummy,' she'd insisted, her child's eyes so vulnerable, her voice so small, Mark had felt another piece of himself die. It was Jade who'd persuaded her out in the end. Mark wasn't sure how. He'd gone into the kitchen, not wanting his baby girl to see his heart break. And Jade had taken her up to Mel.

He glanced to his phone on the coffee table, which beeped with another incoming text. It was probably Lisa again. She'd texted him several times, wanting to talk to him about something important, but 'not work-related'. Whatever it was, it could wait. Mark simply hadn't got the heart. Doubted very much he could talk coherently now anyhow. He lifted his glass to take another swig of whisky, realised he was empty and walked across to the cupboard for a refill, grabbing the bottle and placing it on the table in much the same place as the vodka had been.

Sinking heavily back down on the sofa, the irony that he was doing exactly what he'd condemned Mel for – getting so drunk he couldn't function – wasn't lost on him. The fact was, though, he wanted not to function. He wanted oblivion, escape from the nightmares, both sleeping and waking.

He wanted to confront Cummings in some secluded place, knock his teeth so far down his throat he'd be shitting them for a week. But he couldn't, of course. If he left the house, he'd come back to find the locks changed. The claims Mel was making might have been based on something concocted in her feverish imagination, but it was all way too coincidental. Mark had no doubt that Cummings had taken photos, and that he'd always intended to use them in some way. But he'd been braced for something work-related. He hadn't realised how clever the twisted scumbag was, how low he would sink to destroy him.

What hurt most was that Mel was all too willing to believe it. Kerb-crawling? She clearly thought he was on a par with the sick fucker.

Reaching for another top up of the poison, and knowing it would only make everything look worse in the cold light of day, Mark paused, his hand seeking Hercules, lying faithfully at his feet. 'At least you don't think I'm a complete bastard, hey, girl?'

Mark stroked her velvety ears as she looked dolefully up at him. It could be worse, he supposed. His shirts hadn't parted company with their sleeves. Yet. Picking up the bottle, Mark laughed cynically, and then he began to weep.

CHAPTER SIXTY-TWO

JADE

He didn't hear her come in, unaware of her presence until she sat quietly down beside him. Mark immediately tried to compose himself, pulling himself upright and taking his hands away from his face. He didn't want her to see his weakness, as he thought of it; for her to realise he'd been quietly crying when he'd thought there was no one to hear him,

'It's all right,' said Jade, squeezing his hand gently. 'It's all right, Mark,' she repeated, her heart thrumming excitedly as she realised it was time to show him, to reassure him that it would be. 'We can get through this.'

Closing his eyes, his dark luxuriant eyelashes wet with tears, Mark nodded tightly. 'Can we?' he asked, his throat hoarse, his demeanour so very tired as he squeezed her hand back. But then eased himself away and got unsteadily to his feet.

'Of course,' Jade said, watching him walk across to the window. 'We have to think about the children and do what's best for Mel, but—'

'Which is?' Mark asked, drawing a hand tensely across the back of his neck.

Jade hesitated. *Put the needy bitch in the mental ward* wouldn't be quite the considered, sensitive response he was looking for. 'That has to be your decision, Mark,' she said instead, her tone hopefully indicating that she would understand, whatever decision he came to.

'I know,' he said, staring out of the window as she stood up and walked towards him. 'I'm not sure I can make it, though. The right one, I mean.'

Shrugging disconsolately, he heaved out a heavy sigh and dropped his gaze to the floor.

She wanted to tell him that there was only one decision he could make if he wanted to end the sheer purgatory his life had obviously been for far too long, but... it wouldn't be a decision a man with a conscience could make easily. Reaching a hand out instead, she trailed it lightly over his shoulders as she moved around in front of him.

'You have to think of the children,' she said carefully. 'I just want you to know, I'm here for you. Whatever you need.'

She smiled encouragingly as Mark looked at her. His eyes were slightly unfocused and full of such obvious torment that Jade felt her heart break for him. It was clear what he needed: someone to hold him, to take him to a place where he could abandon his inhibitions and forget all his anguish. He needed to lose himself, with her, inside her.

'Thanks, Jade.' Mark managed a smile back, albeit a smile tinged with sadness – not surprising, given the agony his wife was putting him through. 'I have no idea what I would do without you.' He reached out then, placing a hand softly on her forearm and causing every inch of Jade's skin to prickle with sweet anticipation.

Jade's hands trembled as she made him coffee – strong and black he'd said, when she'd insisted on making it for him. He could barely stand up straight, and his eyes were heavy with exhaustion. She was killing him. That bitch upstairs, she was slowly killing him. He wouldn't leave her, nor would he have her sectioned. He might realise there was no other choice eventually, but Jade was growing tired too. She'd waited too long for him to come back to her. For her sweet little angel to come back to her.

Waiting for the kettle to boil, Jade walked across to the island, where Mark's jogging top was still draped on one of the stools. Picking it up, she pressed it to her face, breathing in the smell of him, the masculine essence of him, suffused with the woody aftershave he wore. She wanted him. She would have him. She would have her baby.

He was fast asleep when she crept back downstairs to check on him, his coffee cold and untouched on the table. Standing over him, Jade's eyes travelled the length of his broad-shouldered physique, semi-naked and bathed in soft moonlight from the window. He cried out as she watched him, struggling with the dark demons that were haunting his dreams.

She would help him chase them away. It was safe to, now that he'd acknowledged his need for her. Jade could still feel the tingle of his fingers brushing her skin, sending shock waves the entire length of her body. It was time. She had to show him. His pain was her pain. She would soothe him with soft kisses, not empty promises. She would stand by him, be there for him, right by his side. A shoulder to cry on. A warm body to comfort him, to make love to. And yes, to take out his frustrations on, vent his emotions, if that was what he needed. She would love him as he needed to be loved.

Freshly showered, her body oiled and perfumed, Jade reached for the shirt she slept in, one of Mark's, and slid it over her shoulders, allowing it to fall softly to the floor.

Gently, she straddled him, careful not to wake him. Her heart ached for him, her pelvis yearned to feel him inside her. *Slowly,* she cautioned herself, through the warm mist in her head, the aura that was Mark in her soul. He would need encouragement initially, gentle persuasion to push aside any guilt he might feel. But it was time.

His eyelids fluttered as her hair brushed his cheek. His poor, bruised cheek. Jade's fingers strayed to his face, her lips following in their wake. A hair's breadth from his, she could almost taste his tongue searching for hers, probing deep into her mouth.

Slowly.

She registered a shift in his position, a stirring in his groin as she allowed herself the sweet taste of him, tracing the thin film of sweat at the base of his neck. Moving downwards, she paused to gently caress a nipple with her lips, the taut muscles of his stomach, his hips; finally reaching her prize. She felt him move as she took him into her mouth, heard him utter a throaty expletive as she worked on him expertly with her tongue.

'*Shit.*' She heard him groan again.

Jade increased her efforts, ignoring the question on his lips – 'Mel?' – and the sound of feet stumbling towards the bathroom overhead. Why was he whispering *her* name? Why wouldn't he let her go?

She couldn't ignore the hand he wove through her hair, the violent expletive that exploded from him as he yanked her sharply up.

'What the *fucking* hell are you *doing*?' Seizing her shoulders, his fingers digging hard into her flesh, Mark shoved her away and scrambled to his feet.

Shaken, Jade crossed her hands over her breasts, watching, stunned, as he hastily rearranged his tracksuit bottoms and reached for his top. 'I… I was lying with you. I—'

'*Why?*' Mark stared incredulously at her.

Seeing an unmistakeable flash of fury spark in his eyes, Jade shook her head, bewildered. 'Because… we're meant to be together. We… You *said*. You said you needed me. That you wouldn't know what to do without me. You promised. The first time you held me, you said you would always—'

'You need to go,' Mark interrupted, pulling his furious gaze away.

But he looked towards the stairs, Jade noticed, relief washing through her. He was worried about being caught. 'It's all right,' she whispered reassuringly, getting to her feet and moving towards him. 'I understand. It doesn't matter. We have the rest of our lives to—'

'*What?*' Mark turned back to her, his expression now one of astonishment.

'To be together,' Jade finished, her mouth going dry. 'To—'

'I don't want to be with you.' Mark was looking at her now as if she were something abhorrent. 'I want to be with my wife!'

No, he didn't. Jade stared at him, confounded. She'd felt his body stirring, his heart beating. He was confused, tired. The alcohol—

'I love my *wife*, Jade. I don't want anyone else. I never will.'

Liar! Anger rose like liquid bile in Jade's chest. 'You wanted *me*!' She pointed out this all too obvious fact. 'You wanted to make love to *me*. You can't deny *that.*'

'*Jesus.*' Mark shook his head, pressed his fingers hard against his temples. 'I was practically fucking unconscious!'

'But not too out of it to lie back and enjoy a free blow job!' Jade retorted, fury now burning like acid inside her.

Mark's studied her, his eyes darkening dangerously, and then he moved suddenly past her. Jade flinched. 'I thought you were Mel. It was Mel I wanted.'

Retrieving her shirt from the floor, he shoved it at her, barely looking at her as he did.

He's lying. Jade's heart stopped beating. *He's lying.*

Desperate to rescue the situation, she stepped closer. She'd got her timing wrong. Moved too fast. He was scared. 'It's all right,

Mark. I understand, really I do.' Arranging her face into a seductive smile, she reached to graze a hand across his cheek, and then leaned closer, attempting to press her lips against his.

Mark stopped her, roughly grabbing hold of her wrist. 'You're fucking *insane.* I want you out. Get your things and go.'

He *meant* it. Shocked, Jade searched his eyes. Eyes that were no longer kind and caring, but cruel, contemptuous and cold. Humiliation and hurt churned inside her. It wasn't her timing she'd got wrong, it was her estimation of *him*, a man she'd imagined to be strong, to be her saviour. But he wasn't strong. He was weak, weaker than his pathetic wife. A user, an abuser, just like all the others. The absolute *bastard.*

Swallowing back her rage, pushing it down to that deep, dark place where so much hurt already festered, she told herself to bide her time until she had more suitable opportunity to vent. 'It's the middle of the night,' she said, composing her features and looking tearfully back at him. Her nakedness, she was aware, would add to her obvious vulnerability. He wouldn't send her out now, a woman on her own in the dark.

Breathing hard, Mark appeared to debate with himself, and then picked up his mobile from the coffee table and selected a number.

Jade watched in disbelief as he spoke to the taxi firm.

'You have ten minutes,' he said, his gaze flicking back to hers as he ended the call. 'Get dressed.'

Jade felt her heart settle like a stone in her chest. 'What about my things?' she asked, notching her chin high.

'I'll send them on,' Mark said impassively.

Noting the unflinching look in his eyes, his utter indifference to her feelings, Jade nodded slowly. He'd shown himself in his true colours. They all did, eventually. So be it. He would live to regret this. She would make damn sure of it. Peeling her eyes away from him, she wrapped the shirt tightly about herself and turned to walk to the door.

She stopped as she realised he was actually *following* her. Clearly, he was going to make sure she left with nothing other than the clothes on her back. Without her baby. *Her baby*, who she'd loved and nurtured far more than his useless bitch of a wife ever had. She wouldn't abandon her, and DI Mark-bastard-Cain had badly underestimated her if he imagined she would. If he imagined for one second he wouldn't suffer for feeding her empty promises, keeping his options open and then callously abandoning her.

Hush, little baby, don't say a word. Jade hummed silently as she walked past the nursery ahead of him. *Daddy loves you, and so do I… Mummy will be back, my sweet Angel.*

CHAPTER SIXTY-THREE

MELISSA

Mel had debated whether to take her medication. She was feeling woozy, again, as she had every morning in what seemed liked forever, but she'd set the alarm and dragged herself out of bed, determined to get some control back over her life, her emotions, for the sake of the children. She would take the tablets, she'd decided, but later, once Poppy was at school. She would speak to the doctor again too. If she hadn't needed counselling before, she thought she might need it now, to help her through the break-up of her marriage.

Willing herself not to go there, not to think about any of it, for fear she might never stop falling, she was stepping into the shower when Mark came into the room. She reached hurriedly to close the door, wishing she could close the door so easily on her emotions, the memory that immediately sprang to her mind causing her stomach to clench painfully: the last time they'd made love. Right here, in the shower. Such meaningful love, she'd thought then. Mark being so gentle, so caring of her needs. She'd thought she'd known him, all of him, every inch, inside and out. But she hadn't. She hadn't known him at all. Mel lifted her face, allowing the cool water to wash the tears from her cheeks.

He was sitting on the bed when she came out, his hands hanging loosely between his knees, looking utterly dejected, so exhausted, Mel's heart would have bled for him, once.

'Where's Poppy?' she asked, noticing the empty space in the bed as she looked past him.

Mark looked at her, his expression one of tired despair. 'Playing in her room,' he said quietly.

Mel nodded, relieved, her gaze flicking to the cot, where Evie was still sleeping.

'I'm not going to take them, Mel.' Following her gaze, Mark sighed hopelessly. 'I just don't want to leave them.'

'With a mad woman?' Mel added facetiously.

'You're not mad, Mel.' Mark rubbed a hand tiredly over his eyes. 'You're depressed.'

'So I'm told. Don't worry, I'm taking the tablets,' Mel retorted, walking across to the dressing table to brush her hair and at least put some foundation on. She had no intention of walking around looking how she felt. Not any more.

'Did you want something?' she asked him. 'It's just that I need to get dressed.'

Mark obviously got the message that she'd no intention of getting dressed in front of him. But he didn't move. 'It's Jade,' he said after a second. 'She's gone.'

'Gone?' Confused, Mel turned to face him. 'Gone where?'

'To her friend's in London.' Mark looked up at her, his expression now uncomfortable. 'She, er, won't be coming back.'

Won't be… Mel stared at him, stunned for a second, and then her anger, her sheer bloody fury with this man she'd thought was her rock, unleashed. 'You know, I'm really not surprised,' she said, her voice loaded with contempt. 'Learning that the man she's working for, the respectable Detective Inspector Cain, is a serial-shagging bastard is enough to drive any vulnerable young woman away!'

'Oh, for *fu…*' Mark heaved himself to his feet. 'Can we not do this now, Mel?' he said, his voice tight with anger. 'The kids,' he added, glancing towards Evie.

Using the fact that she was prepared to argue in front of them against her? Mel looked him over, scarcely able to believe that this was the man she'd once trusted implicitly.

'I came to see if there was anything I could do to help.' Mark shrugged, pushing his hands in his pockets and dropping his gaze, clearly unable to meet hers.

Mel was about to tell him there was; he could collect his things and leave, when Poppy spoke timidly from the door. 'Daddy, are you still annoyed with me?'

CHAPTER SIXTY-FOUR

MARK

Mark snapped his gaze towards where Poppy stood on the landing, looking warily at him over her Bedtime Peppa clutched to her chin, and his heart sank to a whole new level. He looked questioningly at Mel, who looked as confused as he felt.

'Poppet,' he said, walking across to her and crouching down to her level, 'I'm not angry with you. Why do you think I would be?'

Poppy didn't answer, merely pushed her chin further into her soft toy, her huge uncertain eyes searching his – right down to his soul, it seemed to Mark.

'Poppy?'

'Are you going to send me to prison?' she asked, her brow knitted worriedly.

'To prison?' Mark laughed incredulously. 'Why on earth would I do that?'

'Because of the chocolate,' Poppy said, her voice barely a whisper, her eyes now welling with tears.

Was that all? Mark's laugh this time was one of sheer bloody relief.

'I don't want to go to prison, Daddy. It's dark and cold. And they don't let you take any toys, or play, or *anything*.' Poppy's voice quavered and her face crumpled, and Mark reached out for her.

'You don't go to prison for something like that, sweetheart.' He squeezed her tight; felt like crying with her. 'You shouldn't have done it, but I'm guessing you've already figured that out. I'm not angry with you.'

A sob shaking her small shoulders, Poppy didn't answer.

Mark reached to wipe the tears from her cheek with his thumb. 'I love you, Poppy,' he said firmly. 'More than all the stars and all the fish in the sea. Got that? I will never stop loving you, no matter what.'

Poppy flung herself at him, almost knocking Mark backwards. 'I love you bigger than a whole whale,' she snuffled into his neck, locking her arms firmly around him.

'That's a lot.' Mark hugged her hard. 'Come on, sweetpops. Let's go and get you ready for school.'

Taking her small hand in his as he got to his feet, he turned to Mel. 'Shall I drive her there?' he asked hopefully.

CHAPTER SIXTY-FIVE

JADE

It was enough to melt hearts, it really was. Under cover of the trees on the opposite side of the lane, Jade watched Poppy skipping happily to the car alongside her precious daddy, her Bedtime Peppa clutched to her chest. Obviously he'd won her over with his false kindness and oh-so-caring persona. *Lies.* Little did his precious little Poppet know it, but he would hurt her too, abuse her, *lie* to her, just as he had Jade.

Naively, her body not yet grown, her emotions so vulnerable, Jade had forgiven him for abandoning her that first time, despite the initial doubt that had niggled inside her. She'd dismissed it. Made excuses for him, as women did for the despicable, abusive men in their lives. And she'd waited for him. Remade herself for him. Offered herself to him on a plate, and he'd rejected her. The bastard, as if he hadn't enjoyed her going down on him. As if he wouldn't have taken full advantage of what was on offer and fucked her senseless if needy Melissa hadn't stumbled to the bathroom overhead. He was a user. An abuser of the worst kind. Jade's humiliation simmered furiously inside her. It was time Mark Cain realised the grave consequences of using his position to exploit vulnerable young women.

He thought he could just walk away from it. Get away with leading her on and then crushing her under his feet, all the while hiding his deviant nature behind his family, his career, his respectability. He had no idea what the word respect meant. Now it was time to strip away his veneer and show the world what a deceitful, manipulative excuse for a man he was. The public weren't safe with him. His children weren't safe with him. *Her* baby wasn't safe – vulnerable to his twisted whimsies, his wife's mental instability. It was time to redress the balance, turn the tables. To have Mark Cain disgraced and removed to a place where he'd have a lifetime to ponder all that *he'd* lost. It was time to take back what he'd stolen, to ruin him as surely as he'd ruined her.

She sneered as she watched Poppy the spoiled brat chatting to her podgy-faced little pig, her fingers intertwined with her father's.

Time to put away childish things, my lovely.

Mark would never hold his daughter's hand again.

CHAPTER SIXTY-SIX

MARK

Coming back from a jog, which he'd hoped would clear his mind, Mark was turning into his lane when his heart slammed into his ribcage. *What the...?* His gut twisting violently inside him, he didn't hesitate, sprinting towards the house.

'Sorry, sir, I can't allow you through access.' A uniform barred his way as he approached the sea of blue lights. 'There's been an incident. We need to cordon off—'

'Fuck off, this is my house,' Mark shouted, attempting to push his way past the man.

The guy pushed back hard, sending Mark staggering.

'Let him through! It's DI Cain!' Lisa shouted, emerging from his front door. Mark righted himself, his head reeling, blind panic almost choking him.

'Who?' The uniform glanced confusedly back at her.

'Mark Cain!' Lisa bellowed. 'The baby's father! Let him through.'

Evie? No! Feeling something break inside him, Mark scrambled past the officer. His baby. *Christ, please not his baby.*

'Sorry, Mark, he's the new probationer,' Lisa said, looking him over apprehensively as she ran to meet him on the drive.

Mark nodded tightly. 'What's happening?' he asked, his tone short as he desperately tried to keep a rein on his spiralling emotions.

'I'm sorry, Mark... It's Evie. She's been taken.'

Lisa moved quickly forwards as his legs almost failed him. 'Take your time,' she said sympathetically, moving to wrap an arm firmly around him as Mark bent, clutching his thighs and attempting to draw air into his lungs.

Nodding again, Mark straightened up. 'When?' he asked, barely able to get the word past the hard knot in his throat.

'Ten fifteen, give or take a minute,' Lisa said, her tone quiet and measured – a hopeless attempt to reassure him.

Mark reeled inwardly. He'd forgotten to take his mobile with him. He'd been five minutes into his run when he realised, and had debated going back for it, but had decided against it. He'd been out, running, without his mobile while his child was being abducted.

'Melissa fastened Evie into her seat and then went back inside to pick up a box,' Lisa explained.

'A box?'

'A sculpture. She was taking it to the university to be fired,' Lisa clarified, as Mark frantically tried to make sense where there was none. 'She'd left the boot open, so the car was unlocked. When she came back…' Lisa stopped, her voice catching.

Their child had gone. Nausea churning his stomach, Mark closed his eyes, feeling every one of Mel's emotions, every second of the agony she would have gone through. 'Witnesses?' he asked gutturally.

Lisa shook her head. Mark guessed there wouldn't be. The lane wasn't a useful through road to anywhere, providing access only to the local farm and a few houses.

Mark half-turned away, no clue what to do at a crime scene that involved his own family.

'We've been trying to locate Jade.' Lisa cut through his deliberations. 'I asked Mel, but she's not making much sense. Any ideas?'

'Jade,' Mark repeated, cold foreboding washing through him. Could she…? *Would she?* 'She's gone.'

'Gone?'

'Fired,' Mark said tersely. 'Find her.'

'I'm on it,' Lisa assured him. 'Do you have any details? Previous employers, addresses? Relatives we can start with?'

Mark's heart nosedived into the pit of his stomach.

'You did run a background check, right?'

Hopelessly, Mark shook his head. 'Mel said she would. I... didn't push it.'

Lisa drew in a sharp breath, but didn't comment. 'I'll get everyone I can on it,' she said. 'Don't worry, Mark. We'll find Evie.'

Cursing his idiocy, his sheer bloody incompetence at not running the check himself, Mark nodded. 'Where's Mel?' he asked, attempting some sort of focus as he glanced towards the house, their dream home, which had become a house of horrors. Mel would be broken, utterly destroyed.

'Lounge. Distraught, obviously,' Lisa said, and then hesitated. 'She thought you'd taken her, Mark. I thought you should know.'

The news didn't surprise him. It hurt, but it didn't surprise him.

'I've telephoned the health centre and asked her GP to come out.' Aware of Mel's resistance to visit the surgery, Lisa's tone was guarded. 'I thought, under the circumstances...'

Mark nodded. He didn't like the idea, but sedation was probably the only way Mel would get through the first few hours. After that... nothing would help her, nothing but her child safe in her arms would pull her back from the abyss. Mark knew that with certainty.

'We've called in forensics,' Lisa called, behind him. 'And obviously Edwards has all available bodies on it.'

Mark nodded again, grateful for that much. He needed to be at the station, on top of this, but not before he'd seen Mel, tried to reassure her, though he doubted he could.

'Poppy?' He turned back to Lisa, a new fear twisting his stomach.

'We've despatched a squad car to the school. I'll let you know as soon as— Hold on.' Stopping, Lisa checked her radio. 'She's safe.'
And Mark allowed himself to breathe.

CHAPTER SIXTY-SEVEN

LISA

Her heart breaking for them, Lisa paused between calls, watching as Mark walked across to where Melissa stood by the window, her arms wrapped tightly about herself, as if trying to keep the emotion inside. She didn't seem to be aware of Mark's presence, jumping as he reached out to touch her.

'I'll find her, Mel,' he said quietly. Cautiously, he moved closer, gently coaxing her around to face him. 'I will find her, I promise,' he repeated, his voice thick with emotion.

Poor bastard, he looked worse than Lisa had ever seen him. Even after losing little Jacob, when he'd been struggling on all fronts, drinking too much, sleeping little, he hadn't looked so utterly drained.

Clearly as exhausted as he was, Melissa allowed him to pull her closer. Lisa hoped to God they could find some comfort in each other. They didn't deserve this on top of everything else. Relieved as she saw Mel drop her head to Mark's shoulder, Lisa was about to discreetly leave when Melissa spoke.

'Why?' she asked sharply, pulling away from him. '*Why*, Mark?'

Lisa's heart sank as Melissa glared up at Mark, her expression a toxic mix of raw pain and pure anger.

'*Why* did you trash everything?' Melissa demanded. 'Throw your family away? Try to drive me half out of my mind? You *bastard*!'

Shaken, Mark struggled to answer. 'Mel, don't,' he tried, attempting to close the space between them.

'I can't do this. I *can't*. I want her back! I want my *baby*!' Backing away from him, Melissa screamed it.

'Mel, please…' Desperation in his voice, Mark stepped back towards her. 'Please, don't—'

'No!' Melissa lashed out, landing a blow to Mark's arm. 'I want her back! Do you *hear* me?' She hit him again, the flat of her hand curling into a fist, thumping into his chest. 'Where *is* she?'

Mark didn't defend himself or attempt to stop her; he just waited until her blows became useless, ineffectual flails, and then, gently, he caught hold of her wrists. Still, he didn't speak. Silently, he pulled her close and lowered his forehead to hers. 'I'll find her,' he said hoarsely.

Guessing now was a good time to leave them alone, Lisa turned for the hall, pondering the whereabouts of Jade as she went. She couldn't believe Mark hadn't pushed Mel regarding the background check. If only he'd answered her texts. But then, he had been preoccupied, she supposed. And the 'perfect' babysitter had soon installed herself in their lives and made herself indispensable. It might be nothing to do with her, of course. She might be the angel sent from heaven that Mel had seemed to think she was. In which case, Lisa would be extremely interested to find out why she'd been fired. She'd ask Mark as soon as she could. At the station would probably be best. He would undoubtedly want to be hands-on with this, the alternative being to go slowly insane.

CHAPTER SIXTY-EIGHT

JADE

'Jade?' Cummings sounded surprised when he answered the phone. 'What's happening, babe? Where are you?' He sounded caring – as if he gave a damn in reality. The man was a chauvinistic Neanderthal of the worst kind, to whom women existed only to satiate his perverted appetites. He hadn't needed much persuading to play games in the bedroom, throwing himself into his role with gusto. Oh, how Jade would have enjoyed bringing this sadistic little prick down. Her plans regarding the delightful Cummings, however, had changed.

'Babe? Talk to me,' he urged her, an impatient edge to his voice now. 'You need to let me know where you are. You know we have people out looking for you?'

'Looking for me… Why?' Jade made sure to sound puzzled.

'Cain's kid.' Cummings hesitated, as if he might be having an actual thought about anyone but himself. 'She's gone missing. You need to come in and—'

'*Poppy?*' Jade cut over him, alarmed. 'Missing?'

'Not Poppy. The baby,' Cummings went on. 'We need to know what time you last saw her. Whether you saw anyone prowling—'

'*Evie?* Oh God, no.' Jade squeezed her eyes closed, getting into the role as she emitted a heartfelt sob. 'When? *How?*'

'This morning,' Cummings supplied. 'We need to know what time you last saw her. Whether she was—'

'I haven't. I didn't,' Jade cut in quickly. 'Not this morning. I… left. Suddenly,' she said cautiously, as if not quite sure how much to disclose. 'Last night. I had to get out. I didn't want to leave the children, but I was scared and I didn't know what else to do, and—'

'Whoa – scared? Why?'

Jade gulped back a huge breath and sniffled for effect. 'They had a row,' she continued, after a second. 'A dreadful argument.'

'About?'

'I'm not sure. What started it, I mean, but I think…' Again, Jade paused, not wanting to appear keen to divulge.

'It's okay, Jade. Take your time,' Cummings said, attempting to be sympathetic. 'You know you can confide in me.'

Jade rolled her eyes at that. Yes, right. *Hurry up and dish the dirt, you silly bitch,* was more likely what he was thinking, desperate as he was to get something on Mark.

'Melissa,' Jade went on falteringly, 'I think she had an affair. Mark… He'd been drinking, heavily. He was shouting. Really angry. I was upstairs, with the children. I couldn't help but overhear.'

'Overhear what, sweetheart?'

'He was calling her names, awful names. He…' Jade paused for another timely sniffle. 'He thinks the children might not even be his.'

'*Bloody hell!*' Cummings gasped, astonished. 'Well, well, that explains a lot. Poor bastard,' he commiserated – and then chuckled. Clearly, he was highly amused.

Excuse me, distraught victim of crime on the line here, Jade thought, disgusted.

'He turned on me,' said Jade, cutting his merriment short. 'When I came downstairs. Melissa had gone out. I'm not sure where, and he… He turned into an absolute *monster*. I tried to run, to fight him off but he's so much heavier than me. I… I didn't have any choice, Pete. Honestly, I didn't. He…'

Jade trailed off, waited, and sure enough…

'Are you telling me he *raped* you?' Cummings asked, his tone a mixture of utter disbelief, outrage… and excitement. Definitely excitement. He would be orgasmic, Jade had no doubt, revelling at the prospect of using the information to destroy Mark Cain.

Result, she thought. Then, '*Yes*,' she cried, emitting a wretched sob.

'You need to come in,' Cummings said brusquely. 'I'll come and fetch you.'

'No, I'm… with a girlfriend. I'll come to the station.'

'As soon as possible,' Cummings instructed. 'We can't let the bastard get away with this. Don't wash away any evidence, babe,' he said, tempering his tone to something near concern. 'And keep this between you and me for now, will you? I don't want him getting wind we're onto him before we can bring him in. Okay?'

'Uh-huh,' Jade said timidly.

Perfect, she thought, ending the call and turning her attention to the police exiting Mark's property.

The timing would be crucial. She had to get Melissa alone. Which she soon would, it seemed. Jade smiled as one of the officers turned at the squad car to ask Melissa whether she was sure she would be all right on her own, informing her that the family liaison officer would be with her soon.

Jade waited as the squad car drove off and then, checking the road was clear, took a step towards the house, cursing as her phone vibrated. It was Dylan calling, again.

'*What?*' Jade hissed, moving back under cover of the trees.

'What do I do if she wakes up?' Dylan asked. 'Her little cheeks are still all flushed. I'm worried she might start crying again and I—'

'For God's sake, Dylan, she won't wake up. I've given her some Calpol,' Jade snapped. She was anxious to get back into the house while there was a lull in police activity. With Dylan fussing and clucking about like a mother hen, thinking Angel looked a bit peaky, she'd miss her opportunity. He'd even suggested he take her out in her stroller for some fresh air. *Moron.* Jade had paid cash for the room, but the last thing she wanted drippy Dylan doing was perambulating about the Travelodge car park, which would be bound to draw attention. 'I'll be back soon, my love,' she assured him, softening her tone.

Once she'd filled Melissa in about her deceitful bastard of a husband, that was. Which she would need to do soon, before Mark gave anyone his version of events. Clearly, knowing he'd be dropping himself in it if he confessed why he'd thrown her out like so much rubbish, he'd decided to keep that information to himself.

She had to get to Melissa now. There was no other time. Having carelessly endangered her child while she pissed about with her stupid clay statues, Melissa would be teetering dangerously near to the edge. Her grip on reality would be fragile, and she would be susceptible, ready to believe her husband capable of anything. And once she'd seen the indisputable evidence of his perverted sexual preferences, then the weak, self-obsessed woman would fall, and so would Mark Cain.

Letting herself quietly in through the back door, Jade found the kitchen was empty. Poor Melissa must be having a little lie down, she deduced. And no wonder, if she'd popped a few of these little beauties. Seeing the sedatives, Zopiclone, at the back of one of the work surfaces, Jade hummed contentedly and turned for the hall.

Mark's laptop was there. *Oh, deary me.* He really was careless. Though it was only his personal PC, one really would think that, as a policeman, he might have it better protected. Quickly plugging in her phone, she uploaded the desired photo to his desktop. Most of the pictures she'd taken were innocent enough, but the one of him in Poppy's bedroom, the dreadful day her poor little goldfish had died, that could easily be wildly misinterpreted. Mark half naked, removing Poppy's nightie? That would certainly look suspect, particularly in combination with a few of the more risqué sites she quickly saved to his bookmarks – definitely extreme, most definitely illegal, and enough to have Melissa and his colleagues reeling with shock.

Job done, Jade replaced the laptop in its usual position and turned for the stairs, humming silently as she went. *Hush, little baby…*

Hearing a sound from the nursery, she guessed that's where she'd find Melissa, no doubt regretting having neglected her baby. Jade was heading that way when Poppy's door squeaked open and the girl peered out to stare at her like a startled sparrow.

Smiling languidly, Jade pressed her finger to her lips, which was enough to have the brat backing back in and closing the door in a flash. Presumably the dog was in there with her. And it had better stay in there too, or the next noise it emitted in Jade's presence would be a gurgle.

In the nursery, Melissa was standing with her arms wrapped about her in the protective stance she'd adopted since her perfect little world had started falling apart. Rolling her eyes at the woman's complete inability to do anything other than feel sorry for herself, Jade tapped lightly on the door. 'Mel?' she said, her voice loaded with fake concern.

CHAPTER SIXTY-NINE

MELISSA

It took a second for Melissa to register the voice behind her. When it did permeate the thick fog in her head, she wondered whether she was imagining it. She'd imagined she could hear Evie crying in here every time she lay back on her bed.

'Mel? Are you okay?'

Jade? But hadn't Mark said she'd left? Mel could only assume because her situation here had become intolerable.

'I'm so sorry, Mel,' Jade said, tears streaming down her face. 'If I'd been here… If I hadn't run off like that… Oh God, I'm so sorry. I didn't know what else to do. I should have stayed. I—'

Jade gulped back a wretched sob, and despite her own pain, which if God was merciful would surely kill her, Mel felt for her. Jade wasn't to blame. If anyone was, she was – though, in truth, she blamed Mark.

'It's not your fault, Jade. They'll find her.' Even as she said it, the hopelessness, the tidal wave of grief she'd felt since Evie had gone, washed through her afresh, leaving her weak and empty in its wake.

Her sobs stilling to a shudder, Jade nodded. 'I had to come back. I have to tell you something, Mel,' she said, her innocent blue eyes – child's eyes, almost – clouded with confusion and worry. 'I wasn't sure whether to say, but I think you need to know.'

'Know what?' Noting the nervousness now in Jade's eyes, Mel felt an immediate sense of uneasiness.

'I… need to show you,' Jade said hesitantly.

'Show me?'

'Mark's laptop,' Jade said uncomfortably. 'I needed to do some online banking so I borrowed it and… I should have asked him, but…'

His laptop? Icy trepidation running the length of her spine, Mel was already halfway out of the door, heading for the hall, where she knew Mark always left it.

Staring in disbelief at the screen, Melissa felt repulsion flood every pore in her body. It couldn't be true. *It couldn't!* Yet it was there, right in front of her eyes: every sordid detail, every vile pornographic image.

Dear God, not children.

Nausea gripping her stomach, Melissa dragged her horrified gaze away from the graphic images, which would be forever imprinted on her mind, and ran to the downstairs toilet, where she retched the dry contents of her stomach until her insides were raw.

Poppy? Why was that photo on his desktop? *Only* that photo? He wouldn't. *He wouldn't!* Melissa snatched at the toilet roll, pressed a wad to her mouth, trying to stop the violent trembling that shook her entire body.

'Melissa?' Standing behind her, Jade barely whispered it. 'Here,' she said, two small pills in her outstretched hand. 'Take these. Dr Meadows left them, remember? They'll help with the anxiety.'

'*Anxiety?*' Melissa laughed – a laugh bordering on hysteria. It was going to take more than two pills, she thought, desperately trying to quell the nausea as she reached for them, swallowed them quickly down and headed back to the kitchen.

'I've warmed you some milk,' Jade said. 'It'll help line your stomach,' she added, offering her the mug cautiously, as if Melissa might throw it at the nearest wall. She wanted to. She wanted to tear the whole house apart, brick by brick, and everything in it. Erase the nightmare. Dear God, she wished she could erase it.

Melissa took the mug, swilling the contents back for Jade's sake as she sat down and braced herself to browse the rest of Mark's internet history.

Flicking through his bookmarks, her stomach clenched as she realised there were many such sites. Then she turned her attention to his emails. It didn't take long to find a folder marked 'x-receipts', making it the last folder listed in his favourites. Mel's insides turned over afresh as she realised what kind of online purchases he'd made. He couldn't have. Surely to God… She *knew* him. Or she thought she had.

'There's something else, Melissa,' Jade said tentatively as, trying to still the palpitations in her chest, the dizziness in her head, Mel closed the laptop.

What? What else *could* there be? Melissa looked questioningly up to where Jade was standing opposite her, fiddling nervously with her hair.

'The reason I left.' Looking tearful again, Jade went reluctantly on.

She looked more than upset, Mel thought, studying her face. She looked fearful. *Ashamed?* 'Jade?' Her heart thudding painfully now, Melissa urged her on. 'Tell me.'

'He'd been drinking a lot,' Jade said quickly. 'Because of the problems between you, I think.'

Was she defending him? Against what? What had he done?

'I didn't know what to do.' Jade looked beseechingly at her. 'He came to my room. I wasn't sure why. I thought it was to do with the children. I tried to get him to leave. I begged him to, but…' Jade stopped, her face flushing as she glanced quickly down. 'He's much stronger than I am.'

'No.' Melissa reeled. She felt the room shift around her.

'I tried to fight him off, I swear. I should have said something, I know I should, but you were going through so much. I thought it would be better if I just left. I wish I hadn't. I wish…' Swallowing, Jade dropped her gaze back to the floor. 'Evie might still be here, if only I'd said something.'

Melissa stared at her, shocked to the core. She'd loved him. With her whole heart, she'd loved a man who was a complete monster.

'You think he's taken her, don't you?'

'I honestly don't know,' said Jade. 'If he has, I'm sure he won't hurt her, but…'

Pausing pointedly, she glanced at the laptop and then back to Mel. 'Knowing what you know now about his… activities, I really think you should tell the police. For Evie's sake.'

CHAPTER SEVENTY

MARK

Mark had been going door to door with officers, targeting sex offenders and investigating any known links to child trafficking for sexual exploitation or the babies-for-sale trade. They were also visiting parents who'd recently lost babies, in particular bereaved mothers without a support network who might be prone to depression.

As if any parent wouldn't be. Mark had empathised completely as some of them had relived their experiences, his mind playing over memories of his own son, outwardly perfect while his small lungs had struggled to draw their last breath. His tiny white coffin. He'd had to excuse himself as one mother had recounted how she'd nursed her seven-month-old baby in her arms until God had taken her for an angel. Leaving the woman in the care of a female police officer, Mark had sought the sanctuary of his car, where he'd sat with his head on the steering wheel, his heart bleeding steadily inside him.

Glancing around the woodland adjoining the local beauty spot, every square foot of which could conceal a small body, Mark felt a sinking sense of hopelessness. He'd trodden this route looking for Daisy. He'd never imagined he'd be walking it again in search of his own missing child.

Clamping down on his thoughts before his mind wandered too far, Mark reached into his pocket for his ringing mobile.

'Mark, I managed to get hold of Jade on her mobile, finally,' Lisa said, when he picked up the call. 'She's going to come in and give a statement, but I thought you should know her alibi checks out. We have her on the bank's security cameras at the time she says she was there.'

'Ten fifteen.' Mark sighed. Given her unceremonious departure from the house, he'd thought… But he'd been wrong. He wasn't relieved at the news, however. Jade had definitely formed an attachment to Evie, but if she had taken her for whatever reason, Mark had doubted she would hurt her in any way. 'Okay, Lisa, thanks. I'm on my way to see Mel. I'll be back at the station as soon as I can.'

'See you later,' Lisa said. 'Oh, and Mark, about Jade… I couldn't get much sense out of Mel, for obvious reasons, but why did you say she'd left exactly? It's just, it was a bit sudden, wasn't it?'

'Very,' Mark said, and sucked in a breath. He had to give some kind of explanation, but what? *She took advantage of me while I was drunk* would sound pretty lame. And unbelievable. Mark was well aware of that. 'I haven't said anything to Mel yet, but…' He faltered, feeling acutely embarrassed. 'She, er, came on to me. Heavily.'

Lisa was quiet for a moment. 'And you're surprised?'

Not surprised; shocked. And angry, bewildered and humiliated. Ashamed. He wondered whether he'd been responsible, whether he'd led her on in some way. All of the things he'd told victims of sexual crime they shouldn't be feeling, and none of which he wanted to become general knowledge. Cummings would have a field day.

'A bit,' he said instead, glancing up curiously as two officers approached him. 'Looks like I'm needed. I'll catch you at the station, Lisa.'

'DI Cain.' One of the officers looked at him apologetically as Mark ended his call. 'We have instructions to accompany you to the station.'

Accompany him? 'Why?' Mark asked, his stomach tightening as he braced himself for news of Evie.

'DCI wants to have a little chat,' the other guy said, his tone arrogant.

So it wasn't about Evie. Mark felt himself go weak with relief. He looked the guy over, deciding to seek him out later regarding his attitude. Right now, he hadn't got the time or the inclination. 'What about then?' he asked.

Shooting his colleague a disparaging look, the first officer spoke. 'I'm afraid I can't say, sir. We've just been asked to make sure you get there.'

'Sorry, it will have to wait,' Mark said, reaching for his car door. 'I'm going home to see my wife.'

'It's not a request, sir,' the officer responded, his expression hardening as he moved to prevent him opening the door.

Mark looked at him, thunderstruck, and then turned to the second officer, who'd walked around to position himself on his other side. 'We've been told to escort you,' the man said dispassionately. 'We also need to take possession of your phone.'

'*What?*' Mark laughed incredulously. 'You have to be kidding?'

'Never been more serious in my life. *Sir,*' the second officer assured him, his tone now definitely disrespectful.

The officers disclosing nothing on the drive in, other than to tell him there were no developments regarding Evie, Mark still had no idea what was happening. He had a distinct feeling, however, that his colleagues did, as the two men insisted on escorting him right to the DCI's office door. The silence as he was walked through the main office was so profound you could have heard a paperclip drop. The scornful glances didn't do much to alleviate Mark's uneasiness, and the contemptuous sneer he registered on Cummings' face caused his step to falter. It was Lisa's expression, though, one of palpable shock, that stopped him in his tracks.

'Lisa?' he said, his apprehension growing tenfold.

Cummings got to his feet. He didn't speak, didn't utter a word, simply moved to stand by Lisa's side.

Lisa glanced at Cummings, back to Mark, and then looked embarrassedly away.

'Sir.' One of the officers urged him on, taking hold of his arm.

'I know what I'd do with paedo pervs in our own ranks,' someone muttered, as Mark walked on. 'Castrate the bastards and make an example.'

'What the *fuck* is going on?' Mark demanded, as Edwards swung his door open.

'Sit down,' Edwards said shortly, banging the door shut and marching past him to his desk.

Mark stayed put. 'Look, I have no idea what the hell this is all about, but—'

'That's an order, DI Cain. Sit!' Edwards eyed him furiously. 'Now!'

Mark tried to temper his own fury. 'My daughter's missing,' he said, walking reluctantly across to the chair. 'Whatever this is, can't it wait?'

'No, Cain, it can't *wait*,' Edwards assured him, glaring at him until he sat.

Edwards stayed standing, still staring unnervingly at him. 'Now then,' he said, finally, 'would you like to tell me what the hell this shit is all about?'

Mark's first reaction was revulsion as Edwards twirled the laptop on his desk to face him.

His second, overwhelming panic as he realised the laptop was his.

CHAPTER SEVENTY-ONE

JADE

Melissa was taking longer to succumb than Jade had anticipated. She eyed her suspiciously as she blundered up the stairs ahead of her, having dutifully taken her regular meds washed down with a cup of strong, extremely sweet tea. Had she thrown up again when she'd gone to the loo? She really was an irritating cow. Mark was welcome to her. Except, he wouldn't have her ever again, apart from in his pathetic little fantasies.

'I need to go to Poppy,' Melissa said, making her way clumsily along the landing. 'I need to talk to her.'

Talk to her? Jade rolled her eyes sky high. The woman was barely coherent.

'Whoops.' Her mouth curving into a smile, Jade caught Melissa as she appeared to lose the use of her legs and reeled sideways into the wall. 'I've got you,' she said, easing her up and steering her in the direction of her bedroom.

'Poppy,' the woman mumbled, dragging her feet, to Jade's immense annoyance.

'You've had a terrible shock, Mel,' she said caringly. 'You really should lie down. Come on. Let's get you on the bed and I'll fetch Poppy. She can snuggle up with you while I make you both something to eat. How does that sound?'

Mel nodded, pressing her hand to her forehead as she stumbled onwards, her brow furrowed and her expression pained, as if her perfect little world had disintegrated. She was probably contemplating how to end it all. As if she need worry her pretty little rusty-haired head about that with her babysitter here, ready to take care of everything.

Jade was debating whether to bring Poppy in or lock her away when Melissa babbled something about tiny toes and plaster casts, and weaved towards her bed.

Jade watched her go, perplexed. *Bonkers*, she thought, shaking her head. Complete basket case. She really had no idea what Mark had ever seen in her.

The hair was quite pretty, she supposed, looking closely at it as she helped needy Melissa lie back on the pillow. Wavy and lustrous, the copper suited her better. Why she'd ever sought to emulate her by dyeing it blonde, Jade couldn't fathom.

Still, she couldn't blame her for trying.

Turning to the door, having decided to fetch the brat, Jade fluffed up her own hair in the mirror, pouted her full lips and admired her breasts. Mark Cain had missed out big time. She'd have taken him to heights of ecstasy he couldn't imagine in his wildest fantasies.

His loss.

His very great loss indeed.

She was halfway along the landing to Poppy's room when her phone rang. Dylan, again. Jade tutted tetchily, accepted the call, and answered in her sweetest tones.

'It's on the news,' Dylan squeaked in her ear.

Jade stifled her agitation. 'It doesn't matter, Dylan,' she said patiently. 'He'll be in custody by now.' Reviled by his colleagues. Spat on, probably. Jade got immense satisfaction from that. 'They won't believe another word he says.'

'But they're looking for her.' Dylan sounded panicked.

'Not for long,' Jade said, less patiently.

'But what if they believe him? He's a policeman, ain't he? One of their own.' Dylan was talking fast, thinking in clichés. 'And he is their father. What if they come—'

'They won't!' Jade snapped, gritting her teeth hard. God, she was so sick of mollycoddling him. She should have fed him to Inky and bloody Oinky. Though it would probably take them a month to chomp through the useless great wimp.

'They won't, Dylan,' she said, more kindly, when she realised he'd gone quiet. 'The CCTV footage and speeding fine *you* clocked up will see to that.' Emphasising the 'you', Jade thought it better to leave out the one or two other sordid activities the disgraced detective inspector would be charged with.

'CCTV?' Dylan whispered, aghast.

'They do have cameras in red-light districts, Dylan,' Jade pointed out. 'But don't worry, you're the same colouring and height as him. And if anyone should ask, not that they will, I'll vouch for you, obviously.'

'Will you?' Dylan asked, sounding like an uncertain child.

'Of course, my love. I couldn't have done any of this without you. We'll be free soon. Together forever. But you have to keep your head and do everything I tell you.'

'I will. I am,' Dylan replied defensively. 'It's just…'

'Just what?' Jade felt a prickle of apprehension.

Dylan went quiet again. Jade contemplated garrotting him. 'Daisy,' he blurted out. 'I'm worried about her. She—'

'Oh, she's fine,' Jade assured him airily. 'We'll all be together soon.' She glossed over that inconsequential problem in favour of changing the subject. 'How's Angel?'

'Still sleeping,' Dylan said. Jade could hear the bed squeaking under his huge bulk, which meant he was checking on her. 'She looks pale though,' he added worriedly. 'I think she needs a bit of fresh air. Me mum always said a bit of fresh air would put the colour back in my cheeks.'

'Dylan…' Jade tried very hard not to scream.

'I could take her to my house as well, if you like. It wouldn't matter if she cried there, and—'

'Dylan! No!' Jade stopped him in his excited flow, and then sighed inwardly as Poppy's bedroom door squeaked open. She scowled at the child, who was peering at her through the crack in the door with one eye. It was like something from a horror movie, it really was. 'I have to go. If she wakes up, just give her more Calpol,' she said to Dylan, and rang off.

Poppy backed away as Jade advanced towards the door, as if she were some kind of evil witch.

Irked, Jade thrust the door open and marched in. The room was an absolute pigsty, as usual, spoiled little brat. 'Your mother wants you in the bedroom.' She gestured her that way. 'And behave.' She glowered at the girl as she skirted around her, her silly Peppa Pig clutched babyishly to her chest. 'Or I'll eat your fucking goldfish.'

CHAPTER SEVENTY-TWO

MARK

'For Christ's sake, they're websites!' Sweat prickling his forehead and saturating his shirt, Mark dragged his hands exasperatedly over his face and got to his feet. 'Anyone could have accessed them!' He looked desperately from Edwards, seated at his desk, his expression impassive, to Cummings, who'd laughably been drafted in to question him.

'Right.' Folding his arms, Cummings exchanged meaningful glances with Edwards. 'And the image of your daughter? Someone *accessed* your computer to post that too, I suppose.'

Attempting to control his temper, Mark clamped his jaw tight. He could already hear the cell door clanging shut behind him. 'That was *not* taken by me!' he said, his patience fast evaporating. Could they not see the fucking obvious here? That, if he hadn't taken it, then someone else had. Someone who had access to his family and his home computer. Someone who undoubtedly now *had* his daughter. What the *hell* was the matter with them?

'Yeah, you said.' Shaking his head, Cummings looked him over scathingly. 'So, leaving the Category A pornographic images of kids aside for the moment, since we're clearly not getting the right answers, perhaps you could explain this?' He picked up a piece of paper and dangled it in Mark's direction. 'And, just so you know, "it wasn't me" won't cut it.'

Mark noted the colour of the form, green. 'A speeding fine?'

'Correct.' Cummings smiled superciliously. 'Clocked up at two in the morning' – he paused, smirking as he held Mark's gaze – 'in the heart of the red-light district. So much for the father of the year award, hey, Cain. Play classical music while you're doing the business, do you?'

Mark stared incredulously at him. 'No way,' he said vehemently, his heart rate spiking as he realised he was being set up from all angles. 'I haven't been anywhere near there – on or off duty.'

'We have photographic evidence, DI Cain,' said Edwards, still watching him in that supposedly non-judgemental way he had. But the pen he was tapping rapidly on his desk and the fact that he was addressing him formally told Mark he was being judged – and found guilty. Of *this*. 'CCTV images,' Edwards went on, now eyeing him steadily, as he leaned back in his chair.

He waited.

Mark kneaded his forehead. He didn't answer. How could he, other than to say *It wasn't me?*

'We also have a photograph which shows you apparently assaulting a sex worker,' Edwards added, laying the pen down on his desk, as if demonstrating that he'd considered the facts and found him guilty. 'Do you have an explanation for that?'

Tanya Stevens. Mark fixed his gaze hard on Cummings. 'Provided by?' he asked, bile rising in his throat.

'A fellow officer who felt obliged to draw my attention to it.'

'I bet he did.' Laughing disdainfully, Mark dragged his gaze away. 'It was a different time, a different place.'

'To the one you weren't in,' Cummings added drolly.

Mark looked contemptuously back at him. 'You bastard,' he seethed, fury burning impotently inside him.

Cummings nodded, almost imperceptibly, a smirk playing at the corner of his mouth as he turned to perch himself on the edge of Edwards' desk. 'Bit of a shitty thing to do, wasn't it, DI Cain, using your wife's car to fuck prostitutes? Get off on it, do you?'

His wife's? Mark was confused, for a split second. She'd had access to that too. Access to their lives and everything in it. Free access to Mel and Poppy, while he was being detained for Christ knew how long. 'I have to get out of here,' he said, his stomach knotting painfully. 'I need to leave.'

'You should know we've called in a forensic specialist to examine the car, DI Cain,' Edwards said dispassionately.

'A *forensic*?' Mark was astounded. 'Looking for what?' he asked, his panic escalating.

Edwards didn't answer.

'You've been on top of the Daisy Evans case from outset, haven't you, Cain?' said Cummings. 'Obsessed, almost.' He paused, as Mark's shocked gaze shot back to his. 'One can't help but wonder, given your… shall we say, sexual preferences… were you obsessed with finding her, or making sure no one else did?'

Mark felt the blood drain from his face. 'Are you serious?' He looked in utter disbelief between the two men.

'We've been doing some digging,' said Cummings. 'Had a difficult childhood, didn't you, DI Cain? Abused at the hands of your father. That must have been hard to deal with.'

Now he *had* to be joking. Mark shook his head, repulsed by the man and the implication. 'Not in the way you're implying,' he said, his throat tight, his voice calm.

'Really?' Cummings' accusing gaze strayed to his. 'Still fucked you up, though, didn't it, DI Cain?'

'This is *crazy*!' Mark clenched his fists. 'You're way out of order, Cummings, and you know it!' He was now dangerously close to exploding.

'Getting a bit irate, DI Cain? Not thinking of getting physical again, are we?' The perverse pleasure Cummings was taking in this was written all over his face

Mark was close, too close, to taking a swing at him, and the bastard knew it.

'Back off, DS Cummings,' Edwards ordered, his expression now one of complete disillusionment as he stared at Mark. 'We found something in the car, DI Cain,' he informed him solemnly.

'Such as?' Mark asked, his throat dry, his mind racing as he ran through the possibilities, blood being the most likely.

'One of Daisy's shoes,' Cummings provided. 'How did that get there, Cain? I mean, one would assume you'd never met the girl before she went missing.'

Oh, sweet fucking Jesus, no. The news hit Mark like a thunderclap. This wasn't happening. It couldn't be. *Please, God, don't let this be happening.*

'No doubt the forensics examination will yield more,' Cummings added.

'Do you have *anything* to offer in your defence, DI Cain?' Edwards asked him, agitatedly. 'Anything at all that might give me pause for thought before cautioning you?'

Reeling, Mark swiped at the perspiration tickling his forehead. Mel had obviously handed over his computer. Gulping back his nausea, Mark recalled the hatred in her eyes, the way she'd looked at him when she'd believed him capable of manipulating her, drugging her, kerb-crawling, for fuck's sake. And now this. She wouldn't alibi him. She couldn't. He'd been sleeping on the sofa. Panic now tightening his gut like a vice, Mark closed his eyes.

'You've been having a few problems at home, haven't you, DI Cain?' Cummings went on matter-of-factly. 'Arguments, concerning the children? Are they yours, DI Cain? Or was your wife claiming they weren't so you didn't try for custody?'

Mark eyed him, completely bewildered.

'Just wondering,' he said, shrugging, 'whether it might explain why your daughter's gone missing.'

'Where is she, DI Cain?' Edwards asked quietly. 'Where's Evie?'

'Jade,' Mark squeezed the word past the parched lump in his throat, his emotions going into free-fall as he realised where this was leading, 'I have to find her,' he said throatily, turning for the door.

'Jade. This would be the girl who says you raped her?' said Cummings.

Feeling as if an express train had just slammed into him, Mark stopped dead in his tracks. She was framing him, knocking nails into his coffin, one by one, and he could do *nothing*? He hadn't got a snowball in hell's chance of convincing anyone that he'd had no part in any of this. *Christ.* His baby? His family?

He needed to get out of here. A sluggish pulse beating prophetically at the base of his neck, he continued towards the door.

'You really are a lowlife piece of scum, aren't you, Cain?' Cummings said disgustedly. 'Spouting your holier than thou crap. Lording it over everyone, hiding your sick perversions—'

'Enough!' Edwards cut him short. 'DI Cain, you might like to take this opportunity to call a solicitor.'

Mark sucked in a breath, knowing what was coming next.

'Mark Cain, we are legally obliged to inform you that we are arresting you on suspicion of child abduction and offences contrary to the Sexual Offences Act 2003.' Mark could feel Cummings' satisfaction as he cautioned him.

'You do not have to say anything, but it may harm your defence if you fail to mention when questioned something which you later rely on in court. Anything you do say may be given in evidence. Do you understand, DI Cain?'

Mark nodded slowly, his jaw clamped tight. 'I need to go,' he rasped, reaching for the door despite knowing he stood no chance of getting through it and out of the station.

Cummings was on him in a second, locking an arm tight around his neck. 'You're going *nowhere*, mate,' he snarled in his ear.

Two officers bursting through the door to flank him either side, Mark tried to stay upright as Cummings landed a vicious blow to his side.

*

Mark stopped struggling as he was manhandled through the main office, the hostile glances of his supposed colleagues telling him all he needed to know. In their eyes, he really was the lowest of the low. His only hope was Lisa, who knew him almost as well as his wife did – or had. Mark prayed harder than he'd ever prayed as he was escorted past where she stood amidst the audience who'd gathered for the show, wilting with relief as he noted her expression. Not open disdain. Confusion, but not repugnance.

Mark didn't speak. He doubted he could get the words past the fractured pieces of his heart, which were now wedged like shards of glass in his windpipe. He prayed again instead, that Lisa would read the desperation in his eyes.

Lisa nodded. 'I'm on it, sir,' she said simply.

CHAPTER SEVENTY-THREE

JADE

Jade had to work at maintaining her façade as she assured the family liaison officer at the door that Melissa was fine, that she was sleeping and that she would be here for her when she woke. A thought had occurred to her: Mark might well have been charged by now, in which case it was possible police would soon be crawling all over the house like flies over dog shit, searching for evidence. Something else was worrying her, too: her conversation with drippy Dylan. She hadn't been able to properly concentrate, what with the brat peering at her through the crack in the door. He'd said something about taking Angel to his house. He'd also said 'as well'. What had he meant? God, the man was a liability. If he'd got it into his thick skull to do anything off his own bat, she'd boil his balls and make him eat them.

The officer finally handed her a card and told her she'd call back. Jade smiled sweetly, closed the door calmly and then turned to the stairs spitting with rage.

Everything had been going nicely to plan, albeit an alternative plan, and now she was under pressure. She needed to get this done. She needed to get out of here and get to Dylan, who infuriatingly wasn't answering his phone, before the moron messed everything up.

Mounting the stairs, her eyes fixed upwards, her mind on the woman who'd stolen her life, Jade didn't notice the dog until it emitted a low growl behind her. Would the stupid beast not just lie down and die? Seething, Jade carefully back-stepped. And then laughed. The pathetic animal's attempt at a snarl was more a drool, disgusting creature. She noted the whites of its eyes as the dog's eyes rolled, the distinctly wobbly legs. '*Awww*, what's the matter, Hercules? Did the drugs make you feel poorly, hmm? Can't you make it upstairs? Tough *shit*!'

Lunging forward, Jade caught hold of the dog by the collar and heaved it through the kitchen to the back door. She might have been impressed by its loyalty, its heroic attempts to dig its claws in, if it hadn't snapped its head around and bitten her.

Now she was annoyed. *Very.* Assisting the animal out with a vicious kick, Jade slammed the back door and returned to the stairs, blood popping through the teeth marks on her wrist.

Flinging the bedroom door open, Jade locked eyes with the brat, who immediately scurried closer to her mother, as if the woman was capable of doing anything other than lie slumped on the bed. She was still attempting to keep her eyes open, Jade noted, her fuse fizzling steadily. She was obviously fighting the drugs. *Silly bitch.* Could she not just get it into her head that it was time to give up? This was *her* bed. It was *her* man the slut had been sleeping next to. It was time Melissa learned a few home truths, since she was insisting on being so bloody obstinate.

'Out!' Jade glared at Poppy, enough fire in her eyes to let the brat know she meant business. 'Now, or there'll be trouble.' Eyeballing the girl meaningfully, she waited while, sniffling irritatingly, Poppy shuffled off the bed to sidle to the door, where she paused to look pleadingly back at her.

Heartbreaking, it really was. Jade smiled nastily, and then tipped her head back, raised her hand and made swallowing goldfish gestures that had the brat scuttling out in a flash.

Turning back, Jade walked across to the bed, her brow furrowed in concern. 'Oh dear, you haven't drunk your medicine,' she said, looking down at the cold tea on the bedside table.

Melissa tried to raise herself.

She was a fighter, Jade conceded wearily, pushing her back down. 'Not to worry,' she said, leaning down to peer into Melissa's pretty green eyes, noting the hugely dilated pupils with satisfaction, 'you've had enough to ensure you sleep soundly. I'd give in to it, if I were you. The alternative might not be very pleasant. Still, on the bright side, at least you won't have any more nightmares.'

Clearly as stubborn as her brat child, the woman stirred again, attempting to lift her rusty-haired head from the pillow. 'Mark. Where's Mark?' she mumbled, wiping the smile from Jade's face in an instant.

'Bitch!' Jade spat, bringing her hand back to slap the slut's face hard. 'He doesn't want you! Haven't you seen what's been going on right under your nose? *Stupid* cow! It's *me* he wants.' Placing a hand the other side of Melissa, she glared down at her, almost eyeball to eyeball with her. '*Me* he's been fucking, for months. Right here, in *this* bed.'

Her chest heaving with anger, Jade jabbed a finger into the pillow right next to the woman's face. 'Anywhere and everywhere, and every which way. In the nursery, Poppy's room, the kitchen, the lounge, even your precious fucking workshop,' she snarled, making sure to paint a graphic picture for the useless cow to contemplate as she drifted off.

Melissa attempted to focus on her, but couldn't, finally closing her eyes as the truth sank in.

Satisfied, but not finished, Jade straightened up. 'He needs a real woman, a proper mother for his kids,' she went on, driving Melissa's failures home, 'not some whingeing, weak, pot-making freak.'

Jade curled her lip in contempt as Melissa made a last valiant attempt to sit up, groping sideways as she did, presumably in search of her phone. Sadly, it was just out of reach. Calmly, Jade nudged it away.

'Useless.' She sighed, and then turned away, humming. *Hush, little baby, don't you cry…* She headed to the dressing table, extracting a piece of paper from her pocket as she went. It was a nice touch, Jade thought. A goodbye note addressed to Poppy, showing the poor little mite her mother's last thoughts were with her.

Jade smoothed it out carefully, and then, smiling at her own thoughtfulness, she turned back to help Melissa finish her tea.

CHAPTER SEVENTY-FOUR

LISA

Instinct telling her to proceed with caution, Lisa peered through the lounge window. Poppy was standing in the middle of the room, one hand twisting her hair into tight ringlets, her thumb plugged in her mouth. Lisa tapped lightly on the glass. Finally managing to attract the little girl's attention, she smiled encouragingly and gestured towards the front door.

Peering through the letter flap, Lisa mentally crossed her fingers as Poppy cautiously approached. The girl looked traumatised. She desperately didn't want to scare her. 'Hello, Poppet,' she whispered, hoping to put her at her ease. 'Where's Mummy, sweetheart?'

'Sleeping,' Poppy said, around the thumb she was still sucking nervously on.

Leaving her daughter wandering around on her own? Whatever shit Mel had been through, however depressed she was supposed to be, the Mel Lisa knew would never do that.

'I need to see her, Poppy, urgently. Do you understand?'

Poppy nodded. Her eyes were full of trepidation. Picturing her own daughter at that age, feeling how she was feeling, Lisa prayed inwardly. 'Do you think you could be a big girl, Poppy, and help me?'

Again, Poppy nodded.

'Good girl,' Lisa said. 'I need you to open the door, Poppy. Can you reach it?'

Poppy gave another short nod, before she promptly turned around and scooted towards the kitchen.

Not sure where she'd gone, or whose unwanted attention she might attract, Lisa prayed harder, and then blew out a sigh of relief as Poppy reappeared, dragging a chair slowly but determinedly behind her. 'I have to do the bolt.' she said.

Minutes later, Lisa was in, immediately crouching to pull Poppy into a hug. 'Well done. Daddy will be so proud of you,' she said, close to her ear. 'Now, I need you to do something else for me, Poppy.'

Taking her personal mobile from her pocket, Lisa eased back, holding the little girl's gaze with a reassuring one of her own. 'I want you to go to the lounge and stay there. If you hear or see anything that worries you, I want you to press nine three times on my phone, and then the green call button. Can you do that?'

'Uh-huh.' Poppy's nod was resolute.

'Show me where the nine is, honey.' Lisa held the phone up and Poppy duly pointed.

'Good girl,' Lisa said, a wave of relief washing through her. 'Tell them who you are and don't end the call until Daddy's friends get here. Promise?'

'Promise.' Poppy crossed her heart.

Hoping to God she would be safer there than wandering about outside on her own, Lisa steered her gently in the direction of the lounge, quickly checked the other downstairs rooms – the kitchen, downstairs cloakroom and study – and then made her way quietly upwards. Poppy's bedroom door was open; the nursery door too. That room was empty, obviously. Lisa's heart constricted.

The main bedroom door was closed. Beyond that was Jade's room, she assumed. The door was ajar, too tempting an invitation for a detective. Praying a floorboard wouldn't squeak at the crucial moment, Lisa headed that way, aiming to have covered all bases before going into Mel's bedroom.

Jade's things were still there, everything neat and tidy. Way too tidy. Lisa noted the lipsticks on the dresser, lined up like soldiers on parade, the bed made up to hospital standards. Bypassing the dresser in favour of the wardrobe, Lisa flicked through the few clothes hanging there; Mel's mostly, apart from the skimpy babysitting gear the girl was fond of wearing.

Lisa glanced upwards. Seeing a shoebox on the top shelf, she checked over her shoulder and then lifted it quietly out. It was stuffed full of memorabilia – pieces of jewellery, odd bits of make-up, a few old photographs. Lisa wasn't surprised, until she came across one photograph in particular: a little girl, aged around four. A little girl Lisa wasn't likely to forget. But she was very much alive in this picture, giggling as she posed with her older sister, a one-eyed Pooh Bear clutched close to her chest.

Lisa dug deeper, finding a stash of what she recognised as antipsychotic drugs. Her blood ran cold.

A sick feeling in her gut, in her soul, Lisa turned, charging towards the main bedroom. Pausing only long enough to register Melissa lying unmoving on the bed, she sprinted across the room, fumbling to call it in as she went. Shaking Melissa with one hand, she'd got as far as telling the police operator they needed to check out the babysitter when an almighty crack to the back of the skull cut her call short.

CHAPTER SEVENTY-FIVE

JADE

Maybe those crappy sculptures weren't so useless, after all. Jade watched fascinatedly as the blood oozed from the copper's wound, staining the cream carpet a deep crimson. Served her right, interfering cow. Jade had no doubt DI Moyes, with her suspicious eyes, had fancied shagging Mark. She wouldn't be shagging him now, would she?

Jade gave the hopeless policewoman a prod with her foot and then, satisfied she wouldn't be causing any more trouble, she turned towards the door. Some women really were complete bitches, happy to hop into bed with a man knowing full well he was already taken.

Time to clean up, she supposed. Get rid of the whole sorry mess.

CHAPTER SEVENTY-SIX

MARK

Mark had had enough of being questioned, cross-questioned and clearly disbelieved. 'Charge me or let me go,' he demanded, challenging Edwards as he came back into the interview room.

'Sit down, DI Cain,' Edwards said, glancing down at the table, ostensibly to pick up his papers. 'Your claims will be investigated, along with everything else. Meanwhile, try to stay calm.'

Mark stared incredulously at him. 'My daughter's missing!' he shouted, his anger way off the scale. 'I'm stuck here, about to be remanded into custody for serious offences I didn't commit, while I believe my family to be in danger, and you want me to sit down and stay *calm*?'

Edwards turned to walk back out without uttering another word. Had he despatched anyone to his house yet? Even forensics pulling the place apart would be better than Mel and Poppy there on their own. Was he doing *anything*? Mark dragged a hand furiously over his neck. *Fuck it*, he thought, heading towards the door after Edwards, only to find Cummings blocking his way.

'Move.' Mark eyed him levelly.

Cummings smiled flatly. 'You're under arrest, Cain. You know how this works. You're going nowhere.' He grabbed hold of Mark's arm and attempted to shove him towards the seat. That did it. Blind fury driving him, Mark shoved him, hard.

Caught off guard, Cummings stumbled, crashing heavily to the floor. 'You *prat*,' he growled, heaving himself upright.

Mark clenched his fist at his side, itching to punch the bastard's lights out as Cummings advanced on him. 'Don't,' he warned him.

'And who's going to stop me? You?' Cummings taunted. 'Finally lost it, haven't we, Cain? Knew you would, eventually. Didn't have to do much other than wait around, did I?'

Mark looked him over, making no attempt to hide the contempt in his eyes. 'Like falsify evidence, you mean? You're a fucking disgrace, Cummings.'

'That's rich,' Cummings sneered, 'coming from someone who gets his kicks fiddling with kids. I would say your own kids, but you don't know they *are* yours, do you?'

Mark narrowed his eyes. Where was this shit coming from?

'So why rape the babysitter?' Cummings asked, goading him on. Just couldn't resist, could he, the arrogant prick. 'I'd have thought she wouldn't do it for you, given she's over the age of consent?'

'Does it for you though, doesn't she, Cummings? Did she make this allegation before or after you two had had sex, I wonder?' Mark put two and two together and presumably got a correct four, judging by the now smug look on the other man's face. 'You really are a gullible git, Cummings. She's been using you, feeding you information. Wrong information. Do you honestly think she wanted you for your sexual prowess?'

Cummings smiled languidly, still every inch the cocky bastard he was. 'At least I don't have to resort to raping women and kids.'

Mark clenched his jaw. 'You'll get yours, Cummings. It's only a matter of time before someone realises you're lifting drugs from the evidence room.'

Cummings shrugged indifferently. 'Nothing major. No one's likely to miss it. I must admit you did put the wind up me a couple of times. You got way too close to catching me in the act when I picked up Tanya Stevens.'

'Which is why *you* assaulted her presumably?' Mark asked casually. 'Distraction technique?'

Cummings smirked. 'Worked, didn't it?'

'It might have done, Cummings,' DCI Edwards said calmly behind him. 'If you hadn't got quite so cocky with it.'

Paling, Cummings shot around to face him. 'It was self-defence, sir,' he said quickly. 'I had to use force to restrain her. She—'

'Out!' Edwards ordered him.

Cummings hesitated for a second, then, noting the livid look in Edwards' eye, stepped past him and walked apprehensively towards the door.

'Mark.' Edwards looked at him, his expression not quite so openly scathing as it had been. 'The doctor's arrived.' He glanced awkwardly away again. 'If you're ready?'

'Would it make any difference if I wasn't?' Mark asked him disappointedly.

There was definitely sympathy in the man's eyes now, probably because he was about to undergo the humiliation of being swabbed, prodded and poked. But when Edwards turned to the door, it was to find a uniform barrelling into him from the other side.

'Sorry, sir,' the man said quickly. 'Moyes called in. DS Moyes. The call was cut short, but she said something about a babysitter? There's also been an emergency call. A little girl. We managed to keep her on the line for a while. Looks like she was calling from the same location.'

His house. Mark's blood froze in his veins.

CHAPTER SEVENTY-SEVEN

JADE

'There you are.' Jade smiled down at Poppy, crouched behind the chair, her knees tucked up to her chin. 'My, you were hard to find,' Jade said kindly, moving to heave the armchair away from the corner and flush the little brat out.

Extending her hand, her smile frozen on her face, Jade waited.

Obviously realising there was no way to hide, Poppy reluctantly emerged, plugging her thumb into her mouth and nervously taking Jade's hand. Was the poor little mite worried about her mum, Jade wondered, or her soon-to-be-boiled goldfish? Her goldfish, more than likely. The child was just like Melissa, self-centred, no thought for anyone but herself.

'Good girl.' Squeezing her hand, Jade led her across to the sofa, where she could keep an eye on her while she attended to the business of cleaning up. 'Now, you stay there while I get a nice warm fire going, and then we can go for a little walk in the fresh air. How does that sound?'

Poppy didn't answer. Jade let it pass. She was obviously tired. It was way past her bedtime.

'She really is a careless cow, your mum, leaving all these hazardous materials lying around in her workshop.' Jade chatted companionably to the girl, sprinkling liberally as she did. 'Lord knows what she was thinking. I mean, white spirits, on a low shelf?

Honestly, it's a wonder social services didn't cart you off years ago. Being a drink-addled druggy's no excuse for child abuse, is it?'

The first armchair thoroughly doused, Jade walked across to the other, smiling reassuringly at Poppy as she went. 'You're better off without her, my love, and that deceitful father of yours. Trust me, having no parents is better than having abusive parents. They scar you for life.'

The second armchair wet enough for purpose, Jade ditched the bottle, picked up another containing heating oil, and headed for the sofa. 'Almost done,' she said cheerily, unscrewing the top, and then pausing. Cocking her head to one side, she looked the quaking girl over. No, she decided. It was tempting, but she needed the brat for insurance purposes, at least for now.

'Come on, sweetheart,' she said, offering Poppy her hand. 'Let's get you out in the fresh air. These fumes really aren't any good for you.' Tsk-ing at the irresponsibility of a mother who would expose a child to this, let alone the clay and glaze dusts, which must surely be highly toxic, Jade poured out the last of the oil and led the little girl to the safety of the hall.

'Stay,' she ordered. 'If you move, I'll saw your feet off.'

The girl let out a ragged sob. Jade sighed, pulled her matches from her jeans pocket, and held onto her patience. It wasn't her fault she was the product of her dysfunctional parents, she supposed.

'Here we go,' she said, bending as she struck the match, watching the flame dancing in the little girl's watery eyes.

Mesmerised for a second, Jade jumped to her feet before the match burned down, and then, tingling with anticipation, she tossed it into the lounge. '*Whoosh*,' she whispered, closing her eyes, a thrill rushing through her as it caught.

Jade hesitated, making sure the flames leapt and furled before pulling the door to. 'It's going to be the most beautiful bonfire ever. Much bigger than the others I made. There's lots of wood in your house, you see,' she confided conspiratorially to Poppy, taking her hand firmly in her own. 'I'll let you get closer to the next one,' she promised.

The girl was crying in earnest now, gulping back huge snotty sobs as Jade led her to the front door.

She'd feel better after a good cry. Not that Jade ever had. She'd stopped crying once she'd realised tears were pointless when there was no one who cared enough to hear them.

'You really need to feel the heat of the fire on your face to realise the true cleansing beauty of it,' she said, attempting to mollify the child as she pulled the front door open – and then stopped, fury uncoiling inside her as she saw several blue lights rotating outside. The interfering bitch upstairs had got her call through.

Jade's faced darkened as she watched another squad car screeching towards the house, her supposed hero spilling from the passenger door as it careered to a halt halfway across the lawn.

'Too late, copper,' Jade spat, clutching Poppy's hand tighter and stepping back.

CHAPTER SEVENTY-EIGHT

MARK

Undiluted terror gripped Mark's stomach as he took in the scene before him in surreal slow motion. Splintering wood. He could hear beams falling. Hear his house burning.

Windows shattering. Flames crackling. People shouting. Sirens screaming. His daughter's cries – he sucked in a breath, couldn't breathe out – they reached inside him and ripped his heart right out of his chest.

He tumbled forwards, his emotions colliding, his world exploding.

And then he ran.

Wrestling free of the arms that tried to hold him back, ignoring his DCI yelling behind him, he ran.

He kicked at the door, ramming his shoulder, his whole body weight against it – 'Give, you fucking thing!' – and then he was in. Falling into the hall, choking back the fumes that seared the back of his throat, he righted himself, pressing his arm to his mouth as he made his way through the smoke to the stairs.

Noting the open doors on the landing, he didn't pause, but he prayed, a prayer that came from his soul, as he crashed into the main bedroom, his lungs raw from the effort of trying to breathe. Needing to assess the situation, to think strategically through the debilitating panic, Mark closed the door to buy some time, and registered the horror in front of him.

Lisa, face down on the floor, bleeding from a head wound, unconscious at best.

Poppy… alive. Mark silently thanked God. She was sobbing, tugging hard on Mel's arm. 'Mummy, please, you *have* to get out of bed.'

Mel was barely responsive.

A potent mixture of fear and fury raging inside him, Mark snapped his gaze to the tall casement window where, standing precariously on the ledge, her back to the concrete drive twenty long feet below, was Jade. The smile on her face was triumphant, her movements controlled. She knew that Mark knew he had a decision to make: her or his wife? If she fell, if she died, his baby's whereabouts would die with her.

Mark took a faltering step forwards. She edged dangerously back.

'Don't do this, Jade,' Mark begged her, his voice hoarse. 'Please, don't do this.'

'*Why?*' she snarled. Her face, illuminated by the sweeping blue lights outside, was twisted with rage. 'Because you *care?*'

'I care.' Marked took another cautious step. 'I care very much. You need help, Jade. Please, let me—'

'Liar! You pretended you did, but you didn't! You promised me you'd always be there. Made me an *absolute* promise. And you weren't!'

'When? Talk to me, Jade.' Mark moved closer. 'Tell me, I don't understand.'

'Oh, here we go.' Jade laughed. 'The "I'm sorry, I never meant to hurt you" crap.'

'I am sorry!' Mark said, fear slicing through him afresh as she teetered. 'If I did something—'

'I'd lost everything! My whole life burned to ashes! You told me it was going to be all right. You held me and you *told* me, and it wasn't! You lied to me! You left me. You left me to be with that slut of a wife because *she* was pregnant!'

Mark stopped, bewildered. There was no reasoning with her, no talking to her. She was utterly insane.

'*I* was pregnant! Made pregnant by him!'

'*Who?*' Mark shouted, groping desperately for some comprehension, some inkling of what she was talking about.

'It was *her* fault! That spoiled brat of a sister, always whining and seeking attention.'

Mark ran a hand over his face. No idea what to say. What to do.

'It was only a blister from a sparkler, and she screamed like she was being murdered!' she ranted on, sounding more insane by the second. 'She asked for one, over and over, she kept whining: *I want to play sparklers. I want to play sparklers.* I only gave it to her to shut her up, stop her moaning and tittle-tattling, telling tales. She *told* them I'd given it to her. She knew I'd get in trouble. She was always getting me into trouble. She told them I burned her, so I fucking well did!'

'Your sister?' *She…?* Mark reeled incredulously, as the horrific implication of her disjointed ramblings became clearer to him.

'Yes, my *sister*,' she spat. 'Their perfect little princess, who could do no wrong. All of them! Tucked up in their beds, snoring away like they hadn't got a care in the world: her, Miss Goody-two-shoes, lying there with her pathetic thumb stuck in her mouth, looking like butter wouldn't melt. And *her,* that bitch-mother. She knew! She *knew* what he was doing. Every time she left me he did it, touching me, hurting me, grunting and thrusting and apologising – and that whore of a mother just let him! She took that snivelling little brat to the hospital with a tiny little blister, and she *let* him.'

Oh, Jesus. Mark was beginning to see… the images from his dreams, recollections from a call-out he could never quite forget. A little girl curled into a foetal ball in her child-sized bed, her one-eyed Pooh Bear clutched close to her chest. Her older sister, still dressed in her unicorn-print pyjamas when they'd found her, had been shaking from head to foot. Her cheeks, smeared in soot from the fire, had been tear-stained, her cognac-coloured eyes wide and utterly petrified.

Mark swallowed hard. *Grace.*

'You burned them alive?' Astounded, he searched her face, looking for some shred of conscience, some indication she understood the horrendous thing she'd done, was doing.

'I hurt them like they hurt me! I went to the kitchen, and I struck the match and I killed them. And you said it would be all right. You pretended you cared. But you didn't! You're all the same, liars! Users and abusers.' she screamed, over a deafening crash from the landing.

The stairs going? Mark kept his gaze on hers, prayed it wasn't. Sweat wetting his eyelashes, pooling at the base of his neck, he tried to focus as the light bulbs popped. His heart was thundering so loudly he could almost hear it above the cacophony of sirens outside. He risked another step towards her.

Jade twisted around, ready to jump.

'Jade, wait! What happened to her?' Mark shouted urgently. 'Your baby. What happened to her? *Tell* me. Make me understand.'

'*Hah!*' Jade laughed cynically. 'As if you could.'

'Try me.' Mark begged.

Jade didn't speak for a second. 'I thought she was an alien growing inside me,' she said quietly. 'But she wasn't. She was beautiful. So tiny. Blue. Her skin was tinged blue.'

Premature? Oxygen starvation? Mark felt another violent twist in his chest.

'I knew God would take her for an angel when she died. I sang to her when her eyes closed… *Hush, little baby, don't you cry…* She smiled at me. I'm sure she did. My perfect little Angel. I knew she'd come back to me.'

'Evie.' Full realisation finally dawning, Mark almost choked the word out.

'Angel!' Jade glared back at him, her eyes smouldering with hatred. '*You* abandoned me. Tried to take her away from me. I have nothing to live for without her. Now she'll die too. And when she does, remember it was *you* who killed her, Mark Cain.'

Mark didn't dare move, other than to brace himself and pray harder as she moved closer to the edge.

'I'll see you in hell,' she snarled.

Intent on her aim, she didn't notice the hand snaking around her ankle, her calf.

The woman whose child she'd stolen wasn't about to let her go.

'Hell can wait for you, Jade.'

CHAPTER SEVENTY-NINE

JADE

He'd grabbed her. Wrapped his hand around the waist and yanked her away from the window. He'd hurt her. Curled into a ball in the corner where he'd flung her, Jade watched as he handed the brat down through the window. He didn't even glance in her direction as he helped needy Melissa out. She was protesting, of course, whingeing, always whingeing, wanting her precious little baby.

Jade couldn't believe it when he walked past her to gather the policewoman from the floor, the scheming cow who wouldn't have hesitated to steal him from her. Carefully, he carried her to the window, searching her face, as if he was already in love with her, the bastard. It was *she* who needed him. She was choking to death. Couldn't he hear her?

Finally, he turned his attention to her, and Jade shrank back. His breathing laboured, his expression pure thunder, he simply stared at her. There was no compassion in his eyes, nothing. He didn't move to help her when she coughed again – so hard, she was sure her lungs would turn inside out. He barely flinched when the door cracked, and thick grey smoke furled further into the room.

Jade looked frantically towards it. She was going to burn. He was going to let her. Her skin would be blackened and blistered, her eyes would pop. *Oh God…* 'Mark?' she croaked, her throat parched and sore from the fumes.

'Where is she?' Mark spoke quietly, his eyes never leaving hers. 'Evie, where is she?'

Jade looked at him, pleadingly, beseechingly. She couldn't tell. He must know that. If she did, he would have no reason to save her.

Jade's thoughts were cut short as the door blew. 'Mark!' she screamed, as hungry flames rushed petrifyingly towards her.

CHAPTER EIGHTY

MARK

She was barely recognisable as the young girl he'd met eight long years before. An innocent young girl, Mark had thought, and one he'd inadvertently sent out the wrong signals to. She'd obviously had cosmetic surgery as she grew older. Disguised her striking cognac-coloured eyes with blue lenses. She'd been beautiful – on the outside. Broken on the inside. Whether from birth? No one would ever know the workings of a mind that had compelled a young girl to burn her family alive.

There was nothing for him here. The doctors had confirmed cerebral hypoxia from the fire, meaning that, if she survived, lack of oxygen to the brain would result in severe and permanent damage. Despite the full-scale investigation now underway, with absolutely nothing to go on, they weren't likely to find Evie. Mark knew it, but he hadn't said so to Mel. He'd hardly spoken to her, desperate though he was to hear her voice, which had always seemed to anchor him in his darkest moments. He'd been too scared to, knowing it would be a conversation he couldn't bear. She was never likely to forgive him for doubting her, judging her, readily accepting a diagnosis that was wrong. Being involved, albeit unknowingly, in a plan to drive her steadily out of her mind. Accusing her, and then getting so paralytic himself he'd allowed a woman to take advantage of him, manipulating him to the point where he was the accused, locked up like the worst kind of criminal while... He didn't dare imagine what might be happening to Evie. Melissa could never forgive him that. He would never forgive himself.

Swallowing back the grief and guilt weighing too heavily in his chest, Mark turned away from Grace's hospital bed. He didn't really know why he'd come. To see with his own eyes, he supposed. He'd tried to save her, blistering his hands and his arms dragging her out, but it had been too late. He'd gone over that until he'd driven himself almost out of his mind. Lisa had tried to reassure him, telling him she could never have been truly saved. It didn't help. The fact was, crucial seconds had sealed her fate. Sealed his baby's fate.

He couldn't undo it. Couldn't make any of it right. Jade, Grace, whoever she was, had achieved her aim. She'd set out to have him or destroy him, and he'd assisted her every step of the way. *He'd* killed Evie. He was the one who'd destroyed his family.

Kneading the back of his neck, exhausted – sleep only came now to torment him, Mark was deep in thought as he walked the length of the hospital corridor, thinking now about Poppy. He'd let her down too, failed in his most fundamental obligation as a father to protect her. The child psychiatrist had been hopeful, but Mark wondered whether she would ever recover completely from her nightmare. She'd need lots of support and reassurance, and to know without doubt that she was loved. Mark had plenty of that to offer her, so much it hurt. But how was he going to love her from a distance? He'd have to, but how would Poppy cope? She'd locked her arms around his neck and sobbed when he'd told her he had to leave, after visiting her at the Chandlers' house, which was where Mel was staying. How would his little girl know he wasn't deserting her again?

Heading into the reception area, Mark didn't hear Lisa at first, calling him across the foyer. He barely acknowledged her when

she yelled, 'Oi, superhero, look up.' In other circumstances, Mark
might have smiled. His new label down at the station was better
than 'paedo scum', he supposed, but Mark really didn't feel like
a hero. He'd saved Mel and Poppy, but part of his family was
missing. Part of himself was missing.

'Mark!' Lisa yelled, clearly determined to get his attention. 'I
know you have a lot on your mind, but will you please stop feeling
so sorry for yourself.'

Not sure he was hearing her right, Mark snapped his gaze up.

'There's someone here to see you,' Lisa said, a teasing smile
on her face as she approached him. 'I've got a feeling you might
want to see her too.'

Following her gaze, Mark's dormant heart kicked to life in his
chest. The woman he loved, had always loved, would always love,
was walking towards him. And in her arms, nestled close to her
breast, was his baby daughter.

Mel stopped and offered Evie to him. She opened her mouth
to speak, but faltered as Mark gathered Evie into his arms, neither
much caring that they were crying openly in front of an audience.

'They were left in the foyer at Herefordshire Hospital Reception,' Lisa explained. 'Evie's been checked over. She's fine, but—'

'Wait…' Mark tried to process. 'They?'

'Daisy. She's alive.' Lisa squeezed his arm. 'Barely, but there's
a chance. Her parents are with her now. Obviously, they'll need
some support. Social services will make an assessment of her home
situation, but… She's found, Mark.'

Mark tugged in a tight breath, blinked hard and looked
heavenwards.

'There's more,' said Lisa. 'We found Jade's baby. Buried in a
shallow grave in her grandmother's garden. It looks as if she was
born prematurely. Her grandmother died suddenly, apparently,
from a fall. As Grace stood to gain from an inheritance, we're
looking further into that.'

Mark nodded. Despite all that had happened, he still felt sick to his soul that Grace had been abused so consistently as a child. That her circumstances had gone unnoticed, meaning she'd never received the help she obviously desperately needed.

Lisa paused, waiting while Mark caught up. 'Whether she played a part in that, or not, she was sick, Mark. Or else pure evil. None of what happened was your fault.'

'I know,' Mark said throatily. Truthfully, though, he would always wonder whether he could have helped her more, followed up on her progress after visiting her at the hospital, been there should she need someone to talk to, as he'd promised he would.

'Go home, Mark,' Lisa urged him. 'Your family's waiting.'

Mark looked down at his daughter, and then turned to his wife. And he knew. Seeing the look in her beautiful green eyes, the colour of ferns after the rain… there was hope.

'I'll leave you three to it,' Lisa said, turning to give Mel a hug and then sauntering off looking quite pleased with herself. 'Oh.' She turned back. 'Take your time, but when you've kissed and made up, do you think you could collect your dog? She's adorable, but she's giving my kids ideas.'

Lisa rolled her eyes and carried on, as Mark and Mel ignored her in favour of beginning the healing process.

CHAPTER EIGHTY-ONE

DYLAN

Dylan watched from his truck as Mark Cain and his wife left by the front entrance of the hospital. 'I think Jade might have lied to me,' he said, seeing how the man gazed lovingly down at little Angel as he carried her. How his wife kissed his cheek and then threaded an arm around his waist and leaned her head against his shoulder. 'Do you think she lied to me?' he almost shouted, glancing upwards.

She didn't answer him. He didn't expect her to. That was okay. He knew his mum was watching over him. She always had.

Watching them walk to their car, Dylan ran a hand hard under his nose. 'It doesn't matter. I still love her,' he said, with a determined nod. 'And I know she loves me. She showed me how much she loves me.'

Dylan thought about it and made a decision: 'We need to bring Angel home. Be a proper family, just like Jade wanted.'

LETTER FROM SHERYL

Dear Reader,

Thank you so much for choosing to read *The Babysitter*. I really hope you enjoyed it.

If you would like to keep up to date with my latest book news, please do sign up at the website link below. Your email address will never be shared and you can unsubscribe at any time.

www.bookouture.com/sheryl-browne

This wasn't the easiest story to write, as it does touch on subjects that some might find difficult to deal with – loss and mental issues around bereavement in particular. I tend to gravitate towards family, family dynamics and just how strong a family unit can be when faced with adversity. Yes, I do sometimes write from personal experience. Even then, though, careful research is called for in order write about such issues sensitively and honestly. I would like to thank those people who have shared their stories with me and also those people who have been there for me: my family, my friends, not least my wider circle of friends that now includes wonderful bloggers, reviewers and readers who encourage me every step of the way.

Thank you. I really could not do this without you. If you have enjoyed the book, I would love it if you could share your thoughts and write a brief review. Reviews mean the world to an author and will help a book find its wings. I would also love to hear from you via Facebook or Twitter or my website.

Keep safe everyone and Happy Reading.
Sheryl x

sherylbrowne.com

SherylBrowne

SherylBrowne.Author

ACKNOWLEDGEMENTS

I would like to offer a massive thank you to the team at Bookouture, without whom *The Babysitter* would never have been born. Special thanks to Helen Jenner, whose patience, enthusiasm and editing skills have made the story the best it can be, and to Peta Nightingale for loving the initial idea enough to give the book its wings.

Special thanks also to Kim Nash for her quiet determination, absolute professionalism, unstinting support and belief in me, and to all the other lovely, friendly and super-supportive authors at blogger and author events organised by Kim. We share the highs and the lows and realise we have one thing in common that drives us on – our love of writing.

I owe a huge debt of gratitude to those bloggers and reviewers who have taken time to read my books, review those books and shout out endlessly for me. I so often say I couldn't do this without you. I simply couldn't. Your passion leaves me in absolute awe. Thank you! Huge thanks, too, to Shell Baker, who led me by the hand around the maze that is often Facebook groups – gave me a push in the right direction when I needed it and who works her socks off for authors.

Final thanks to every single reader out there for your tremendous support – every book sold, every positive comment and every review spurs a writer to keep on writing when the going might get tough – and to Drew, who was there, quietly encouraging his mad mother on, when it did.

One thing that I have learned from these special people around me is to never be afraid to reach out. So often when you do, you find someone has been there, and that that someone cares.

St. Julians

14/5/18